... This is Poppy ...
worked as a journalist, editor and book reviewer ... ...ntly teaches journalism and creative writing. Poppy lives in Queensland, Australia, with her husband and two beautiful children.

Praise for Poppy Gee:

'Beautifully atmospheric and superbly gripping, BAY OF FIRES is a stellar debut. Poppy Gee . . . had me eagerly turning the pages late into the night as she carefully tightened the screws of suspense'
Lisa Unger,
New York Times bestselling author of HEARTBROKEN

'A thrilling murder mystery set on the coast of Tasmania, BAY OF FIRES is my favourite book of the fall. Poppy Gee's heroine is tough and absolutely winning'
Amanda Eyre Ward,
author of HOW TO BE LOST

BAY OF FIRES

POPPY GEE

headline
review

First published in 2013 by
HEADLINE REVIEW
An imprint of HEADLINE PUBLISHING GROUP

First published in paperback in 2013 by
HEADLINE REVIEW
An imprint of HEADLINE PUBLISHING GROUP

1

Cataloguing in Publication Data is available from the British Library

ISBN 978 0 7553 8785 4

Typeset in Aldine by Palimpsest Book Production Ltd,
Falkirk, Stirlingshire

Printed and bound in Great Britain by Clays Ltd, St Ives plc

Headline's policy is to use papers that are natural, renewable and
recyclable products and made from wood grown in sustainable
forests. The logging and manufacturing processes are expected to
conform to the environmental regulations of the country of origin.

HEADLINE PUBLISHING GROUP
An Hachette UK Company
338 Euston Road
London NW1 3BH

www.headline.co.uk
www.hachette.co.uk

For William, Scarlett, and Miles.
And for Mum, Dad, Lucy, Sophie, and Steven.

Preface

The storm broke the night before the body of the second missing woman was found. She was face-down in the sand halfway along the longest beach in the Bay of Fires. Red polka-dot bikini bottoms were tangled below the woman's hips. Sand maggots fed on her back wounds. Seaweed twisted through her hair, which was the only part of her that still looked human. She was swollen from days of floating in salt water before the sea finally spat her out on the high-tide line.

It was the day after Boxing Day when the fisherman discovered the body. He was wandering along the shoreline, taking pleasure in the heavy silence of dawn and the strangeness of the beach, newly carved by wind and rain. The sun had barely surfaced over the ocean horizon. The crisp sand, littered with marine debris, gleamed in the day's freshness. Beneath a shapeless mountain of green eucalypts, the lagoon shimmered in purple darkness. It was full. Soon the Chain of Lagoons would overflow, pouring through the grassy dune and gutting the beach to meet the ocean. A sharp undertow sucked on a steep wall of wet quicksand, making it dangerous for swimming. This part of the seashore was visited only by fishermen, surfers, and the occasional shell collector.

The fisherman's were the only footprints on the beach.

Chapter 1

Six beer caps filled the pocket of Sarah Avery's cutoff jeans. She checked her watch; Christmas lunch was over, but the afternoon was hours from ending. Lame jokes printed on slips of paper found inside Christmas crackers and long-winded stories that she had heard before became louder. It was time to get out of here. Sarah crumpled the paper crown she was wearing into a tight ball and flicked it under the table. She muttered something about checking fishing conditions. No one noticed her grab the bottle of Bundaberg rum, her gift to herself, from the top of the gas fridge. No one tried to follow as she left the family holiday shack, and that satisfied her. The thought of being alone on the rocks with her father or his mate Don was excruciating. From the outdoor cold box she took a six-pack of beer and a liter of Coke and shoved them into her Esky fishing cooler.

She did not relax until she was steering the car, in a pleasant alcohol-infused idle, along the gravel road. At the wharf she parked behind the boatshed. Low greasy cloud sweated over the ocean horizon. Close to the shore the sea was choppy. She could leave the car here and walk back to the shack if she wanted to. On the backseat was the wicker picnic basket her sister had given her for Christmas. What a stupid gift, she had thought, as she thanked Erica that morning. Now she realized it was handy. She took one of the cups and poured herself a rum and Coke.

Runabout dinghies, partly filled with rainwater and seaweed, bobbed tightly on their cable wire restraint. Some had not been taken out to sea in years. They remained here, tied so severely they were barely able to float. Perhaps she should come down with a box of salt and pour it into the point where the cable was drilled into the rock. Better off being a shipwreck than like this.

Halfway through her drink, a muscular guy wearing his cap back-to-front emerged out of the scraggly casuarina trees. He trod carelessly on the native pigface, a purple-flowered succulent vine that protected the dune from the wind. She watched him skim stones across the little harbor and smoke a cigarette. He tossed the butt into the sea. Sam Shelley – all grown up. The last time she had seen him, maybe seven years ago, he had played Chinese checkers against her and Erica. He had cried when he lost. To cheer him up, Sarah had taken him fishing at the jetty and helped him reel in a beautiful leatherjacket.

He said he remembered her and sat in the passenger seat, fiddling with the stereo, adjusting the mirror, storing his cigarettes in the rental car's empty glove box. Several soft hairs that his razor had missed grew from his cheek.

Sarah didn't offer him the first beer; he asked. That point

would seem important to her when she recalled the evening later.

On Boxing Day the beach shacks huddled under one endless cloud of cold moisture. Sarah sat alone, watching the heaving sea through the window. It was perfect weather for reading, and there was a fly-fishing article in an old *Reader's Digest* Sarah wanted to have a look at. Unfortunately, Sarah's parents had invited their best friends, Pamela and Don, over for a game of Celebrity Head. They had played some kind of game every afternoon in the week since Sarah had arrived, while summer rain blew sideways from a chilled gray sky. Her sister, Erica, said Sarah had brought the rain with her. Indifferently she agreed and took another large mouthful of beer. Noisy rain popping into bowls and saucepans strategically arranged under the leaking roof forced everyone to raise their voices as they drank Ninth Island champagne from glasses marked with individual charms. For the fun of it Erica had attached a charm to Sarah's stubby. It was a single stiletto.

No one noticed Sarah's sadness; they barely noticed as she stood up to light the gas lanterns. She had told them that boredom had been her reason for quitting her job at Eumundi Barramundi Farm. Man troubles, too, she had added, when Erica pressed her. They all assumed Sarah had been rejected. Fair enough, Sarah didn't blame them; it was a safe assumption about a plain woman like her. It was easier for them to digest than the truth. Sick, perverted, mental; those were the names Jake had shouted across the wet asphalt that night. Her family didn't need to know that. One by one she held a matchstick beside the soft wicks, filling the shack with milky light. Conversation drifted around her like a familiar, itching blanket.

Sarah had a sour feeling of déjà vu; they were talking about the same things they had talked about for as long as she could remember. Jane Taylor, the angry woman who ran the guesthouse, had let her dogs run unleashed on the beach and one of them had chased a child. That was irresponsible, Sarah's mother, Felicity, said; Pamela agreed wholeheartedly.

Deep in the national park on the east coast of Tasmania, the Bay of Fires was a holiday community. People drove for hours from Launceston or Devonport every summer to open up their shacks or rent one of the humble fishermen's cottages or pitch a tent in the camping ground beside the lagoon. Two people lived here year-round, Jane Taylor and Roger Coker, who kept to himself in his green cottage. There were no more than a dozen shacks, no room for more than a dozen tents at the campsite. Even now at Christmas, the busiest time of the year, the beach remained quiet enough to suit Sarah. Everyone said the Bay was crowded, but it was nothing compared to a tourist-packed Queensland beach in January.

Beer bubbled up the back of Sarah's throat and into her nose. She swallowed and concentrated on the conversation. Simone Shelley had bought a new wave ski and had offered John and Don a lesson. Felicity, or Flip as everyone called her, and Pamela decided that was half funny, half pathetic. Simone was flirtatious, but that didn't bother Flip and Pamela, so they said; it was more that she wasn't warm, she wasn't comfortable around women. Pamela ran the corner store and was pleased to share local news. She said the campers were drinking a lot more than in previous years; she could tell by how much ice they bought from her.

She could tell other things, too, such as why certain people couldn't lose weight, judging by what they bought from her store. It didn't seem to occur to anyone that an apple or a banana in Pamela and Don's store cost three times the price of a bag of potato chips. The campers presumably brought their own fruit and vegetables from Launceston.

The only customers who could afford Pamela's fruit were the relatively well-off people who owned holiday shacks – professional people, doctors, teachers, business owners. Flip and Pamela were pharmacists. Flip owned a pharmacy in town, but Pamela had never used her degree. Instead, Pamela and her husband, Don, had worked in real estate and done so well they were semi-retired now. They ran the local shop in summer and then closed it and retreated to Queensland for the winter. Pamela and Flip had been best friends since studying pharmacy together. Sarah assumed they had been equally annoying back then: Pamela had been crowned Miss Pharmacy, Flip first runner-up. It was a story they still liked to tell – and with no embarrassment.

'Sarah's turn.' Erica wrote on a piece of paper and passed it to Sarah. Sarah licked the back of the paper and stuck it to her forehead.

'Am I a woman?'

'Yes.' A circle of grinning faces surrounded her.

'Am I married?'

'No.'

'Am I alive?'

'No.'

Sarah couldn't think of another question. She didn't care. The celebrity head was probably some pop star she had never heard of.

'Give me a clue.'

'You're an elderly virgin.' Erica's laugh was a hoot.

'Who is it?'

'It's not you!'

'Erica. Let her work it out.'

Sarah ripped the paper off her forehead. Everyone groaned. She was Queen Elizabeth I.

'Good one.' She tipped her head back and poured the warm flat froth at the bottom of her stubby down her throat.

Outside, pink light was visible through cracks in the darkening sky. Red sky at night, shepherd's delight. Although it was raining now, tomorrow would be clear. She would still leave. The week had dragged on long enough. The weather didn't bother her. In fact she preferred it; bad weather brought schools of salmon close to the beach and kept the tea tree-stained lagoon pleasantly childless. It was the Bay of Fires that she remembered from her childhood, when all the shacks were tiny Fibro fishing cottages and there was never a queue at the boat ramp.

Erica cupped her hand around another slip of paper as she wrote.

'One for you, Pam.'

Pamela stuck it on her forehead.

'Am I a woman?'

Flip and Erica shouted yes.

'Am I a bitch?'

'Yes!'

'Am I Simone Shelley?'

Raucous laughter drowned the rain. It woke Henry, who poked his head up and barked. Sarah couldn't feign a laugh.

It had been a mistake coming here. After living and working for seventeen months in the cheerful nosiness of Eumundi, Tasmania's isolation had appealed. Ninety kilometers down a gravel road to coastal wilderness. No electricity, no telephones, no television. Bay of Fires: summer population, seventy; winter population, two. But the isolation was not as reassuring as she had imagined. A week, a month here, nothing to talk about but Simone Shelley's alleged flirtations, untrained dogs, and fat people. Before long they would want more details about Sarah. It was the intimate details of other people's lives that nourished them. So far, Sarah had listed bare facts: she had quit her job and broken up with Jake.

She didn't know that she could keep her secret hidden. Kindness would be enough to shatter her fragile shell. The problems that had forced her self-imposed exile from her life up north would provide her mother and Pamela hours of intense discussion. Worse would be their disgust if they found out that she had messed around with Sam Shelley, Simone's seventeen-year-old son. If she was honest, she hadn't given his age a thought. And on Christmas Day, no less. It was so bad it was almost funny. But she had not drunk enough to laugh.

Sarah looked around the room at her family and their friends. If they turned on her, she could handle herself in an argument. But to be the focus of their concern would be unbearable. Sarah twisted the top off another bottle of beer.

Sarah went to bed too early and woke in the dark, with nothing to do but wait for day, prey to a contorted parade of raw memories. She tried to control her thoughts by focusing on work. On the barramundi farm there was order, systems, programs that required finite concentration. Before she quit she had been improving staff training. She'd taught them to diagnose diseases that the caged fish suffered. Each ailment had specific symptoms: gill disease, skin lesions, sores, viruses similar to those humans could contract. Lying in bed, Sarah visualized each symptom. Some were psychological, and she concentrated on recalling each troubling behavior, such as fish swimming unusually, or sitting at the bottom of the tank, or floating on the top, gasping for air.

Some of the blokes on her staff never got it. Glorified tank cleaners. Not that she'd ever say that to their faces; she had encouraged them to take pride in their work. But still, how many times did she need to remind them to be alert to the reactions of the fish every time they brought in new water or new breeding stock? Old anger temporarily contained her shame. She focused on her breathing, counting each breath, releasing it slowly. Maybe she was the problem. She had high expectations of people and got frustrated when her expectations weren't met. But so what? If they didn't like it, she could handle that. She only wanted them to reach their potential. Some of them had never had a chance; one older bloke had spent so much time moving in and out of prison, he had never had a proper job until Sarah made him full-time. No doubt some of the Eumundi Barramundi staff were glad she had quit. She could see them standing around the Pineapple Hotel pool table, laughing about her over Friday afternoon beers.

People were more of a challenge in land fish farming, as opposed to ocean fish farming. Storms and sudden shifts in currents, hot autumns and freezing springs, pollution; there were many unpredictable elements in ocean fish farming. The thing is, you expected these to occur. On a land farm, you were supposed to have total control of the environment.

Quiet and dark, that was how barramundi liked it. It was her job to make the environment as friendly as possible for the fish. Healthy fish lived a peaceful life, rippled currents on the surface of the tank their trademark. She imagined herself submerged near the bottom, slippery skins slicking past her, flipping somersaults in the cool darkness. On the tank floor, the sun would belong to another world. Oxygenized water bubbled upward to the top. She closed her eyes and allowed herself to be absorbed into the undulating swirl of four tonnes of barramundi. The distraction worked for a while until the madness crept in, her thoughts more frightening than any bad dream.

As soon as light appeared at the sliver where the mold-stained Ken Done curtains did not join up, she slid out of bed and hung a towel around her neck. She closed the shack door on Mum's and Dad's and Erica's sleep noises, escaping before the cups of tea and conversations that would follow her from the solitude of the couch to the wooden chair under the old beach umbrella on the front veranda.

Dad had mowed the track to the beach. It was reassuringly wide, but Sarah set each foot down with a deliberate thump and hummed to warn the poisonous black snakes that thrived in the area that she was coming. It was a childhood habit and she was barely conscious of it. Dad had done a good job of mowing the track, especially for someone who was not used to doing it. Sarah's parents had a gardener who came weekly. When Sarah had lived at her parents' home in Launceston, it seemed her dad had never had time to do anything more than tend his herb and flower gardens, his time stretched between his job as a lecturer in history at the university and his research on Tasmanian tin mining in the nineteenth century. Her father still made Sarah lists of handyman-type jobs to do whenever she came home.

Erica had mentioned that she had the same gardener tending the lawn at her place, which was a smaller version of the family's red brick and red tile roof Federation-style home. Erica worked as a flight attendant, her boyfriend, Steve, as a pilot, and they said they didn't have time to do it themselves. Sarah wondered what other aspects of their parents' lives Erica and Steve would eventually emulate. She could see Erica educating her children at one of Launceston's private schools and spending the next decade watching rowing regattas, netball matches, and ballet recitals in lieu of a social life, as their parents had done. It was not the life Sarah desired and this had been one of the reasons why she had moved away from Launceston as soon as she finished university.

At the bottom of the track she kicked off her sneakers and leapt across the smooth granite rocks and onto the chilled sand. The storm had cleared and the beach was empty, a slender pale arm curling between spiky yellow sea grass and the ocean under a scrubbed-clean blue sky. Curly brown seaweed and twists of orange string, driftwood and fishing line, broken shells, globs of smashed jellyfish, and bits of plastic littered the beach beneath the shacks. The sea was too rough for swimming. The usually clear green water churned sand. Clumps of dirty yellow froth like beer scum stained the beach. If Erica were here, she would crinkle her nose and say it smelled like raw sewage, but Sarah liked the salty, fishy smell that remained after the storms, that pungent aroma of decomposing seaweed. It was good for fishing.

Twenty minutes' walk down the beach, the dune flattened around a purple lagoon. Sarah tossed her towel on the sand and waded into the swimming hole without fuss. Smashed sticks, gum leaves, and other debris flushed from the gullies floated on the surface. She scooped water over the goose bumps on her thighs, wetting her sagging nylon one-piece, splashing her shoulders and face, smoothing her unbrushed hair back into its ponytail. The sun rose slowly in Tasmania and a chill breeze rippled the water. A school of tiny silver baitfish darted toward her, then away. She took a breath and dived. Underneath, she opened her eyes. The water was so cold it felt like her eyeballs had frozen.

The storm had created a new deep pool at one end of the lagoon, conveniently near a good jumping rock. She swam toward it. The distant sound of breaking waves was accompanied by the high screech of seagulls and the gentle lap as Sarah sidestroked through the water. For a moment she forgot everything. The lagoon was wrapped in quietness now, though before long it would be as noisy as a public swimming pool. Sarah had mentioned this to Erica last night and her sister had agreed, cheerfully, as though this was a good thing about the lagoon. Sarah couldn't stand it. The men in new Christmas board shorts following kids flapping on blow-up fluorescent-colored toys; mums yelling instructions; old women keeping their hair dry breaststroking up and down; and that awful blind friendliness of people who think they know you and want to ask stupid questions when all you want to do is press your shivering body flat against a hot rock and close your eyes.

When she got out she was cold. Wrapping the towel around her shoulders she walked along the beach, away from the shacks. The sand was warm under her icy feet. A man was coming toward her. As she got closer she realized it was Roger Coker. He swung his fishing bucket with his good hand, his rod wedged tightly under the other arm. She couldn't remember the last time she had spoken to him; it had been years since she had spent more than a weekend here. Roger was an awkward man, and she had always made a point of being friendly to him, conscious that it took him a certain amount of effort to initiate a conversation. Sarah curled her lips into a parched smile.

'There is a girl. Down half a mile. Dead.' He blinked and looked out to sea.

'What are you talking about?' Sarah resisted the urge to take a step backward; Roger was standing too close to her.

'Smells bad, worse than rotten squid.'

'A dead person?'

'Murdered.' His breath smelled like sour milk.

'On the beach?'

'Stabbed.'

His long white finger pointed to the unprotected end of the beach. With the rough swell that lingered after the storm, the only other person who might walk that far would be a shell collector. But there was no one else wandering along the tideline picking up polished creamy cowrie shells, Chinaman's fingernails, or the flat shells with a hole perfect for threading fishing line through. Apart from Roger, Sarah was alone on the beach.

'The Shelleys' is the closest phone,' Sarah said.

'No. No. I'll use the phone box at the shop.' Roger's gumboots dragged through the sand toward the shacks.

Sarah watched him for a moment, then followed his boot prints back along the shoreline. In the morning sun her shadow was long, a thin black ribbon that moved one step ahead of her toward the dead woman.

The smell hit her first; rotting flesh, as foul as road kill festering in the sun. Her stomach heaved but she didn't slow her pace. From a distance the body looked like a seal, curled and dark on the sand, the outgoing tide lapping her legs. Up close the blackened and bloated body was swollen around bikini bottoms. Her top half was naked.

A crab crawled out of the raw tissue. The stench was unbearable, but Sarah couldn't turn away. Covering her nose and mouth, she walked around the body. Roger's footprints formed a circle in the sand; none came close.

Sarah wasn't squeamish. Crouching down, she rolled the dead woman over. Her head was floppy like one of the dead fairy penguins tossed onto the beach by winter seas. Her empty eye sockets stared at the new sky. Sarah registered the polka-dot pattern of the bikini bottoms and reeled backward, her hands clawing at the sand as she scrambled away. Adrenaline shot through her system, at once sickening and strangely pleasing. She had not expected to recognize the corpse.

She sprinted toward the shacks, ignoring the splintering sensations in her ankle tendons as she pounded across the hard sand.

Chapter 2

Ocean swell muffled the police car's engine. The windows rattled and the chimney pipe swayed and tapped against the tin roof as two policemen came up the ramp. Erica tied a sarong around her waist. Sarah sat on the banana lounge and inspected her hands. Every nail had broken unevenly. Two nails were split up the center, ruined from repairing filter systems and replacing gutters. What could she tell the cops? She had been anticipating their arrival, had silently rehearsed what she would say; now they were here, her thoughts were beyond her control.

They took her statement while she sat there in her Speedos and a T-shirt that said *The Liver Is Evil and Must Be Punished*.

'I saw her in the guesthouse. I might have said hi.' Sarah didn't elaborate on the conversation she had had with the Swiss woman. 'I took Jane Taylor, the guesthouse owner, some mullet a few days ago. Can't remember when exactly.'

She wasn't lying. What passed between her and the pretty backpacker was nothing. It wouldn't interest the police.

Thinking about it made Sarah's stomach churn sluggishly. The younger, gravel-voiced policeman demanded to know why she had tampered with the crime scene.

'The danger is you destroyed evidence.'

'I know. I'm sorry. I don't know what came over me.' Sarah tried to read his face but it was inscrutable, his pen poised over his pad as though he expected some kind of confession. 'She's been soaking in the ocean for God knows how long. You won't get the killer's DNA.'

The older policeman stood with the sun behind him so that a shadow fell across her body. He had his hands deep in his pockets and his hips thrust forward. She wasn't intimidated. Sarah had been the only woman on the barramundi farm. She had been in charge of eleven men: hard-living, hardworking blokes who didn't hold back. She had been one of two women in her year studying aquaculture. At Hash House Harriers running club she was the only woman. She could hold her own from the ponds to the pub and anywhere else it counted.

'I am sorry I touched her.'

'It's all right.'

Sarah reached for a glass of water beside the banana lounge. She rolled the water around inside her mouth. It was warm and had a faint taste from the tank. They were correct; she shouldn't have touched the body.

'I felt sorry for her.'

If she started describing the twisted bikini, the legs splayed revealing unkempt pubic hair, the crawling lice, or the sand caked in her fingernails, there was a chance she would cry. If she started crying, there was a chance she would not be able to stop.

'What do you think happened to her?' Sarah asked.

'Too early to say. The forensics personnel will take the body to Hobart, and the postmortem will take place in a week or so. We'll get the toxicology reports first. The cause of death always takes longer. Of course, we can't release the findings until the family is located,' the older cop said. 'If she is a Swiss national, as the guesthouse owner suggests, that could take time.'

The younger cop added, 'But young women don't get killed for no reason.'

'She was raped?' Erica said. 'Oh my God.'

'That's a guess until the autopsy is completed,' the older policeman cut in. He stepped forward, and Sarah was out of the shadow of his body. Sun pierced her eyes and forced her to squint. 'If you remember anything . . .'

'This is like in the movies,' Erica said. 'If we remember anything, we'll come down to the station.'

'Yes, Erica. It's just like in the movies, except it's not, and someone did actually die,' Sarah said.

Embarrassment flushed Erica's face. She blushed easily. Cried easily, too. Everything came easily to Erica. The only thing Erica struggled with was failure. Sarah had often tried to assuage her younger sister's disappointment. The desire to protect Erica remained in Sarah, but right now it was dormant, too deep to be tapped.

Ashamed and unable to apologize for her meanness, Sarah turned away.

Not long after the police left, the shack became crowded. Elbows resting on the veranda railing, Sarah watched through the binoculars as the police removed the body. She ignored the chatter and the feeling that she was just another nosy resident. The forensics people worked slowly. One person was taking photographs. Another, crouched beside the body, was writing in a notepad. More men, in plain clothes, watched. There were no women documenting the crime scene.

Behind Sarah, her mother and Erica bustled about with the teapot and leftover Christmas cake and shortbread biscuits, as though this was a high school parents and friends fundraising morning tea and not the aftermath of a murder. Slurping tea from chipped cups, the visitors swapped bits of information with barely contained excitement.

It seemed the Swiss woman had been walking to the rock pool in the middle of the day, a few days before Christmas, when she was killed. No one even knew she was missing until Roger found the body. If he hadn't found her, there was a chance she could have washed away on the next high tide. Someone said that she had sunbathed topless every afternoon at Honeymoon Bay and laughter simmered through the crowd. They became silent when someone else added that the woman's parents would probably fly out from Switzerland to take her body home. Sarah was the only person who had spoken to the woman, a fact she didn't volunteer.

Anja Traugott was alone in the Bay of Fires Guesthouse when Sarah strode in, looking for Jane. Anja had tried to speak to her. She was not Sarah's kind of woman. Her accent, dumb and sexy at the same time, was irritating.

Sarah had been back in Tasmania for less than a day. Everything felt irrelevant except her own reeling sadness. Sarah told herself her unfriendliness had nothing to do with the woman's pale, pinup girl prettiness, or the fact that her clothing, tiny cutoff shorts with breasts almost falling out of her red and white bikini, was better suited to the Gold Coast than a Tasmanian national park. She wasn't jealous, she was just preoccupied.

But as Anja had traced her finger along Jane Taylor's wall map of the local coast, shades of blue pillowing out from the long curving beach to the continental shelf, Sarah had stood mutely, the plastic bag of mullet she was bringing Jane hanging limply by her side.

'The rock pool is a two-hour walk from here,' Sarah had said before leaving the woman staring at the map.

Sarah had been to the rock pool that morning, and the water, usually so clear you could see the delicate seaweed fronds growing on the bottom fifteen feet down, was blurred with fish guts and scales. Gulls scratched over bloodstained rocks where someone had cleaned fish. But Sarah had not mentioned this.

Sarah gripped the binoculars with damp fingers. Her hands were sweating. There were other walks she could have suggested; traversing the nearby apple and turnip farm to see the wild northern beach or hiking along the sandy Old Road past the local rubbish dump, known as the tip, and up to the burnt bridge where wildflowers were in season, tiny pink and lemon petals among parched banksia and wattle. Any of those would have made a nice walk for a tourist.

Through the binoculars Sarah watched as two people in white jumpsuits lifted the body into a bag, and then onto a stretcher, and carried it to a white van parked behind the grassy dune.

'It's quite disgusting that you touched that dead woman,'

Erica said with a grin. 'Mum's worried they'll make you a suspect.'

'Mum's got no idea.'

'Yeah.' Erica took the binoculars. 'Oh. She's gone.'

There was disappointment in her voice as she turned and announced the news to the people gathered on the veranda.

A solitary bodysurfer hurtled down the face of a seven-foot wave in the post-storm swell beneath the shack. The wave crashed, and he disappeared into the beating foam. Sarah counted silently. It was a good thirty seconds before he emerged from the white water. It would be like being inside a washing machine in there. He stood up, twisted around, and dived under an incoming wave, just before it exploded with a force Sarah could hear from the veranda. His forceful strokes were those of someone who had done years of swimming training in the pool.

She had not seen him since Christmas night at the wharf. She had woken the next morning on cold sand, daylight penetrating her closed lids. She could smell something acrid and hear flies buzzing. Her hair stuck to her face, pasted across one eye, and she desperately needed a drink of water. She sat up, squinting in the overcast morning glare. She was in a sand dune. Her fly was undone and one of her sneakers was not on her foot. She could not remember passing out.

She was alone, her skin clammy and her guts sick. Her head reeled when she stood up. She peeled the damp clump of hair off her face and pushed it back. The ocean and rocks fluctuated and she felt seasick. It looked like the sand dunes beyond the wharf, although her hungover mind was not sure. She couldn't remember walking up there. The last memory she had was of being in the car, listening to the clinking of moored boats and rain on the roof. Sam, her seventeen-year-old one-night stand, had left, of that she was fairly certain. She could not remember leaving her car.

Flies buzzed around something at her feet. Creamy vomit, a chunky pile of regurgitated Christmas lunch, sat centimeters from where her head had been. She fingered her clumped hair; the smell was foul. She retched, stomach muscles convulsing in a bid to dredge her guts. Yellow bile came out, acidic and rancid.

Erica's voice brought her back to the present, the hot veranda and the swirling swell below.

'Sam Shelley.' Erica leaned on the railing beside her. 'He is H.O.T. Hot.'

'You're learning to spell. Don't tell me Qantas are educating their trolley dollies these days? It's really great.'

'We're not just there for our looks.' Erica laughed; meanness was wasted on her. 'Go and get the binoculars so we can have a closer look.'

'No.' Sarah felt saliva spray from her mouth. 'Someone is dead, Erica. Get a hold of yourself.'

In the surf, Sam was being pummeled in knee-deep water. He braced his hands on his knees and bent forward, probably hacking salt water out of his nose.

Sarah went inside and lay on the couch. Erica and her mother treated her like she was ill, offering her toast and watching her closely for signs of something. Signs of what, she didn't know. Did they expect her to break down in floods of tears, shaking with shock at what she had touched? That wasn't going to happen. At least they weren't asking any more personal questions. She closed her eyes as Erica placed a cup of tea beside her. The attention was pleasing.

The scent told Sarah the tea was Earl Grey, her favorite. Without tasting it, she knew it would contain one sugar, and have been topped up with cold water so it was barely hot, just how she liked it. Jake didn't know how to make her tea; he had always needed to ask her. These were things sisters knew about each other.

The thought saddened Sarah. It was only because she was feeling so horribly wretched that she felt this antagonism toward Erica. Over the years Sarah had made compromises for her younger, less resilient sister. When she was ten, Sarah had nodded mutely as Jane Taylor yelled at her for telling Pamela that Gary Taylor had been seen in town buying head lice shampoo. In fact it was Erica who had spotted Jane's ex-husband in the chemist's and shared the information.

'We don't need talk that the guesthouse has a nits epidemic,' Jane had said as Sarah stood stunned beside the lagoon one day. 'Shut your little gob.'

They had looked alike then, before puberty hit, two chubby, curly-pigtailed girls, and many times one had been mistaken for the other. As puberty arrived, Sarah took up rowing, developing her thick-muscled arms and legs, while Erica played tennis socially and maintained a girlish figure. These days no one would mix them up, although people did comment, pleasingly, on their similar catlike brown eyes.

Sarah had lied, concealed information, remained silent, for Erica. At seventeen, when Erica crashed their parents' car driving drunk, Sarah took the blame. At twenty-two, when Erica and her boyfriend accidentally left a condom wrapper underneath the hammock at the shack, Sarah had pretended it was hers. Sarah wasn't a hero. She just didn't care what other people thought of her. Erica, on the other hand, crumbled at a whisper of disapproval.

There were things about Erica that Sarah would never understand. For instance, Erica had currently taken four weeks' annual leave and planned to spend the entire time at the shack. Steve would come and go as his pilot schedule allowed. Who would choose to spend four weeks in a two-bedroom shack with their parents? Sarah was only here until she worked out what to do next. Sarah told herself she should be grateful Erica was here – at least she would have company.

'Thank you for the tea,' Sarah said, sitting up. 'It's nice.'

From the shack's veranda Sarah watched the road. She still felt ill. It wasn't the revolting smell, or the mutilated flesh, but the thought of that woman's final hours that gripped her. There were kind ways to kill, if you wanted something dead. On the barramundi farm, fish that were to be processed were put on ice to slow them down. Sometimes they put a mild anesthetic in the ice slurries to slow them down even quicker. Sick fish that needed to be destroyed weren't treated so kindly. Sarah preferred to put sick fish on ice, but some of the staff were ruthless and chucked the fish in the trash bin alive. For twenty minutes the creatures would flap away on top of one another until they ran out of air.

Walking on the other side of the road in the gutter beside the farm's barbed wire fence was Roger. If he had looked down toward the shack he would have seen her, motionless on the swing she had built herself when she was nine years old, her fists balled on either knee. Sarah watched him pass, a solitary shape huddled under the morning's expansive pale sky.

The fishing section of the Bay of Fires general store was a mere shelf. There were several bags of hooks, floaters and sinkers, reels of line, some butterfly nets, and an overpriced Alvey surf rod that had been there almost as long as Pamela and Don Gunn had owned the shop. Sarah knew the contents of that shelf as well as she knew the contents of her tackle box, and as she walked down the hill toward the shop, she envisaged which size hooks she was going to purchase. The wind had dropped, and there wasn't time to muck around if she wanted to catch anything today. She also didn't want to get embroiled in a long conversation with Pamela.

Several people were sitting in front of the shop, under a plastic banner saying *Real Espresso Coffee*, $2. Sarah vaguely recognized them; they belonged to an extended family who had camped at the back of the lagoon from Christmas until Australia Day ever since she could remember. The woman straddled the picnic table's wooden bench. She held a pie in front of her mouth with two hands and a can of Coke was wedged between her sprawling thighs. Her wide bra straps cut into sunburned skin flaking off her shoulders. Unfortunate looking, or salt of the earth, was how Mum or Erica would describe a woman like that.

Everyone did it, made assumptions without bothering to find out the truth. Until she moved up north she had thought it was a Tasmanian characteristic, the result of living in an insular place. Of course it wasn't. More than once Sarah had been mistaken for a lesbian. She kept her shoulder-length hair slicked away from her face and held back with a plain rubber band. She never wore makeup, and her clothes were functional: bobbled T-shirts left over from her university days or aquaculture conferences. Jeans and old clothes were practical when you were feeding fish.

The woman outside the shop was speaking through a mouth full of pie. It was hard to tell if the two men were listening. They smoked and drank iced coffees while looking down the road. The short man finished his drink and popped the carton under his foot. He tossed it through the air toward the bin as Sarah approached. Milk droplets rained in front of her.

'Bunghole, you're a bastard,' the woman said, adding for Sarah's benefit, 'Sorry, love.'

'No problem.' Sarah forced a smile.

Keith Gibson, known to everyone as Bunghole, was jockey-small with a solid beer gut. He wore a blue wife-beater and tight grubby jeans that slunk down over his flat bottom. He wasn't looking at Sarah; he was distracted by something happening on the other side of the road. A policeman Sarah had not seen before leaned on the open door of his car, staring down the gravel toward the boat ramp. There was nothing to look at except an empty paddock of yellow clumpy grass on one side and shabby peeling paperbarks hiding the beach on the other. Parked in the black sand at the top of the boat ramp was an empty boat trailer attached to a dusty sedan. Sarah pushed her way through the multicolored fly strips; Pamela would know what was going on.

Coins clunked on Pamela's counter. 'Here's your change.

Sixty cents. Where are your manners? Good boys. Thank you.'
Pamela spoke to the young boys she was serving as though
they were her own children. She turned to Sarah, her blond
bobbed hair swinging as she shook with excitement.

'Sarah. Sweetheart. Your mother told me what happened. I
can't believe it. You poor thing.' Her fingertips were flashes
of vermilion darting through the air. 'You know, I saw Roger
Coker lurking in the phone box when I opened the curtains
this morning.' Although there was no one else in the shop,
Pamela lowered her voice. 'I said to Donald, he's probably
ringing the sex line.' She put her hand over her mouth and
laughed. 'I can't believe I said that, given what's happened
today. No one can believe it; murder in paradise. Two murders
in paradise.'

Sarah picked up a bottle of Hartz mineral water. There was
no point trying to speak until Pamela had finished.

'My heart goes out to the Crawfords. I can't imagine how
they're feeling. The same beach where Chloe was last seen.
The same jolly beach.'

Australia had fixated on Chloe Crawford's disappearance.
Her family had rented one of the fishing shacks down at the
wharf for a week last summer. Sixteen-year-old Chloe had
taken one of the shack's surfboards down to the beach late
one afternoon, the hazy hour before dusk when anyone who
knew better would not dare to swim for fear of sharks. From
what Sarah could remember from the news coverage at the
time, Mr and Mrs Crawford were bush folk. He had a massive
beard; she wore her hair in two long plaits. Chloe was their
only child.

The surfboard was never found, nor were Chloe's shorts,

T-shirt, towel, and sunglasses which her mother had seen her leave with. It was unlikely that Chloe was simply lost at sea. Sarah's parents and Pamela and Don had helped search; everyone had. They had not found a single trace of the girl.

Pamela took a deep breath and exhaled with both hands on the counter. 'Everyone is saying there's a serial killer. I'm not joking, Sarah.'

Sarah tried not to laugh. There probably was a serial killer out there, but Pamela's blatant excitement about it was comical. It was as if she had won one hundred dollars on a scratch-and-win ticket.

'I feel sick thinking about it. I need something to do.' Pamela ducked her head under the counter and pulled out a green bottle of disinfectant. Citrus-scented vapor rose as she sprayed the counter in fast bursts.

Pamela wiped the counter, speculating on how authorities would contact the dead woman's family in Switzerland and describing the reactions of customers as she told them the news. One woman had wondered if the ocean was now contaminated and whether it was safe to swim.

'I don't understand why you went up there. It's not what anyone needs to see,' Pamela said. 'You'll have nightmares.'

'I'll be all right.' More than once Sarah had wondered how her mother could stand being best friends with Pamela. Gossip dressed up as concern never fooled Sarah.

'Anyway. You saw Roger . . . at what unearthly hour were you on the beach?'

Measuring her words in terms of how they would sound repeated to the next customer, Sarah told her the story. For once Pamela listened carefully, nodding as she slid candy cobbers, teeth, bananas, freckles, and milk bottles into piles for her one-dollar lolly bags.

'It's awful,' Pam interrupted, raising her voice as an elderly man and woman entered the shop. 'I've been coming here every summer since I married Donald, and I cannot believe that someone could be killed – murdered, for goodness' sake – in a sleepy holiday village like this one.'

The couple looked up from the ice cream freezer. Sarah pretended to be fascinated by the overpriced tackle. There was no way she was going to be drawn into a discussion about Roger Coker and Anja Traugott with strangers.

The man paid for two Billabong ice creams and they stood there eating them as Pamela repeated the story. She was unstoppable.

'The police think she was dumped out at sea in a boat. They're down there now, talking to the fishermen,' Pamela concluded.

'You'll scare your customers away,' Sarah said when the couple finally left. 'If people think there's a psychopath living here, they might all pack up and go back to town for the summer.'

'Good. I'm sick of everyone already and it's not even January. Take them.' She waved away payment for the fishing hooks.

Pamela followed Sarah outside. The police car had gone, and the sunburned woman was climbing into the passenger seat of a sky blue Hilux, indifferent to her floppy shorts riding up so the baggy beige cotton of her underpants showed.

'Make sure your father locks the front door tonight, sweetheart. It bothers me that they sleep with it unlocked.'

'You too, Pamela. Keep safe.'

'Please. No one's going to be messing with an old girl like me.'

In the driver's seat of the Hilux, Bunghole pressed his cigarette to his mouth with curled fingers. Ferret, Sarah thought, and then caught herself. She sounded like Mum and Erica and Pamela. The woman slammed her door shut, and they all gave the thumbs-up as the truck skidded onto the road.

'Aren't those campers revolting?' Pamela waved as the Hilux jolted away.

There was a ledge at the southern end of the gulch where Sarah had once caught seventeen cocky salmon in one afternoon. Many summers had passed since. The orange lichen-covered rocks were smoother against her bare legs, the water colder and clearer than she remembered. She took a squid tentacle out of the bait container and slid it onto a hook. The second hook she baited with a pilchard. She cast out and waited.

In her twenties when she used to fish here, she had nothing more pressing on her mind than the fish she would catch. Sure, she worried about pointless things, people usually. Jane's sad smile when children stopped to pat one of her dogs as she walked by the lagoon; her mother's need always to check with John before she did anything; Pamela's tendency not to listen properly, which Sarah felt was caused by her thoughts being helplessly elsewhere. A person's dignity was fragile, capable of being fractured by a glance or the wrong word. She used to worry about other people; now it was herself she could not stop thinking about.

Three lines later she saw Roger Coker, high on a rock above a swirling kelp eddy. His presence startled her; she had thought she was alone. He waved a finger before turning away and hiding his face toward the ocean. Roger was strange, but not as strange as everyone enjoyed believing. He wasn't that much older than Sarah, maybe forty, but he had the surrendered, hunched posture and parched skin of a man who had lived for much longer. Sarah remembered him wandering the beach when she was a child, wearing a long-sleeved shirt and trousers even in the middle of January, never swimming, sometimes sitting shyly near the mothers or paddling in the shallows. He became even more self-conscious when Sarah and Erica turned into teenagers. He still waved and smiled but didn't try to speak to them anymore, often spending hours crouching half hidden in the dune grass, watching the families splashing in the lagoon.

Slowly reeling in empty line after empty line, checking the baits and recasting, Sarah began to breathe more easily, and each swing of the rod became smoother. Her eyes slid along the watery horizon to Sloop Rock and the point where the wooden jetty, built for the trains carrying tin, once stood. Everyone said that was where the woman had been murdered and thrown into the sea.

Her finger felt the line tighten and she wound it in. The cocky salmon had gone for the pilchard. Its mouth opened and closed, its body writhed, as she slipped the hook out of its flesh. A quick twist to the neck and it was dead. The fish stiffened and spasmed; she tossed it in the bucket. She removed the squid tentacle. When she cast out again, both hooks were loaded with a pilchard.

The salmon were funny like that. On any given day they would prefer either one bait or the other. It depended on what was around; if they had been feeding on a school of pilchards, they would take the squid bait. If, like today, she was catching them with pilchards, it meant the ocean was probably full of squid. It would be a good idea to return with the squid jig tonight.

Sarah squinted to see through the haze caused by shiny afternoon light. The water slapped the rocks with more insistence, the black mass of kelp shifting and folding with the waves. She didn't hear Roger climb down the rocks.

'I didn't have nothing to do with that girl,' Roger said. 'Nothing.'

'You scared me,' Sarah said.

He grinned, showing the blackened broken teeth, reminding her of the nickname Smiley they had secretly called him since they were teenagers.

'Murderer. They called me a murderer. I know them. I've seen them with their parents.' He was muttering and looking out to sea, so it was difficult to understand what he was saying.

'What do you mean?'

'Those kids.' He gestured beyond the lagoon, toward the camping ground.

He produced a shell from his pocket, one of the common sturdy crustaceans that the tide left in arcs along the beach. It formed a creamy circle in his dry, leathery palm. He slapped his back and the top of his head, demonstrating where the shells had hit him.

Sarah finally understood. 'They're children. Don't worry.'

'I never met the Swiss woman. When the first one

disappeared, I was up in the Douglas Aspley chopping wood with Uncle Les. Don from the Bay of Fires shop saw us getting petrol for the chainsaw in Douglas River. Can you tell them?'

'No one thinks it was you, Roger.'

He crouched down to inspect the contents of her bucket. The top of his bent neck was dark red and freckled; beneath it was a slender stretch of delicate skin so pale it was possible it had never been exposed to sunlight.

'Cocky salmon. Pilchards will catch something. Squid's running.'

His way of articulating her thoughts rattled her. He was peculiar. She didn't mind talking to Roger Coker here on the rocks in sight of the shacks, or anywhere on the main beach, but she wouldn't want to be alone with him any other place. One summer when she was seventeen or eighteen he had followed her across the rocks.

'I'd make a good husband,' he had said as though they were continuing a previous conversation. 'I own the house. I don't drink like some blokes. I'd let my missus work and go into town . . . whatever you wanted.'

She had told him she had a boyfriend. It was a lie, but he had nodded as though he expected this, squatting with his hands cupped around his eyes. She could see the reddened skin of his stumpy hand, chafed where his fingers should have been.

'If you're not interested, you can tell your sister. I don't mind,' he had said.

As creepy as the conversation was, it still made Erica and Sarah laugh.

His was a lonely life. He lived in a blackberry vine-covered cottage with old newspapers for curtains and rusting car skeletons in the yard. No one cared how many fish he had caught when he came home each night. She imagined having sex with him before she realized what she was thinking, immediately halting the image of his inexperienced panting, his dirty fluids contaminating her body.

Think of something else, quickly. Pamela said he had had a girlfriend once, a shy, chubby woman who bought toilet paper and kitchen cleaning spray at the store. Someone saw them walking on the beach. Apart from that, no one had seen Roger with anyone, except the uncle who came down to fish a couple of times each summer.

'Any idea who murdered that woman?' Sarah said.

'Nope.' He replaced the lid on her bucket. 'It's not hard to kill a person. It is harder to kill a snake than a person.'

A larger wave washed up behind her, cold seawater smacking over her head and shoulders, so she yelped. Roger laughed his high-pitched giggle, eerie in the long, quiet afternoon.

'Don't worry about a bit of water. The only thing a pretty lady like you needs to worry about is that you'll be next.'

When he was gone, Sarah turned back to the ocean. After every encounter she had with Roger her skin felt damp and prickly. Although she hadn't touched him, had never touched him, he left her with a foul residue of intimacy that made her guts slide.

Knee-deep in the shallows, Don wore the flaccid expression of someone lost in thought. Sarah splashed water at him and he startled. Amicably he splashed back. He had seen dolphins. There had been a pod of them, maybe as many as seven, pirouetting out of the waves. It was worth waiting for. They watched in silence for a few minutes.

'Pamela said you had a boyfriend up in Queensland?' Don said.

'Not anymore.'

'Oh. What happened?'

'You know. Ended.'

'Got it. Some blokes don't know a good thing when it's staring them in the face.'

'Something like that.'

She waved goodbye and continued making her way to the point where she planned to swim. The hard wet sand felt pleasant under her bare feet. Sarah was glad that Don didn't ask any more questions. He never said much; it was one of the things she liked about him.

Initially, that had been one of the things she liked about Jake. As she got to know him, his silences lost their sexiness. Jake was dissatisfied with everything: his car that kept breaking down; his flatmate who earned more than him doing fly in, fly out for a coal mine up north; his dog that wouldn't obey an instruction; and, eventually, he was dissatisfied with Sarah. She should have realized what was happening sooner, taken a gauge from the increasing tension of their squabbles or the lack of real conversation between them. Instead, his discontent had festered until it exploded that night at the Pineapple Hotel. Maybe if she had had someone to mull it over with, things would have turned out differently. But she was hardly a woman who found the dissection of a relationship to be a worthwhile conversation topic.

Sarah had little time for talk. Consequently she had few

female friends. That didn't bother her. She was comfortable in a world where neurotic conversations about weight, husbands, job stress, or other people's business, followed by confidence-boosting pep talks, did not exist. She would miss that about the fish farm, where insults about one another's weight, attractiveness, or genitalia were routine. Nothing was off limits. Even others' families were targets. If the guys became too revolting, she concentrated on the computer spreadsheet or double-checked that the automatic feeder was set correctly and pretended she hadn't heard.

Sometimes they tried to shock her.

'You ever been put on the spit, Aves?' one of the guys asked one day.

Sarah had a thick hide; she wouldn't have lasted fourteen years in the industry otherwise.

'I'm not giving you visuals for your wank bank. Get back to work.'

She was the boss, so the blokes had no choice about that.

Thirty meters offshore was a rock reef covered in shiny black mussels. To harvest the mussels, you had to float across slippery fingers of bull kelp and haul yourself onto the rock. As kids Sarah and Erica had often dared each other to jump over the tangling kelp fronds and into the sea. Sarah climbed up and surveyed the tightly packed shellfish. Panfried in butter and sprinkled with chopped parsley, they were a snack Erica and Flip enjoyed. They were too chewy to be Sarah's favorite food, but her mother often commented on how well they went with champagne. Sarah chose ten of the biggest, ripping them off the rock with a firm hand, and placed them in a plastic bag, which she tied onto the strap of her bathing suit. They would enjoy the treat.

As she prepared to dive back in, a childhood memory halted her. Once, on this very rock, Erica had shoved her. She had lost her footing, rough shells grating the skin off her thighs as she slid into the sea. In those terrifying minutes as she sank and struggled in the kelp, Sarah had thought she was going to drown.

This time, being extra careful to avoid the kelp, Sarah dived long and low. She emerged some distance from the rock. Immediately she recognized the hum of a thirty-horsepower Yamaha motor. She treaded water and tried to look over the rock reefs and the incoming waves, but she couldn't see the vessel. It was safe to assume if she couldn't see the boat, the driver couldn't see her. It was dangerous to be swimming where she was. She twisted around and began to swim to the beach. If the boat driver was preoccupied, or not watching where he was going, the propeller could kill her. Sarah swam faster, stopping every few strokes to look for the boat. It was getting louder but she still could not sight it.

'Ahoy!' she yelled.

There was no reply. The approaching engine noise came from the other side of the rocks. Boats – even a small dinghy like the tinny coming toward her – had no business in this cove. There were no pots to check, and it was rocky enough to make line fishing treacherous. Sarah swam, her long hard strokes propelling her toward the beach. As she turned to breathe, she saw the tinny meters away, bearing down on her. It was too close. Whoever was driving hadn't seen her.

She duck-dived, remaining under for as long as she could

hold her breath, scissors-kicking in the direction of the shore. When she was certain the tinny wasn't above her she came up for air, gasping. Her eyes and ears felt like they were bleeding. She was too puffed to try and shout an insult at the skipper. Fool.

Sarah floated on her back, waiting until her breathing was under control. It sounded like the tinny was heading north, back to the boat ramp. She wished she had seen some identifying information on it, the name, the color, even a glimpse of the engine. He shouldn't have been in so close. He could have run her over, his propeller butchering her, killing her. Perhaps Anja was the victim of a hit-and-run? She would not have had any idea of the dangers associated with sharing the water with a tinny driven by a moron.

The long-ago night after Erica had pushed her in, Sarah had curled up on her banana lounge bed, listening as her parents discussed how fortunate it was that Sarah fell in and not Erica. Sarah was well able to look after herself, they agreed. She had turned her face to the pillow, biting into the chunky foam to stifle the aching sob. Her brain had flicked from the terror of being submerged under the kelp, to her parents' apparent indifference to her vulnerability, and back again. Just for once, she had wished to be the fragile, needy daughter.

But no good would come of dwelling on the past. Over the sound of the waves and her ringing ears, she could hear the motor fading. She swam toward the beach.

Sarah spread an old road map of the Tasmanian east coast on the kitchen bench, studied it, and penciled a cross at the place where the woman washed in. Her mother was leaning over the sink, brushing her teeth. The sloshing of the brush in someone else's mouth was not a sound Sarah was used to hearing. She looked up from the map to see her mother watching her.

'Why are you writing on the map?' Flip said.

Sarah shrugged, swirling the beer in the can. Her mother rinsed her toothbrush. Usually they used the little bathroom at the end of the veranda to brush their teeth.

'Newsflash, Mum. Anja Traugott and Chloe Crawford were young. I think you'll be safe using the outside bathroom.'

Sarah meant to reassure, to tease; her mother recoiled. There was a moment when she could have apologized, but it passed. Sarah concentrated on the map.

Strange things had happened on this isolated beach. Almost ten years ago, half a dozen perfect square holes, two meters deep, were found dug in the sand. Newspaper reports suggested a midnight boat delivery of contraband – drugs or smuggled crayfish. But like on the morning Roger found that woman, no one heard or saw anything suspicious.

Sarah remained silent as she watched her mother lock the shack door. They had never locked the shack, not even when they visited the nearest town, a ninety-minute drive on corrugated gravel, for groceries. They never lit all four gas lanterns or closed the curtains of an evening, but tonight someone had done so.

As her family settled into their beds, Sarah remained at the kitchen bench, sipping her beer. Erica's boyfriend, Steve, had arrived earlier in the evening. He was a pilot, and his hat was on the counter. Sarah spun it around on her finger, recalling the fuss Mum and Erica had made about how handsome he looked in his Qantas uniform. She could hear Erica and Steve talking in their bedroom, their voices low and friendly. Dinner's heated scent, cheese and pasta, lingered. She wished she could open a window, but it wasn't worth the alarm it would cause.

In Eumundi her house was never completely closed, not even at night or when it rained so hard the house swayed to an oceanic rhythm on its old legs. Up north, nature was not restrained by brick walls and insulation. Curious possums wandered through the living room, and rats used the frangipani tree as a ladder to access the kitchen window, both creatures leaving bite marks in the avocados in the fruit bowl. Moss grew in the bathroom and palm fronds pushed through the wrought iron veranda railing. Even the cobwebs had mold growing on them.

She opened the gas fridge and tried to replace the beer cans she had drunk. Doing so now was better than doing it in the morning, when the task would be incorporated into Erica's running commentary. It was difficult to stack the cans on the top rack without making a noise. She knew she didn't need another one. She knew she should drink some water and go to bed. Instead, she took another can of beer back to the bench. Fine soot had fallen from the lantern wick onto the counter. With her finger she traced the letters JW in it, looked at them for a moment, and erased the initials with a swipe of her fist.

She was home, but homesickness overwhelmed her. What for, she did not know. There was nothing to go back for. She folded the map of Tasmania tightly, pinching the brittle old paper so hard it tore.

* * *

Her head hurt when she woke in the morning. The water bottle she had taken to bed was empty. Hanging from the ceiling above the top bunk was an old wooden surf rod, its rusty sinker dangling directly over Sarah's face. This was the bedroom she had slept in every summer holiday since she was a child, and it had not changed. Rat-chewed boogie boards were wedged in the wardrobe, a yellow sticker saying *Brownies Are Beautiful* peeled off the door, the shaggy green seventies bedspreads and doughy polyester pillows smelled from being in storage all winter. It wasn't so much a bedroom as a hole in the wall. The bunk and the cupboard only just fit inside the space. There was no door, and she could see the kitchen and the ocean through the window above the sink. Anyone walking past could look in and see her, too.

She could hear Erica and her boyfriend in the kitchen. Steve had picked Erica a flower while she made him coffee. It was a tradition they were copying from Flip and John, who had begun every day of their thirty-six-year marriage with the ritual. Jesus. They lacked the imagination to dream up their own thing. They were so cheesy, and Sarah was about to tell them when she heard Pamela's voice.

'I was interviewed this morning and you'll be pleased to know I'm innocent,' Pamela called as she entered the shack without knocking. 'The police have three names they're interested in. All local men.'

Sarah heard her mother gasp.

'Who?' Erica said.

'Everyone's saying it's one of those men who camp behind the lagoon. Roger Coker found the body, which makes him a suspect. Of course, there was talk he had something to do with Chloe Crawford's disappearance, way back then.'

'He's an official suspect?' Erica asked. 'Goodness.'

'There's a yellow station wagon driving around with a group of surfer boys whom the police would like to speak to. I said they hadn't been into the shop.'

'Roger Coker has the right profile,' Erica said. 'He was mistreated as a child. Neglected. Abused. Remember when Don saw Roger running along next to the car and horrible old Mrs Coker hanging out the window hitting him with a rope?'

'Maxwell saw that. Not Donald. I'd forgotten,' Pamela said.

'It was good that she died,' Flip said.

The gas in the hot water system clicked and hummed, and there was the flush of water rushing through the pipes as someone filled the kettle.

'I don't know that Roger is capable of murder,' Erica said. 'He's too gentle, too shy to hurt someone. Remember when he ran over the possum and then came up here to ask Dad to put it out of its misery?'

'Call me a snob, but the people who camp around here become more unsavory every year,' Pamela said. 'I was saying to Donald, it's the rubbish that bothers me. When you camp, you take out whatever you take in. And it's high fire danger, but Donald and I could smell campfire smoke yesterday.'

'That rubbish was revolting last year,' Flip said. 'I'll never forget all the broken glass bottles and cigarette butts we picked up off the beach on New Year's Day.'

'Was that the fishermen?' Sarah called as she swung down from the top bunk.

'Most likely. We collected an entire garbage bag full of rubbish. I'll tell you something you won't read in tomorrow's paper.' Pamela lowered her voice. 'I apologize, it's gruesome. They believe that girl was killed with two different knives. And the intensity of the attack suggests someone psychotic who hates women, or was under the influence of drugs.'

'The impression I got was that the police wouldn't confirm any of that until they have the autopsy results, and that wouldn't be for a week.' Sarah came out of the bedroom. 'It's a suspected murder, a suspected rape, or whatever.'

'I'm just saying what everyone is saying,' Pamela replied. 'We would be foolish to wait for a postmortem result to confirm there is a killer on the loose. Someone killed that woman.'

'Maybe,' Sarah answered. There was some sense in what Pamela said.

'Maybe we should go back to town,' Erica said.

'There's no need to panic.' Pamela sounded confident. 'The police are advising people to be cautious. Nothing more. We need to be alert, that's all.'

'Be alert, not alarmed,' Sarah said.

'They're not going to catch anyone.' Erica shook her head. 'There are posters up in every small town from the Fingal Valley to Bicheno and up to Ansons Bay and they still haven't found a trace of the Crawford girl. There's always something on television about her. This is just a tourist. As if the police have a chance.'

Everyone paused. From the road came the sound of male voices, raised in anger. Erica ran into the bedroom to look out the window.

'It's Don,' Erica said. 'He's yelling at someone. Funny. I've never heard him shout.'

The shack shook as the three women ran outside to see. Sarah remained at the table, eating another slice of Pamela's cake. If Don was going off his rocker, he would be embarrassed afterward. He certainly wouldn't want an audience.

At the bottom of the beach track Sarah paused to breathe in the cool, calming air. Beyond the rush of the ocean and the cawing seabirds she heard someone cough. There was no sign of another human; no shoes or folded towel.

She weaved through the rocks toward the sound. As she drew closer, she rethought her decision. Approaching a person you couldn't see was a mistake. She should have either walked straight back up the track or bolted across the rocks to the open beach, where at least the visibility offered her some kind of protection. Here, locked between giant boulders, no one from the shacks could see her. Each breath she took felt strained, as though she were at altitude. Someone was there; she could hear the sound of feet sliding in the sand. She took another step closer and saw the bag. It was a plain green cloth bag, the kind people use to carry their groceries. Poking out the top was fishing line, a weathered milk carton, and, chillingly, an old-fashioned corrugated fishing knife with wide-set, rusted teeth. It was not sharp enough to make a swift, clean kill. When she was a girl, she had seen her father use one like that to dislodge abalone. She looked around, but the beach was empty.

As she moved away, a hand landed on her shoulder. She screamed. A man shouted. Sarah spun around, fists clenched and rising.

It was her father. 'What are you doing?' she said.

'What?'

'Dad, you fruit loop. Is that your bag?'

'I beg your pardon,' John said. 'Yes, that's my bag.'

Sarah marched to the bag and peered in. As well as the knife and fishing line there were scraps of fishing net, a plastic ice cream container, a collapsed sandy beer can, and pieces of different-colored glass. He was picking up rubbish. She sat down too quickly, like wet sand being dumped out of a bucket. It hurt her coccyx.

'You scared the hell out of me,' she said.

John glanced at his rubbish bag. 'Why?'

Sarah started to laugh. 'Don't worry.'

It was not worth trying to explain her brief suspicion. It was ridiculous. Her father shrugged and continued with his rubbish-collecting mission.

Hundreds of footprints dimpled the icing-sugar-white sand, and discarded police tape flickered in the dune grass. A gentle onshore wind hummed into a discarded polystyrene coffee cup. There were no other signs that the dead woman, Anja Traugott, had lain there.

Sarah picked up the coffee cup and strode into the dune, ignoring the grasses swatting her legs. Behind the rise the terrain flattened. Banksias and pigface clung to the sandy soil. She stopped in a small clearing which was accessible from the gravel road that ran along the back of the beach. A low wooden sign announced *No Camping. Day Use Only*. Tires had torn the white sandy surface, the weight of several cars ripping into the ground so the black undersoil showed through like a bruise.

Balancing on the sign, Sarah scanned the coast. Dainty clouds rushed south high above the horizon; beneath it the sea had the calmness of a barramundi pond. A pair of hooded plovers circled her, their distance reassuring.

Sturdy, steady waves broke at the place where the sea had delivered itself of Anja Traugott. Impulsively she ran toward it. At the ocean's edge she stripped away her clothing until she was naked, throwing it in a pile on the sand. She dove under the first small wave, enjoying the coldness. Mistaking her father for a killer was not a good move. Maybe she and Erica would laugh about it later. Or maybe, with the benefit of hindsight, she would pinpoint it as the moment when she started to lose it. Calm down, she told herself, and allowed the undertow to suck her body in.

The undertow was stronger than she'd anticipated. It sucked her down to the bottom, each wave tumbling her in a death roll. Blinded by the stirred-up sand, she flailed her arms as she struggled to find the surface. She swallowed water and her chest burned. It was uncomfortable but she didn't panic. The key was not to swim for the safety of the shore but to give in to the ocean and swim with it. She pushed through the back of each wave, and eventually, in what she hoped was a diagonal direction, she swam out to sea until she felt the pressure ease. Behind the billowing greenness the ocean was as it looked from the beach, and she floated on her back until her breathing slowed.

She noticed the man only as she emerged from the water. He was watching her from the dunes, hands on his hips, legs apart. She didn't know him. He looked scruffy. His shirt was tucked into his pants, not in a fashionable manner but in a way that revealed he wasn't interested in how his clothes looked. He ducked his head, and she remembered she was naked. Pervert. If he wanted to have a go, he would want to be quick.

She started dressing herself. He had his back to her. She was aware of a weird thrill that started in her stomach and pumped out to her extremities. Even her fingertips tingled. It reminded her of the artificial adrenaline rush she experienced the one time she had taken acid at university. He was probably a tourist. If so, he was a moron, lurking around the murder scene like that. She decided to tell him so. Without taking her eyes off him, she marched up the beach. Her shirt stuck to the wet salt on her skin. It made her back itch. Old mate up there was going to get an earful.

Chapter 3

Hall Flynn turned left off the four-lane Midlands Highway and onto the crumbling Fingal Valley Road. The sun was too low to be shielded by the visor, and he squinted through the shards of light, trying to anticipate corners he could barely see. The seventies-style sunglasses he had found outside the Gunners Arms on Saturday night did nothing to help. He slowed as he drove through each empty little town, considering buying some better frames from a petrol station, but nothing was open; even the bakeries had yet to position their *Open* signs.

In sprawling clear-felled paddocks on either side of the road, the occasional lone tree was dwarfed by its own long shadow on grass in the last stages of greenness. Early graziers cut down all the trees except a few, which they left to shelter the sheep. What they did not know was that a tree left alone in the middle of the paddock would die. Trees needed shelter too. Sheep trampled the ground around a single tree, affecting its roots, making it susceptible to bugs and disease. Hall sighed. By

February the ground would be dry, the sheep's white fleeces dusty and blending with the dirt. Hall would report the usual drought stories, interviewing cattle and sheep farmers who complained about not having enough feed to last the summer and the cash crop farmers who moaned about diminishing yields of potatoes, carrots, or canola. He found it hard to be sympathetic; the farmers who cleared every last acre of their land were the same ones who wondered why precipitation levels were falling. Not that he would ever say that outright; it was a journalist's job to keep his opinions to himself.

The road curled away from another empty main street, mimicking the leafy line of the South Esk River. Hall wound the window down carefully so it wouldn't get stuck. The morning air chilling his face carried the sweet wetness of rotting river bracken. Damn, it was good to get out of Launceston.

When his editor called him late last night with the assignment, she had tried to sound detached but she couldn't hide the anticipation in her voice. A murder. Near the very beach a pretty teenager had disappeared from last summer. This was a story that sold newspapers.

'Serial killer is the obvious angle, of course. Inept police, inept local MP, too. Who's next? Focus on their fears. Vox pop the man on the street. Set the agenda,' she said. 'And I need a photo of the dead woman.'

'I think I know how to handle it, Elizabeth,' Hall said before thanking her for the story.

He was surprised that she had chosen him to cover it. Why hadn't she handed it to one of her favorites, kids with double degrees and shorthand so shoddy they had to record their interviews on their mobile phones? They were the ones getting all the good assignments. Last year someone retired and the state political reporter position came up. Hall had applied. Over the twenty-three years Hall had been on the *Voice*, his assignments had included council, police, courts, state parliament, agriculture, and arts. His CV was quietly impressive, and he had assumed that the job would be his. But Elizabeth hadn't even given him a formal interview; she had handed the job to Ned Keneally. The guy had worked on the paper for less than two years, for Christ's sake.

'You're too good at what you do,' she had said when Hall fronted up to her office. 'You're good with country people. They trust you. You know all the councilors, from Break O'Day to The Nut. All the issues. We can't lose you.'

Elizabeth had tossed him a heap of front-page stories to compensate: a murder-suicide up at Mathinna; a garage amphetamine factory in Trevallyn; the Victoria Museum theft of seven nineteenth-century stuffed animal specimens, including a Tasmanian tiger, which his reporting had helped recover. This barely assuaged him. Hall had restrained his bitterness, but it remained within him, quietly malignant.

Concentrate, he told himself as he steered his car onto a narrow crumbling road that curled around a eucalyptus-covered cliff face. He grinned as he drove past a sign that announced *You Are Now Entering St Mary's Pass*. Someone had scratched the 'P' off. There were more signs within the pass, warning of falling rocks and active wildlife, and enlisting large vehicles to sound their horn before each blind corner. Hall's Holden was not that big, but he followed the instruction anyway, honking continuously and keeping his foot on the brake until he rolled out the other side of the pass. He didn't want to speed, but he needed to get to the Bay of Fires by ten a.m. According to his editor, some locals were gathering at that time to perform an emu parade on the beach where the woman was found. The emu parade involved participants lining up shoulder-to-shoulder and slowly walking the length of the beach, searching for clues. It was called an emu parade because participants resembled emus pecking the ground for food. Obviously they hoped to find something that the police might have missed in their line search the previous day. Hall doubted they would find any new evidence, but it would be an easy way for him to make some contacts.

At the entrance to Bay of Fires National Park, the road turned to gravel and his radio lost transmission. A cloud of dust hovered behind Hall as he steered his jarring vehicle along the rutted surface. Fire had ripped through toward the end of last summer, and the blackened eucalypts were woolly with new leaves. If Hall recalled correctly, the local community had enacted emu parades back then, traversing the burned landscape in a human chain, looking for remnants of the missing teen. They found nothing, not even her surfboard, let alone her bones.

Hall breathed in the charcoal-clean scent of burnt bush. There was the faintest trace of salt on the air, an aperitif to the ocean which the flashes of blue shining through the canopy told him was not far away. He emerged through the trees and onto a long straight road running beside an empty white beach. It looked about four or five kilometers long, curving around the sea and ending beneath a rocky headland. Somewhere on this beach the dead woman had washed in.

A serial killer made for copy that was human interest, crime, and politics. He had a lot to do. So far all reports, newspaper and radio, were based on a police report and a couple of phone interviews. Hall began going over the different angles in his head and then stopped himself. The angles would appear on their own after he started interviewing. This was a good story. No, this was a great story.

Moored in the wind high on the headland was the Bay of Fires Guesthouse. Hall parked beside a battered Land Cruiser and walked up the ramp. He liked the place immediately. It was an old Nissen hut, the kind built to withstand tropical storms. The faded green corrugated iron roof was curved like a giant beer barrel. It looked like it had withstood its fair share of bad weather. He walked up and down the veranda, inspecting the building, wondering how it had come to end up on the Tasmanian east coast.

Inside it was larger than he anticipated. Bench seats fit snugly beneath the curved roof, and tall windows overlooking the ocean were decorated with shell and driftwood mobiles. The furniture was dingy, the yellow rug stained, and the green linoleum peeling, but the sky and sea lit up the room. No one answered his greeting. Downstairs, the dormitory-style rooms all appeared to be unoccupied.

He found a tall thin woman in the side yard, pegging towels on a Hills Hoist swirly washing line. She wore skin-tight jeans and a snakeskin belt.

'Morning,' called Hall.

'Oh, hey.' She spoke holding a clothes peg between her teeth. 'You the journo?'

As he moved closer, he breathed the sweetness of her last cigarette coming off her clothes and skin.

'I guess I am.'

'Well you either are or you're not.'

Hall laughed, but he wasn't sure if she was trying to be funny. Inside the guesthouse a telephone rang. The woman tossed the pegs on top of the washing basket and marched toward the back door.

'Come on, then.' She didn't check to see if he was following.

'Bay of Fires Guesthouse.' As she answered the phone, she shoved a form and a pen at him. Her rings were loose on her fingers. 'Yes, I'm the manager.'

Her voice remained unfriendly; the wrinkles around her lips rose and sank as she spoke. 'Suit yourself.' She hung up the phone. 'Okay. Grand tour. Get your bag. There's no valet service here.'

Her name was Jane. She showed him around, describing the facilities in a rehearsed manner. Downstairs there were two bunkrooms, two bathrooms, and Jane's private quarters. Hall averted his eyes from her denim-clad buttocks as she took the stairs two at a time. 'How long are you staying for?'

'A few nights to start with. Not sure. Depends what my editor wants.'

'The room's yours for as long as you want it.' Except for the distant roar of the ocean, the guesthouse was quiet. Jane paused in the doorway of one of the upstairs bedrooms. 'I take it your wife doesn't mind not knowing when you'll be back.'

Hall repressed the twitch of a smile. This gruff woman was sussing him out. If this was how she behaved toward potential suitors, he wouldn't want to see how she treated men she didn't like.

'No wife, so no problem,' he said, making sure to avoid her gaze. He didn't want to give her the wrong idea. Hall recalled a frightening Stephen King novel about a nurse who kept a man captive in her house. If he remembered correctly, that man was a writer too.

'Right. This is you,' Jane said.

'Good day for the beach,' Hall said as Jane winched open his bedroom window and shoved a piece of wood in the frame to hold it there.

'Don't talk to me about it. I should be turning people away.' She swiped her hand across the bed, dusting something off, before she spoke again. 'No one's staying. I had a group of ten here last night; they all left this morning. Women decided they didn't want to stay. More people are coming on the weekend, at least. Right now I've got twelve beds, one guest. You're it.'

'That's hard,' he murmured in the voice he reserved for grieving families and business owners going broke.

'Summer's our make or break down here. Easter to the November long weekend this place is dead. High season now and they're not coming. It doesn't help; all your muckraking.'

'I haven't written a word on Anja Traugott,' Hall said truthfully, meeting her gray eyes.

Strands of salt-and-pepper hair had fallen out of her topknot. She tucked them behind her ears, and the end pieces of hair scooped out to the sides.

'Her parents are coming to get her stuff. You tell me what I'm supposed to say to them.' She crossed her arms.

'You tell them she was a lovely person and that you are sorry for their grief. That's all you can say.'

'I don't want this to be happening.'

'Sure.' Hall unzipped his laptop case.

'I suppose you'll want to interview me, seeing as how I was the last person to see her and that. The coppers say I'm an important witness.' Her laugh was bitter. 'I can only tell you what I told them. She took her camera, went out for a walk at about one p.m. Didn't come back. You want me to tell you what she was wearing?'

'Listen. I'm not interviewing you now. I need to make notes. We'll sit down later. Do it properly. Where did you say the men's room was?'

She stepped past him and into the hallway. With her thumb, she jabbed toward the stairs. 'Down to the left. Make sure the button pops up when you flush; it's almost had it. You want a cup of tea when you're done? Come outside and I'll talk. But don't mess around. I have to go to town to meet the bus.'

'Okay,' he relented, and she finally smiled, showing teeth that looked like they had never been cared for by a dentist.

Walking carefully so the floorboards didn't creak, Hall bypassed the bathroom and entered the first bunkroom. The beds were made, white sheets folded back over gray blankets. Otherwise the room was empty. The next room was set up the same except one bed was unmade. A backpack leaned against it and a book was on the nightstand. Hall picked it up. *Bruchstucke des Zwielichtes* was the title. He couldn't read German, but it looked like a work of literary fiction rather than a romance, which he had half expected it to be. Did that mean Anja was an intelligent woman? He looked at the backpack. There wasn't time to open it now; if he asked nicely, Jane might let him have a look. If not, he would investigate the bag when she went to meet the bus. The room wasn't locked.

Hall peered out the narrow window. It looked over a succulent garden and a paddock in which a chestnut mare stood beside a barbed wire fence. A cul-de-sac on the point gave access to several new shacks. You couldn't correctly call them shacks; their sharp lines and walls of glass positioned to frame certain views suggested the clever touch of an architect, unlike the original Fibro dwellings. In the other direction he could see the lagoon, a purple smudge on the edge of the beach.

It must have been winter when he came here with Laura, for it was too cold to swim. A family of black swans had watched as Laura waded in the lagoon. With her floral skirt hitched around her waist, her face drenched in dappled autumn sunlight, she had looked like one of Renoir's women. One of the birds had thought she was too close and flapped and hissed with its neck stuck out. At the time Hall had been frightened for Laura; now he wished it had bitten her.

In his notebook Hall wrote the date and time. Perched on the bench seat opposite him, her back to the ocean, Jane ineffectively swatted the cigarette smoke floating in the air.

'So.' Jane propped her lighter on top of the Holiday cigarette packet. 'Where do you want me to start?'

'Start at the beginning, when she first got here.' He sipped the tea. It was too hot and burned his lip. Jane didn't notice.

Anja Traugott had arrived on the bus from Launceston five days before Christmas. She had spent her time reading in the garden, sunbathing, taking walks around the beaches. One afternoon she hired snorkeling equipment; another morning she joined a couple of other guests and canoed around the lagoon. Jane had been grouting her window ledges and saw Anja leave the guesthouse on the day she went missing.

'It's not my fault no one realized she was missing right away. I don't keep tabs on everyone who stays here. She'd paid for a week,' Jane said.

She pulled weeds out of the herb pots as she spoke. Jane had been away on Christmas Day. Boxing Day she was busy clearing the beach track. It was on the day after when Jane went to clean the room that she realized her guest was absent.

'When I heard someone had washed up on the beach that morning I rang the cops right away. I have nothing to hide, mate,' she said.

'Why haven't they taken Anja's bag?'

'I knew you'd snoop in there. Someone special is coming up from Hobart to look at it. No one's supposed to go in there.'

'I didn't touch anything.' Hall was not apologetic. 'Tell me about the man who found the body.'

'Roger Coker. He's retarded.' Jane wasn't being malicious. It was clear to Hall that as far as she was concerned, her version of his mental capabilities was factual. 'One time someone gave him a bucket of red paint and he painted everything in his house red. Pots and pans. Kitchen table. His lawn mower.'

'How do you know that? Do you visit him?'

'God no. I wouldn't step inside that dump. Everyone knows about the paint.'

'Do you think he did it?'

Jane lit another cigarette and took a long suck, blowing the smoke hard out the side of her mouth. She filled a dog's bowl with water from a tap attached to a corrugated tank. Hall turned to a fresh page in his notebook, numbered it, and waited patiently for her to decide what she was going to say.

'Probably not.'

'So who did?'

Jane shrugged. 'Your guess is as good as mine.'

'No it's not.' Hall was irritated by the interview. 'You've lived here a long time and you know everyone.'

'I'm not going to name and blame. I've copped enough of that myself to know what it's like.'

'What do you mean?'

'I mean what I mean.'

She stubbed out her cigarette in an old Vegemite jar almost full of butts. She screwed the lid back on before looking him in the eye.

'I was married once. This place was more upmarket then. When Gary was here. No backpackers.'

'Right.'

'Well, if you want to know what happened to him, you won't need me to tell you.'

'People talk.'

'You got it, Scoop.'

Jane pulled a cigarette out of the box, tapped it upside down on the lid. Her lips pinched. He sensed the conversation was ending. He closed his notebook and waited. It was an old trick and it always worked. To fill the time he tried to name the herbs on the patio. Basil, flat parsley, rosemary, normal parsley; there were more but he did not recognize them. A flock of gulls swooped overhead, casting fleeting shadows on the table. A dog he couldn't see barked and dragged its chain.

'I'll just say this. I wouldn't be surprised if Roger Coker knows more than what he'll tell the police. He's not as stupid as everyone thinks.'

'You think he did it?'

'Don't twist my words.'

She returned the unlit cigarette to its box and stood up. She checked the time on a cheap digital watch that had a plastic band.

'It must be hard running a business on your own,' he offered.

'Oh, well. I'm still here, at least.'

Headlands loomed over each end of the beach. On Hall's map they existed as small curves on the edge of a blue vastness. Standing in the dunes, Hall studied his map of the coast, correlating the markings on the map with the landmarks he could see: the Old Road winding around the other side of the Chain of Lagoons, the cleared hilltop of Franklin's Farm, the point where the old tin railway had once run on a wooden jetty out into the ocean to meet cargo ships bound for Hobart. There was a turning circle toward the end of the beach, and he could see vehicles and people gathering for the emu parade. He checked his watch; it would start in fifteen minutes.

Hall jotted a couple of impressions of the beach in his notebook. It was a rugged, isolated stretch of coast. Beautiful and wild. There had been a program on *Stateline* some time ago about the large number of persons whose lives ended in the Tasmanian wilderness. In the past two years there had been four bushwalkers, two rock fishermen, a white-water rafter, a child who wandered away from a campsite, and several teenagers including Chloe Crawford. Some were dead, some were still missing. The program raised the question: Was Tasmania an island of murderous criminals, or had these people been swallowed by the rugged, unforgiving landscape? It was a good question.

He was about to return to his car when he saw a woman striding toward him. Water streamed from her dark hair, and she clutched a jacket around her that was the same muted green as the coastal scrub. She didn't seem bothered by the spiky dune grass under her bare feet.

'Can I help you, mate?' She didn't smile back.

'I don't know.'

'You're aware this is a crime scene?'

'I am.' She was having a go at him. This could be fun. He fiddled with his camera, ignoring her.

'Well, what are you doing here?'

'Looking around.'

'Looking around?'

'Research.'

'What kind of weirdo lurks in the dunes after someone has been murdered there?'

'No one was murdered here.'

'Yesterday . . .' She faltered.

Her eyes were bright and her breath ragged. She wasn't having a go; she was scared of him. He imagined how he looked, a middle-aged man wearing chinos and a crumpled business shirt, creeping around in the sand dunes. His curly reddish-brown hair was bouncing out of the neat combed lines he had urged it into when wet that morning, and his lined face could just as easily owe its weathered appearance to a life of crime as to twenty years of bushwalking in extreme Tasmanian weather. He wore an earring, too, a single silver stud, which the blokes at work reckoned helped in making Launceston's underworld trust him. From his shirt pocket Hall took a card.

'I'm a reporter,' he said. She didn't take the card. They watched each other over the blowing yellow grasses. 'In any case, what kind of weirdo approaches a strange man in the dunes where a murdered body was found?'

'Who do you work for? You don't look like a reporter. Is that your car?'

They both looked up at the Holden, its big round headlights watching them from the top of the dune.

'My other car is a Ferrari.'

'Let me see that.'

'It's worn out.' She fingered the curling edges of his business card. 'You sure you didn't pick this up somewhere?'

He didn't answer.

'The *Tassie Voice*.' Her laugh was prettier than she was. 'I guess if you were making it up you'd have a card from *The Australian* or something.'

'Of course. Who would pretend they worked at the *Voice*, right?' Hall turned to leave.

'You looking for clues? Speak to Jane Taylor at the guesthouse. That's where the dead woman was staying.'

'I know.'

'You planning to interview the person who found the body? I'll answer all your questions if you give me a lift up the hill.'

In the passenger seat she sat sideways, watching him drive.

Aware of her bare toned legs, he concentrated on keeping his eyes on the road. She said her name was Sarah, and she drilled him with questions without any self-consciousness. Who had he interviewed? What did the police think? Was there a suspect? Hall wasn't used to driving on the gravel and couldn't think to answer her properly.

'Who do you reckon did it?' he asked.

'I've got as much an idea of that as I have of what happened to Chloe Crawford. None.'

'Usually in small communities like this, people don't ask who the murderer is; they simply say who they think the murderer is.'

'I honestly do not know. It was brutal. I don't believe anyone around here is capable of that.'

Hall slowed as he drove past a crowd milling in a clearing beside the beach. They were mainly civilians, but he noticed a couple of men wearing orange and white vests, the uniform of State Emergency Service's volunteers. The police, assisted by a dozen SES volunteers, had conducted their official line search yesterday and found nothing. Today there was no designated crime scene; the tape had been removed. There was no point trying to preserve an exposed area indefinitely.

'Tell me, are they locals who are conducting their own line search?' Hall asked.

'You got it. Everyone's really upset. They all want to try and help.'

'You're not joining them?'

'I've had a look.'

'Find anything?'

She shook her head. 'Neither will they. There've been two

high tides since Anja Traugott washed in. Nothing stays still on the beach.'

The road was curving when Hall felt the wheels slide. He wasn't driving fast, maybe forty kilometers an hour, but the gravel corrugations offered no grip. They skated past blurry brush and paperbarks. The Holden slid sideways on the ruts and Hall gripped the wheel, trying unsuccessfully to aim the car toward the middle of the road. He shouted helplessly. His car was veering off the road. It wouldn't stop. It was going to crash.

'Take your foot off the brake, mate,' Sarah said.

He lifted his foot and the car lunged forward. The wheels responded to his steering. They bounced down the middle of the road. Hall felt sick in his guts. He swore, then apologized for doing so.

'It's slippery.' Hall's knuckles were white from clenching the wheel.

'The faster you go, the safer you are, you see? More grip.'

'Right.'

At the top of the hill, where the view of the ocean was unencumbered in either direction, she pointed at a small blue shack. Red geraniums grew through the fence, and the concrete tank was painted in a bright mural of sea creatures. She climbed out of his car and waited for him to drive away.

Sarah waved, her face glowing with a wide grin, as he urged the standard H gear stick into first. Damn that stupid corner. She was nice. Pretty in a natural kind of way. Not all done up and fake like the women he drank with at Launceston's various happy hours. He honked a couple of times as he drove off and immediately regretted it. If his embarrassing driving hadn't blown it, the horn honking would for sure.

Driving back to check out the emu parade, he considered her advice about driving faster. But the road was sandy in parts, and he let the Holden roll along at twenty kilometers an hour, his hands clenching the wheel and his head craned forward like someone's grandmother.

Sarah's words resounded in Hall's head. Nothing stays still on the beach. She was right. The emu parade had walked the length of the beach twice and found nothing. The people gathered here interested Hall. It was likely one of them was the murderer. It was likely to be a man, too, given the violent nature of the dead woman's injuries. Hall watched everyone but approached no one. He wondered if the murderer would seek him out. In case of this, he wore his media lanyard and made a show of jotting things down in his notebook, so it would be clear to everyone that he was a reporter.

Three men spoke to Hall of their own accord. John Avery owned a shack and had written a book on the history of the area, which he offered to lend to Hall. Don Gunn, who wore an SES volunteer uniform, had assisted with the police line search yesterday. He ran the shop near the boat ramp. Don took his boat out every morning at six to check the cray pots, and Hall was welcome to come if he wanted to view the coast from the sea. The third person was a young American man called Sam, who pointed out an almost invisible speck on the horizon which he said was one of the racing yachts doing the Sydney-to-Hobart. None of them seemed like murderers.

While Hall was in conversation with Sam, a woman called out to the young man from across the undulating dune. From a distance she looked young enough to be his girlfriend, and the wheedling way in which she called him confirmed Hall's assumption. She didn't come over. Instead, Sam stopped speaking halfway through his sentence and excused himself. Hall watched them walk toward the surf, the woman giving the young man her sandals to hold, while she picked up what looked like pieces of driftwood.

Later that afternoon Hall called the police, right before he filed. Lucky he did. A canvas beach bag had been found near a rock pool located at the southern end of the beach. It contained Anja Traugott's wallet, a booklet issued by the Tasmanian Wilderness Society outlining how to treat poisonous snake and spider bites, a hairbrush, sunscreen, and a digital camera. The wallet contained money, so she had not been robbed. There wasn't time to do anything more than type it up and file it.

Work was on Hall's mind as he shaved with cold water in the yellow-tiled bathroom at the guesthouse. He dried his face on a stubbly towel. Twice it slipped off the towel rail when he tried to hang it up, and he tossed it into the sink in frustration. He was worried about the story he had just filed. His three-hundred-word update on the discovery of Anja Traugott's beach bag was padded out with a vox pop of local residents describing how the murder and missing person investigation were impacting their lives. As he put on a clean shirt, he considered whether it was sensational enough to satiate the editor. The thing was, if you had to ask yourself that question, you knew the answer.

He closed the bedroom door behind him. A broom whisked the wooden boards on the deck outside. It was the only sound in the late afternoon stillness.

'I'm going to the Abalone Bake,' he called.

He didn't notice the leather handbag on the table until after he spoke.

'I might as well show my face.' Jane leaned the broom against the wall. She wore an ironed black blouse tucked into her tight jeans and a slick of coral lipstick on her lips.

'I don't usually bother with these things,' she told him as they walked down the hill, her fluttering fingers tracing her bag's worn leather. 'Not my cup of tea.'

They paused at the edge of the park. On the beach beyond, children were playing cricket. Hall breathed in the tepid sea air. It was laced with the salty garlic aroma of barbecuing seafood. Laughter and conversation drifted up. He quickly counted around thirty people, lounging in deck chairs, cross-legged on picnic rugs, or standing sloshing ice in plastic cups. Their curiosity was shameless. He could imagine what they were thinking as they stared at the woman in her cowboy boots and lipstick and the freshly showered journalist beside her. Hall tried to look friendly.

Jane dug her elbow into his waist. 'Watch out, you'll be the news yourself tomorrow. You and me both.'

Hall had a good memory for names. He recognized most of the people from the emu parade and the door knock he had done immediately after it. There was John Avery and his wife, Felicity, or Flip as she had insisted. Simone (she pronounced it Simmon) was a blond American woman, who was in fact the mother of the young man. She was very friendly and had given him a glass of freshly squeezed orange juice when he knocked on the door of her holiday house. The shop owner was Don Gunn and the attractive woman with him was his wife, Pamela. She had invited Hall to the Abalone Bake when he was in the shop earlier that day.

Pamela waved. Carrying two plates she marched over, shaking her hair out from behind her ears.

'Flip is collecting the money.' Pamela's gold bracelets jingled. 'It's seven dollars a plate. I already paid for yours, Hall.'

On the plastic plate she handed Hall was a pile of what looked like hot moist shreds of curly leather and a slice of lemon.

'I won't have any, thanks, Pamela.' Jane rummaged in her handbag.

'You're funny, Jane,' Pamela said. 'Coming to our Abalone Bake and not eating.'

'I didn't say I wasn't eating. I'll have a sausage. Just not that. It's disgusting.' Jane strode down the slope, an unlit cigarette between her fingers.

'She's had a hard life,' Pamela told Hall. 'I'm always a little bit careful what I say when I speak to Jane. She upsets easily.'

Through introductions and small talk, Pamela's hand remained firmly on Hall's arm and her cushiony breast kept bumping against him. She did most of the talking while he nodded, chewing and chewing a strip of abalone. It was gristlier than the toughest calamari he had ever eaten.

'Wash it down, mate.' John pushed a glass of red wine into Hall's hand and smiled with porcelain veneers that were too white for his softening face. 'Did you learn anything today?'

Hall was aware people were waiting for his response. He shrugged in a noncommittal way and sipped the wine.

'I wonder if the murderer is here now?' said the young guy who had pointed out the boats to Hall at the emu parade.

'That's not funny, Sam,' Pamela said. 'Don't even joke about it.'

'Defensive, Pamela,' Sam said. 'What are you hiding?'

'Don't be ridiculous.' Pamela bristled.

For a moment Pamela reminded Hall of Laura's good friend Sue, an antiques and oddities dealer who wore pearls and often took offense at harmless banter. Hall had tried to avoid Sue whenever Laura dragged him along to social events that required partners.

'Forget the murder for a minute. We think you should do a story on Erica,' Flip said.

Hall looked from Flip to Pamela. They wore similar pastel-colored shirts with the collars turned up and gold fob chains. Even their hair was cut in similar shoulder-length styles. Considering how ratty the shacks around here were, the people who owned them appeared well off, compared to most Tasmanians. Their cars were new models, BMWs and expensive four-wheel drives, and most of the yards contained boats or jet skis. Pamela's husband, Don, wore a Rolex, although it could have been a fake for all Hall knew.

Hall tried to keep his tone cordial. 'Who?'

'My younger daughter. She makes greeting cards. Pammy's nearly sold out in the shop . . . wait there, I'll get her.'

'It's okay.' Hall had often wished for a dollar for every ridiculous story idea suggested to him. The less likely the idea would become a story, the more insistent the person was.

'Flip, you're so boring. The story the *Voice* needs is Sam's.' Pamela paused in arranging the sauce bottles and beer cans which were stopping the tablecloth from blowing away. 'He wrote a letter, put it in a bottle, and threw it out the front here and it landed in New Zealand. A girl his age wrote back to him.'

'It's stupid,' Sam said.

'That's not stupid, that's a great story.' The punters loved stories like that. Hall wanted to ask for more information when someone's Labradoodle thrust its nose into his crotch. It could probably smell his cat. He pushed it away, as gently as possible. He was not a dog person.

'Henry. Scoot.' Pamela shooed the dog away. 'Tie him up, Flip. Now, Hall. Let me know if there is anything else I can tell you.'

'Pammy knows everything about everyone,' Don called.

Pamela swatted him. 'Watch out or I'll tell him all your secrets, darling.'

It was funny that she should say that. There was something familiar about Don. His low, articulate voice and his deferential manner of pausing between each sentence gave Hall the feeling he had met him before. He wondered if Don recognized him. If it was from a situation Don regretted – a court appearance for drunk driving or domestic violence – they would both pretend to have forgotten. It was easier that way. It could have been during the police raid on a Windmill Hill brothel which Hall had attended last year. Those blokes had all been well-to-do guys like Don Gunn. If that was the case, Hall didn't care. Other people's sex lives were not a topic he was inclined to pass judgment on.

Metal tapped against glass. John Avery cleared his throat; some people were still talking.

'Quiet, children,' called Pamela, and the chatter subsided.

Obviously comfortable in front of a crowd, John spoke about the tradition of the Abalone Bake and the importance of getting everyone together. He spoke with the precise enunciation of a private-school-educated man. Behind him, Jane slipped into the shadows along the edge of the park and lit a cigarette. She didn't speak to anyone. He could venture over, make some small talk. He always felt sorry for people who were nervous in crowds. But tough luck tonight. He was here to work, not chaperone misfits to community functions. Hall focused on what John was saying.

'We love this place. I've been coming here every summer since I bought my block of land twenty-seven years ago, you see. Eight thousand dollars.' John lifted his glass, and red wine splashed onto the grass. 'Worth a bit more than that now. We all are.'

'John,' Flip cautioned.

'We all feel the same. What has happened here breaks my heart and I know it breaks the heart of everyone standing before me.' He poured himself more wine, took a sip, and added, 'I don't know what happened to Chloe Crawford and I don't know what happened to the Swiss woman, Anja . . . Anja.'

'Traugott,' called Pamela.

Anja Traugott, an unlikely name for Tasmanians to pronounce. Soon everyone would know her name. Chloe Crawford was a name that sparked discussion in any pub across the state. Everyone had an opinion. Some thought the teenager from the west coast had staged her own disappearance and run off with a boyfriend. Hall understood her family was deeply religious, so this was possible. Others surmised she had been raped and filmed for pornographic purposes and her body buried on a remote and impenetrable bush block owned by one of the local dubious motorbike clubs. A few thought she had fallen into a mineshaft while bushwalking. Everyone had a theory, but no one knew for sure. Despite a massive search, not one of her personal belongings had been recovered, not her surfboard nor any of her clothing. She had one bank account with the Commonwealth Bank, and it had not been touched. Uncertainty fueled speculation. Hall didn't know which story he believed; all he knew was that it made good newspaper copy.

'I don't know what happened to Chloe Crawford, and I can't explain why Anja Traugott was murdered,' John repeated.

'Serial sex offender,' Pamela muttered loudly enough for everyone to hear.

Don put a hand on Pamela's arm, which she shook off.

'Don't shush me, Donald,' she said.

As John continued, Hall noticed Sarah for the first time that evening. She was sitting on a picnic table, drinking beer out of a bottle and peeling off the label. Tanned and almost as tall as he was, she looked capable of skippering a maxi-yacht. When she saw Hall looking, she rolled her eyes. She was laughing at everyone. He wasn't sure if she was laughing at him, too, so he just nodded and looked away.

At the beginning of his speech, John had made eye contact with everyone. Now he kept glancing over the top of the crowd, his gaze returning to his audience briefly before being drawn back to something on the rocks. Hall turned to see the distraction and realized many others were doing the same.

The fading light made it hard to see clearly the hunched figure causing the murmuring. Against the gray ocean, Hall could make out what looked like an old man holding a stick. A woman's voice rose above the whispers. 'Roger Coker makes my skin crawl.'

'Boo!' Sam said, right in Hall's ear. His breath was hot on Hall's neck.

Hall didn't have a chance to tell him to back off. From that point, everything happened quickly.

Dogs barked, women screamed, and everyone scattered. The Labradoodle was flat on its back as a black dingo-like dog snarled on top of it. The cause of the trouble, a plate of barbecued meat, was upturned on the grass. As the dogs fought, someone stepped closer to break it up, but the black dog lunged, a chain attached to its neck swishing across the ground. The man jumped back. The black dog dove onto the plate, gobbling up the sausage and seafood. The Labradoodle barked and the black dog lunged and bit its neck. Everyone screamed.

'Do something, Donald!' Pamela handed Don a metal barbecue spatula.

'No,' Jane shouted as Don hit the black dog.

He belted the animal's back several times with the metal instrument. It made a hollow whack and pierced the skin. Blood spurted across black fur and the dog cried.

'Enough, you piece of shit,' Jane told Don as she scruffed the dog's neck.

'Control your animal!' Pamela yelled.

'Who do you think you are?' Jane called over her shoulder as she dragged her whimpering animal out of the park.

Don looked confused, standing there holding the spatula

with his mouth open as though he didn't know what he was doing. Everyone slunk away, and Pamela turned on her husband.

'What were you thinking, Donald?'

'You gave me the bloody spatula.'

'That was psychotic. She'll press charges.'

'Shut up. Just shut up.'

Jane let the dog go as they walked up the hill. It trotted along by her side, its tail down. Her handbag slapped against her leg, forgotten. From the rocks Roger Coker watched the spoiled gathering. The man was motionless, as much a fixture on the landscape as the granite boulders and scraggly banksias.

'They're a bunch of dickheads, if you haven't worked it out yet.' Sarah pressed a beer into Hall's hand. It was fresh from the Esky and cold water trickled down his arm.

'Is that right?' She didn't seem to care if anyone heard her.

'They're mad; there is a group of them going round telling everyone not to swim in the lagoon. They think it's too close to Roger Coker's house, and it's hidden from the road, so therefore they deduce that's a possible murder site.'

Hall laughed, although he could see she was partly serious. 'Are you okay?'

'Fine. Why?'

'Some people get post-traumatic stress disorder after seeing what you saw.'

'I'm not as fragile as I look.' She tilted her head back and finished the last of her beer. 'Help yourself when you want another.'

They watched the park empty. The dog fight had ruined

the mood. Simone Shelley smiled at Hall as she walked past him, looking for her son. Sam was with some of the older kids milling around the swings. Sam stood out, his blond good looks and substantial physique setting him apart. He was better dressed, too; his khaki shorts and T-shirt looked newer and more expensive than what the other kids wore.

'I'm staying for a bit,' Sam told his mother. 'I'll be up in an hour.'

Hall didn't hear what she said, but Sam reluctantly followed her out of the park. Everyone was scared to be alone tonight. Standing with Sarah in the long twilight's soothing dimness, Hall did not want to return to his empty room. As though she could read his thoughts, she suggested they take a nightcap down to the water's edge.

'And then I'll walk you home,' she said. 'It's not safe to walk on your own in these parts. Too dangerous.'

'Very kind of you.'

She grinned, revealing a dimple in her cheek. His confidence had diminished since he turned forty. These days it took a dozen games of pool, sixty bucks' worth of bourbon and Coke, and the Batman Faulkner Inn's jukebox had to be playing the right kind of song for him to muster the courage to leave with a girl. He always went to their place, and he never brought them home. Somehow, as pointless as it was to think this, it felt a betrayal of Laura to bring another woman into what had been their bed.

Right now Hall was far too sober to consider having sex with anyone. He liked the straight-talking country girl sitting next to him, and common sense told him to say good night. Cut his losses before he made a fool of himself.

It was her smile that made him stay. Her smile was easy, glad, as though she had nothing more pressing on her mind than enjoying a cold beer on a warm evening.

It was hard to tell how late it was. The sky above the ocean was brighter than in the city. There was a chance it was almost midnight; the sun did not set until nine o'clock and it wasn't dark until an hour after that. The grass, rocks, and sea had melded into one. Hall looked over the ocean, drinking Sarah's beer as he listened to the waves rolling. He couldn't tell if Sarah was drunk; her speech was clear and she was steering the conversation. Earlier she had told him that men found her intimidating. Now she was saying she would make a good mistress.

Hall said some silly things too which he knew, in a vague drunken way, he would regret in the morning. He told her an old story about the time he and Laura were locked inside the public toilet block in the city park. The toilets were notorious for attracting unsavory characters, and Hall had stood outside the cubicle door while Laura was in there. The caretaker, not realizing they were inside, locked the padlock. It was a winter evening, and they were stuck there for three hours, rattling the gate and calling out, until someone came past to help them. Hall had been so young then, barely thirty years old.

It was a funny story and Sarah laughed. But what was he thinking? Everyone knew you didn't talk about your ex-girlfriend when you were chatting up a woman.

Sarah stood up. 'Do you want to see the fishing shack where the girl who disappeared last summer was staying?'

Hall did, but he would have preferred to see it in the

morning. He needed to get some sleep. He had a lot of work to do tomorrow. Sarah didn't wait for him to answer. She was already walking across the rocks, carrying the Esky.

The shack was one of three timber huts overlooking the gulch. It was uninhabited, Sarah told him. The other two shacks had been let to holidaying families, as usual, but the one where the Crawford family had stayed remained vacant. There was a padlock on the door but they did not go close enough to look. It was spooky, hiding behind the gum tree with Sarah, peering out at the derelict hut. Boats screeched eerily on their moorings in the little harbor and he could hear tiny rapid waves lapping the sand. A curtain inside the shack was partly open and Hall fancied he saw something looking out at them.

They shared the last can of beer, passing it back and forth. When the can was finished, Sarah crumpled it with both hands and stowed it in her Esky with the other empties. She turned to leave. Hall picked up the Esky and they followed a sandy track back toward the road. It was not a bad thing that they had run out of beer.

The walk back to the guesthouse seemed to take a very short time. In his bedroom he opened the curtain to let the moonlight in and slid the window open so they could hear the waves crashing below. As long as he had had at least six drinks, he had the confidence to know what women liked. Anything less and he found himself walking home alone to open a bottle of red wine and switch on the television. Tonight he had drunk more than enough. He sat beside her on the bed and began his routine. It started with soft kisses on her cheek and neck, his fingers gently tugging the ends of her hair. The second stage involved the removal of clothing, and this he did gently too, one button at a time, one garment at a time. Sarah was wearing a flannelette shirt with the pocket ripped off. Underneath, her skin glowed in the soft light. He undid her hair elastic band and loosened her hair. It was longer than he thought it would be; honey-golden waves that smelled freshly washed. Her plump lips smiled each time he touched her. Most alluring to Hall were her eyes, those hazel eyes watching him kiss her, conveying both intelligence and a heartbreaking vulnerability. She was beautiful and he told her so.

'You don't have to talk me into anything.' She pulled him onto her.

Hall tried to remember the things that women liked, but Sarah's exuberance made him forget. The bed was old and rocked against the wall. It was loud. He thought about making a joke, but she was ignoring the noise. In the silent guesthouse the banging of hard wood on plywood was excruciating. He couldn't believe that he was thinking about Jane Taylor right now, but the guesthouse owner would have to be deaf not to be awakened by the racket. He braced the bed head with his hand until Sarah was still.

In the morning he boiled water on the gas stove for coffee. Sarah watched the ocean with her back to him.

'Such a contrast of color,' he said. 'Those reddish granite boulders and the ocean. Makes you want to run down and jump right in.'

'Yeah.'

'Maybe not. It's always colder than it looks.'

'Yes.'

He tried a different topic. 'I heard there were middens in the area; where are they?'

'Don't ask me. That's a can of worms.'

He couldn't recall much of what they had talked about last night. He remembered swaying up the road and trying to scare each other with tales of serial killers. He remembered standing outside the guesthouse and contemplating inviting her in for a cup of tea when she grabbed his hand and led him up the ramp. The floor creaked with each careful step, and he put a hand over her mouth to muffle her giggles.

While he waited for the kettle to boil, he read the signs on display. The sign above the sink said *Wash, Dry, and Put Away Your Dishes*. The signs on the fridge said *Name Your Food* and *Complimentary Milk in Door is for Tea and Coffee Only*. There was no sign outlining Jane's policy on unofficial guests. He was relieved when he heard the guesthouse Land Cruiser wheels skidding across damp grass as Jane left to meet the bus coming from Launceston.

Chapter 4

High sun filled the shack with a light so bright it hurt Sarah's eyes as soon as she removed her sunglasses. She forced a casual greeting, hoping they would assume she had been out fishing.

'Catch anything?' Her father didn't look up from his muesli.

'It's too early to tell,' Erica said.

Sarah ignored her and poured herself some tea.

On the counter beside the Weet-Bix box the newspaper was open. The headline announced *Murder in Paradise*. Below it was a half-page color picture of Honeymoon Bay, obviously borrowed from the newspaper's travel archive. It showed the teardrop-shaped cove on an aquamarine, breezeless, waveless day. But the *Voice* was such a rag; it wasn't even the right beach. Honeymoon Bay was three or four beaches around the coast from where the body was found. The tiny photograph of Anja Traugott was unflattering; she wasn't smiling, yet the Swiss woman still looked pretty. Sarah stared into the newsprint face. Her bowels contracted. She winced; the pain was worse than was warranted by the alcohol she had drunk. God, what was wrong with her?

And there was his name. Hall Flynn, the journalist she wished she hadn't met. It was late when she arrived at the Abalone Bake, and she had drunk several cans of beer quickly, watching as everyone clamored around Hall. How bored they must be with one another, she remembered thinking. But she was no different. A few drinks and an aversion to a ridiculously jolly walk home with Mum and Dad was all it took. Company was all she had desired, not sex with a middle-aged man she had only just met. He was probably married, for all she knew.

At least she hadn't spent another night lying in bed, staring into the darkness, regretting things that were impossible to change. She started reading the article.

The language was dangerous. Hall Flynn used words such as 'mutilated,' 'autopsy,' and 'massive manhunt.' Emotive phrases such as 'frenzied attack' and 'second woman to go missing' prompted Sarah to swear quietly. Hall Flynn had interviewed Jane Taylor.

'We're in shock. Who walks onto a beach, kills someone, and walks off?' Jane was quoted as saying.

The next words Sarah read caused bile to rush up the back of her throat. She swallowed. A bag had been found near the rock pool. A striped canvas bag. The article did not specify the color, but Sarah knew it would have red and white stripes. She had seen the bag when she spoke to Anja in the guesthouse.

'What does it say?' Erica leaned over Sarah's shoulder.

'You can have it when I'm finished.' Sarah put her hands over the page. It was a childish gesture, but she wanted to read the article alone.

Chloe Crawford's family had refused to comment. Sarah

wondered how Hall had approached that conversation. Not an easy interview. The parents were from Zeehan, a mining ghost town on the west coast. They had remained in the decrepit fishing cottage that they were renting for three months, leaving only when their money ran out. Pamela said they had walked every beach, hiked around the back of the lagoon, visited all the old mineshafts searching for signs of their daughter. Twice a day the father drove the Old Road, where Chloe had cycled the morning of the day she disappeared. Together they stood on the beach where she might have died, gazing out to sea. They didn't make any friends; Pamela thought they blamed the community for their daughter's disappearance. She said after having met them she wouldn't have blamed the daughter for running away. Bible bashers, she described them. They left without saying goodbye, without knowing what had happened to their daughter.

Sarah frowned at the newspaper. 'That's annoying. It doesn't say anything realistic about how Anja's death might have happened. Or how long she was in the sea. She could have been thrown off a boat twenty nautical miles out to sea; the current runs strong enough to drag her back in.'

'No one would hear your screams out there.' Erica was studying her reflection in the mirror, and she did not look up.

'Maybe she wasn't even murdered. Maybe her injuries were from shark bite. If she was walking around to the rock pool, she could have slipped in.'

'Several sharks, from your description of the corpse.'

'The kelp is so thick around those rocks it would be very difficult to climb out. Swiss people can't swim. I would struggle to swim back to the beach from there. *You* wouldn't make it.'

'Whatever,' Erica said. 'The woman was raped. By a violent psychopath who hates women; that's what everyone is saying.'

'Pamela's not everyone.'

'They found her wallet. He wasn't after that. Unless he was disturbed while he was on the job. But you'd think if someone was close enough to disturb them, they would have heard something.'

Although Erica's comments were not baseless, her attitude was flippant. Sarah stared at her sister, who was still gazing into the mirror. It was an old mirror, bordered with shells that Erica had glued onto it one long-ago winter's afternoon. As a teenager Sarah had accepted that her younger sister existed within the confines of an expansive comfort zone. Erica's life experience had been rose-tinted. She was a person whom people wanted to be around, a woman who was nearly always happy, who was beautiful and who found most things agreeable. There was nothing wrong with that. It wasn't Erica's fault. But it gave her a limited perspective.

Yesterday Erica had vowed not to walk on the beach alone until the killer was caught. Sarah draped her bath towel around her neck and tugged on the ends harder than was necessary. This wasn't an Agatha Christie plot, something that could be solved by puzzling over the breakfast table. Maybe if Erica had seen the body and could still smell the stench of decomposing human flesh, she would shut up about it. Like the smell of rotten prawns or the urine-soaked lane behind the Pineapple Hotel, death's scent lingered in Sarah's nostrils and the back of her throat.

Erica didn't know the full story. Only Sarah knew the rock

pool was foul with fish waste that day. It didn't change anything, and they didn't need to know.

Sarah pressed her forehead against the salt-streaked window, the glass warm on her skin. There was no wind, and waves were breaking neatly on the beach. Sufficient swell curled across the reef beyond the point; there might be something biting out there.

As she watched the waves she noticed a solitary figure in a green army jacket throw a line off the rocks. You had to observe him carefully to see if he was getting anything; he moved each fish from his line to his bucket without his usual jerkiness. Most people watching Roger fish would think he had caught nothing. Sarah knew this was exactly what he intended.

A towel collapsed over Sarah's head. A pair of hands slammed her shoulders. She jolted and gasped.

'Did I scare you?' It was Erica.

'That's not funny.' Sarah was furious.

'Sorry.'

'Bring back the serial killer.' Sarah kicked the chair out from under her so it screeched on the linoleum floor. 'I'm going for a shower.'

'No showers please,' John called as Sarah headed for the bathroom. 'The tank's only a quarter full.'

Sarah went to the beach to bathe. Cold water temporarily relieved unwanted thoughts. Underneath, coolness eased the throbbing in her head and washed away the alcohol's clamminess and the limpid softness of a stranger's fingers on her body. She flipped and rolled, blowing bubbles as she shimmied along the ocean floor. Sarah stayed underwater until her lungs tightened in need of oxygen. As she finally came up for air, she saw that she was not the only person in the water.

Whitewash frothing around her, Simone Shelley was bent over a wave ski. Her drenched sarong clung to the pink bikini she wore underneath. Short, steady waves battered the board against Sam's legs as he held it steady for his mother to climb on. They hadn't seen her. Sarah kicked slowly, swimming toward the submerged rock islands to hide. She watched as Sam guided his mother through the relatively calm water between the rocks, wading out until he was chest-deep. With a shove, he set her adrift. Simone laughed, and the sound, silvery and girlish, drifted across the water to Sarah.

Sarah swam behind the rocks. She had no recollection of what had happened on Christmas Day with Sam, and she was too ashamed to face him. At least she could remember last night more clearly. She had barely spoken to Hall when they went back to the guesthouse. He had tried to talk to her; she had focused on the job. She didn't like talking in bed. Jake was the same. It was one thing they did well together, especially if he was sober. He was fit and could do it several times in a night. They did it anywhere. Once they did it on the ground next to the vegetable patch she was building. Far beyond the mango tree's luscious canopy, the cloudless sky was enormous. Pungent smells of decomposing garden beds and Johnson's topsoil mix gave her a physical sexual memory that remained impossible to erase. Damn it. She was as useless as any bloke she knew. Given the chance, she would sleep with Jake again, despite everything. The knowledge made her angry.

She forced herself to swim. Slicing through the water, she took long deep breaths and focused on her stroke until it physically hurt. When she stopped, she was about two hundred meters away from the beach. Behind the break, where sharks and unpredictable currents made others afraid to swim, the solitude was therapeutic. Ocean breezes flicked shouts from the beach upward in pleasing distant puffs, as inconsequential as the faraway squawks of seagulls.

At the base of the granite headland was the cove where Anja Traugott had sunbathed topless in the days before she died. Scrubby green bushes protected a tiny patch of white lapped by blue. Anja had folded a white T-shirt over her eyes and dozed. Breasts bare and open palms facing the sun, she wore nothing but the polka-dot bikini bottoms that were on her corpse. Everyone knew this because Don, walking the beach on his chiropractor's orders, had almost tripped over her. Pamela had told the story again last night.

'He was so embarrassed. You can just imagine Donald trying to sneak away, so big and clumsy.'

Flip and Erica had laughed. Don, listening as John described a recent lecture he had delivered on the history of Chinese settlement in the area, pretended not to hear. Pamela had gleaned a lot of information from someone who had apparently seen nothing more than a glimpse of a topless woman, but no one commented on this. The conversation had turned to the pressing concern of melanoma risk.

'I've always said, Europeans have no clue about the hole in the ozone layer. Everyone sunbathes nude in Europe – I always did as a girl during vacations in the Mediterranean – but it just isn't safe this far south,' Pamela had said.

Sarah swam toward the cove. She lay against a rock that, under the midday sun, was almost too warm. Disjointed, uncontrollable images swam blindly through her head: Jake's angry voice shouting across the Pineapple Hotel pool table, waking up in the sand dunes on Boxing Day, Jake's flatmate slamming the door in her face when she went looking for him, her own loud voice opining to Hall last night. Stuff it. You couldn't change the past.

Eyes closed, she dug her nails into the lichen until they were gritty with sand. She swallowed and swallowed again, searching for something else to think about. There was a collection of shells in the shack, gathered years ago on long walks around the national park's empty beaches and rocky points. She tried to remember each one, visualizing the milky surfaces and brownish corrugations until her mind stopped racing. Cuttlefish, pen shell, fan mussel, cone shell, angel's wing, bubble shell, screw shell, smoky Venus, butterfly, cowrie, witch's fingernail; each appeared briefly in her mind.

Soothed by the silent recitation, Sarah pushed herself off the rock, ignoring the flecks of lichen and sand stuck to her. She peeled down her one-piece and inspected her body. Ugly stretch marks clawed her breasts, a reminder of the weight she put on the winter she fractured her ankle and couldn't exercise. Her abdominals were hard and white. She reclined slowly onto the sand, her abs taking her weight. She took pleasure in their strength.

Above the beach, the row of shacks hobbled along the hill blurred between the bright sunshine and acres of blue sky. Was anyone watching? Everyone owned a pair of binoculars to spot wildlife. Dolphins followed the waves close to the beach, mollyhawks swooped over dark shadows of mullet schools moving through the shallows, and, twice a year, pods of whales passed. Any movement on the sand was enough to raise people from their armchairs; a lone surfer far down the shore break would arouse mild interest, and a few guys towing each other in a donut suspended behind their tinny was sufficient. A couple of shacks had telescopes installed on their decks, sweeping metal barrels that could see sailors moving on the deck of a Sydney-to-Hobart yacht sailing kilometers out to sea. Sarah turned her palms upward, the sun hot on her chest, her toes buried in warm sand.

It was funny how people looked so different in daylight. Hall's long sideburns and aviator sunglasses had seemed like a stylish retro nod last night; today the bristly sideburns looked unkempt and the plastic glasses cheap. His business shirt was unironed, his trousers too long and the bottoms frayed and dirty where he had trod on them. He had more freckles than she remembered, and more gray in his reddish hair, which was damp. She was close enough to smell the citric sweetness of his shampoo. He wanted to know where she was going.

'Nowhere. Just to the boat ramp. Dad and Erica were checking their cray pots.'

He slapped his hand on the roof of the vehicle and told her to get in. She hesitated. In the paddock behind his car, bunches of fraying yellow ryegrass swayed above dusty clumps of turnips uprooted for the cows to eat.

'What's the matter? Are you feeling bad for taking advantage of me?' Hall's deep voice reminded her of the announcer on Eumundi Classical FM. 'It's okay. I'm not holding it against you.'

He took off his glasses, and his green eyes fixed on her. Sarah forced a chirpy laugh.

'Judging by how hungover I was this morning, I think it was the other way round.'

'I've had a day's practice driving on the gravel now, if you're worried about that.'

It would be rude to decline his offer of a lift, but she didn't want to go with him. Despite the previous night's intimacy he was a stranger to her. He was waiting for her to do or say something. If he was just trying to be nice for the sake of it, he could save his breath. She wouldn't be offended.

'Well, if you don't need a lift . . .'

'No,' she said. She was surprised to feel sorry for him. 'Oh, what the heck.' She walked around to the passenger side of his car. 'Follow the road.'

She had not noticed how dirty his car was the other day. Loose newspaper pages and three used coffee mugs cluttered the floor, clothes were strewn across the backseat, and something heavy and metallic shifted back and forth in the boot as the car bounced on the corrugated road. She smelled engine oil and dust. The edge of the bench seat sank away, and she kept sliding toward the door. Head aching, she braced one hand on the door's armrest and busied herself with sipping the discolored tank water in her water bottle. It was insane how slowly he was driving.

Words to fill the few minutes it took to drive to the boat ramp evaded Sarah. Usually the conversation after the night before came easily to her. Flirty small talk over a final beer and a cigarette as she waited in pale new light for one of the town's three taxis, making plans she wouldn't keep. If a man drinking in the Pineapple Hotel's public bar wasn't married, you could bet your last buck he either was a sugar cane laborer or a fruit picker, or worked at the Eumundi Barramundi Farm. Sarah would know. She wasn't proud of this but didn't care either. When you called the shots, you knew where you stood.

Hall signaled to go around a bend in the road. He took driving seriously, sitting upright and watching the road with his hands in the ten-and-two position. Occasionally he glanced out his window but only for a second. She felt like she was a teenager being driven home from a party by her father. It was very different from being in the car with Jake, who, in the six months she had known him, hadn't left his vehicle outside the pub once. He nearly wrote it off many times. One night they were fighting about something and the car swerved off the road and wiped out someone's tin can letterbox. It got caught on the front bumper and clanged all the way home. In the early days things like that made them laugh.

'Abalone Bake Park,' Hall said as they drove past the sunburned patch of grass next to the shop.

'Mmm,' she said.

She remembered most of the night, more than she wanted to if she was honest about it. A swollen half-moon had cast a thick white path of light across the black sea as they sat on the rocks and drank the last of the beers. Behind them the Abalone Bake wound up and people drifted away into the night. Clean salty ocean air blew away the smells of frying garlic and seafood. Waves they couldn't see gushed and frothed on the rocks, and at some point they sat in a way that their bodies were touching.

Meandering up the gravel road, Hall and Sarah had joked

about the murder case and tried to hold each other upright. Neither had mentioned the thing they both knew was about to happen. Between sheets softened from constant washing she had straddled him, pinning his shoulders and arms and hips to the hard mattress with a forcefulness that now made her cringe. The most embarrassing bit was when she pressed her mouth on his neck, drunkenly tugging at the softness under his jaw, and he had pushed her away.

In the morning she had woken up surprised to find herself squinting in the strange predawn light coming through the guesthouse window. Hall was awake, tapping on a laptop. Her mouth felt like the bottom of a birdcage. She needed to use the bathroom. If only she were at home.

Through the thin walls Sarah could hear someone walking around, the hollow sound of a door opening and closing. Jane Taylor would raise her penciled eyebrows in surprise if Sarah came out of the bedroom with Hall. It was out of the question to explain to Hall that this wasn't the first time she had been an unofficial guest here. He watched as she searched for her underwear at the bottom of the bed, turning away only as she pulled her underpants on. On the floor was the unmistakable silver square of a condom wrapper, torn in half.

In the confined space of the car Sarah tried to breathe inaudibly. She couldn't bring herself to check if there was a mark on Hall's neck. His hands on the steering wheel were the closest she could come to looking at him. Patches of rust-colored hair, some of it gray, grew on his knuckles, and his fingernails were longer than hers. She took another little sip of water and wished he would drive faster.

★   ★   ★

Tasmanian crayfishing laws stated that each person holding a license had to be present when his or her pot was pulled. It was supposed to stop overfishing; a person couldn't drop six pots a day on behalf of absent friends.

In the boat motoring toward the broken concrete boat ramp, Sarah counted four heads. She was in no doubt they had cleared five pots. She crossed her arms. She wouldn't say anything. Don knew how she felt about illegal fishing. They'd had the conversation more than once.

Hall stood beside her with the wide-legged stance of a farmer, his shoulders broad above stringy hips. He took a couple of photos. There wasn't much to photograph; submerged kelp-covered rocks prevented a pure reflection of the sky, and the water looked dirty. Six or seven tinnies tugged at the ropes leashing them to wire cables drilled into the rocks on either side of the bay. Low tide meant the ropes, tied to bow and stern, were too short, and the tinnies jerked as if they were hog-tied.

As the boat got closer, she recognized Erica perched on the bow, waving with her whole arm. Behind her was Sam Shelley. He didn't wave.

Don cut the engine and Erica jumped off the side, landing in thigh-deep water. Wash sprayed over her as she guided the boat through the shallows. It looked like fun.

'Good catch!' Erica shouted.

Sarah didn't react. Hopefully Hall would be oblivious to Erica's double entendre.

'Thirteen,' Erica said. 'We would have had more, but an octopus got into Pamela's pot. Nothing left but two heads.'

'That always happens to Pammy.' Don grinned. 'You should put out your pot, Sarah.'

'I'm all right.' The thought of being in a boat and making cheery conversation with the lot of them was abhorrent. She preferred to fish alone.

'I've told you I'm happy to put it out for you,' Don offered.

'Where is Pamela?' Sarah asked, pretending to look around. No one answered.

Sarah waded over to the boat and unraveled strands of weed coiled around the propeller, flicking the green ribbons into the breeze. It was beyond her why Don flaunted his readiness to break fishing laws in front of a journalist. He wasn't stupid. He knew a lot about fish and was an astute businessman. Before they bought the shop Don had sold real estate. He had made so much money from that business that now he and Pamela escaped every Tasmanian winter, flying two thousand kilometers north to their beach house at Queensland's exclusive Noosa Heads. Their lifestyle was something that most Tasmanians would only ever dream of.

From the bow of the boat, Sam was watching Erica. Her bikini bottoms were showing through her wet shorts. Sarah glanced at Hall, wondering if he had noticed too, but he was busy picking bindii prickles out of his socks.

Don slid his empty trailer down the ramp with the ease of a man who had done it many times before. While he winched the boat onto the trailer, John approached Hall. It was horrible watching her father talk to the man she had just had sex with.

'I've written half a dozen letters to the *Voice*,' John said. 'No reply. No attention is being paid to that abomination on the point. Who's running that rag?'

'I'm afraid I'm not up to date with the issue,' Hall said. 'Not my area.'

'They've painted it Mardi Gras purple. Stands out like cat's balls. You can see it two nautical miles out to sea. It doesn't comply with the local environmental plan; that's what makes me really angry.'

'Let me think of the name of the guy you need to talk to.'

'What's the point? The *Tassie Voice* won't publish real news.'

Sarah felt herself deflate. She tried to catch her father's eye. It was futile. If she did manage to make eye contact, he was just as likely to make a big deal out of it and ask her what she was trying to say.

'Dad, admit your interest,' Sarah said. 'He owns a block behind the massive new shack, so he's not being completely honest.'

Black snake fast, John whipped his head around. 'You are missing the point. This is about preservation of local amenity. Corruption, too. If that council isn't corrupt, it's stupid.'

Sarah could hear herself in her father. She had even used the same expression when she was angry, accusing someone of not understanding, dismissing their interpretation of a situation. When Dad was riled, he didn't listen to anyone. Hall didn't acknowledge the rudeness.

'You're quite right, John,' he said. 'And don't get me started on the paper. I've been there twenty-three years and it's not what it used to be.'

Inside the cray coffin thirteen creatures writhed, their muscular pincers tied with string. As everyone admired them, Hall began a conversation with Sam. Sarah watched as the situation got worse. It sounded like Hall was writing a story about

Sam. Hall was a nice guy; he looked genuinely interested. He made plans to meet Sam at the Shelleys' shack. Her hands felt clammy and her stomach heaved. What was she doing here?

Sam climbed up into Don's boat, which was now hooked onto the back of his Range Rover. Don gave Sam directions on where to stow each piece of equipment. Sarah unfolded her map and handed it to Don.

'Show me which way Chloe Crawford walked to the beach the day she disappeared. And where did she ride her bike that morning?'

'Why are you asking me?'

'You headed up one of the search parties, didn't you?'

Don sighed. He didn't want to look at the map. Reluctantly his plump index finger landed at the turnoff to the lookout. He traced the dotted line as it curved around the back of the lagoon, past the old rubbish tip and across the two burned bridges, and back onto the graded gravel road that ran parallel to the beach where Anja Traugott was found.

'Chloe rode her bicycle along here. Then she left it at the fishing cottage where her family was staying and took her surfboard to the beach.' Don tapped the map at the main beach, where Chloe had been heading with her surfboard.

'No one knows how far along the beach she walked, do they?'

Don shook his head. 'Or even if she made it that far at all. Perhaps she decided to avoid the surf and enjoy the lagoon's calm water instead. A lot of people do.'

'Hang on. Why does it matter if she went up into the scrub, when she was last seen walking with her surfboard to the beach?' Sarah asked.

'It was a beautiful day. Everyone was outside. But no one saw anyone they regarded as strange. Personally I think someone saw her when she was riding on the Old Road and then took her back up into the scrub. We don't know.'

It was a popular theory that someone had encountered Chloe in the bush and followed her down. Wild duck hunters, guys taking target practice on beer cans at the old rubbish tip, people gathering firewood or picking wildflowers; there were various reasons why people ventured along the Old Road.

'People saw her paddling the surfboard in the lagoon, did they?'

'There were lots of reports that were never confirmed. People thought they saw her but weren't sure. It was hot the day she went missing. I'll never forget it. I was driving back from Douglas River and my right arm got badly sunburnt from hanging out the car window. I never understood what she was doing riding her bike in the midday heat.'

'She wasn't riding in the midday heat. She dropped her bike back at the rented cottage at lunchtime. That was the last time her parents saw her.'

The black-sand bush tracks would have been cool under gum tree shadows in the morning. Chloe wasn't reported missing until evening. The first search party carried torches, their vehicles panning the thick bristly scrub with hopeless yellow beams.

Don was remembering incorrectly if he thought Chloe had been riding at lunchtime. Considering he had helped search for her, you'd think he would recall an important detail such as her exact movements on the last day she was seen. It showed how people's memories could not be relied upon.

'I'm not lying,' Don said.

Sarah stared at him. Why was he being defensive? Chloe disappeared ten months ago. It was long enough for a person to get time frames mixed up.

'What were you doing at Douglas River?' she asked.

'Twenty questions. That's where we bought the chemical toilet from. There's a guy there that builds them. And we had been to visit Max,' Don said.

The mention of Max stalled Sarah. Maxwell was Don and Pamela's only son, a nice guy who she had grown up alongside. He was doing eighteen months at the minimum security prison farm for a robbery motivated by his gambling addiction. It wasn't a topic anyone felt comfortable discussing.

'Anyway, do you reckon the same person who took Chloe Crawford killed the Swiss woman?' Don said.

'Maybe, maybe not.' Sarah shrugged. 'But I don't think Roger Coker was involved either way. Unlike Pamela.'

'Pammy gets excited, that's true, but she usually ends up being right about most things.'

'Is that what you think too?'

'Why are you asking me? You were pretty friendly with that reporter last night. Did he tell you any inside information?'

'I wasn't that friendly with him.' Sarah was aware that up in the boat, Sam was listening to the exchange. He shielded his face from the sun, and she could not see his expression.

'Never mind.' Don chuckled. 'There are two kinds of men who wear earrings. Pirates and poofters. He's not a pirate.'

'He's not a poofter.'

Hall was walking up the boat ramp. He was only meters

away. She hoped Don would not add anything more to the conversation.

A Hilux truck towing a blue and white powerboat approached. Bunghole. He leaned out his window and waggled his fingers in their direction. Don didn't react. It was difficult to tell whether Don even saw Bunghole; his eyes were hidden behind reflective sunglasses and his thick red-skinned face was immobile.

'I heard you and Bunghole had words,' Sarah said.

'Not really.'

'Come on, Don. Everyone heard you.'

'The problem with Keith is he thinks he can do whatever he likes. He continually puts his pot too close to other people's. He knows he's doing the wrong thing.'

The Hilux reversed. Bunghole swore as he accelerated too hard and the wheels spun in the sand. Hall pulled Sarah out of the way. She wasn't about to be run over, but it was a nice gesture.

Hall and Sarah stood in the dusty wake of Don's trailer, seagulls squawking and circling the fish scraps on the beach.

'I was going to get an ice cream,' Sarah heard herself say. 'Want one?'

In the shop Hall peered at the collection of greeting cards displayed between the newspaper stack and licorice laces and the till. Each card had a photograph of a local scene glued to it. Sunsets, pristine white beaches, layers of blue-shaded water; snapshots that fell well short of being artistic, in Sarah's view. Some were supposed to be comical: crayfish wearing Christmas-themed oven mitts or holding barbecue tongs.

The words *Photography by Erica Avery* were printed on the back of each, along with the location or a description. Pamela sold them for five dollars each.

'Those ones walk out the door.' Pamela arched an eyebrow as Hall examined a crayfish card. 'They're hilarious, aren't they?'

'I like this one. What beautiful photography.'

Hall held up a card that depicted the three fishing shacks near the wharf. The image had been taken from a boat in the ocean on an overcast day, and the dilapidated trio of huts, with their shabby weatherboard and rusted corrugated iron roofing, appeared to Sarah as if they were at the world's end. The shack closest to the dune, the one with the blackened brick chimney and pink geraniums, was where the Crawford family had stayed. She had a vague memory of looking at it last night with Hall.

Sarah directed Hall to the ice cream freezer before Pamela could get started on Chloe Crawford. A chill puff of air rose from the freezer as Hall slid the lid open and chose an ice cream called Gaytime. He didn't make a joke about it, either.

'I can't decide,' Sarah said, and Hall closed the freezer lid.

Condensation fogged the glass so she couldn't see in. On the sign above the freezer, half the ice creams were crossed out with thick black pen.

'I felt sick when Erica told me what Roger Coker said to you when you were fishing,' Pamela called to Sarah as she took Hall's money.

'What did she say?' Sarah selected a small container of Valhalla triple fudge ice cream.

'He said that you're next, didn't he? I wouldn't pay too

much attention to him, but I hope you've told the police. Don was furious when I told him.'

'It wasn't like that.' Sarah watched Hall leave, the plastic strips hanging in the doorway slapping behind him.

'I don't want him coming in here,' Pamela asserted. 'Look.'

Pamela pointed to a thirty-centimeter gap on a bottom shelf at the back of the shop. Packets of pink toilet paper were stacked on one side of the empty space, cans of mosquito repellent and fire starter coils on the other.

'If people want a can of Whiskas, it's in the storeroom. They can ask me.' Pamela's lips compressed into a fuchsia-colored pout. 'Roger Coker can drive to town to buy his cat food now . . . and anything else he needs.'

'Now you're acting crazy,' Sarah said.

'Darling, don't be like that.' Pamela played with the tips of her hair. 'I'm not having it. We're not all imagining things, Sarah. I think you're foolish, fishing alone down at the point in the dark. There's no one around to help you. Donald said he saw you on Tuesday night.'

'I didn't . . .'

'You're not being careful, darling. I worry about you and Erica. How well do you really know someone?' Pamela point-edly looked at the empty doorway and back at Sarah. 'Don't worry about it, sweetheart,' she added, gently, when Sarah offered her some coins.

Eating ice cream as they rocked on the park swing set, Hall told Sarah he had been invited baitfishing that afternoon with Don. There were many responses she could have made. She could have pointed out that nets caught entire schools of mullet or parrot fish, as well as seahorses and crabs that didn't survive. She could have questioned the point of sacrificing several kilograms' worth of decent table fish just to catch one kilogram of crayfish. Instead, she made a pathetically female comment.

'Erica's going.'

When he didn't say anything, she felt the need to explain.

'I don't know why I said that,' she admitted. 'About Erica. She might as well be married.'

'Right.'

'Erica and Steve have been together forever. They're in the honeymoon stage, all the time. Very close. Like that.' Sarah held up crossed fingers to show Hall how close Erica and Steve were.

'I get the picture.' Hall looked uncomfortable.

Fat March flies rose and fell around the melted ice cream on her hand, looking for somewhere to land. Hall swung back and forth, his sneakers dragging on the ground. Some children ran into the park and climbed up the slide. A family came up the beach track, the father lugging buckets and spades and beach chairs, the mother carrying two small children, both crying. It was too hot to be at the beach, and she felt their agitation.

Hall spoke before she could say another stupid thing.

'I can't eat those triple fudge ice creams. They're too rich for me.'

'If you're going to have an ice cream, you might as well indulge.'

'I agree. I'm glad you're not one of those women who count calories.'

His comment implied longevity and that her personality

traits might actually matter to him at some point in the future. But maybe she was overthinking things. She scraped the last bit of ice cream out of the container. While she enjoyed the last mouthful she snapped the wooden spoon in half.

'You've done a number on your finger,' he said.

They looked at her left hand. Her index fingernail, what was left of it, was black. Raw flesh on her fingertip was covered by a translucent sheen.

'Dodgy hammer,' she said, and he laughed. 'I was renovating an old Queenslander I've got up north.'

His warm laughter encouraged her to talk as much as uncomfortable silences did. She described the house and the work that she had done. She had been installing a section of heavy wrought-iron balustrade when she hurt her finger. Hall was still looking at her hands. Calloused fingers and dirty nails; he was probably repulsed by the thought that they had touched his naked body last night. She crossed her arms so he couldn't see them.

The fluty sound of children singing drifted across the park as Sarah and Hall rocked on the swings. It was peaceful until Sarah realized that the children were singing, to the tune of the 'Teddy Bears' Picnic' song, about Roger being a serial killer. When they were little, Sarah and Erica had loved that lilting tune.

'Do the police reckon it's him?' Sarah asked.

'His name hasn't been mentioned specifically.'

'He didn't have to report it. He could have left the body on the beach and the next high tide would have removed it. Or parasites and sea crabs would have demolished the evidence.'

'How well do you know him?'

'Not well. I'm happy to fish with him. I'm as guilty as anyone of giving the guy shit. He is a freak. When we were kids we used to dare each other to sneak up to his house.'

It was a story she could tell Hall. Max Gunn, Pamela and Don's son, had called the dare. There was a rumor that Mrs Coker kept a pet black snake under the veranda and fed it fish heads and dead rats through a hole in the boards. It was supposed to be seven feet long with the girth of a four-kilogram salmon. One bite and you'd be dead; no time to drive to St Helens for help. Sarah was close enough to smell the cat piss coming off the sunken couches out front when Roger opened the door. Spittle came out of his mouth as he yelled at her to clear out. His urgency warned of high summer mating season and aggressive snakes. She sprinted toward the gate Max held open, trying to ignore the bindiis piercing her feet.

'The thing was, there was no snake,' Sarah told Hall. 'There was a wasp nest he was worried about. His mum had a thing against snakes; she used to make him shoot them.'

Hall half laughed but didn't make any other comment. His feet dragged arcs on either side of the swing.

'There's a story in that, too.' Sarah couldn't stop talking. 'Mrs Coker hated snakes. Even had a dead snakeskin hanging from the front fence to warn other snakes not to come into her yard. She was a nut. She died after she got bitten by a baby black snake which she disturbed in the wood stack.'

'Did she?'

'Yeah. The bite itself might not have been fatal, but the shock stopped her heart.'

In the silence that followed she could hear her own uneven breaths. She wished she hadn't told him the story; there was no point to it. At least she hadn't told him how the game of dare had ended. She and Max had run from the Coker house to the lagoon. They swam and afterward climbed into a rock cave. In the damp half-light she had dared him to kiss her and had steered his childishly plump hand inside her bathing suit.

Afterward she had felt ashamed, as though something incestuous had happened. She had swum across to the dark cold water on the other side, where she knew he was scared to swim, pulling herself out on rough rocks slippery with the slime in which the fish bred. It hurt his feelings, but she avoided Max after that, refusing to accompany him and Erica when they flew his kite, not talking to him when Pamela and Flip cooked dinner for their families together. The rest of that summer she had devoted to running, jogging shin-shattering lengths of the beach and pounding the sandy fire trails until her lungs felt like they were made of mulch. It was not until years later that they had started talking again, over beers in the university bar.

Hall seemed to be waiting for her to say more. To change the subject she said, 'Anyway. Enough about me. Tell me about one of your favorite stories that you've worked on.'

Hall liked the question. He told her about a ship's bell that was found following a house fire in the Launceston suburb of Windmill Hill. Experts from the museum traced the bell to an iron steamship that had set sail from London for Hobart in the 1880s. The steamship was last sighted by a sealing sloop off Tasmania's northeast coast. Weather records from that year showed that gales had lashed the coast with waves so strong they broke the glass of the Derwent Lighthouse at Iron Pot, ninety feet above sea level. It was thought there were no survivors, but the finding of the bell proved otherwise.

'I love my job when I get a story like that,' Hall said. 'Rewriting history.'

Sarah understood Hall's passion. She felt the same fascination with her fish. When you were immersed in satisfying work, it could feel like the most important thing in the world.

She swung a little bit on the swing. The park was now empty except for the two of them. A light breeze swept off the ocean and the flies had gone.

That night Sarah couldn't sleep. To halt the crazy thoughts trapped in her head, she ran through the process she had taken to restore the iron balustrade of her house. The job of dismantling and carrying the balustrade into the backyard for sanding and painting had been harder than she anticipated. Jake had helped her number each panel. If you neglected to do this, the guy at the hardware shop had advised, it would be an impossible puzzle to resurrect. There were seventy-eight pieces, each heavier than the last. When the backyard was a graveyard of white squares, she and Jake had swung their legs from the empty balcony and drunk beer and watched the pink galahs perched on the frangipani's bony branches.

Locking up that house to come back to Tasmania was hard. There was plenty of work to do; it needed foundation repairs, she had patched the roof but was only halfway through insulating it, and she hadn't finished painting the window frames. Jake said she had used him for free work. That was bullshit. She would have done it without him.

Instead of herself she focused on the murderer. She imagined a man sitting on a brown couch in a room lit by a game show flickering on a portable television set. He would be drinking a can of Wild Turkey, one hand parked in the hairy space between his hip and groin, his eyes too intelligent for the surrounds. On the coffee table would be a small wooden bowl containing chopped marijuana, which he would smoke from a homemade plastic bottle bong, his hands thin and shaky as they held the lighter. His unmade bed would be visible through a doorway, piles of unwashed linen beneath curtains he never opened.

It was an odd psychology, to calm oneself with thoughts of a violent offender. Strangely, it worked, and she drifted into a dreamless sleep.

Growing beside the road were red waratahs and flexing kangaroo tails which blurred in Sarah's peripheral vision. The air above the sandy fire trail was hot, the bush floor so dry it was crackling. Bushfire weather. Sand was a difficult surface to ride on; the wheels slid and the gears on the bike were rusty and didn't always work. Ordinarily Sarah would have cut her losses and turned for home. It was as though she was addicted to tracing the last paths of those two women. There was nothing logical about it.

At the rubbish tip she paused. She leaned her bike against a gum tree and strolled into the dump area. Two trenches in an L shape were half full of junk. It didn't smell too bad, not like the city tip. She peered in, looking for interesting rubbish. There was an old bed headboard, a discarded cray pot, a stained mattress with wire coils poking out, a rusty fridge, and black plastic bags of domestic trash. Nothing that looked suspicious.

As she rode away from the tip, Sarah thought she saw a movement, a flash of color in the bushes. But then it was gone. Her imagination had been active since she saw Anja Traugott's body. How far Chloe Crawford had ridden along this road was unclear. Somewhere between the turnoff from the main gravel road and the first burned bridge, along an almost uninhabited stretch of the Tasman Sea, Chloe had vanished. The police had pulled everything out of the old dump and didn't find her body, surfboard, or clothing. But the tip was too obvious. According to Hall, if the two cases were linked, the killer was clever, methodical, and careful to cover his tracks. This kind of sociopath would traipse through acres of eucalyptus scrub and prickly wildflowers to find the right spot to torture and dispose of his victim.

Anja Traugott had not been killed for her money. Police found her wallet containing fifty dollars in her bag at the rock pool. Her attacker was creepy; he had taken the bikini top as a memento. Unless it had fallen off in the ocean. Maybe he had wanted to take the wallet but was interrupted. Perhaps she fought back harder than he anticipated. Hall reckoned it was an accident that the Swiss woman's body was found. The murderer might have thought that currents would drag the body out to sea, where the great whites would eat it. There were often shark sightings around here. Hall's theory could be correct, but it depended on where exactly Anja entered the water. From the headland near the rock pool the current sucked straight out to sea. Closer to the shore was a trough that swept directly along the coast. Based on this, you could rule out Roger Coker, Bunghole, and anyone else who knew how the currents ran. Any fisherman worth his weight in mullet understood the complexities of the currents.

In the canopy above, the bush birds had halted their eerie

calls. Sarah slowed her breathing and tried to hear what had silenced them. Sometimes the appearance of a black snake quieted the birds. Apart from dry winds rustling leaves there was nothing. And then she heard it. Rubber sliding on sand; it was unmistakable and it was getting closer. Someone was riding up the track behind her. She changed down a gear and picked up speed. They wouldn't catch her, not likely; she had plenty of energy. The problem was this road was a dead end. The bridges had burned years ago, and it was impossible to cross any of the rocky gullies with a bike. Unless she ditched the bike and went cross-country, the only way out was the way she had come in.

Her fear felt strange; it was laced with excitement. She continued riding, listening to the sound of the stranger closing in on her. Where the road widened, she stopped. Through the bottlebrush she glimpsed the cyclist pedaling hard with his head down. He was moving quickly, not an easy thing to do on the sandy track, which meant he was as fit as Sarah, if not fitter. He emerged, and she wished it were the murderer.

Sam slammed his brakes on and skidded the back wheel sideways, spraying her legs with warm black sand.

Since Christmas Day she had seen him three times. At the boat ramp they had said hi, nothing more, and on the beach and at the Abalone Bake she had pretended not to see him. Embarrassing details fizzed through her head. Worse were the details she could not recall. These could not be dismissed with a sarcastic comment. She turned to face him. Get it over and done with.

'Hey.'

'Hey.'

'I owe you an apology,' Sarah said.

She avoided looking him in the eye. Instead she looked down, at his legs, which were muscled and shaved. His arms and laterals were as thick as an adult's. She remembered her mother saying Sam rowed and swam for Hutchins, the private boys' school in Hobart where he boarded. She had seen him surf; he was obviously a natural athlete.

'What for?' Sam said. 'Coming on to me?'

'You wish. It was the other way around.'

This time she watched his face. Her comment had been a worthwhile punt. He reddened and scuffed his toe in the dirt sheepishly. His shoelaces were not done up properly. Man, he was young.

'You're too young to drink,' she continued, ignoring the feeling of déjà vu that occurred so frequently these days. 'Not that I care. Some people would give a shit, though.'

'Who gives a damn?'

'Yeah. Have you told anyone?'

'Who am I going to tell around here?'

There were other things she wanted to know, physical details such as who had made the first move, and how much she had told him about herself, and whether he had still been there when she crawled up into the dunes. No way was she going to ask him any of that.

Phlegm caused by the cigarettes she had smoked the night they hooked up – Sam's cigarettes – irritated the back of her throat. Even though it was now five days later, she could still feel the tobacco's effect. She wasn't used to it. She coughed, but that did not dislodge the mucus, and she had to use more force, which made a rude hacking sound.

'You're all class, aren't you?' Sam said as she spat into the dirt behind her.

It was a fair call, and one that she would usually enjoy retaliating to. Given the circumstances, it was better not to push her luck. Little shit.

Sarah said, 'Tell me, where were you when that backpacker was murdered?'

'What?' Sam was startled.

'I'm asking everyone. Just wondering.'

'Don't know. Probably surfing.'

'What break?'

'Are you Inspector Gadget?'

Sarah ignored the question. Everyone knew where they were when Anja Traugott went missing. It was like when Princess Diana died, or the Twin Towers collapsed. Judging by how flustered he looked, he was probably doing something embarrassing.

'Were you choking the chicken?' Sarah grinned.

'You'd know.' He stepped toward her and she could see the acne scars on his cheeks. A flashback from that stupid night appeared in her mind; his face was so soft that at one point in her drunken stupor she had thought she was kissing a girl.

'What's wrong?' Sam asked.

'Nothing.'

'You look like you're about to have a big cry over something.'

He grinned, and she remembered when he was nine or ten and had turned up at the lagoon with a hessian sack clutched in his hand. Sam had held the bag up, shaking it, and told everyone there was a blue-ringed octopus in there. When he threatened to set it free in the lagoon, everyone screamed and raced up onto the rocks to get away. Sarah had kept her distance. She liked blue-ringed octopuses, but their bite was fatal. There was no antidote for their paralyzing venom, which would kill an adult in three minutes. Sarah had always felt a bit sorry for the soft-bodied creature. The male died soon after mating, and the female, who laid fifty eggs and carried them around under her arm, died months after the eggs hatched. Blue-ringed octopus were intelligent animals and not aggressive unless they were threatened. They should never be put in a bag. When Sarah told Sam this he had laughed. Dangling the sack, he halfheartedly chased people farther up the rocks. Eventually he stopped. It turned out there was nothing in the bag but a pile of seaweed.

Sarah thought of reminding Sam about the incident but changed her mind. She did not want to prolong the conversation.

'Race you back,' she said.

'Want to bet on it? Ten bucks.'

'I don't want your pocket money.'

She could have whipped him – not easily, but she was pretty fit at the moment. Instead she let him ride ahead so that he would think he was beating her.

Sarah thought over the conversation as she packed her fishing gear that afternoon. Sam's cockiness was unnerving. Usually, younger guys were easy to be around. Their self-absorption was a buffer to Sarah's insecurities. They didn't expect anything from her. They were into the same things she was. Lots of men her age liked to watch motocross or boxing on television; not many wanted to have a go themselves.

Jake was a natural athlete. He had a welted scar that twisted down his bicep like mangrove roots, collected during a mountain bike race. It was when he told her he raced that she'd decided to hire him. His previous job experience on the salmon farm at Tickera was not extensive.

If she was honest, part of the appeal of younger men was their lack of inhibition. Like her, most young guys drank unreservedly. That was how she had ended up in the disabled toilet at the Pineapple Hotel the first time she went there with Jake. In the bathroom, which smelled of piss and shit and vomit, Jake told her she was a great fuck. The band was blasting a song from Hunters and Collectors, and she heard him only because he repeated it several times.

But Sam Shelley was seventeen years old. Most women her age were married with children, worrying about things like how to pay a mortgage on one wage and which kindergarten to send their kid to. Not dwelling on what an idiot they'd been on the drink the other night. Sarah Avery needed to get her shit together.

Onshore gusts clipped the tops off majestic sets of six-foot waves and veiled Sarah in sea spray. Sand swirled, and the water twisted into an undertow that sucked at the beach. It was just the sort of place you wouldn't want to swim; perfect for chasing salmon. Schools of black back salmon were visible in the water, clouds of dimpled silver riding in the crest of each wave. She grunted as she swung the rod, sinking the surf popper lure bang in the gutter twenty meters offshore.

'Got a fright the other night. Night you all were cooking abalone it was.'

'Stop sneaking up on me.' Roger must have come down from the dunes; she would have noticed him if he were on the beach.

'There was a thump out the back.'

'Possums?'

'I thought it was.' He sat down cross-legged and cupped sand in his hands. His arms were thin, too thin to restrain a strong woman.

'Sounded loud, like a V8 taking off up the driveway. I got up to have a look.'

She felt the bite and played with the fish, gradually bringing him closer to the shore. It was likely she would get a few bites today. Black back salmon and the younger, feistier cocky salmon fled when the ocean was flat and bright. On days like this, unsettled swell washed food into the water colony and the salmon followed. She admired the cocky salmon. He swam with the waves, used their force to propel him to prey. She was only half listening when Roger spoke again.

'Dead devil. Road kill. A week old, from the way it smelled.'

Stunned, she allowed the line to slacken. 'Someone threw road kill at your house?'

Roger described the black furry animal he had found sprawled beside his doormat, its mouth and eyes wide open. In the morning he grabbed the stiffened devil by the back legs and dropped it under the paperbarks behind the fence. Hot soapy water and a hard-bristled brush couldn't remove the brown bloodstains from the timber planks on his deck. The tufts of fur caught in the wooden cracks reeked with the putrid smell of a carcass rotting for days in the sun. Burnout marks remained on his driveway. Roger grinned as though the story was a joke he was part of.

'I can still smell it on me.' Roger sniffed his fingers.

'You going to tell the police, Roger?'

'I hear plenty of noises around my place and none of them get to me.' Roger's chapped lips twisted over his broken teeth as he imitated the noises made by various animals that lived around his house. Possums thumped up and down his pitched roof, fighting with catlike screams; a bird's nest stuck to his kitchen window was full of whimpering baby sparrows; rats scratched under his floorboards.

'A blue-tongued lizard, this big, lives under the tank stand.' Roger grinned. 'I call him Louis. He likes sausage mince the best.'

'Tell me. The skid marks on your driveway. Were they continuous or broken?'

'Continuous.'

Sarah nodded. 'You're a good man. You don't deserve this.'

The cocky salmon was losing energy. Her finger monitoring the tautness of the line, she could sense his surrender. She wound him in slowly. Roger held the surf rod while she slipped the hook out of the fish's mouth. They grinned at each other, silent acknowledgment of their teamwork. There was something about Roger that attracted and repelled her. He was not her intellectual equal. Physically, he was strong but not well built. His arms were too long for his body, his legs and neck so thin they appeared to undulate like sea grass. He would never meet someone who would love him. It wasn't possible. Sometimes she thought about being his wife, and the thought made her sick.

'I've seen you outside at night, fishing, whatnot. And I saw you up at the tip yesterday,' Roger said. 'You were wearing a yellow shirt with a white bear on it.'

Using both hands, she broke the fish's neck with a quick twist. It stiffened and she held it until it spasmed.

He thumped her fishing rod handle in the sand. 'Don't go up there on your own.'

Hall had written two articles for the day's newspaper. Sarah supposed they were what he had referred to as a beat-up. Basically the murder investigation was not progressing. In the first article the police claimed that with so many tourists in the area, it was difficult to confirm possible sightings of Anja Traugott. The second article referred to a police statement issued back when Chloe Crawford vanished.

'At this stage we are treating this as a missing person and are trying to locate the young girl concerned. At the moment there is nothing to suggest she is not alive.'

The police refused to confirm whether the two cases were linked. Someone in the Bay of Fires had to know something. Jane Taylor had said it from the start: a person doesn't just walk onto a beach, kill someone, and walk off without a single person seeing or hearing something. Perhaps someone knew something and didn't know it was important. People were hopeless; you could not trust them.

Sarah had learned this the hard way. In November, when the pumps had kept shitting themselves, Sarah had not allowed herself to go home for more than an hour at any stretch. Anxious that the emergency alarm would not transmit to her mobile phone, she slept on the couch in her office. Pump failure meant no oxygen and the fish would die. The fish farm had emergency oxygen, but those pumps had played up too. Every time she left the farm, she feared she would return to tanks full of dead fish. It would be devastation – she could lose all her stock, from babies to adult fish. Human error on a land farm could cost hundreds of thousands of dollars in a few minutes. She had vowed not to take another land farm job again. An ocean-based fish farm was quite different. Farming was safer at sea; if something went wrong, the ocean protected the fish. At sea the oxygen never ran out.

Sarah gripped the edges of the newspaper. The headline blurred. Her head hurt in a dizzy, disorienting way, as though her skull contained a swarm of wasps. As she pushed the paper away, she glimpsed herself in the window reflection. She looked haggard, gaunt, ugly. Unblinking, she stared at herself. This was what a person capable of being heinous looked like. She didn't want to think about Jake, but images from that final night in Eumundi forced themselves on her.

His hands on the bonnet of her car. In the headlights, his eyes hollow, his nostrils flared. Faceless witnesses watching from the dark edges of the Pineapple Hotel car park. His sour beer breath spittle on her face and his index finger drilling her chest. Riding mountain bikes and renovating had made her biceps strong, and when her fist smashed his nose, it popped like a balloon. Blood spurted and he hopped backward across the car park in surprise. Shouting profanities, he ran toward her and knocked her to the ground.

Pinned on the wet asphalt underneath Jake, she tried to turn away from the blood streaming from his nose. He grabbed a fistful of her hair and forced her to look at him. He put one finger against his nostril and did the fisherman's whistle, snorting blood over her hair and face and neck. She could taste it, the salty warmth mixed with sweaty rain and wet tar.

Maybe if Sarah had stopped then, had closed her eyes and waited until he heaved himself off her, maybe things would be better now. Tit for tat, they both got what they deserved. Instead she had kneed him hard in the balls, and when he was in the fetal position, howling, she had straddled him and managed to smash his face with a closed fist before someone pulled her off him.

Elbows on the kitchen bench, she dropped her head, her shaking, cold fingertips barely holding its weight. Shame engulfed her. Her chest tightened, and for a moment she thought she was going to cry, but no tears came, just a raw, soundless sob, like a person who had been shot in the lung.

Chapter 5

The police had a suspect. The detective wouldn't give Hall his name but said it was someone they had spoken to in regard to the murder of Anja Traugott and the disappearance of Chloe Crawford. Hall called Ann Eggerton, the police media officer. She confirmed that the police were talking to a man who lived on the east coast, was unemployed, and had prior convictions.

'Give me a break, they have a suspect,' Hall jeered. 'I bet they're blaming some poor bloke who's got no more criminal record than you or me. It's bullshit.'

'No. They've picked him up three times for poaching crayfish and he's been convicted twice.'

Hall grinned down the phone. Gotcha.

Company expenses wouldn't cover the cost of renting Jane's room for a fortnight, Hall knew that. But he deserved a break, and it would be good to have somewhere with generator power to charge his laptop and write his stories. After all, it wasn't like he could type them up on the picnic table outside Pamela's shop.

He thought Jane might have sounded more pleased about the arrangement.

'Suit yourself.'

'I'll pay for two weeks,' Hall said. 'I'll have to go back and forth to Launceston, but I might keep some gear in there. You don't have to clean it when I'm gone.'

'Wasn't planning to.'

'Fine.'

Hall sat down and Jane watched him, her face contorting as though she was chewing the inside of her cheek.

'I don't want charity.'

'Good. I wasn't planning on giving you any.' He opened his notebook, studying it until she marched away.

Hall was reading the paper at the big table, circling typos. Page seven had five; one case used *their* instead of *there*. It was ridiculous. Shame on every one of those subeditors. Attention to detail had gone to the dogs since the *Voice* downsized from broadsheet to tabloid. A man's voice greeted him and he startled, spilling hot tea that made the newsprint run. It was John Avery, smiling that wide white grin so hard he appeared ill at ease. He must have come up the inside staircase. Hall introduced himself again, in case a memory lapse was the cause of John's discomfort.

'I know who you are, Hall. Everyone does. And I still haven't given you my book,' John said. 'Maybe it's of no interest.'

'*Trail of the Tin Dragon* . . . Was that the name?'

'Yes, quite right. This was the entry point; the Chinese miners made their way across to the Blue Tier from here. It's an interesting story.'

'I'm very keen to read it.'

'Well, in that case, swing by this evening. I'll have it ready for you.' John backed out of the guesthouse. 'In fact, stay for dinner. We have a few friends coming over. Just another barbecue.'

'What can I bring?'

'Nothing. I'm a wine connoisseur, you see. Amateur. But I'll open one of the reds I've been saving.'

After John left, Hall folded up the sodden newspaper and boiled the kettle again, pondering what he knew about the man. He was a senior lecturer in history at the University of Tasmania's Launceston campus but had not taught any classes for a while. At the Abalone Bake, Flip had mentioned her husband was working from home on a research project of some kind. She had added that it was her income as a pharmacist that permitted him to do so. So, John worked alone; he knew the area's topography, above ground and below; and he had a bad temper. Hall had noted this at the boat ramp when John snapped at Sarah. A bad temper didn't make him a murderer, though.

He was surprised at how pleased he was at the chance of seeing Sarah again. From what he could tell, she was not his type. The woman was obsessed with fish. The topic had snuck its way into nearly every conversation they had had.

Sarah called herself a fish doctor. In southeast Queensland she ran a barramundi farm where they grew fish from babies into four-kilogram adults. They produced four hundred tonnes of fish each year in huge purpose-built ponds in the middle of paddocks. He had heard of fish grown in cages in Bass Strait and the Tamar River, but not in paddocks. According to Sarah, the advantage of land farming was that the environment could be controlled, which meant higher stock intensity. Ocean-based fish farms were cheaper to run, but you were at the mercy of the ocean's unpredictable weather patterns. It was scientific, and she hadn't dumbed it down as she talked about water quality and grading fish.

'Grading is sorting them by size. Fish are cannibalistic. If you have three fish of different sizes, all of a sudden you have one big fish,' she had explained. 'I know the fellas aren't doing their job if I see a monster fish swimming around in one of my tanks.'

He had laughed although he suspected she wasn't joking completely. It was only when she was speaking about fish or fishing that she maintained eye contact with him.

Hall checked his watch. Four hours until dinner. He made a mental note to remember to ask John for the book before he mentioned it; otherwise John might think Hall was there only in the hope of bedding his daughter.

Hall knocked on the door of the green Fibro cottage. While he waited he patted a silky black cat purring around his leg. Something scurried under a broken sofa on the porch next to him. He glanced over his shoulder. He couldn't help it. This place reminded him of a job he had done early in his career in the Dover Street public housing. The guy he was looking for had shoved him so hard on his arse that his back still ached weeks later.

'Snake weather, this is.'

Hall spun around. Roger stood in the long grass, a shovel in his hand. His buttoned-up shirt was frayed at the collar, but it was tucked neatly into his jeans. He seemed friendly.

'Black snakes. You seen one?' Roger continued.

'No. I've been told to be careful.'

'Especially on the high rocks at the back of the beach. That's where they sleep. They're all poisonous down here. Venomous. Leave them alone and you'll be okay.'

Hall introduced himself and explained he wanted to interview Roger for a general story on people in the area. It was almost true.

'What for?'

'The *Voice*. I'm a reporter.'

'I won't bother, thank you,' Roger said.

Roger opened the door to his cottage. Hall caught a glimpse of a tidy kitchen sink and a wall calendar showing a native bottlebrush.

'The snakes are more scared of you than you should be of them,' Roger said before closing the door in Hall's face.

In the Averys' kitchen the women swooped. Pamela perched Hall on a wobbly stool, Flip poured his beer into a glass, and Erica gave him a papery biscuit smeared with duck pâté. He didn't know whether to bite it or shove it in his mouth at once; the risk with biting it was that it might crumble everywhere. Better to eat it whole, he decided.

His mouth was full when Pamela said, 'Everyone's wondering whether or not you're married.'

It meant either they knew something had happened between him and Sarah and consequently thought he was the kind of man who cheated on his wife or, on the contrary, they were trying to set him up with her. Either scenario was embarrassing. He chewed the biscuit slowly, watching them wait for his response. In Erica he could see what Flip had looked like as a younger woman. They had the same neat brown hair and delicate features, the same self-assured smiles. Air hostess smiles, he thought, remembering that Sarah had said her sister was a flight attendant for Qantas. Women with that kind of smile made him nervous.

'Never been married.'

'You're a bachelor,' Pamela said.

Behind her on the wall was a poster showing a multitude of brightly colored fish. It advertised a fishing reel: at the bottom were the words *It will catch them every time*. Hall chewed another biscuit and waited for the follow-up question. It would be one of two: either whether he owned his house or how much he earned. The question about whether he wanted children usually came later. It was part of the reason why, when he broke up with Laura, he had decided to date only women under the age of thirty. Of course there were other benefits to dating younger women, if you could call what happened between midnight and dawn dating.

'Sarah said you're originally from Buckland. Are your family still on the farm?' Erica opted for the asset question.

'Just my father. Mum died a few years ago.'

He smiled kindly while they searched for a change of subject.

Watching Sarah during dinner, he doubted she had put them up to it. She didn't seem like the kind of woman who would care; she hadn't even changed her clothes for the meal. Her hair was pulled back in a clumped salty ponytail, and her black T-shirt promoting the 1997 World Aquaculture Conference was at odds with the creamy color palette the other women were wearing. Her face was more delicate than he remembered, a prettiness diminished by her gruffness. Apart from recommending Flip's hollandaise sauce, Sarah hadn't spoken to him all night. Maybe it had been presumptuous of him to come.

When he arrived, Sarah had been standing out the back with John and the other men, drinking beer around the barbecue. Now she was shooting off opinions on every topic. Apparently Erica's partner, Steve, had installed the shack's new chimney incorrectly.

'Rattles. Kept me awake all night. I couldn't sleep,' Sarah said. 'There's a few things around here I need to fix.'

'You like fixing things?' It was the first time Hall had spoken to her directly that night, and he immediately regretted the lameness of his comment.

'Love it. Forget tidy modern homes. Give me a diamond in the rough any day.'

Someone else interrupted before Hall could reply. He concentrated on the delicious food. Before long the conversation turned to the two missing women.

'Chloe Crawford was such a pretty thing and polite, too,' Pamela said. 'She came into the shop a few times. Actually, I think she was having a little flirtation with Sam Shelley.'

'I remember you saying that,' Flip said. 'Didn't Simone put a stop to it?'

'That's right.' Pamela laughed. 'The two of them were eating ice cream on the bench outside and Simone turned up and took Sam away. The poor kid. He can't even have an ice cream with a girl.'

From what Sarah had told him at the Abalone Bake, Hall knew Simone was a wealthy widow who made her money running a home furnishings import business. She shopped in

Indonesia and Thailand and shipped items back to Australia and the States. Her late husband, who was Australian, had owned the dirt on which her beach house stood. Immediately after his death she had demolished the old Fibro beach shack on the site and built the glass and green copper structure. Her son was being educated in Hobart – at a boarding school. Given her circumstances, Hall could understand why she was a bit overprotective of young Sam.

Toward the end of the meal Sarah started an argument with Don over whether yachtsmen deserved to pay for their own rescue operations if they ran into trouble on the ocean.

'Some yachtsmen are decent sailors, I agree with you, but many are just lunatics who expect the taxpayer to pick up the tab,' she said. 'No, no, I'm not talking about Simone Shelley's husband, so don't bring me into that one,' she added to Pamela.

'I didn't say anything,' Pamela said.

'Pammy doesn't need any help moaning about Simone Shelley.'

'What is that supposed to mean?' Pamela said.

'Nothing.'

'Shut up, Donald. You're drunk.'

'No I'm not.'

'You've drunk two bottles of red. No one else is touching it.'

'I'm not counting your drinks.'

'You don't need to. I've had two champagnes.'

In the silence Flip piled calamari and crayfish onto Hall's plate from platters on which parsley sprigs had been arranged around fleshy white meat and prawns with gleaming dead eyes.

'Give me a break,' Don said.

'We've had a nice night,' Flip said. 'Come on.'

'No, I'm sick of him. He's always like this.' Pamela's voice cracked.

'Like what? I've done nothing wrong.'

'Of course you haven't.'

'My darling wife, I'm going.'

'Where? Prowling around on the beach, looking for half-naked women to perve on? You won't find any out there tonight, sorry to disappoint you. They're all dead.'

'Now listen here, Pamela. I'm going home to bed.' Don's voice was controlled, but his lips were stiff as they ejected each word. 'To be honest, I'm getting a bit tired of hearing your opinions. Everyone is.'

'Go, Don, let it rip.' Sarah laughed, and Hall realized she was drunk.

'Hush, Don,' Flip said. 'Everyone's a bit worn out from this . . . thing.'

The door closed behind Don. John started to follow him, but Flip pushed him back into his chair. He glared at her.

It was clear these people were not used to confrontation. They seemed shocked, like witnesses milling around the edge of the highway after a car crash, not sure whether to comfort one another or leave the scene. Flip patted Pamela's hand, and Steve had bowed his head in his hands as if he were praying.

Hall excused himself to visit the bathroom. John gave him directions: go to the end of the veranda and it's the blue door.

'Don't get locked in there.' Sarah grinned.

As Hall stepped outside, he could hear Sarah laughing. Hall smiled. She could not have been that intoxicated at the Abalone Bake if she remembered his story of being locked inside the city park toilet block. At a dinner party once, he had told the tale and it had made Laura cross with him, as though there were something embarrassing about being accidentally imprisoned in a lavatory. Sarah was not so highly strung.

When Hall returned from the bathroom, Sarah was stacking the plates. Hall helped. Superficial chatter around the table concealed the discomfort caused by Don's exit. In the kitchen Hall placed the plate stack he was carrying on the bench. He was tired. He felt slightly sick from the rich food. He had never seen so much seafood on one table. Years ago, he recalled, a guest at his family's farm had brought a crayfish and his parents had not known how to eat it.

'What's it like being so popular?' Sarah said.

'I am?'

'A journalist. I don't think anything so exciting has happened here since, well, since a body washed up on the beach.' Sarah tipped eight sets of cutlery into the empty sink. 'I'm crass. I shouldn't joke about it.'

'Being a journalist doesn't impress everyone.'

'Neither does being a fish farmer, trust me.'

'I've got a story to follow up near the St Columba Falls in the next day or so,' he began.

He had not planned to ask her to come with him. He wanted to. It was a country pub in the nearby Pyengana dairy farm region, somewhere on the road to the St Columba Falls. The map showed gravel roads crossing cattle bridges and a green dotted line climbing through a national park. Tasmanian roads were notoriously underused. If he got lost on one of the forestry roads, if he got a flat tire, it could be days before someone else drove past.

In the shack's silence the gas lanterns buzzed. White moths

beat the glass like butterfly whips. Sarah opened another beer, her cheeks billowing as she swirled the liquid in her mouth.

'I'll buy you lunch,' he said.

'Got nothing else to do.'

Erica giggled, and Hall realized everyone was listening to them.

'Hush, Erica,' Steve said.

Sarah glanced across the room to the dinner table. She spun the beer cap on the bench. Hall worried that she was changing her mind.

'Thanks for asking.' Sarah slung a green satchel over her shoulder and picked up her fishing rod. At the same time John poured a glass of port and handed it to Hall.

John started talking about his book, and Hall remembered why he was there. He tried to concentrate, but all he could hear were Sarah's feet thudding down the ramp into the night.

'Johnny, aren't you concerned about her being down there alone?' Pamela bustled into the kitchen and pulled on pink rubber washing-up gloves.

'When did anyone in this shack ever listen to me?' John read the time on his watch. 'I'll go for a walk in a little while, make sure everything is safe.'

Hall considered following Sarah to the beach. Fishing by moonlight with Sarah was infinitely more appealing than drinking port on a stomach full of seafood. But it was John who had invited him for dinner, and it would be rude to leave now. He would finish the drink and excuse himself.

Before he left, Hall had another look at the fishing poster. He searched for the snotty trevally. Earlier Sarah had confessed her secret for catching snotty trevally. She used raw chicken breast. Underwater, raw chicken resembled jellyfish which the fish usually ate.

'Don't quote me. It's never been scientifically proven. But it's the only explanation anyone can think of, because a snotty trevally who only eats chicken is going to be one very hungry fish.'

Hall had laughed; it was the kind of fact he liked.

The snotty trevally was silver with a blue and green back and small rubbery lips. She had a black dot on her cheek, like a beauty spot.

Pamela's huge four-wheel drive headlights were inconsequential under the late night sky. Their bucketed light was dwarfed by the immense blackness. Sitting beside Pamela as she drove him back to the guesthouse after dinner, Hall tried to remain impartial as she explained exactly how obese the Averys' Labradoodle was. Apparently Henry ate scraps from the table during every meal.

'Henry is so fat he'll get arthritis. It's in their genes. I've told Flip.'

'Well, you're not helping. I saw you feeding him crayfish tonight.'

'Cray meat doesn't keep.' Pamela waved a hand in the air indifferently. 'We get so tired of it. I've got nine in my freezer. Nine! They take up too much space.'

If he was talking to a bloke, another journo or any of the guys he played pool with on Wednesday nights, he would have questioned the sense of continuing to drop pots when they had already caught so many. You're fucked in the head, mate, he might comment with a grin, and the other guy would shrug and tell him where to go. He'd get the point, though.

Instead Hall said, 'I heard there was a murder in your crayfish pot.'

'No. I haven't put my pot out for days.'

'That's funny. I was at the boat ramp yesterday morning and Erica said an octopus broke into your pot.'

'I'm too busy working to put my pot out.'

It was easier to tell if someone was lying if you didn't look at them. Practiced liars knew about holding eye contact and maintaining a calm expression. Their voices were harder to control. Pamela's voice changed just enough to confirm what Hall already knew. He exhaled, slowly, and let the topic slide. It was cruel to have a go at a woman who had just had a public row with her husband.

Stories that would never be written had always teased Hall. The facts would remain with him, forming into impotent leads in his mind as he tried to fall asleep at night. Knowing that something needed to change and there was nothing he could do about it was irritating. When Sarah had complained about how many pots everyone was throwing in, Hall knew he was onto another story that was dead before it started.

The road curved steadily past the wharf and Pamela slowed down. The headlights picked up a figure moving down the beach track to the water. It was Don; his bald head was unmistakable.

'Was that . . .?' Hall said.

'No.'

'I thought I saw Don.'

'I thought I saw something too, but it was an animal, a wallaby perhaps.'

Hall waited in the dark garden of the guesthouse. When her lights vanished, he walked back the way they had come. At the top of the wharf track, in the shadow of an old boathouse, Hall stood. He listened to the boats creaking on their ropes, the slip-slop of the waves. This was silly. He didn't know where Sarah had decided to fish, and it was unlikely Don Gunn was a murderer. Still, he held his breath for a minute longer and tried to hear something more sinister than the rustling of bush rats feeding on fishing scraps.

In bed that night Hall's mind was too alert to let him sleep. He had not drunk too much, but he felt overstimulated as he tried to correlate the conversations with the work he needed to do. Anxiety, a long-absent yet familiar variety, also nagged at him.

Thankfully he hadn't felt that unpleasant undercurrent for a long time. For pretty much two years after Laura left, disquiet had gnawed him, at any time, whenever anything reminded him of her. Certain books or films he knew she would like, the smell of the Nivea body moisturizer she used, women who wore their hair long and untied, and songs by the Waifs. The Waifs were a band he hated, but for a long time, if they played on the office radio, he feared he was going to cry. It would be seven years since she left this February. The first few years had been very dark for Hall. It was a long time to get over a breakup. Some of his friends had given up on him. They were the ones who were still mates with Dan.

He hadn't thought about Dan and Laura for ages, not in a

loathsome way. He had seen Dan a couple of months ago, outside the Penny Royal Arcade. Dan had waved, Hall had crossed the road. And why shouldn't he? Dan was a man who'd waited until Hall had an out-of-town assignment and then got himself invited for dinner at Laura and Hall's home. They had been sitting at the little wrought-iron table on the sunny side of the veranda, eating cornflakes, when Hall returned earlier than expected that terrible morning. The casualness of the scene, Laura wrapped in Hall's dressing gown, Dan wearing an old tracksuit, suggested to Hall it had been going on for longer than he wanted to know.

There was an old joke about a man whose wife runs off with his best friend. Someone asks him, 'How are you coping?' 'Pretty bad,' the man replies. 'I really miss him.' But it wasn't like that for Hall. Once he got past the wretched, cruel business of being heartbroken, the humiliation as he pieced together the puzzle to discover that quite a few people knew about the affair before he did, the violence he wanted to inflict on Dan, his final suffocating pain when he realized Laura would never beg Hall to take her back; when all that was out of his system, he had missed them both, in different ways.

And here he was again, feeling nervous, like he was bush-walking and could not find his location on the map. But the feeling was not as sickening and helpless as how he had felt when Laura left. Just like being lost in the bush; his anxiety was laced with endorphins, the sweetness of a challenge that was almost, but not quite, beyond him. He had asked Sarah to come for lunch with him. It would be good for him. And, he hoped, it would be nice for her too.

He opened John's book, grateful for a constructive

diversion. The book contained maps of the area, some dating back to the late 1800s. Others were more recent, detailing the mines that had been rehabilitated in the 1990s. The government-led initiative had seen some shafts filled in and others gated or blocked to protect humans and animals from danger. Hall would get an expert to suggest that a body could be disposed of in one of these mineshafts, get the police to comment on it, sex it up with an emotionally loaded quote from someone like John Avery, and there was a nice story. Better check the copyright issues related to John's book. There were the pictures, too. A good Saturday double-page spread.

He wound down the reading lantern and closed his eyes.

On the morning of New Year's Eve, Hall's battery-operated alarm clock rang at five a.m., rattling the wooden nightstand. He was at his desk in the office in Launceston four hours later. The first part of the drive had taken him longer than he anticipated. He slowly negotiated the unlit gravel roads, mindful of wombats, wallabies, and devils. He was thankful he hit nothing except that which was already dead. In hindsight, he should not have left so early. It would have been more sensible to wait until the sun came up, but he was anxious to finish his work in town and return before nightfall.

Driving back to Launceston, Hall was conscious that there was something eluding him, a piece of information he needed to consider. The first thing he did when he arrived at the office was examine a map in John Avery's book that depicted the coastal hinterland. There it was: Atherton's Lookout, a village on the other side of the Blue Tier mountains, roughly one hundred kilometers from the Bay of Fires. Once prompted, the facts snapped mechanically through his mind. Five or six years ago a teenage girl vanished from Atherton's Lookout. She had ridden a horse up the forestry roads. The horse returned, but she didn't. Hikers stumbled across an old timber hut, high in the mountains, recently used, recently abandoned. Police had looked into the possibility that a deranged hermit had abducted the girl and was keeping her for company.

Hall looked up the article. The photo was not particularly clear, but the girl was uncannily similar to Chloe and Anja, the same fine features, the pale good looks. To this day she had not been found. There was no escaping it; it looked like paradise, but the east coast was rotten at the core. He put the information in a folder to think about later.

The office was pleasantly quiet with only a skeleton staff present due to it being New Year's Eve. Elizabeth didn't speak to Hall when she walked past his desk. His index fingers whacked the keyboard as he pretended to be consumed by his notes. He spent the day on the phone, typing as he interviewed, following up on old stories. A family who survived carbon monoxide poisoning after firing up a barbecue inside their house; a light rail linking Riverside with Invermay (despite the *Voice*'s persistent campaign, an expensive light rail was never going to happen); and the residents of Peace Haven nursing home had finally raised enough cash to start building their smoking gazebo. Good on the old fellows; that was the only story that made Hall smile.

As Hall proofread his smoking gazebo story, it occurred to him that one of the gentlemen driving that gazebo agenda had a brother who reared racehorses on the east coast, not too far from the Bay of Fires. Bennett was their surname. If Hall remembered correctly, Allan Bennett was the name of the horse trainer. Perhaps a man involved in the shadowy business of horseracing might have knowledge of the local fishing underworld and be able to help Hall locate the crayfish-poaching suspect the police spokeswoman had mentioned. It might not come to anything, but it was worth a phone call. He looked up the number and dialed. No answer. He would try again later.

There was a Post-it note on his computer reminding him that he was welcome at a party that evening at the home of one of his colleagues. He would make his apologies another time. There were a lot of people going and the friend would not mind if Hall was absent. In any case, Hall had arranged to interview Sam later in the day.

Tonight, Simone had invited everyone to her beach house for champagne. Hall had not asked if Sarah would be there, but it sounded like Simone's invitation was inclusive. Driving him home last night, Pamela had told him that she and Don, and the entire Avery family, were going. The party was a Bay of Fires tradition.

'She'd be so upset if we didn't go it wouldn't be worth it,' Pamela had said.

At two p.m. Hall turned his computer off and wandered out casually, hoping it would appear that he was on his way to the bathroom rather than leaving the office. There was no need to go home. When he had popped in that morning, Marsha, his cat, had ignored him from the neighbor's sunny veranda. Inside his house, her biscuit bowl remained full; she had not been home for a few days either.

Light summer ocean sky welcomed him when he pulled

onto the Bay of Fires road several hours later. Wide sky, acres of ocean, and smells that were now familiar: salt, seaweed, seafood cooking outside one of the shacks, rusty fishing gear and old boats and diesel.

Simone and Sam Shelley's holiday house, or shack, as they called it, was built from glass and untreated cedar weatherboard that had faded to gray. It had expensive green copper pipes. It was a misfit with the scrap metal and recycled timber construction of the neighboring fishing shacks, Hall thought as he knocked on the door. When Simone opened it, barefoot and wearing a white sarong, she tipped her head to the side and smiled as though they had known each other for a long time.

Inside, the floors were Huon pine and the walls paneled with blackheart sassafras, the couches low and lined with green and brown cushions. Sheer white curtains billowed with air straight off the Tasman Sea. In the garden below, a dozen chairs were arranged around a table overlooking the ocean. Vases of yellow and blue flowers were set on the table, obviously in preparation for the evening's party. Simone stood beside him and admired the view. Her closeness was disconcerting. Hall opened his notebook. He could not see Sam.

'Coffee or champagne?'

'Thanks. But I don't drink when I'm working,' Hall lied. 'Coffee would be great.'

'In that case I'll save the champagne for tonight. How do you like your coffee?'

'Any way it comes.' Hall didn't know how he liked it; at home he drank instant coffee.

As the coffee machine groaned into action, Hall looked

around at the candles in glass hurricane lanterns and huge tropical shells. He had never seen shells so large. On the table was a book titled *Underwater Archaeology: Submerged Treasures*. It was the kind of book he would have liked to peruse, but he suspected Simone would interpret his interest in the wrong way.

Sam Shelley thumped down the staircase taking it four or five steps at a time and sat opposite Hall.

'How much are you paying me?'

'Checkbook journalism is not my thing.'

'Geez.' Sam had his mother's wide blue eyes and ragged blond hair that flopped over his face in an effort to hide the pimples on his forehead and temples. 'What do you want me to say?'

Last summer Sam had written a letter and stuck it in a plastic soft drink bottle. Standing on the point, he tossed the bottle out to sea. Six months later a square blue envelope with New Zealand stamps on it was waiting in the Shelleys' post office box. On the beach of Granity, a small town on the west coast of New Zealand, a fifteen-year-old girl had discovered Sam's bottle. It was a straightforward quirky warm fuzzy.

'What do you think? She's hot, huh?' Sam pushed the photograph toward Hall. 'Just my type.'

'Sam!' Simone said.

'Nice rack, too.'

'That's disgusting, Sam.'

'Mom, we're men. If you don't like it, don't listen. Mom's always disgusted about something,' Sam told Hall. 'She *found* my porn stash.' Sam adopted a high-pitched voice and mimed someone flicking through a magazine stack. 'Naked people, that's disgusting! Doggy style – disgusting! Shaved – disgusting! Teens, that's disgusting! Amputees – disgusting! Asian – disgusting!'

'I get it.' Hall cut Sam off.

'That's enough,' Simone snapped.

If Simone had not been there, Hall would have laughed. Sam did a decent impression of his mother. Hall studied the photo of an attractive girl hugging a large black dog.

'Mom thinks she used to look like that when she was young,' Sam said. 'Smokin'.'

'I didn't say that,' Simone said.

'That's what you told me.' Sam grinned. 'You said it.'

Hall could believe Simone was once a dainty blond girl like the teenager in the photo. She looked young to have a seventeen-year-old son.

'What blows me away,' said Hall, cringing as he heard himself adopt the foreign lingo of a younger generation, 'is how the bottle made it that far. How far is it across the Tasman?'

'Sixteen hundred kilometers. My bottle survived huge head-winds, thirty-five-knot northerlies. Crazy cross-currents. Storms. Still ocean. Below the fortieth parallel are the worst ocean weather conditions in the world.' Sam tossed each fact to Hall with a short glance. 'And it could have got swallowed by a shark or a whale.'

'Impressive oceanography.'

'Dad taught me.'

'My husband was a sailor. He completed the Sydney-to-Hobart twice.' Simone pointed to a framed photo of a sailing yacht. 'That was his pride and joy.'

If Pamela was to be believed, Simone's second husband drowned after receiving a head injury from the boom of his yacht. It had happened on a holiday in the Bahamas, and Simone had been on board. The first husband had died after a massive heart attack. 'Some people say she poisoned the first husband with rhubarb pie,' Pamela had said, and then she laughed, shaking her head to show she wasn't really one of them. Hall endeavored to differentiate between news and gossip; he tried to avoid the latter, but some people were talked about more than others.

After the interview Sam went out back to find an empty soft drink bottle.

'There are a lot of rumors going around about the murder,' Simone said. 'I'm frightened being here alone.'

'Sam's a big lad.'

'Hall, he's a kid.'

'They'll catch the guy soon.' Hall tucked his notebook into his shirt pocket. He followed her out to the veranda.

'I suppose you were at the doctor's seafood feast last night?' Simone asked. 'I wasn't invited.'

'Is he a doctor?' Hall's stomach was still queasy from all the rich seafood he wasn't used to eating. He looked around for Sam. Who was or wasn't invited somewhere was none of his business.

'He has a Ph.D. in history.'

'Interesting family. I suppose you've known them awhile, have you?'

'Sure.' Simone leaned against the railing. 'Things used to be different around here. I remember barbecues on the beach every afternoon, everyone sharing the catch of the day. Things have changed.'

'Oh well. Everyone's coming here tonight, aren't they?'

'I hope so. I've got twenty-four bottles of champagne in the fridge.'

No one had explicitly told him why they didn't like Simone, but he could have a good stab at guessing. Her sexiness didn't bother Hall. It was honest. Hall felt more comfortable around Simone than he had around the women last night. She was not the sort of woman who would elicit promises from him that he wouldn't want to keep.

Over the years, over a ten-dollar steak on Fridays at the pub or in hushed conversations at the piss trough, other journalists had told him stories about getting action while they were on the job. He had never done it. The facts were, for the last seven years since Laura left him, strangers were the only women he had slept with. It was all he could handle – giggling, ridiculously drunk women who were barely half his age and didn't seem to care that he didn't want to see them again. Girls who thought the Tarkine Tigers were a band and were impressed with stories about Launceston's criminal underbelly. Girls who tasted sweet from the red cordial they drank with their vodka and were grateful for each drink he bought them.

Sex, however uncomplicated, was not what Hall was looking for. The revelation pleased him and he whistled tunelessly as he admired the view from the veranda. The sky above the mountains had the faintest red tinge, the promise of an amazing sunset. It was not good light for taking photos. When Sam returned with the soft drink bottle that Hall wanted him to hold in the photo, they arranged to meet on the headland in the morning instead.

'In that case, would you like to drink a glass of champagne with me now?' Simone asked.

'I still need to go to the campground,' Hall said. 'I've been down there twice already and no one has been there. I haven't spoken to any of the campers yet.'

'I invited a couple of them tonight.'

'They declined?' Hall could tell as much from her tone.

Simone nodded. 'I assume you're coming back?'

'Yes, absolutely. Thank you.' Hall was definitely coming back.

Simone's smile widened.

As he walked across the garden to his car he realized she had misinterpreted his motives. He would return because he wanted to see Sarah – not for the expensive champagne, or whatever else Simone was promising.

The campsite was impressive. Past the four-wheel drives and boat trailers were several three-room tents erected in a semicircle in a clearing beside the lagoon beach. One had a handmade wooden kitchen, complete with a sink and running water. Another had a massive BeefEater barbecue and beer fridge. All had plastic tables and chairs, shade cloths, and clotheslines out back. Hall inhaled: onions were being cooked. How nice to be on holiday, wearing a tracksuit, drinking beer, and cooking dinner on your barbecue. Everything about camping appealed to Hall.

'We got company!' a woman yelled. She was not unfriendly, but she didn't return Hall's smile.

It had been the same on the beach yesterday; suspicious sideways glances and children playing close to their parents. The man who came forward to greet Hall was the man Don Gunn and John Avery had snubbed at the boat ramp. He introduced himself as Keith Gibson.

'But they all call me Bunghole. Even my missus. We've been camping here for over twenty years, me and my brother-in-law,' he said. 'We could claim land rights.'

Hall pulled out his notebook and jotted down the date and time: December 31, 6:11 p.m.

'Sorry to turn up this late in the day,' Hall said. 'I've been down a couple of times but I seem to miss everyone.'

'We'd be out fishing,' Bunghole said. 'That's what we're here for.'

Hall nodded.

'So what do you want to know?' Bunghole didn't wait for Hall's answer. 'The cops are fucking hopeless. Took them three days to come down and talk to us. We got kids here. The women won't let us go fishing, they're so scared. We have to take the whole lot of them with us or one of us men has to stay at the campsite. It's fucked.'

Hall glanced at the people sitting in front of the tents. The adults were smoking or drinking, and the kids were eating sausages wrapped in bread. They were all listening to Bunghole's rant.

'Some of the blokes are talking about taking things into their own hands. It's got to that point.' Bunghole threw his hands in the air, emphasizing that this turn of events was out of his control.

'What's going to happen next, one of the kids will get raped and murdered,' called a woman who was sitting in a hammock. 'The police need to do something.'

'We all know who did it,' Bunghole said. 'Cops know too.'

'Who?'

'No. You work it out. Not my job to solve this crime. Cops should be doing that.'

'They need evidence.'

Bunghole swore. 'They're too stupid, too lazy. The fellas are pissed. I can't stop them. I don't have a badge, do I?'

Hall asked permission and took some quotes and a couple of photos. The campers watched him work. The simmering agitation made him uneasy. He had seen it before at logging protests, right before things got out of hand.

John and Don did not like Bunghole. At first the reasons Hall could see for this dislike were enough to make him sympathize with Bunghole. Not everyone attended a private school – and thank God for that. But when a group of men openly disliked an individual, there were usually good reasons. Sarah had mentioned there was a fishing issue. No matter what your background, every man knew the rules when it came to buying rounds, respecting one another's women, and not cheating in sport.

'It seems to be a common complaint, the lack of police presence around here,' Hall told Bunghole, as he took one last photograph of a teenage boy holding up the large fish he had caught that day.

'You're on the money. And look, sorry if I sounded agro before,' Bunghole opened a can of beer. 'We're just all upset. Anyone who's got a daughter can't help but wonder what it would be like if something happened to her.'

Bunghole dug into an Esky and offered Hall a beer. Hall accepted the can. Simone's party did not start for an hour or so, and he did not want to arrive early.

They sat in camping chairs overlooking the glassy lagoon. A couple of other people joined them, including Bunghole's wife, Darlene. Nestled behind the dunes, the campsite was protected from the cold wind blowing off the sea. Dark shadows from the mountains lengthened across the lagoon's surface, contrasting with the shimmery bronze patches where the sun still reached the water. It was a pleasant place to relax and Hall wondered what his answer would be if Bunghole invited him to stick around for the remainder of the evening.

'When you look at this view, you wouldn't think anything bad could happen around here,' Hall said.

'Maybe it didn't,' Darlene sighed. 'Maybe they both just drowned.'

'I reckon Chloe Crawford ran away,' said one of the teenage girls standing nearby.

'No. Not from here.' Darlene stretched her legs out. 'It's ninety kilometers back to St Helens. There's no bus or taxi. Someone would have seen her if she tried to walk out.'

'Someone could have picked her up,' Hall suggested. 'I doubt it though. Why would she take her surfboard but not a bag of clothes?'

Bunghole was surprised when Hall mentioned Gary Taylor.

'Gary Taylor? There's a name I haven't heard for a while. Darlene – you've had three kids since we saw him last,' Bunghole said. 'Speed was the name he called himself. I used to drink with him, years ago, at the top pub before it burned down. Someone said he left with his girlfriend. Who knows? He didn't check in with me before he went.'

'Did you like him?'

'I drank with him.' Bunghole softened. 'I felt sorry for his missus. After Speed left, I used to take her a bit of crayfish or flathead if we had some to spare.'

'You were sweet to do that, love.'

Five children played on a canoe in the lagoon. They were having fun, shoving one another into the water. A yellow station wagon, with surfboards on the roof, carefully entered the campsite. Music thumped from the vehicle's open windows. A group of young people jumped out. Bunghole stood up and told them to put his ice and beer in one of the Eskies.

'What kind of shenanigans will be happening down here tonight?' Hall addressed Darlene. They'd answered all his questions so far, and given him a beer, and he didn't want the entire conversation to be about the investigation.

'We'll have fun,' she said. 'We always do.'

'I'm going to stick my head into Simone Shelley's place,' Hall said.

'Oh, yeah.' Darlene was ambivalent. 'She has a party every year. She always asks us, but I think we're a bit crazy for that lot. What do you reckon, love, do you think they could handle us?'

Bunghole chuckled. 'It might be a bad move.'

Darlene laughed too. A little girl ran out of the water and stood in front of her, shivering and whining.

'What?' Darlene looked at her. 'What's your problem?'

Hall thought she was going to reprimand the child. Instead, Darlene put her can in the drink holder of her chair and went to the tent area. She returned with a beach towel, which she wrapped around the child. When she was seated again, with the girl nestling on her lap, she turned to Hall.

'You know what scares me, Hall? The person who did this is going to get away with it.' Darlene took a long drink of beer. 'It's just the feeling I've got. In this world, some people always do their time and other people never have to face the music. It's not fair, but more than that, it just makes me sick when a person has done something as evil as this.'

Hall parked his car at the guesthouse and walked along the cliff path that led to the Shelleys' holiday house. After drinking a second beer with Bunghole at the campsite, he was later than he intended to be. He went through the motions: he accepted a glass of champagne and a canapé from Simone, he greeted John and Don and met some of their friends, he patted the Averys' dog when it snuffled up against his leg, and he helped himself to a plate of salad and barbecued meat from the buffet table. The whole time he looked for Sarah. He had known it the minute he walked into the garden – she was not there.

Hall was standing with the other men around the fire, making small talk and swapping stories, when Erica confirmed what he already knew.

'She was here for five minutes and then she went fishing,' Erica said. 'She's very unsociable.'

Hall ate a forkful of potato salad. He pushed the food around on his plate as he chewed. 'Did she mention anything about tomorrow?'

'Your field trip to the back of beyond?' Erica grinned. 'She knows about it. You do realize nothing will be open on New Year's Day, don't you?'

'Where I'm going they're expecting me.'

'Well, that sounds very nice.'

Hall remained with Erica while he ate. She was easy to listen to; she smiled and laughed a lot. She didn't ask him any work-related questions or mention Sarah again, and he appreciated it. She told him that, when she was a teenager, she had done work experience for a week in the *Tasmanian Voice*'s photography department. She loved taking photos. She had accidentally got the job at Qantas after applying alongside a friend.

'Working for Qantas is great, don't get me wrong. I like looking after people,' she said. 'And not many employers let you take four weeks off in the middle of summer.'

Steve joined them and chuckled as he heard Erica's comment. Hall had not had much of a chance to speak to Steve, but he seemed like a good bloke. A few minutes ago, while Hall was listening to Erica, he had seen Simone fussing over Steve. Hall had a feeling that Simone's flirtatiousness was something he and Steve might have a bit of a laugh about, if ever it came up in conversation.

'Mate, I take it you're not on holiday for as long as Erica?' Hall said.

'I wish. I used up all my annual leave on a ski trip,' Steve said, smiling at Erica as she slipped her arm through his.

Hall found himself looking around the garden once more for Sarah. She had not come back. He excused himself and walked over to where Simone sat. He thanked her and said goodbye. He explained he had an early start the following morning and that he had been up since five a.m. No one seemed to mind, and he didn't care if they did. He was more disappointed by the evening than he cared to admit.

Outside the Shelleys' garden, Hall peered down the track that led to the beach. Tree branches on either side arched together to form a dark passageway. He couldn't see the ground.

Somewhere down there on the dark rocks, Sarah was standing alone next to the pounding sea. Damn, if only he had not paid the campers a visit tonight.

He didn't mind missing New Year's Eve. It seemed his choices these days were either to drink copious amounts of alcohol in a crowded bar or in the home of a work colleague, or watch television coverage of the fireworks exploding off the Sydney Harbour Bridge in the solitude of his lounge room. At least tomorrow he would wake up with a clear head for the drive to Pyengana with Sarah. Who knew – maybe she was thinking the exact same thing.

Early on New Year's morning the sun was like a huge ball of molten lava rising on the ocean horizon. It was breathtaking. Watching it from the water's edge, Hall didn't move in time. The wave was swollen and it smashed hard across the rocks. It was too late to run. The force knocked him sideways. Fortunately his camera was looped around his neck, but it still slammed against the granite as he fell. He scrambled for higher ground, his hands clumsy. It was only when he paused to glance back at the sea that he saw Roger Coker watching him.

'Be careful,' Roger said. 'Not safe where you were standing.'

'You're telling me.'

'People die, get washed off the rocks.' Roger giggled. 'More chance of that than being murdered. Everyone forgets.'

Roger's eyes were bluer than the ocean. His were eyes that were used to looking – not being looked at. He shifted his gaze from Hall's stare.

Before Hall had time to think of a leading question, or even to wish him a happy New Year's day, Roger was gone. He waved as he walked away; he knew Hall was watching his back.

Hall cut across the rocks and followed a track that eventually joined the gravel road. Enjoying the cold, salty air, he strode along until he reached the gulch. There was no sign of anyone. He went to the end of the jetty. Across the water were the three fishing shacks. Cars were parked out in front of the first two, and beach towels hung from wooden chairs lined up on either side of the doorways. It was still early – probably everyone was asleep. Trying not to feel nervous, he walked back along the jetty and up the slope to the hut where the Crawfords had stayed. Being careful not to squash a pretty geranium, he pressed his face to the dirty glass window. Inside it was basic. There was a table, a double bed, and a bunk. A vase of fake yellow daisies was set on the table.

'What are you doing?' Hall heard a man shout. 'Clear off.'

Hall jumped. A big fellow glared at him from the open window of the next shack. Hall decided not to bother explaining he was a reporter. He waved and walked as fast as he could back to the road.

A chill wind shredded the tops off waves, tossing water high and fortifying the air blowing across the rocks with salty sleet. Hall shivered.

'Colder than a witch's tit,' he said, and Sam chuckled.

He didn't know why he said that. It was not an expression he ordinarily used. In fact it was one of Dan's expressions. Dan often used rude clichés to describe things: a difficult shot on the eight-ball table was tighter than a nun's nasty, and when it was time to leave he said he was off like a Jew's foreskin.

He didn't care who heard him. Watching football once, Dan had told Laura the Hawks were so useless they couldn't get laid in a whorehouse. Later she told Hall how much she disliked Dan. That was one of the issues that still rankled Hall. When the hell did Laura decide she could put up with the gutter talk?

Forcing himself to focus, Hall positioned Sam. Framed by ocean, it was a decent shot. Sam pretended to hurl the empty Coke bottle over the edge as Hall took the picture. At first Sam smiled without showing his teeth. After a few shots, he relaxed and grinned more naturally.

Sam shook his hair out of his eyes. 'I like the clicking sound your camera makes.'

'It's fake. That sound you hear is actually recorded. That's the sound people think cameras should make, the way they used to sound. This is a digital camera, so it should be silent.'

'Cool.'

'So who do you reckon did it, Sam? Off the record. Old mate from the green cottage?'

'No.'

'Don from the shop?'

'He'd like to do something like that, but he wouldn't want to get his hands dirty.'

'His wife?'

'No.' Sam laughed.

'Raped, bashed, thrown into the ocean alive. Who is capable of that?'

'Stop. I feel sick.'

Hall stopped shooting. Sam was no longer smiling.

'She's an idiot. Walking around on the rocks, right up close to the ocean. You can get washed off like that.' Sam clicked his fingers. 'My dad drowned, and he could swim. He played water polo for Australia when he was my age.'

'Is that what you think happened to Anja?'

'I don't know.' Sam struggled to control himself. 'Who do you think did it?'

'I've got a fair idea.'

'You're full of it.'

'I know.' Hall grinned and took one more shot.

Hall warned Sam not to talk to any other reporters about the bottle story. He said it out of habit more than any genuine concern; it wasn't as though Sam had a personal interest in receiving media attention.

'This will be in Saturday's paper. After that I don't care who you talk to.'

The last shot Hall took was not of the ocean or of Sam. Instead, he turned around and focused the lens on the row of the shacks scattered along the hillside overlooking the sea. The guesthouse was the highest dwelling; the round roof huddled in the heath and clematis like an owl on her nest. Roger Coker's green roof was barely visible. The Averys' blue shack, fenced neatly on all sides, was set farther back than the others in the row.

Hall sat on the hard wooden chair at his desk in the guesthouse. He was due to pick up Sarah in half an hour. He dialed Allan Bennett's number again. Even though it was New Year's Day, Hall did not want to waste any more time. This time the phone was answered.

Bennett was chatty and he insisted Hall call him Benno.

They had a jovial conversation about a range of things in no way connected to the murder investigation. Finally Hall asked Benno if he knew of a reclusive person who lived on the east coast and had several crayfish poaching convictions.

There was a pause.

'I don't know him, but I do know of a man who fits that description,' Benno said. 'A large, red-haired bloke who lives in a cabin somewhere in Goulds Country. That's the old tin-mining bushland about seventy-five miles back from the coast.'

'Okay.' Older Tasmanians usually measured in miles, as opposed to the newer metric system. Hall made a rough calculation in his head and jotted down one hundred and twenty kilometers. He was driving near Goulds Country with Sarah later today. He'd better make sure he had enough petrol.

'Have you considered that sometimes a man has his reasons for not wanting to be found?' Benno said. 'There might be nothing illegal in that.'

Sarah was waiting for him in the shadow of the concrete tank. It was the first time he had seen her wear something other than shorts and a T-shirt. Her white shirt accentuated her tanned skin and her snug jeans showed the curve of her hips. She strode over to his car, climbed in, and slammed the passenger door. The powerful way she moved was that of someone very sure of herself.

'Happy New Year,' he said. 'I was sorry not to see you last night.'

'Did you go to Simone's?'

'Just for an hour.'

'Oh,' she said, and he wondered what she was thinking.

It felt good to leave the coast and its rutted gravel roads behind, to accelerate on sealed roads through the grassy fields and old tin-mining villages where no one was worrying about shameless crime scene voyeurs or whether a strange man on the beach was a pervert or not. It felt even better to have Sarah sitting beside him, her bare arm stretching in his direction along the back of the bench seat. They were almost identically proportioned, he remembered. He had been vaguely conscious of this as they stood face-to-face when they first met in the dune. Usually he had to look down to make eye contact with women. When he kissed her on the rocks after the Abalone Bake, it was confirmed; their hips and chests fitted neatly together. The memory was arousing.

Hall turned up the volume on the car stereo. It was one of his favorite songs, Lee Kernaghan's 'High Country,' and he sang along, fingers tapping on the steering wheel. It was pleasant to be with a woman who didn't talk constantly. Laura had liked to listen to Radio National and comment on what they were discussing, which meant Hall missed hearing the next thing they said. Sarah didn't talk at all. She crossed her arms and watched the road. When he had woken up beside her in the guesthouse, her sleeping body had been supple, her toned muscles malleable around him. He wondered if she would come back again.

She exhaled and uncrossed her arms.

'Are you okay?' Maybe she was bored.

'Yeah.' She looked out the window. 'Is it hard interviewing people about awful things?'

Hall was surprised. 'Sure. They've been interviewed so many times it can be difficult to get them to say something new.'

'No, I mean, do you feel bad for asking?'

'Feel bad?' He didn't really think about it; if a phone call needed to be made, or a question asked, he did it. It was his job. She might think he was unfeeling if he admitted that. 'Yes, it can be difficult sometimes.'

'How horrible.'

'Sometimes it's not. People want to tell their story. When I was a cadet reporter, I had to do doorstops at three in the morning, usually after someone's kid wrapped himself around a telegraph pole. There was probably only twenty minutes between when the police broke the news to them and I turned up. That was tough.'

'I'd shut the door in someone's face.'

'Some did. You knew when you knocked on the door how you were going to be received. The nicer the house, the shorter the time the door remained open. You have to be quick.'

'Rich people don't talk to reporters?'

'Educated people don't.'

In Hall's experience, working-class people were more likely to welcome you, offer cups of tea and candid comments, and lend photographs of their dead or injured children. One time Hall left with a family's photograph album. He told the grieving family it was to allow his editor to select the photo they were running of the boy bashed to death outside a Launceston nightclub. In truth he took it to prevent any rival news outlets from obtaining a photograph before the *Tasmanian Voice* went to press.

'The Crawfords weren't excited to talk to me, but they were accommodating. They still hope their daughter will come home. Let's talk about something else.'

'I can't get it out of my head.'

'It would be frightening, finding a dead body.'

'Yeah.' She shrugged. 'I spoke to the Swiss woman, probably on the day she died.'

'I didn't know that.'

'She asked directions to the rock pool.'

'Go on.'

'I'd been at the rock pool that morning. It was filthy. Some loser cleaned his fish in it.'

'You told her that?'

'No. That's the point. I didn't tell her that. There was no point her trekking up there. You couldn't swim in it. It stank; flies and dried guts over the rocks.'

Hall shifted down to second gear, doubling the clutch so the engine gave a satisfied hum. So that's what was bothering her, kept drawing her to that desolate stretch of beach in half-light and rain.

'You wouldn't be the first person to blame yourself for someone else's act of evil.'

'I don't blame myself.'

'Guilt is a waste of time. When your number's up, it's up.'

'I don't agree. That's too fatalistic. People have to be responsible for their actions.'

'So Anja Traugott is responsible for choosing to walk on the beach the day a sexual predator goes hunting.'

'You reckon that's what happened to Chloe Crawford, too?'

There were five scenarios Hall had listed in his notebook. Chloe was run over on the Old Road and fell down a steep embankment; possible, but where was the body? Tasmanian devils were capable of eating an entire corpse, bones, hair, and clothing. They rarely left any scraps when they dined. But where was the surfboard? Scenario number two: Chloe was run over, and the motorist panicked and hid her body; unlikely. Three: misadventure, she fell down a mineshaft or drowned; again, where were her surfboard and gear? Four: misadventure, but someone found her surfboard and kept it, and was too scared to come forward following the media attention. Five: foul play was the likeliest scenario. Chloe Crawford was practically a child, so it was not likely that money had been a motive. The suspected rape and murder of the Swiss woman, who had a similar build and appearance, reinforced the likeliness of this scenario. Anja Traugott's autopsy would help confirm this theory. Unfortunately, it was not likely that Chloe had simply run away. Hall wished it were as simple as that.

'Sorry to say it but yes. Foul play is the most likely. If it wasn't the case, some trace of her would have turned up by now.'

'Foul play,' Sarah repeated.

Chapter 6

Bumping along in the Holden, Sarah listened to Hall sing. He wasn't a good singer. No range, he hissed every 's' sound. It was awful. And he had got the lyrics wrong. She looked out the window and wondered if he even knew he was singing. They might have slept together, but he was still a stranger.

Listening to him, she tried to swallow the laughter pressing inside her. It was no good. She didn't want to laugh at him but she couldn't help it. The more she tried to hold it in, the more she wanted to laugh. When she did, it startled Hall enough to make him put his foot on the brake.

'Is that your real laugh?'

She nodded.

'What? My singing bothering you?'

'You're really bad.'

He kept singing.

They were going on a date. An old-fashioned date. She wasn't really a date person, but she had washed her hair and borrowed a shirt from Erica. All hers were dirty; she hadn't bothered to do any washing since she left Eumundi. They would end up at one of those quaint tearooms on an old dairy farm, sitting at a wrought-iron table with sandwiches and pots of tea in the shady garden. Maybe they would stop at the cheese factory café for a coffee on the way home.

She had been on only one date with Jake, if you could even call it that. They biked along the winding Yandina road to Coolum and ate fish and chips in a park beside the beach. That was nice. Afternoon rain drenched them as they rode home, heavy Queensland rain that fell in sheets from a ripe purple sky. They took turns at riding in front. Every time a car went past, dirty road water sprayed over them. It was fun. They had fun together. What had she done? What was wrong with her?

'You okay?' Hall glanced over. 'You look sad.'

'Yeah.' Sarah had forgotten where she was. She tried to think of something to say before he asked any more questions. Lately even the briefest kind word could make her throat close up, that strangulating feeling of needing to cry. She asked him a question about the murder investigation. While he spoke, she focused on the dirty windscreen. Splayed insect legs and wings fringed the wipers like broken lashes.

A couple of kilometers before the St Columba Falls, Hall turned right onto a bumpy dirt road. A squat weatherboard farmhouse with picnic tables on its narrow verandas came into view. At least twenty motorbikes were parked out the front. Disappointment seized her; she had been here before. The pub was a waterhole for the local dairy farm workers. It served schooners and counter meals, and, for one dollar, punters could purchase a stubby of beer slops to feed to a leathery pig housed in a wooden shed.

'The Pub in the Paddock.' She didn't undo her seatbelt. 'I haven't been here for years.'

'We don't have to eat here if you don't want to. I can do my story and we can go somewhere else.'

'So you planned to have lunch here?' Her girlish fantasies of a country garden picnic, or a glass of wine and some delicious cheddar cheese at the Pyengana cheese factory café, were embarrassing. He was waiting for her to speak. 'It's fine,' she said, and it sounded insincere. 'Really, it's great.' That sounded worse. She pulled at the door handle and it flipped back and forth. 'You'd better help me open my door.'

Inside, the pub smelled of yeast and hot chips, stale tobacco, and pine air freshener. A television set above the bar blasted commentary from a dog race. Blinking into the dimness, Sarah felt exposed. Her white shirt was too ruffled, her handbag cumbersome. She shifted it from one hand to the other and smacked her lips, greasy with Erica's lipstick in Cotton Candy. Slowly she wiped her hand across her mouth to remove it.

Bikers paused at darts or pool, expressions hidden behind facial tattoos and beards. At the bar, a flannelette row of farm workers peered from beneath caps. There was only one other female in the room, a ruddy-cheeked woman eating lunch at the bar.

Hall ignored the empty tables by the far window. He sat on a green bar stool and swung sideways, one foot on the rung, the other on the floor.

'What's your party poison?'

The blokes on the other side of the bar listened with undisguised interest.

'Coke.'

'Have a beer with me. Or a wine if that's what you prefer . . .'

The punters turned to Sarah to find out what drink she wanted.

'So what'll it be then?' The barman patted the bar mat, pleased to play a part in the performance.

They decided on Boag's Draught and watched as the barman cradled two glasses under the beer tap, moving them side to side, working the liquid into a perfect creamy dome.

They should have gone fishing. Away from these busybodies, who weren't even pretending not to eavesdrop, there would be heaps of things to talk about. They should have gone fishing, or walked up to the rock pool, or taken the canoe out on the lagoon. Even a game of Scrabble in the shack would be more fun than this. She noticed his ring then. It was plain, a dull silver band exactly like a wedding ring, but worn on his right hand. It hadn't been there before. Hall cleared his throat and she looked at him expectantly.

'Tell me something about yourself,' he said.

It was the type of question that irritated her. How on earth was she supposed to reply? He was a journalist; surely he knew a better way to open a conversation.

'It's funny. What do people really want to know when they ask that question?' Her voice was straining to be calm the way her mother's did when her father wasn't listening or had forgotten to do some mundane task. 'I don't like lazy people. I like fishing. I sleep with my mouth open. But you probably already know that.'

She laughed but the sound lacked any real humor.

'No one wants to hear that kind of boring stuff.' He sipped his beer. 'Surprise me.'

No question about it, she could surprise him. But did he really want that? The last man she had surprised had not enjoyed the experience. There was a fine line between surprise and shock. How about if she told him that she had lost count of the actual number of men she had slept with once she clocked fifty. That three of them had been guys who were employed under her supervision at the fish farm. Jake had called her a sexual predator when she told him that after a few too many one night. At the time she had thought he was joking.

'Tell me something about you,' Sarah countered.

Hall was happy to talk about himself. He told funny stories about people in the newsroom where he worked. He made a joke about his ex-girlfriend who now ran, with her new boyfriend, a pub called the Ball and Chain Inn. Sarah had drunk there before. It was a beautiful heritage building opposite Civic Square. It was what he didn't say that interested Sarah. He was leaving something out.

Sarah knew what it was like to miss someone when you knew you shouldn't. On Christmas Day she had taken Erica's mobile up behind the tank stand and tried to call Jake. It was the only place where there was coverage. Jake hadn't answered; it went straight to his message bank, and she hung up. What would she have said anyway? She wasn't going back. Sarah took a slow breath, immobilized with guilt. You could apologize for punching your boyfriend in the face, but it didn't undo the act.

Hall was fiddling with his cutlery, trying to unravel it from the paper napkin, when their lunch arrived. On Sarah's plate a T-bone soaked in pepper sauce took up most of the space.

The lettuce, tomato, and slivers of purple onion looked fresh. She remembered the Pub in the Paddock was known for serving prime steak. Her plate certainly looked healthier than Hall's lunch; deep-fried curls of seafood sat in a cane basket with a packet of tartar sauce balanced on top. He whistled in appreciation. A crinkle-cut chip fell off and Hall stuck it in his mouth.

The food was good quality and the beer was cold. They ordered two more beers and talked easily while they ate. He was interested in fish farming, in particular whether or not it was sustainable. From the stickers on his car she suspected he was a hardcore greenie and she censored some of her opinions. He also asked her about crayfish smuggling. Ten years ago he had visited the Bay of Fires to report on six square holes that had been dug on the main beach. They had appeared overnight, during winter, when the area was particularly desolate. Two meters deep and evenly spaced; at the time the holes were believed to be the site of a well-planned drug delivery. Now Hall wasn't sure.

'I remember that!' Sarah said. 'I was at the shack when it happened.'

She wondered if they had walked past each other on the beach, driven past each other on the road. Behind her, someone shoved coins into the jukebox, and Cold Chisel's 'Flame Trees' began.

'Enough about me . . . tell me, why did you end it with your boyfriend up north?' Hall said. 'Or am I being too nosy?'

She was expecting the question, but when it came, she couldn't think of a short answer. Her brain tried to unscramble the strands of events leading up to her departure from

Queensland. She didn't want to lie. She might have mentioned Jake the night of the Abalone Bake, but she couldn't remember. That was the problem with one-night stands that didn't end when they were supposed to.

'Put it this way. Something happened with Jake that irrevocably changed the situation. Nothing more to say.'

Sarah glanced at Hall and then looked away quickly. It wasn't an outright lie, but she knew she was misleading him.

'I get it,' Hall said.

She appreciated that he didn't make a big deal out of the subject. It was a shame they didn't catch up last night at Simone's party. Hall would have been a good person to have a few New Year's Eve drinks with. He wouldn't carry on the way most other people did, hugging and kissing each other at midnight like there was something to be excited about. She had walked to the Shelleys' with Erica and Steve, half-thinking that when Hall turned up she would see if he wanted to come fishing with her. She had waited for what seemed like ages before she left.

Fishing alone last night was not as enjoyable as it usually was. She had cast out halfheartedly, listening to the music and laughter of the party drifting down the hillside. Her efforts had been a waste of time, but still, fruitless fishing was better than enduring the forced merriment of New Year's Eve. Finally, she carried her empty fishing bucket home. From the beach track, she could see the party. Candles and lanterns lit the garden. Sarah almost returned, but she had spilled a container of bait on her jeans and could smell it. She wondered if Hall had had a good night.

'Was it a fun party?' she asked.

'I think so. I had an early one in the end.'

Sarah smiled. 'Me too.'

They had almost finished eating when Hall leaned across the bar and addressed the barman. Sarah didn't hear what Hall said.

The barman was thoughtful as he opened the glass washer. 'There is a guy who sounds like him. Doesn't come in much. Doesn't talk to anyone. Just puts twenty bucks in the slot machine and drinks his beer and goes.'

They watched the barman wipe inside the glass washer. His arm jerked as he rubbed at some hard-to-remove gunk at the back and the machine rocked, making an embarrassing squeaking noise that sounded like Hall's bed at the guesthouse.

'Who did you just ask him about?' Sarah murmured.

'Nothing much . . . just another story which will probably fall over.'

Hall finished his beer. She wondered if he was thinking about the squeaky bed. For something to say, she told him about Roger and the Tasmanian devil that had been tossed onto his porch. Hall murmured something about vigilantes but didn't comment further. She sounded like Pamela and her mother cloaking their gossip with pretend sympathy.

'The burnout marks on Roger's driveway were continuous,' Sarah added.

'So?'

'It's impossible to do a continuous burnout in an automatic; the tire rubber stops burning briefly as the gears change. You have to hammer it in first to do a good burnout. I'll show you later.'

'No thanks. My car doesn't like doing burnouts.'

'The point is, there are only three manuals in the Bay of Fires at the moment. Yours. Roger's Valiant. And Bunghole's Hilux. And you weren't driving anywhere after the Abalone Bake.'

'You're an undercover detective,' Hall joked, but he made a note in his spiral notebook.

She was relieved when Hall stood up and pulled his wallet out of his pocket. The date was almost over.

'How much do we owe you, mate?'

They waited while the barman searched for their tab on a cork board at the end of the bar.

'Thirty-three dollars will do it.'

Hall opened his wallet and looked inside. It seemed like he was waiting for her to do something, so she reached into her bag for her purse. She handed Hall a twenty-dollar note, which he accepted. There was no automatic credit card machine, just the old-fashioned card cruncher. The barman arranged a yellow page and swiped the imprint of Hall's card. Hall explained why he was there. He described the story he wanted to write about the pig as a color piece. He sounded more excited about it than he had explaining it to Sarah earlier in the car.

'Does he still drink beer?' Hall asked.

'She. Alice's all woman. And she'd drink any of these guys under the table if we let her.' He pointed his thumb over his shoulder at the bikers throwing darts.

'Is that right?' Hall wrote in his notebook.

'My word. The weekend before Christmas she left Boonie for dead.'

'No way, mate.' Hall's voice became deeper and his vowels slowed in imitation of the bartender's rural drawl.

'Mate.' The bartender nodded. 'I wouldn't lie. She drank seventy-six full-strength stubbies in the one session. She dropped after fifty-four, but she's a trouper, Alice; she kept going lying on her side.'

'That's disgusting,' Sarah said.

'You're telling me.' The bartender grinned, but he was missing the point.

Hall negotiated a free bottle of beer for the pig since he was going to do a story on it and they went outside. As they walked toward the pig's paddock, Hall slid the twenty-dollar note into the back pocket of Sarah's jeans.

The pig was asleep and looked dead. Her head lolled back, and the elongated nipples on her rubbery black belly touched the dirt. Flies hopped across wiry hairs on her back. A sign in front of the pen stated, *Hi, I'm Alice! Geez I'm dry. I'd love a beer*.

'Tell me who Boonie is?' Hall asked while he fiddled with his camera.

'David Boon?' Sarah said. 'Tasmania's most famous cricketer. He drank fifty-two stubbies of full-strength on a flight from Australia to England on the way to a cricket tour. He's a legend for it, apparently. Everyone knows Boonie.'

'I don't write sport.'

Sarah held the beer bottle while Hall took some shots, testing the light and finding the pig's best angle. The pig shoved her nose through the chicken wire, snorting in the direction of the beer.

'I want you here.' Hall demonstrated, crouching down and holding the bottle through the fence. The grass was worn out in the spot he chose. She shook her head.

'Just for fun,' he said.

'No way.'

'Please.'

Sarah took the bottle from him and offered it to the pig. Alice gulped.

'Hold the bottle out more. Turn toward me. Smile.'

The camera clicked and the bottle throbbed in Sarah's hand as the pig sucked out the slops. She was close enough to the animal that she could have touched it, could have rubbed a finger along her rough snout, flecked with coarse hairs. The sow's eyes blinked, milky and knowing. This was the highlight of her day, a tourist bringing a beer. Later tonight the cook would tip a bucket of kitchen scraps into the pen and she would scratch around in the dark, treading on bits of tomato and bread as she sniffed out her dinner. When the night became cold, she would huddle under the corrugated iron shelter, staring out at the shadows of the cows in the next paddock.

'Why don't you do a story about prisoner pigs being force-fed beer by idiot tourists?' Sarah said.

'I will,' he said. 'It'll be my follow-up to this one. The animal rights protesters will be on the phone first thing in the morning. They're very reliable.'

Before the drive home Sarah went inside to use the bathroom. The toilet paper was pink and rolled out from under a swan-shaped toilet paper holder. She could have been in someone's grandmother's bathroom if it weren't for the advertisement about date rape on the back of the door. She layered toilet paper across the pink plastic seat and ran over their conversation. Hearing how he planned his newspaper stories was interesting, made a change from the talk of intensive versus extensive and semi-intensive farming techniques. She probably shouldn't have criticized the pig story, but then he hadn't seemed offended, so maybe that didn't matter. Now she was overthinking it again.

As she washed her hands, the woman who had been sitting at the bar earlier came in. Almost everything about her suggested a femininity that had succumbed to a male world; her thick brown Blundstone boots, her hair cropped short, her sullen expression and ruddy skin. Small gold hoop earrings were her one concession that she was something other than one of the guys with whom she worked and drank.

'How's it going?' she greeted Sarah. 'First date?'

'Sort of.'

'I knew it. I said it to my mate Mick. I said, those two are on a date,' the woman disappeared into the cubicle. She began urinating, a heavy stream, and raised her voice so Sarah could hear. 'Hold onto him, lovey. He looks like one of the good ones.'

'Lucky you're here,' Sarah called back. Immediately she forced a laugh to soften her sarcasm. The woman was only being friendly.

Blunted and sleepy from the afternoon beers, Sarah gazed at the blur of dairy pastures out the window. At the T-intersection Hall took a wrong turn, but she did not notice immediately. Instead of turning right and going back the way they had come, Hall had turned left onto the Blue Tier road. It had been a long time since Sarah had traveled up here. It was part of the area her father had researched for his Ph.D. If you followed this road all the way to the end, you would arrive at Goulds

Country, an almost abandoned tin-mining town that was noted for being the only remaining settlement in Tasmania built completely from timber. On the way there, lost in the scrub, was an old miners' graveyard that contained gravestones from the 1880s, as well as many short, grassy unmarked mounds – the graves of babies who never stood a chance. In the surrounding forest was the brick chimney stub of a burned-down church, several hiking tracks that led to lookouts, and gnarled wooden huts, few and far between, inhabited by hippies or the inbred, according to talk. It was an inhospitable tract of bush and barely managed farmland. Narrow and rutted, the road weaved upward, enclosed by thick, ancient gum trees. There was nowhere to turn around.

First Sarah wound her window down, all the way. She was wearing slippery sandals, impossible to run in, and she pushed them off her feet without undoing them. She opened her handbag, took the twenty-dollar note Hall had given back to her, and shoved it into her jeans pocket. When Hall glanced over to see what she was doing, she pulled out Erica's lipstick and pretended to examine it.

'Bit bumpy to try and put that on,' Hall said. 'Although I'd like to see you try.'

If he was a murderer, he would be passive-aggressive. She wondered how he would try to do it; he probably had a tire iron or a handgun shoved down the side of his seat. Her only chance was to get out of his car and run. Hard. She would run deep into the scrub and hide. Later, when she was sure he had gone, she would hike downward until she hit one of the dried-up creeks and then follow it out.

The radio wheezed, and he asked her to choose a CD from

the glove box. She didn't want to open it. Her mouth felt dry. Adrenaline coursed through her; flight was her body's desire. It would be logical to assume that Hall Flynn was not going to kill her. He was too normal, too nice. But what if Sarah's gullibility, lack of preparedness, stupidity, put her in a vulnerable position?

'You going to tell me where we're going?' she said. It was his last chance. She was ready to throw herself out of the moving car.

'No idea.' Hall laughed with embarrassment. 'Wrong turn, sorry. I was hoping you wouldn't notice. I'm just looking for somewhere to turn around. It's spooky.'

'You're not wrong. This is the place you would move to if you wanted everyone to forget about you. I bet there are a heap of dodgy characters living up here.'

'Reckon you could live up here?'

'I could.' Sarah relaxed. She hoped he had not noticed her taking her sandals off. Her fingertips were damp on the leather seat. 'Bit far from the ocean, though.'

Five minutes later they passed a driveway cut through the trees. Hall reversed into it, turned around, and they returned the way they had come.

Waiting for the bream running on the incoming evening tide, Sarah contemplated the strange location of the guesthouse. It overlooked a narrow granite reef where, even on a calm day, noisy seagulls fought each other for space. Occasionally a big wave scattered the birds into the sky. In stormy weather, surf exploded across the kelp-shadowed water, swallowing the shore rocks and threatening to wash away the succulent garden of Jane's place above. There was no beach below the guesthouse, just the rocky point and black bull kelp. You couldn't swim there. When the wind blew onshore, as it did for eight months of the year, salty gusts drenched Jane's windowpanes and rusted her window latches so some were permanently stuck. It was a rough tract of ocean, but Jane liked to boast that in the thirty years she had lived there, not once had the waves trespassed on her property.

Hall had dropped Sarah home after lunch and said he had work to do. She imagined him sitting at his laptop, writing up the pig story, checking through the notebook for a new angle on the murder investigation. He had talked about journalistic ethics and the public's right to know. Lucky for her he didn't know about her evening with seventeen-year-old Sam Shelley. The newspaper Hall wrote for would love a story on that: *Fish Doctor Hooks Illegal Catch*. Jesus.

Eumundi Barramundi was a publicly listed company. That meant the public had a right to know a certain story about her. It was the kind of gossip the local Eumundi rag liked to print in lieu of real news. They would print a clever headline: *Fish Farmer Goes on Bender and Loses 5,000 Fish* or something. Her laughter was stunted. There was nothing funny about losing three tonnes of prime barramundi. Maybe it was real news. If she had not quit, she would have needed to sack at least three casual staff, an event that would send a nasty ripple through a tiny place like Eumundi. No point paying people to feed fish that didn't exist.

Above the spindly branches of the casuarinas and banksias the Nissen hut's curved roof fit snugly under the night sky. Only two lights were on, one in an upstairs bedroom and another downstairs in Jane's room.

Apart from the gently slapping ocean, there was no sound; no distant dog barking or an outboard motor dragging a net for mullet. She cast out and wound the line in. Nothing was biting. The bream were more timid than she remembered. She lightened the weight and checked the bait before casting out again. Still waiting for a bite, she pulled her hair out of its tight ponytail and shook it. Loose hair fell around her face, soft on her cheek. She sang; lyrics from 'Flame Trees' that used to make her feel sad now had new meaning. For the first time since she left Eumundi she wasn't analyzing the harsh accusations and insults that had sounded in her mind as loudly as if Jake were right there, puffing his beery breath over her. It was a relief to let her thoughts flow naturally.

Reluctantly, when she could no longer see the watery horizon, Sarah packed up. She shoved the bait container and hook jar into her satchel, wound down the fishing rod, and secured the line. Her knife had sardine blood on it. By torch-light Sarah dipped her knife in the ocean, wiping it on a rag she kept for this purpose. The blood wouldn't come off and she dipped again. Tentacles emerged from the water without warning, wrapping around the knife and tugging at it. Sarah didn't flinch. She released the handle and watched the blue-ringed octopus slide beneath the rocks. It was her favorite knife, but she didn't care.

The color photo ran the next day in the *Tasmanian Voice*. Sarah's face, grinning as she offered the bottle to the pig, was stretched across most of the page. The caption underneath the photo said *Here's cheers . . . Sarah Avery shares a beer with Alice the pig*. It wasn't even true. She looked hideous; her watery eyes were bulbous and her gums were showing. What on earth was Hall thinking? Erica laughed so hard her eyes welled up with tears. Even Don, who was usually so kind, chuckled as he counted the takings at the kitchen table.

'Stop it, Erica. Not everyone is photogenic,' Pamela said.

Pamela had things to discuss. Yesterday she had spotted a man riding a jet ski up and down between the reef and the point. Don had seen a bronze utility truck parked all day at the boat ramp. The man jet skiing was too far out for Pamela to be certain, but through her binoculars it looked like Jane Taylor's estranged husband, Gary.

'There aren't that many red-haired men around here.' Pamela bit her lip. 'Keep it to yourselves but I did put in a call to the police. I just told them what I saw. And that he fit the description of Gary Taylor.'

'I can't remember Gary Taylor ever driving a bronze ute,' Erica said. 'What does Jane say?'

'Well, I'm not going to ask her. She'll bite my head off.' Pamela opened a packet of chocolate Wagon Wheels biscuits and offered them to Sarah and Erica. 'She's always been strange. Do you remember when he left? You were teenagers. She didn't tell anyone. I was still getting mail for him – which she collected every week – and he had been gone for a year. She never said a word.'

Sarah remembered. Talk about Gary and Jane had begun before he left. They used to come to the Abalone Bake and the odd barbecue. She remembered her mother commenting on how they always drank more than anyone else and argued without caring who was in earshot. Sarah could not remember hearing them argue; she had observed a man who seemed nervous around children, and who was overweight and shy. She couldn't imagine him having fun on a jet ski.

'I feel sorry for Jane,' Sarah said.

'I don't. I've wasted enough time on her over the years. You can't help someone who won't help themselves. Here, have another biscuit.'

'Maybe help is not what she needs,' Sarah said.

'When Gary left, she had a lot of debt. I recommended her for a couple of cleaning jobs. I've never chased her too hard for her account here, either. I'm not like that.' Pamela bit into a biscuit, catching the falling crumbs in the palm of her hand.

'Did the police think the jet ski person was suspicious?' Erica said.

'They don't say much. Ask that reporter, Sarah. He'll know. But I do predict Jane Taylor will receive a visit from the police very soon.'

Judging by Hall's conversation with the barman at the pub the other day, it seemed he was already on to it. Sarah sighed. Pamela's doggedness had an edge to it.

'Well, if he is back, it needs investigating. I've seen that jet ski here before and I can't remember when, but I feel like it might be around the time Chloe Crawford went missing.' Pamela spoke defensively. 'Why does a man leave the town where he has lived all his life without even saying goodbye to anyone? Why does his wife never mention it? She just carries on as though he is still living there, and then these girls going missing out the front of their place.'

'Of everyone's place,' Sarah said. 'Poor Jane.'

An ugly red washed Pamela's paleness. Her expression stiffened with bravado. 'She's going to have to live with it. If you behave strangely, people will talk. That is the way it is. People talk. Jane Taylor isn't stupid. She knows.'

'Hey, Don,' called Erica. 'Are you putting your money on Gary Taylor?'

'I think there's enough of an argument to charge Coker,' Don said. 'I don't know why they haven't put him in a holding cell by now.'

'They can't lock someone up just because everyone thinks he's weird,' Sarah said. 'Next you'll be arguing to lock up anyone who is Jewish, Gypsy, or homosexual.'

Don gave her a keen look and continued counting the money without replying.

Pamela and Erica were looking at the photo again, giggling.

'Enough.' Sarah closed the newspaper.

The station wagon slowed to a stop several meters in front of Sarah and Erica as they walked up the hill from the shop. In the passenger seat was Darlene Gibson – Bunghole's wife. She had been with Bunghole outside the shop when he had almost hit Sarah in the head with his milk carton as he tossed it into the bin. Today Darlene wasn't smiling.

'Keith has got nothing to do with this.' Darlene folded sunburned arms on the open window.

'Who?' Erica asked.

The woman rolled her eyes. 'Bunghole.'

Sarah and Erica laughed.

'Who's accused Keith of anything?' Sarah immediately thought of the roadkill that had been thrown at Roger's cottage. Had the police somehow heard about that? She knew Roger would not have reported the incident.

'We've seen the way you lot look at us. You're stuck up. And you're not pinning this shit on us.'

The kids crammed in the backseat – at least four – complained, and the woman in the driver's seat yelled at them to sit down.

'We've got our own theories,' Darlene continued.

'You're doing the talking,' Sarah said. Her curiosity about what the campers thought was going on was greater than her desire to tell it like it was.

'I'm not going there. It's what a lot of people are saying.'

'Go on.'

'Nup.'

'Bald Don,' shouted the woman in the driver's seat. She put her foot down and the car accelerated, gravel spitting out the sides.

'What the . . .?' Erica said. 'I thought they blamed Roger.'

'I don't think they really do believe Don did it,' Sarah said. 'They just hate him because he bullies them about where they fish.'

Could Don have done it? Years ago, a popular Launceston schoolteacher had driven back to town from school camp at Waddamana, murdered his wife, and returned to the school camp that same night. It had taken the police six months to charge him, in which time he had played a perfect grieving widower.

Don was not a murderer. Sarah dismissed the thought. She had known Don all her life and was certain he would never do a thing like this.

'We all need to calm down,' Sarah said as they started walking again.

★   ★   ★

Using an old knife, Sarah pierced the black back salmon's belly, sliding the blade from the stomach to the head. Cartilage crunched as she sliced under the gills.

'Do you feel bad for doing that?' Hall said.

'Nope.' With a firm tug of the gills, the guts slid out. She tossed them into the ocean.

'Do you feel sorry for the fish?'

'Not if I'm planning to eat it. They don't suffer.' She realized he was teasing her. 'Much.'

'How come you don't keep the fish in a bucket of water?'

'Stresses them out. It gives them physiological problems. The more stressed out they get, the flesh gapes, and they toughen up. Better to break their neck.'

'You twisted its neck.'

'Yeah. Some people use a dongometer, something to whack it with. English trout fishermen spend hundreds on ivory-handled dongometers.'

'Really?' Hall said.

He was looking at her intensely, and she had a brief, strange feeling that he was about to kiss her. He didn't.

She slid a fresh squid tentacle onto her hook and cast out. Wind was picking up, twenty knots and nicely onshore. Good fishing weather. Hall sat on the rock beside her. Usually she liked fishing alone; Hall, however, was easy company. He appreciated solitude.

She could hear happy conversation coming from the shack. All summer Sarah's parents had invited friends over for drinks before dinner. She had taken to returning to the shack when the cool evening air was quiet and the only sign of guests was the empty glasses by the sink and a half-eaten cheese platter or chip crumbs in a plastic fish-shaped bowl on the table. Tonight their voices didn't heighten her loneliness; instead, their distant gabbling was as innocuous as the ocean's breath.

Alerted by the silence, Sarah held her fishing rod between her and everyone else in the shack. Something was wrong. On the couch, her mother, Pamela, and Don sat in a row, like people waiting for a bus. Steve and Dad were smiling so hard she wondered if they were drunk. She noted that each of the champagne glasses on the table had one of her mother's silver charms attached to the stem. Paralyzed, like a cornered animal, Sarah waited for the dreaded words to come. In the expectant hush of contained excitement, everyone beamed idiotically.

'I'm getting married!' Sarah felt Erica's words under her skin. Her cheeks became numb; the muscles incapable of smiling.

Erica held out her hand, showing five diamonds on a slender silver band. Sarah leaned her fishing rod against the wall and dumped her bag on the floor. She unbuttoned her jacket. Was it hot in here? She hung her jacket over the back of a chair and turned to look at her sister's hand.

'Cubic zirconia?'

'No! It's real.' Erica crossed her fingers. She was always crossing her fingers, an annoying gesture. She did it to wish Sarah luck at fishing, or when she dished up a new recipe.

'I know. They don't make cubic zirconia that small.'

A chair leg grated against the floor and someone coughed. Erica's hand dropped and she glanced from her mother, to her father, to Sarah, standing there in her old Hash House Harriers T-shirt, stained with fish muck.

'Erica's ring is eighteen karat, Sarah,' Steve said. 'I didn't mess around.'

'Don't look at me like that,' Sarah said, taking Erica's hand. 'I'm joking.'

Erica's manicured fingers felt warm in her own small cold hand. Sarah was genuinely happy for her sister, but the happiness was a long way inside her and too fragile to vocalize. She examined the ring.

'It's a beautiful ring,' she said. It was enough to relieve the silence.

'It's exquisite.' Pamela beamed. 'And worth every cent, Steven. What do they say? A month's salary that lasts a lifetime.'

'And the rest,' Steve said.

Sarah sat at the table and drank some champagne while Erica described how it happened. Steve had proposed on the beach that afternoon, after playing a song on his guitar which he had written about love and finding a soul mate, having children, and growing old together. Erica was teary as she told the story. It was so pathetic Sarah didn't know what to say, so she busied herself fitting a charm to the stem of her glass.

Erica and Steve had been together for six years. Everyone knew they were going to get married one day, so it wasn't as though this engagement was a surprise. They'd never even had a breakup, as far as Sarah knew. By the time she and Jake had been seeing each other for six months, they had already split up three times. For the last four months of their relationship, they had broken up almost every weekend. Sarah drained her glass and held it out for some more. Don poured champagne almost to the top.

'Those new sinkers will be in the store in a few days,' he said.

Sarah nodded. His offering of a conversational lifeline was welcome, but she couldn't even think about fishing right now. She glanced at the ring again. Five perfect diamonds, scraped from the bowels of the earth in some distant ruined place. Really, who could bear to wear one?

Erica was sitting on Steve's knee, her laughter sharp. Steve was drunk and slouching lower and lower in his chair. Fortunately Sarah was sober enough not to comment. Sarah's face ached from smiling. Her mother stood to announce a toast. Flip tittered, and champagne splashed from her glass as she raised it.

'To Erica and Steve. To see your child happy is the greatest thing.'

Pamela made a funny noise. Makeup bled around her eyes. She was teary. It took Sarah a moment to realize that Pamela was not crying in happiness for Erica but was thinking about her only child, Max, who was in prison. Sarah thought about Max being locked up occasionally. She had been to visit him once, last year, when she attended a conference in Hobart near the prison farm. He wasn't happy to be imprisoned, but he wasn't doing too badly, either. He told her he was relieved to be getting some help for his problems. Pamela had always struggled to accept that Max needed help.

'Sit down, Felicity,' John said.

Pamela pressed her hand to her lips, as if to restrain her emotion. While it was easy to avoid discussing gambling and anything about prison in general, it was the unpredictable, happy moments that upset Pamela more.

Flip hugged Pamela. There was a fuss as Erica searched for the tissues. Sarah found them on top of the fridge. She handed Pamela the box, glad to have something to do. Assuaging Pamela was a relief from pretending to be happy for Erica.

Erica was the first to forget about Max. She held the ring up, laughing and repeating, 'I can't believe it!' and 'You are so naughty!'

Sarah watched the ring move about the shack, pressed to the neck of the champagne bottle, disappearing and reappearing in Erica's hair, a dragonfly alive in fuzzy lantern light. In Sarah's pocket were three bottle caps from the beer she had drunk earlier in the evening as she fished. She turned them over, pressing her fingers against their rough edges, mentally adding the three glasses of champagne she had just drunk in the shack. Who cares, she told herself, draining her glass. She was drunk now, so there was no point slowing down.

Her mother and Pamela were remembering engagement stories. Pamela was twenty-two when she married, which was young by today's standards. Mum and Dad were twenty-four and twenty-five when they got married in the quaint St Helens chapel. Erica was thirty-two.

Of all the men Sarah had known, there were only a few she would have considered marrying. When she was at university, Max Gunn had been interested in her. There was nothing between them, but he had more or less said he was keen on something serious. That was before his gambling got messy. Looking back, she realized he had ticked most of her boxes, but that was before she even knew she had boxes that required ticking.

Who really wanted to be married, though? Look at Mum

and Dad. They barely touched each other; if they kissed, it was on the cheek, never on the mouth. It had always been that way. They functioned well together, tolerated each other's company, but if that was all you wanted, you might as well marry your dog.

Under her father's chair, Henry slept, oblivious to everything. It was nearly midnight when Pamela and Don finally left. Yawning, happily tipsy, Flip and John kissed their daughters and hugged Steven and went to bed. Sarah remained at the table, finishing the champagne. It was flat and warm. Erica squeezed toothpaste onto Steve's toothbrush and handed it to him. As Sarah watched, she silently congratulated herself for not commenting. He went to bed to wait for Erica. Poor guy; gets engaged and doesn't get a celebratory fuck. The shack was too confined, the walls too thin. Maybe Erica would give him a silent blow job. Sarah chuckled.

Sarah put the empty champagne bottle on the bench beside the other two empty Moët bottles Erica was saving to use as candlesticks. Men wanted wives like Erica, the kind who would match her tea towels to her oven mitts and slow-cook casseroles with seasonal vegetables from her own garden. Erica was an air hostess, the ultimate training ground for wifely perfection.

As though she sensed the drift of Sarah's thoughts, Erica sat on the stool beside her and started rehashing the proposal.

'Yep, you told me that already.'

Sick of listening, Sarah stretched. She wasn't tired but she needed to be alone. In the dark bedroom her head spun. She was thirty-five, too young to be spending evenings listening to her parents' friends reminisce, too old to hide on the top bunk feeling jealous and mean. Mindful of her potential hang-over, Sarah drank from her water bottle until her stomach felt uncomfortably swollen.

Erica finished tidying up but she didn't come to bed. She was probably standing in front of the mirror, looking at the ring on her finger. The shack was quiet, just the wind blowing down the hill to meet the ocean's constant hum. Henry's sloppy drinking from his bowl sounded like a human whimper.

Sometime in the night Sarah woke up needing to urinate. She couldn't find her flashlight. Without it she was reluctant to use the toilet at the end of the veranda. There were spiders, mainly daddy longlegs, living in there. Although they were harmless, it was creepy to think you might sit on one accidentally. Instead she went into the backyard and squatted on the grass.

She was almost finished when she heard the low howl of devils fighting. Startled, she tried to hurry. It had been a long time since she'd heard their screams; a vicious, chilling sound like that of a woman being strangled. The convicts had thought it was Satan's laughter when they heard it two hundred years ago. Devils were misunderstood – usually their noise was their bluff to protect a carcass – but their capacity to rip one another's head off and their high pain threshold meant that humans were sensible to maintain a respectful distance. They could fight for hours.

Sarah pulled her underwear up and looked in the direction of the noise. It had stopped. Two thoughts ran through her mind. One, devils didn't become suddenly silent. Two, if it wasn't devils fighting in the bushes, what on earth was it?

She sprinted back inside the shack and locked the door behind her.

The shack was quiet when Sarah woke up the next morning. There was no sound, no chairs squeaking or newspaper rustling. Everyone was gone. She didn't care where.

In the empty kitchen she drank a glass of juice and stared blindly at the wall, not seeing her mother's collection of fish-painted plates hanging there. Her meanness hung around her shoulders like a heavy and ill-fitting coat. She should apologize to Erica but she knew she wouldn't. They never had. Transgressions passed without comment, forgotten and forgiven.

Erica knew there was something wrong. Even Hall had guessed. On their date he had asked her about Jake. She didn't mention the fight in the Pineapple Hotel car park, or how she had driven drunk as far west as the car would go before running out of fuel. She had woken up on the side of the road in blasting afternoon heat. Birds were fighting over something in the cane field beside the car.

The fish were dead by then. Tanks eerily silent with three tonnes of drowned prime barra. When she worked it out later, the pumps must have broken down around midnight, closing time at the Pineapple Hotel.

Juice splashed over her hand and onto the floor. She was not aware her hands were shaking. It wasn't just her hands but her entire body, engulfed in wretched sadness. When would this end?

Dusk and the ocean brimmed with sharks. So everyone said. There was also a consensus that between nine p.m. and dawn, the hours of darkness, it was unsafe to be outside. The fear was stupid. Both women had disappeared in the afternoon, so if there was going to be another murder or disappearance, chances were it would be another daytime tragedy. Sarah had scattered the burley mix she had made from bread crumbs and diced mullet heads. Judging by the lack of interest in her burley or her bait, the fish were absent. That meant there were probably no sharks in the water tonight. Sarah leaned over and dipped her hand in the luke-warm seawater.

Bored with catching nothing, Sarah left the rocks and followed a trail worn by wombats and quolls. She hoped to spot a quoll, a small native catlike creature with delicate white spots. Quolls were shy, though. There was more chance of seeing a wombat.

Spiderwebs spanning the path stuck to her face and hair as she pushed through. The track ran along the top of the rocks before winding down to the beach. She hadn't thought about the murderer while she was fishing on the rocks; now every wind moan in the dunes made her snap her head around to reassure herself there was no one there.

From the beach nothing delineated the spot. There was a garland of flowers in the clearing near the road, but you couldn't see that from the beach. The spot where Anja Traugott had washed in was marked by an eroded sand wall, a broken driftwood arc, and creepy shadows from the dune grass. Sarah stabbed her fishing rod into the ground and walked toward the dunes. She was sinking in the soft dry sand when she heard the noise, a faint metallic scratch, like a knife being pulled. Frozen, she listened hard. There it was again. Fuck.

She had to get out of there. She spun around, sprinting to retrieve her rod. Running perfectly on the hard sand, she knew no one would catch her. It wasn't until the adrenaline rush eased that she realized the sound was her sinker, taut and scratching against her rod.

The table was set with mismatched plates. The salad tongs had handles in the shape of fish. A baking dish of lasagna sat on a breadboard Sarah had made for grade eight woodwork. For a moment Sarah had the unsettling feeling of déjà vu; she could have been stepping into the shack fifteen years ago.

'We were worried.' Her mother was accusatory. 'Dad's driven down the road looking for you.'

'I didn't see him.' Sarah tried to conceal her irritation. She was thirty-five, not fifteen. 'That smells delicious.'

'Clean yourself before you sit down. Mum, she stinks,' Erica said.

Sarah dropped the bucket with a clatter. There was water in the sink and Sarah soaped her hands in it, rubbing hard to get the scales off.

'Please. That's the washing-up water,' Erica said.

'It's fish, Erica. It's organic.'

She sat down and rubbed her bare feet on the dog, asleep under the table. Opposite, her mother and sister continued eating. The backs of their heads made twin reflections in the salt-smeared window behind them. It reminded Sarah of the doll heads Erica and she had practiced hair and makeup on when they were young. Erica had cut the hair off hers and then cried. Sarah had handed her own doll over and been complimented on her generosity. In truth, she had hated the doll, hated its bright blue eyes, too-long lashes, and pearly lips.

She filled her plate and only half-listened as her mother and sister talked. Wind collected pace, rattling the loose chimney pipe. About time it picked up; she hadn't caught anything for days. She was planning where to fish tomorrow when the door opened. Sarah heard her father's voice.

'I didn't find Sarah but I found someone else foolish enough to be wandering around in the dark.'

Sarah swiveled around. Simone Shelley, wearing a white sundress and a leopard-print scarf around her head, stood uncertainly in the doorway. She clutched the shoulders of her son.

'Oh, no. I'm so embarrassed. You're having dinner.' The American accent made her seem confident, almost sexy, like a character in a television show.

Simone had knocked on Pamela's door, and on Jane's, but no one had a spare bed. She was too frightened to stay in her shack. There had been a noise downstairs and she refused to let Sam go and look.

'Everyone knows we're alone.'

Flip dropped the fish tongs into the salad bowl. 'You've got your phone if you need it. Go home and make a cup of tea. You'll be all right.'

'That's what I told her,' Sam said.

Sarah tried to read his expression, but he wasn't looking at her. He obviously didn't want to be here. Fair enough. She had not wanted to be at the Shelleys' place on New Year's Eve either. She had only gone because it would have looked strange if she didn't. She was paranoid Simone knew something about whatever had happened on Christmas Day down at the wharf.

There had been one awkward situation on New Year's Eve. Sarah had gone to Simone's kitchen to fetch Pamela's wine cooler bag. Simone and Flip had paused at their task of arranging cheeses and crackers on a platter, and were discussing something serious. For a horrible moment Sarah thought they were talking about her.

'She likes being single – it suits her fine,' Flip was saying crossly.

Sarah had grabbed Pamela's cooler bag off the bench and walked straight back to the garden. The conversation fragment she had overheard unnerved her. She felt ill for a few minutes until she realized that, based on their body language and the fact that they had not reacted when she entered the kitchen, they were most likely talking about Jane Taylor. She did not want to know what her mother was saying about Jane.

In any case, Simone had invited everyone to her party, and now she had insisted on dragging Sam up here to the Averys' shack. These were good signs. It meant Simone wasn't worrying about anything. Still, Sarah thought, she would feel better if they left now.

Her mother, too. Flip turned the tap on and began washing dishes. If it had been anyone else, her mother would have welcomed them in. Years ago, Simone had alienated many of her female neighbors. She had asked them to babysit her son while she scuba-dived with their husbands, she had worn string bikinis when everyone else wore one-pieces, and she had spoken about traveling to places they had not heard of. Flip and Pamela were happy to attend Simone's New Year's

Eve party, to include her in large activities such as the Abalone Bake, or even to sit with her occasionally on the beach. Their tolerance for Simone ended there.

Simone was not the kind of woman Sarah usually felt sorry for. Tonight she did, for the simple reason that Simone did not understand why she was being turned away.

'Mom. They don't want us here,' Sam muttered. 'Let's go home and turn in.' He was looking at Sarah.

Erica stood up, smiling her too-perfect smile. 'Have a drink with us before you go home. Everything's less scary after a drink.'

Simone and Sam sat down on the window couch underneath the colorful toy parrot swinging upside down on his perch. Simone's gaze moved from the gas fridge with the stickers peeling off it to the piles of curling magazines and newspapers on the coffee table and the dusty children's books on the bookshelf. One of those books Simone had given to Sarah and Erica when they were little girls. It was about a scary toymaker called Weezy who created dolls that came to life. One of Weezy's dolls was evil, and the book had been one of Sarah's favorites. For ages Erica had been too frightened to listen to Flip read that book.

'Such a long time since I've been here.' Simone smiled. 'Cozy.'

'What scared you tonight, Simone?' Flip said. 'It's not as if we just found out about the murder.'

'Sam was talking to some fishermen down at the wharf and very cleverly told them how worried I was, being all alone in the shack. I just couldn't stay there.' Simone twisted her buttery hair into a bun behind her head, held it for a moment, then let it fall around her face. 'We went to the guesthouse first. Jane was very rude.'

'What did she say?' Sarah imagined Jane, her twitchy face devoid of sympathy, taking pleasure in telling the glamorous American to walk.

'She was full up. She said, and I quote, "Go bother the Averys. John won't mind chasing the mice out of the old bunkroom for you."'

'I cleaned it out when we got here. I borrowed her Land Cruiser to take the mattress with the mouse nest in it to the tip,' John said.

'I feel like crying. It's terrible to be knocking on people's doors.'

'Don't be silly.' Flip dropped a heavy pot into the sink. 'Simone, I would offer you a bed but as John said, all our spare mattresses were ruined.'

'The Dolphin Motel is never fully booked. Give them a call,' Sarah said. 'It wouldn't be more than fifty bucks a night.'

'That's an hour's drive from here.' Simone shook her head. 'Longer, at this time of night, with all the wildlife on the road.'

Everyone watched Erica light candles with the gas gun. It clicked and clicked, igniting a weeping column of wax wedged in an empty port bottle, stubby wicks in abalone shells, and candles welded to saucers with their own wax. In the kitchen Flip was scrubbing the sink with Jif and a wire brush. It was clear she had no intention of sitting down.

Simone sighed. 'That poor woman. You know, Sam found her bikini top.'

'Shut up, Mom,' Sam said.

Simone took a sip of wine, smiling as everyone paid attention. Sam had found it caught in kelp at the gulch while he was cutting abalone off the rocks that afternoon.

'What end of the gulch?' Sarah asked.

'Southern. Near where you're always fishing.'

'After the jetty?'

'That's what I said.'

Sarah visualized the currents running from the rock pool and around the coast. Even with a strong westerly, it was unlikely an object would drift past the jetty. The natural movement of the currents was toward the long main beach, or even the little cove where Anja had sunbathed. It was almost impossible for something to drift from the rock pool, along the coast, around the headland, and then into the gulch. It was hard enough to steer a boat along that route.

'You've just solved part of the puzzle.'

'What?'

'The only way that piece of clothing could have landed there was if it was tossed off a boat. Maybe Anja was killed on a boat.'

'Hall said the same thing when Sammy gave him the bikini top,' Simone said.

'You gave it to Hall?'

'He was about to speak to the police, so he said he'd pass it on.'

Of course he was. Hall would say anything to score an exclusive story. Conversation became less stilted as they discussed the murder case. One thing Simone and Flip agreed on was the campers: they thought it was inappropriate that they discussed the murder in front of their children.

'How did you know it was Anja Traugott's bikini top?' John said with a grin.

'I talked to her a couple of times.' Sam glanced at his mother. 'There's no one else around here to talk to.'

Simone smiled at Sam. 'All the pretty girls like Sammy. Why wouldn't they? I tell him, when you are fishing, you are allowed to throw a few back. Same goes for girls.'

John laughed with Simone. 'Good advice,' he said.

At the other end of the table Sarah tried to keep a poker face while blood rushed to her cheeks. Common sense said Simone was not having a go at her. But Simone's comment was strange and her accompanying giggle sly. If she knew what Sarah had done, of course she would be furious.

Sarah excused herself to get another beer. The outdoor Esky was full of melting ice and Steve's Cascade Lights. She thought she had left some full strength in the fridge and went back inside to have another look. Everyone was laughing at a story Sam was telling about Hall cross-examining him. Rummaging through the plastic bags of veggies, soft cheeses, and half-eaten dips, she realized Erica had been right to insist the Shelleys stay for a drink. There was no point pissing anyone off. She tugged at an egg carton to see if there was any beer behind it, and a block of butter banged to the floor. She rammed it back in, not caring what it squashed. This fridge was overpacked. And there was no beer in it.

On the top of the fridge was her bottle of rum. It was what she had drunk on Christmas Day, and she hesitated before twisting off the lid. She swayed the open bottle neck under her nose, enjoying the smell, sweet like burnt sugar. One wouldn't hurt.

She returned to the patio and took a bottle of Coke from the outdoor Esky. Clutching the Coke, cold water dripping from her hand, Sarah turned to see Sam standing in the doorway.

'You got a license for that hot dog stand?'

'What?'

He pointed at her groin. Her fly was undone, his finger wavering in front of it. She grabbed his outstretched finger and twisted it hard enough to make him yelp.

'Mommy, don't hurt me.' Sam mocked her in a high-pitched voice.

She could smell dried sweat on his skin. Unwashed and unscented; the smell of teenage boys. Sarah released his finger. Compose yourself, she repeated silently.

Inside the shack's lit cocoon, Simone and her family did not appear to be listening to their conversation. Sam's arms braced either side of the doorway, blocking her entrance. He had the swagger of a man who was owed money and was about to collect it. She wanted to tell him to piss off. Instead she said, 'How are you doing, Sam?'

'All right. If you're going fishing tonight, I'll come.'

'Not tonight I'm not.'

'Where do you figure there might be some action tomorrow?'

The question veiled a plea. He had asked the same question as she left the New Year's Eve party to go fishing. She knew the hollow yearning, the desperate drive to avoid aloneness. His need was not unlike her own. Still, she couldn't help him. It was hard enough right now to look after herself.

From a dirty sky the moon printed a silvery path across the sea. Beneath the formless coastal scrub, the ocean pitched on and on. Sarah tried to breathe evenly. Something broke in the Esky as she returned the unopened Coke bottle.

Sarah followed Sam back inside the shack. Erica was admiring Simone's scarf.

'Sam chose it for me.' Simone smiled, pleased with Erica's compliment. 'He's helped me buy quite a few of my clothes.'

'Hidden talent,' Erica said.

Sam was expressionless. It was hard to know whether he was uncomfortable with his mother's attention or indifferent. In any case, it would give Flip an example to share with Pamela of Simone's smothering parenting technique. Sarah had heard Pamela and Flip comment on it in the past – when they weren't complaining of the times Simone had dumped her son with them so she could go diving.

Later, when John drove the unwanted guests home and Flip and Erica busied themselves closing the curtains, Sarah repacked her fishing bag with the squid jig. Her sister and mother were laughing; the sound ebbed with the low tones of cruelty. They were titillated by the novelty of turning away Simone Shelley and the anticipation of telling the story to Pamela tomorrow. Even the act of closing the curtains was exciting. They never closed them except when they shut the shack at the end of summer. Tonight, they pinned the gaping sections together with clothes pegs, admiring each other's handiwork. Sarah's fingers curled in so tightly she could feel the bluntness of her nails on her palms.

Sarah switched her torch on to check if the batteries were working. There was no point trying to go out right now; Mum and Erica would have a fit. She poured herself a glass of wine and waited for them to say good night.

By torchlight she knotted the line and attached bait. She cast out, then switched the torch off. No one needed to know exactly where she was standing. Her finger tingled and she realized she had cut herself. She pressed the wound to her mouth and sucked. Blood's warm saltiness triggered memories that made her shudder: Jake standing over her and spitting on the ground; the peppery smell of wet asphalt; the taste of beer and blood and his foul-smelling, slobbering breath; his lazy drawl hurling cruel insults as he stomped away into the night.

She searched her mind for the happier memories, but they were slow to surface. Humid evenings eating dinner on the back veranda while November thunderstorms shook the roof. Drinking cups of tea while strolling through the bamboo and palms in her overgrown garden. In that house they had talked about everything they hadn't talked about during the day. At work they didn't speak; at home he wanted to know everything: who was calling her, where she went to buy groceries after work, what she thought of the other guys on the fish farm. She was flattered by his close attention; the intensity of his feelings was something she was not used to. He was insistent, that's what he was. Like the vines pushing through the cracks in her floorboards and gaps in the window frames; you could snap them off, but they'd be back in a few days.

The radio reckoned it was thirty-four degrees, and Sarah reckoned they were right. You could see the heat spiraling out of the sand, which was too hot to walk on with bare feet. She was planning to take the canoe for a paddle through the Chain of Lagoons, across the small one where everyone swam, under the bridge and into the broad deep water, past the campsite and the burnt bridge to a silent place shaded by the mountains.

As she dragged the double canoe out of the grass, she saw Erica. She was moping around in the shallows, her camera hanging from her neck. Yesterday Steve had had to go back to Launceston for work, and Erica was feeling sorry for herself. Sarah whistled to attract her attention.

'Come for a canoe,' she called.

Erica rolled her camera in a towel and left it in the dune. She carried the paddles while Sarah dragged the old wooden canoe into the water. Dirty rainwater containing dead insects had pooled on the seats, and Sarah scooped it away with her hand, hoping Erica wouldn't notice; she could be funny about things like that.

Erica sat in the front seat, Sarah behind, and they paddled in unison across the lagoon. Under the bridge the air smelled off, like old flower water left in a vase. Swallows had built nests from sticks and sea grass, and mounds of bird droppings covered the beams. Sarah could tell it was the first time since they launched the canoe from the beach that Erica was actually putting some grunt into each stroke. She was scared of the shadowy quiet space, the way the dark lagoon water made hollow sounds as it lapped the mildewy pylons. They were about to pop out the other side when Sarah jammed her oar in.

'Easy oar,' Sarah said as the canoe swung sideways. 'Stop. Look over there.'

Don's black four-wheel drive was parked in the rushes, not on the wide beach nor on the edge of the gravel road behind. Only the top of the vehicle and the long antenna of Don's two-way radio was visible.

'What is he up to?' Sarah held on to the underside of the bridge so the canoe wouldn't float away.

'Probably nothing. Can we go before a bird poops on us?'

'Just wait.'

Sarah's eyes followed the run of the beach as it wrapped

around the water before disappearing into the mountain's shadow. Nothing looked unusual, except for Don's car, almost hidden beside the lagoon.

'Maybe he's sitting inside it, masturbating,' Erica said.

'No. There's so many better, more private places to do that around here.'

'I was joking.'

The screaming started then, a woman's frantic high-pitched scream. Sarah started paddling. In front of her, Erica fumbled with her paddle.

'Hard strokes, Erica, hard,' Sarah said.

The scream came from the west, which was the direction of the campsite. The woman sounded terrified and incoherent; her words swallowed by fear. Sarah concentrated on making each stroke deep and strong, matching Erica's pace. The canoe picked up speed. They were about to discover something truly awful. Sarah regretted that Erica was with her. Erica would not be able to cope with it.

They rounded the sand peninsula and could see the campsite tents and fire smoke. The screaming woman was waist-deep in the lagoon, fully dressed, beating the water with her arms. Thirty-odd meters offshore a toddler drifted in a blow-up dinghy. Two swimmers were swimming toward him, the imprecise, hardworking strokes of people who had never been properly taught to swim. The woman, presumably the mother, gestured to Sarah and Erica.

'I can't swim. Cooper can't swim,' she cried. 'Help him, please.'

Sarah and Erica steered the canoe toward the child. The swimmers reached him first.

'Easy oar,' Sarah told Erica and they stopped paddling.

The child was distressed, crying, as the swimmers towed him back to the beach. The mother waded through the water to meet them, yelling, 'You little shit, Cooper!'

As his mother lifted him out of the boat, she cuddled him. She swung the little boy onto her hip and carried him up to the campsite, calling her thanks over her shoulder. The rescuers, two teenage girls, carried on playing with the blow-up dinghy.

'Oh my God, I thought Don Gunn was murdering someone,' Erica panted, still breathless from the physical exertion.

'That's what it looked like.' Sarah whacked the water with her paddle. 'Frickin' hell. And I thought I was coming here for a relaxing holiday.'

The sisters had almost reached the bridge when they saw Don. He raised a cylindrical tube toward them in a salute. It was a yabby pump, used to extract the crablike creatures from the sand. Its stainless steel glinted in the sunlight. He was standing on the bank, dressed in navy shorts and a white polo shirt. Don's attire was usually appropriate for attending lunch in a nice restaurant or going sailing on a yacht, even when he was carrying out an ordinary task like collecting sandworms for bait. They waved back at him.

'Pamela sells Dynabait for ten bucks and he pumps his own yabbies to save money,' Sarah said.

'That's nothing. I busted him reusing a teabag when he made me a cup of tea the other day,' Erica said. 'My favorite is when he brings his cheap no-name wine and drinks Dad's good stuff.'

Their laughter rang across the lagoon, causing Don to look over, which made them laugh more. Sarah was glad to share a joke with Erica. It felt good. She had contemplated apologizing for her awkward behavior on the night of Steve's proposal but felt as if it wouldn't sound sincere. As they paddled toward the shore, Sarah cleared her throat.

'Hey, Eric,' she said. 'I'm happy you're marrying Steve.'

'I know you are.'

Sarah poked a finger into her mother's skin. The pressure made a white indentation that reddened immediately. Flip was extremely sunburned. She had been with Pamela, floating on air mattresses on the lagoon all morning. Now her shoulders and chest were dark pink, like an overripe peach.

'Curse Pamela.' Flip fanned herself with a *Country Style* magazine. 'She wouldn't let me leave. She's scared to be on the beach alone.'

Flip had overheard some kids plan to dig a channel between the lagoon and the ocean. The lagoon was swollen from the unseasonal heavy rain, and the children planned to surf on the torrent of water that would explode across the beach and into the sea.

'I said to Pamela, someone will drown,' Flip said. 'It's very dangerous.'

'No it's not. Lying in the sun until your skin peels is dangerous,' Sarah said.

'Girls, one of you run down to the guesthouse and fetch some aloe vera from Jane,' John said without taking his eyes off his book. 'I'm sure she has some with all those herbs and things she grows.'

Sarah eyed her mother's damaged skin. Aloe vera would not prevent it from peeling, but it would help take the sting out of it.

'I'll get it,' she said.

Flip's comment about the lagoon rankled Sarah as she walked down the hill to Jane's guesthouse. The lagoon was ready to explode. As a kid, Sarah had always dug the lagoon out. Everyone came and watched as the brown tea tree-stained water charged into the azure. People brought surfboards and rubber donuts to ride the frothing current. Someone could drown; Mum was right. But someone could drown on any given day in the unpredictable surf here. There was never anyone on the beach to hear cries for help. Anyway, she and Erica had dug out that lagoon almost every second summer. Damned if she was going to let someone else do it for her.

As she passed the gum tree glade beside the wharf, she saw the writing. It was in red paint on the timber palings of the largest boatshed. Either last night or first thing this morning, someone had scrawled in capital letters: COKER IS A KILLER.

The Nissen hut's curving roof cupped the day's warmth. There was no answer when she knocked on Hall's bedroom door. She waited for a moment, feeling like an intruder in the empty guesthouse living room. From the garden came the sound of wood being chopped.

Jane acknowledged Sarah and continued chopping. Sinewy muscles pumped under the folds of loose skin on her arms as she swung the axe. Her hair had slipped from its topknot and stuck out from her head like tangled fishing line.

'Jobs like these make me think a man around here wouldn't be completely useless.' Jane wiped sweat from her forehead with her sleeve.

Erica had speculated about Jane's sex life as they canoed across the lagoon that morning. She claimed Jane had never had a boyfriend after her husband left. Erica wondered whether celibacy was a conscious decision for Jane, or whether it had happened slowly, the thought of taking a lover much like a chore you planned to get around to doing but never did and ended up forgetting about. It was a saddening thought. There were different levels of aloneness, Sarah knew, some more lonely than others. Sarah had been glad Erica was sitting in the front of the canoe and could not see her expression.

Watching the older woman swing the axe, Sarah noted that Jane still shaved her armpits. Erica would interpret that as a sign of hopefulness. Depressed, Sarah tried to remember why she had come.

'Dad says you've got a heap of aloe? Mum's sunburned.'

'He did, huh?'

Jane leaned the axe against the wood block. Sarah followed her across the patio. Under a veil of white netting, basil, rosemary, parsley, and mint flared in pots beside brick plant baths of tomatoes and fat red strawberries. Jane found a plastic bag that had been shoved in the wood stack under the barbecue. She broke several fronds of aloe vera and dumped them in the bag. Sarah moved aside as Jane pushed a pot under the netting with her foot. It made a sharp scraping sound on the brickwork, which woke a black dog in his kennel. He lifted his head and barked.

'Shut up, you.' Jane stooped to drag her fingers across the loose dirt in each pot, pulling out a clump of stray grass and tossing it in a pile.

Sarah offered the dog her fingers, and he rubbed his nose across them. His fur was matted from saltwater. Jane walked her dogs on the beach twice a day. Sarah had seen her throwing a stick into the waves, the dogs racing each other to bring it back. Even during the recent storm, when the rain was coming sideways and the ocean plastered anyone who ventured near it with freezing water, Jane exercised the dogs.

'Simone Shelley came up last night.'

'What did she want?' Jane continued weeding.

'You know.'

Jane didn't answer.

'I guess you were fully booked.'

Jane tossed a handful of weeds into the pile. 'No.'

'I thought you didn't mind her.'

'I used to clean for her. She rents her place out when she's not here. One lot of her friends left the place so filthy it took me seven hours. She only paid me for four.'

'I didn't know that.'

'Why would you? Anyway, she didn't need a bed. She just wanted company.' Jane shrugged with the indifference of someone for whom loneliness was as much a part of her life as chopping firewood and washing floors.

They fell silent. The breeze was like a heavy blanket that morning, catching more heat as it moved through the crackling bush and over the farm's parched paddocks. A car came up the road, slowing as it approached the sandy turning circle in front of the guesthouse. It wasn't Hall's. Sarah didn't recognize the car. Jane stood beside her and they watched as it stopped, engine still running.

'Guests?'

'Stickybeaks more like it. Sticking their noses in where they are not wanted.' Jane glared, one hand shielding her eyes from the sun. She shook a gloved fist at the car and it accelerated away toward the shop and the boat ramp.

'Where's Hall Flynn?' Sarah tried to sound casual.

'No idea.'

'I offered to take him fishing, that's all. Later. Doesn't matter. I'll go without him.'

Jane was arranging the netting over the herbs and didn't answer.

'I guess he's out looking for murderers,' Sarah said.

'He won't find one.'

'Why not?'

'It's hard to find someone who doesn't want to be found.'

'They've still got a lot of people to talk to.'

'Good luck to them.'

Jane's guest had been killed. The murderer could have been inside the guesthouse. He could easily come back. The nearest neighbor was a kilometer away. Jane must have been over all this in her mind.

'Are you afraid?' Sarah asked, but she knew the answer before Jane spoke.

'Got the dogs.' Jane banged her gardening gloves on her thigh. A cloud of wood dust billowed out. 'I better get back to work.'

Chapter 7

'There was a great story on Apple Isle TV news last night,' Elizabeth said as soon as Hall answered his phone. 'Vigilantes frustrated with police have taken the law into their own hands following the unsolved murder of Swiss backpacker Anja Traugott. A local man has been victimized with a dead devil thrown at his house in the night. Furthermore, a piece of graffiti at the nearby wharf accuses the same man. Police plead for calm.'

The last bit Elizabeth said sarcastically.

'I'm assuming Apple Isle TV gave no attribution to me.' Hall had not seen the previous evening's news bulletin.

'Why would they? That piece you filed barely covered the facts. I gave it a rewrite myself – the chief sub didn't know what to do with it. But still, the TV news had a much stronger story than we did.'

Of course the chief sub wouldn't touch it. He didn't want to be sued for fabrication.

'I'm not comfortable with beating—' Hall said.

Elizabeth interrupted. 'If you're not filing, there's no point you being there, is there? As much as I'd like to give you a company-sponsored beach holiday.'

After the phone call Hall slammed his car door hard. He used so much force that the side mirror cracked, which made him more irritable.

A good story took groundwork – talking to locals, waiting for people to return your calls. The vultures at the television and radio stations often let newspaper journalists do the grunt work for them. He felt worse because the devil story should not have appeared in the paper at all. Vigilante stories encouraged destructive behavior, copycats and the like. The problem was that Elizabeth had called him five times that day. It was a slow news day and she needed something.

Why was he even surprised? Hall had known when he typed it up it would get subedited into a sensationalized version of the facts. Unfortunately, that was what sold newspapers – and kept people tuning in to the six o'clock news.

From Pamela's kitchen window, Hall watched the crowd gather in the park. Milling around the two policemen in the center, the radio girls clutched handbags and microphones as their heels sank into the grass. Near the road the Apple Isle TV crew waited beside their company car; the cameraman smoked and the producer wrote on his clipboard. Hall knew the presenter, an attractive woman who was peering into a side mirror and rubbing makeup on her jawline. Anyone who'd ever had a drink with her knew the only thing she cared about was to get a job with CNN. A car rolled down the hill and everyone looked up. It was a black four-wheel drive and it didn't stop. The media pack resumed their conversations, and Hall's toes curled in his leather boots.

Behind him at Pamela's kitchen table sat Anja Traugott's parents. They were a slight couple, their faces bleached of emotion. They drank coffee silently as Pamela and the police media officer, Ann Eggerton, discussed the problems of designating an official nudist beach.

'I'm not a prude, but it's the caliber of person it attracts that bothers me,' Pamela was saying. 'Flashers and perverts and the like.'

What a ridiculous topic to be discussing while two bereaved parents sat by, waiting to beg the public for information on their daughter. Hall took a hard bite out of his bacon and egg roll. The paper had sent down a photographer, and he was using his zoom lens to shoot the locals who were lingering at the edge of the park. Some shifted in the hot sand on the beach while others hung back behind the swings and slide, all curious to see the parents of the murdered woman. As Hall watched, the Apple Isle TV presenter marched over to her cameraman. Whatever she said made him slide his phone into a pouch on his belt and heave his camera onto his shoulder. If she'd known about the exclusive shots the *Voice*'s photographer had just taken inside Pamela's kitchen, she would have been furious. The thought made Hall grin.

The photographer had taken some great shots of the grieving parents, candid pictures that told a thousand words. The only photograph Hall still needed was a decent one of Anja. Her parents had supplied a photo which the police had distributed. It lacked personality. Anja had worked in a bank, and the photograph looked like it had been taken for professional purposes.

A chair squeaked against the cork floorboards as Ann Eggerton stood up.

It was time.

Hall held open the colored plastic strips while the Traugotts trundled out. Mrs Traugott's eyes were bloodshot, her face taut. She had cried the entire time Hall had interviewed her. Now she held a white handkerchief to her chest with both hands; it would have made a good shot. Mr Traugott retucked his black shirt into his black slacks. He nodded at Hall. Earlier, tears had streamed down his face as he tried to verbalize, in someone else's language, how it felt to lose his daughter.

'What went through your mind when the Swiss consulate told you it was likely that the woman found on the beach was your daughter?' Hall had asked. It was one of his least favorite questions; the answer was so obvious it often angered interviewees. Hall filled three pages with notes and decided it was enough; this story would write itself.

'I better go and see what's happening out there.' Pamela flipped her *Closed* sign around and sighed as though she had no choice.

As Hall followed the group across the grass, he noticed John Avery standing among the onlookers, one hand on the shoulder of each of his daughters. Hall couldn't see Sarah's face, but as he passed, John pulled Sarah and Erica closer together and spoke into their ears. Flip stood off to the side, her hands shoved inside the pockets of her shorts, an uncharacteristically boyish stance. Simone and Sam were there too. They were standing closer to each other than a mother and teenage son usually would, their bare arms touching. Disconcerted, Hall looked twice at them. There was still space between them, and perhaps they were simply scared, but their stance gave the impression of two people very much physically aware of each other. It was a fleeting impression and then it was gone, and Sam was slouched beside his mother, looking bored while she glanced around for someone to talk to.

The press conference began. Ann Eggerton introduced the mayor, the senior inspector, the Swiss consular officer, and the Traugotts and handed out a press release, which Hall put in his pocket without reading. The senior inspector explained that toxicology reports showed there were no drugs or alcohol in Anja Traugott's body at the time of her death. The cause of death was drowning; the examination of her body was continuing, however. He explained that it was difficult to clarify what injuries had occurred before or after she drowned. The senior inspector was tactful in the presence of the Traugotts; the real aim of the press conference was to encourage members of the public to come forth with new information.

Hall stood a few paces behind the jostling reporters as Mr Traugott answered their questions in broken English. Mrs Traugott said nothing; Hall was not sure how much she understood. Twelve minutes later the media officer thanked everyone for coming and the pack surged around the Traugotts. Two uniformed police officers steered Mr Traugott away as strangers tried to press cards into his hand. His wife was already gone.

'We're finished for today.' Ann Eggerton often became flustered at large press conferences. She held her hand up, indicating the press needed to back off. 'You all have what you need.'

The Apple Isle TV producer nodded as Hall left the park; Hall kept his sunglasses pointing straight ahead.

His Holden took four attempts to start. Glancing up, Hall saw Simone Shelley talking to the Apple Isle TV producer. A wide straw hat hid her face. He eased the gear stick, glancing once more at them in the rearview mirror as he drove away.

Hall spotted the flowers as soon as he got out of his car. Roses, tied to a heavy piece of driftwood. They looked fresh. Bingo. Taped to the plastic wrapping was a large photo of Anja. It looked like it had been taken on a summer camping trip: she was tanned and happy; there were trees and a river in the background. He couldn't have hoped for a prettier photo. So much better than the passport mug shot the *Voice* and every other media outlet had been running.

Carefully Hall peeled the photo away from the flowers and slipped it into his pocket. In his room at the guesthouse he scanned and e-mailed it to the office. Afterward he held the photo for a minute, thinking, before putting it safely away in his laptop bag. Other reporters could track down their own photo. Wind could easily be blamed for its loss.

Sitting at his desk in the guesthouse, Hall read over his list of the people who attended the press conference. Beside each name he noted who that person suspected of the two presumed crimes.

Each person he had interviewed in the past week had happily made an off-the-record suggestion. Often these revealed more about the accuser than the possible killer. Most of the wealthy folk in the shacks thought it was one of the blokes who camped and fished at the lagoon. Hall had interviewed many of them, although it was difficult to speak to them all. Several times he had found the camps empty, everyone fishing or swimming or boating. For their part the fishermen thought it was either Roger Coker or Don Gunn. Pamela had changed her mind; currently she suspected Gary Taylor, although from what Hall understood, she had not seen him for more than a decade.

Simone Shelley had laughed that throaty laugh when Hall pressed her for her thoughts on a suspect. He had sat beside her for a short time on the beach, where she was relaxing, holding a book, watching her son surf.

'That's not the way to make small talk with a woman, Hall,' she said. 'You could ask me what I am reading; that would be nicer.'

He glanced at her book. *Señor Barton's House*. It was not a title he recognized.

'It's about a utopian Australian settlement that was formed in Paraguay in the 1890s,' she said. 'The New Australia, they called it.'

Hall was intrigued, but he refused to be diverted. Simone had a way of derailing a conversation, quite charmingly, so it would not go where it needed to go.

'Simone, you're levelheaded,' Hall said. 'What happened to those women?'

She sighed and stretched her legs on her towel, pointing her painted toenails into the sand. She had lovely legs. 'I think humans underestimate Mother Nature, Hall.'

Only one person suspected John Avery.

'Have you interviewed Dr Avery?' Sam Shelley had said when he gave Hall the bikini top.

Hall had said yes. He thought he had. But later, as he filed his breaking story on the dead woman's bikini washing to shore, he realized that although he had spoken to John Avery many times, he had not actually interviewed him or quoted him in any article. It rankled Hall that Sam had noticed this and he had not. He stared out the window until his screensaver flashed.

John Avery had taken the gas bottle into St Helens to be filled, Sarah explained as Hall followed her around the side of the shack. A glass of red wine was beside her tackle box on the wooden table. She picked it up and sat down, gesturing for him to do the same.

'Went diving earlier. Did a bit of redistribution. Relocation project, you could say.'

'You did what?' Sitting across from her, he could smell the wine on her breath.

'Along the back wall of the gulch, north of where I took you fishing, best real estate.' She didn't check to see if he was following her erratic conversation. He grinned as he realized she was drunk; it was the middle of the afternoon. 'Most successful crays live in those sea caves. Deep and quiet, good views. Fat cats of the sea. You didn't see any buoys near there, did you? No one puts their pots there. Too stupid. They get enough, though. Not tomorrow. Nothing tomorrow. Should have left them one, just to let them get excited. Oh, well.' Sarah laughed, and when the effort made wine splash out of her glass, she flicked it off her hand and laughed some more. 'Oh, well. Maybe I'll be kinder next time.'

'You took everyone's crayfish out of their pots?' Hall said.

'Yep. Released them.'

There was a big straw hat under the table, a sombrero, and she put it on. She wasn't as tough when she was drinking; the dimple was ever present and her skin flushed in a girlish way that made her freckles seem brighter. She tightened the hat string under her chin, jumped up, and handed him her half-full wineglass.

'You have mine,' she said.

An empty mug lay on the grass and she poured a dash into it, swished it out, and then poured herself a generous measure. The bottle label stated it was a Peter Lehmann Stonewell Shiraz from 1992. He wondered if John knew she was drinking it.

'Pamela was telling me about those middens,' he lied, feeling only slightly guilty.

'She knows jack.' Sarah took the bait. 'I'll tell you.'

Hall nodded encouragingly and sat back to enjoy the glass of wine.

The rock wall was exactly where Sarah had said it would be. It was positioned between a new barbed wire fence that marked the perimeter of Franklin's Apple Farm and an unprotected beach. The rocks were football-sized stones that would have been gathered from the paddocks behind. There were days of work in that rock wall. The farmer would have parked his tractor in the middle of each paddock and loaded the trailer with as many rocks as the suspension could handle. Driven the tractor over to the edge of the property and unloaded. Days of backbreaking, repetitive work.

Too much effort just to build a wall in the middle of nowhere.

Hall recalled what he knew about the farm. He was fairly sure it was owned not by one farmer but by a superannuation consortium. It was old, the original apple orchard established on the site in the 1880s. The main entrance was on the other side of the property, on Anson's Bay Road, where the original homestead and packing shed still existed. Here on the fringe Hall estimated fifty head of cattle were run, probably just to keep the grass down. Neat bushy lines of the orchard were visible on the distant hills.

Not far out was the granite island where, Sarah had said, the Aboriginal people had caught seals. Apparently the people from the Tasmanian east coast were the only Aboriginal people in Australia who swam. Sarah reckoned that underneath the farmer's rock walls had been the middens. It was the right location for a shell midden site. Hall had seen some on the southwest coast. They were deep round pits, ten feet wide and ten feet deep, and contained thousands of sun-bleached mussel and abalone shells. Sometimes they contained the remains of cooking fires, tools, bird or animal bones. They were an archaeological treasure chest; you could tell what time of year the Aboriginal people used the midden from the type of bird bones found there.

He stared at the man-made rock wall, imagining the site of feasts and long-forgotten conversations. As well as being a dining room, the middens doubled as an animal trap. The Aboriginal people used to arrange bait along the edge of each pit and hide inside. When an unsuspecting seabird set down on the bait, it would have been thumped on the head.

Sarah said she had seen the middens there, had walked up to them every summer until the farmer covered them. Hall believed her. Unfortunately, the only way to confirm a shell midden had existed there would be to remove every rock. Even then, if the farmer had any brains, he would have bulldozed the original formation and destroyed the pits. In reality whoever owned the farm had little to fear, so the destruction would have been pointless. It was unlikely an Aboriginal land rights claim would be made, as there were not many, if any, survivors of the east coast tribe. Fear fostered such an ugly reaction.

Hall drafted the lead in his head, then the second and third paragraph, and listed who he would speak to before he acknowledged the futility of writing a story like this. Destruction of the middens would be impossible to prove and defamatory. Hall's political leanings had caused trouble in the newsroom before. He already had two letters of warning sitting in his desk drawer. Last year when he received his first warning for his editorial on the Franklin River loop road, he had thought the chief of staff was fooling around. Even when he received the second written warning, he had found it hard to be apologetic. This time it was clear-cut; he had refused to write a story about a woodchip company donating money to a primary school. Elizabeth did not see his point that the story was an advertorial.

Three warnings and you were out. Hall didn't love his job as much as he used to, but he didn't want to lose it. He photographed the rock walls with the ocean behind them, and then again with the paddocks behind them, and recorded a description of the area in his notebook. That was all he could do for now.

★　★　★

Jane poured a large serving of gin over ice cubes and added a drizzle of water from the tank-stand tap. She took a sip and smacked her lips.

'Good. I needed that.'

Hall arranged sausages and onion rings on the barbecue plate. It was handmade, a blackened metal square resting on three walls of charred bricks. He had spent twenty minutes arranging wood underneath it, trying to get the temperature right. Jane didn't offer advice and he was glad. The sausages were the cheap supermarket variety, he noted from the packet. He should have organized some fish. Never mind. Food tasted better when it was cooked outside. The meaty smell reminded him of camping trips by the farm dam during school holidays. One of his brothers would simmer lamb chops on an open fire while the rest of the brothers swam and built wobbly rafts from dead wood.

Jane hadn't mentioned it, but he knew she was worried. Agitation motivated each movement she made – the steady gulps of gin, the flick of her finger as she tapped ash from her cigarette. Nothing about her was still. When she wasn't drinking, she propped her glass in a potted plant and added wood to the fire or flipped the onion rings around the hot plate. Even her hair kept moving, the wiry coils undulating out from the bun.

He felt sorry for her. There was talk her estranged husband had been seen near the old jetty in a faded bronze Ford utility with unpainted panels on one side. He was hard to miss, a beefy red-headed bearded man. Apparently he had driven up the tip road. Several people had noted the dust cloud rising behind his car as it traveled down the straight road running beside the beach.

'Can anyone believe that man turning up now?' Pamela had said. 'You wouldn't read about it.'

John Avery said Gary Taylor had been working in the mines on the west coast. Erica Avery thought he was doing time at Risdon, a maximum security prison near Hobart, although she was not certain of his crime. No one said anything pleasant about the man. Years ago when Gary Taylor lived at the guesthouse he owned a runabout dinghy. More than once he had been spotted lurking near other people's buoys; those were the days when empty pot after empty pot was pulled and nobody caught anything.

Hall had mentioned to no one his suspicion that Gary Taylor was living a lot closer to the Bay of Fires than anyone realized. He still had not been able to confirm whether Taylor was the twice-convicted crayfish poacher the police were interviewing in relation to the murder investigation. There were several unemployed men in the area with this type of record. Certainly Pamela was right in saying it was a bit strange, Gary turning up now after all these years. But there was a difference between news and gossip. Jane's bitterness suggested to Hall that Gary Taylor had left her for another woman. If this was the case, he didn't know why everyone persisted in discussing him. It was cruel; losing your partner to someone else was a pain Hall understood all too well.

The heat from the wood fire hurt his legs and forced him to stand back. He drank beer and watched fat stream out of the sausages. Jane folded a slice of white bread around a sausage, squirted tomato sauce on top, and handed it to him.

'Sorry,' Jane said.

'It's fine. I like sausage sandwiches.'

She frowned. 'No. Sorry I'm not much fun tonight.'

'What's on your mind?' Hall felt disingenuous. Casual dinner conversation was not the entire reason he had agreed to eat with her.

'Nothing.'

Jane finished her drink. She held her liquor well. He had noticed her sipping gin during the afternoon while she washed salt from the windows. It was understandable she would want a drink. That morning her final booking had canceled. She had asked Hall to proofread a flyer offering her services for ironing and cleaning.

They talked about the middens while they ate. Jane didn't blame the farmer for covering them up; Hall was not interested in arguing. She snorted when Hall mentioned Sarah's concern that certain people in the area took more than their fair share of sea spoils.

'I don't have a lot of time for Pamela and Don Gunn but I can tell you this: their catch is not a drop in the ocean. They don't eat that much. And it's not like they're taking it to sell in their Chinese restaurant or something. Sarah Avery was complaining about that, was she? Everyone's got their axe to grind,' Jane said.

Eventually the conversation returned to the murder.

'You know,' said Jane, scraping the spatula along the barbecue plate, 'some of the bus drivers coming down from Launceston have been telling people where the beach is. They're making a big deal out of it, like it's a tourist attraction.'

Hall stoked the fire but watched Jane's face as he said, 'I'm more interested in that fellow driving the bronze utility.'

'You know who it is.' Jane sucked her lips in.

'Why do they call him Speed?'

'Don't be mistaken. He's not stupid. Gary's got it all happening up here.' She tapped the side of her head. 'Everyone from Ringarooma speaks slowly.'

Without prompting, Jane outlined the brief, bitter history of her marriage. Gary Taylor could be blamed for pretty much all of Jane's problems, from her childlessness to the back-breaking hours she worked to keep the roof over her head.

'Nineteen is too young to marry,' she said. 'Look at me now. I'm stuck here.'

'How did you meet?' Hall asked.

'God, a long time ago.' Jane poured herself another drink. 'Raspberry picking. Sounds bloody romantic, doesn't it? It was a summer job for a gang of us kids. You picked all day, drank all night. We all camped out in the farmer's shed and I tell you, once the lights went out, some of those blokes were like a bunch of goanna lizards, crawling over each other trying to get a bit, not caring who it was with.'

Hall cringed. It sounded dreadful.

Jane laughed. 'Gary took me under his wing. He was older, twenty-two. He said, "You're too special for those louts to get their hands on." We liked each other. Had the same sense of humor.'

Her cheeks flushed, which Hall assumed was from embarrassment at having spoken so candidly.

'"Special." I'm not the first girl to fall for that line.'

'I'm sorry that your marriage ended.'

'I don't even think about it anymore,' Jane said. 'Don't worry about me. I still have a personal life.'

'Do you think it is strange that Gary has turned up after so long?' Hall knew more about Gary Taylor than his question implied, but he was undecided on how much to tell her.

'Do I think it's strange Gary turning up now? Nothing that man does will amaze me. Look, he read something in the paper . . . something I said. He's full of it.'

'So you've spoken to him?'

'Yeah.'

'What else did he say?'

'Drop it. You're barking up the wrong tree. Gary's not your man.'

'I have never said he was.' Hall sighed. 'All this angst. If only beautiful young girls didn't go walking on the beach alone.'

'Well, they shouldn't. Girls who don't want trouble shouldn't go running around screaming for attention.'

There was a hard edge to Jane's voice. Hall waited for her to say more, but she only shook her head. She flicked her cigarette lighter on and off and smiled for the first time that evening. 'I nearly forgot. I was talking to someone who is angry with you.'

'Yeah?'

'Apparently you weren't supposed to put that thing about Roger Coker in the paper. Vigilantes throwing Tassie devil roadkill at people's places.' Jane laughed and lit a half-smoked cigarette she had put out when they started eating. She blew smoke toward the ocean. 'You reporters, you're all the same. I better be careful what I say.'

Hall swallowed the froth in the bottom of his stubby. 'What else did Sarah say?'

'She was yapping on. Reckoned you tricked her into saying

something. She's worried Roger Coker's going to be hassled even more now. It was all over the TV last night. I said who gives a rat's? You can't worry about other people.'

Jane propped her pointed boot on a stump of wood. He hadn't picked her as someone who enjoyed telling a person something they wouldn't like to hear. A mosquito pricked the back of his neck and he slapped at it in disgust.

'If people don't say it's off the record, how the hell am I supposed to know?' he muttered.

A fat round moon was high over the ocean horizon. Darkness, unfortunately, was hours away. Hall opened another beer and sat down next to Jane. There was no point taking his frustration out on her. Her wanting to talk about someone else's problems for a change, he couldn't hold that against her.

It was nearly midnight and Hall was getting ready for bed when he heard a male voice coming from somewhere in the guesthouse. It was muffled and for a moment he could not be certain he had heard anything at all. He opened the door to his room carefully, so it wouldn't squeak, and listened. From deep within the guesthouse he heard the shuffling of furniture on floorboards, followed by Jane's laughter. Perhaps she was listening to her transistor radio. He shrugged off the thought that something was not quite right and leaned out his window.

Ten minutes later he was still gazing at the night sea, conscious that the guesthouse was now silent, when he saw a solitary figure moving down the empty road. In Launceston he wouldn't have noticed a person walking at night on an unlit street. Here it was clearer. He recognized her posture first;

striding out, her back erect. It was Sarah. Her fishing rod bounced against her shoulder as she walked.

By the time Hall had tied his bootlaces and crossed the guesthouse yard, she was no longer in sight. He waited until he was well away from the guesthouse to call out.

'Anyone feel like coming fishing with me?' His voice sounded strange in the silent night, as if it belonged to someone else. There was no answer and he couldn't help feeling foolish.

'Hello?' he called less confidently.

At the shortcut to the gulch, she was waiting for him. She must have been standing there for several minutes, listening to his footsteps crackle on the gravel, hearing him breathe and cough and look for her.

'Boo,' she said.

'Hope I didn't scare you.'

'You wish.' Her teeth gleamed in the moonlight; he liked the way they weren't perfect, one front tooth leaning against a corner of the other. Her sister had perfectly straight teeth. Sarah had told him that her sister had worn clear braces, which cost twice as much as normal metal ones, but they had been necessary as Erica was a promising ballet dancer as a teen. Apparently metal braces could be detrimental to a dancer's prospects in competitions.

'You've got balls, wandering around out here by yourself at night.' Immediately he wished he had not used that expression. 'You're gutsy.'

'Not gutsy. Just extremely fit.' She had mentioned that one of the reasons she had been unconcerned about approaching him on that first day on the dune was that she knew she could outrun him. Did that mean she thought he looked unfit? He touched his stomach; it wasn't as hard as it used to be, but it wasn't all that soft, either. Maybe she noticed the move for she added, 'You look pretty fit yourself, so I guess we're safe tonight.'

They walked past the gulch and onto a slender stretch of sand called Witch's Cove. At the end of the beach they sat on a rock, facing the sea. Sea lice glowed like tiny fairy lights in the body of each wave.

'That article about Roger. I regret that it ran.'

He explained about his impatient editor and the news cycle pressure. He kept it brief; he didn't want to give her the impression that his work colleagues did not respect him.

'No worries,' she said.

'Jane mentioned you were upset about it.'

'I don't upset that easily, Hall. I'm worried about Roger though.'

She leaned back against the rock. In the moonlight her hair had the reddish hue of an Antarctic beech in summer. He wasn't sure, but the way the fabric of her shirt was sitting it appeared that she wasn't wearing a bra. He wondered if she was expecting him to take the lead. Without alcohol dulling bravado he felt as though he was on stage and about to be judged, like the bulls in the livestock show at Agfest, blinking at the audience, not comprehending what was expected of them. The rock was digging into one of his legs and it hurt.

'What's wrong?' she said.

'Nothing.'

'Tell me. You're acting weird.'

He felt like a boy on a first date.

'Are you married or something?' she said.

'No!'

'You think I'm ugly and wondering why you got with me the other night?'

'No!'

How could he explain to this confident woman that he had not made love sober for seven years? The problem was not that he was worried he couldn't perform; it was that he would disappoint her. That afterward she might lie beside him, cuddling in his arms, but secretly be thinking that she had had better. Ragged with frustration at himself, he turned back to her. It was too late. She was picking up her fishing rod.

In the kitchen, waiting for his tea to steep, Hall munched Vegemite toast and watched Jane follow her black dogs down the beach track. The bigger one was older and limped, trying to keep up with the younger one, which raced toward the surf. Jane put a hand to her mouth, probably whistling through two fingers, commanding the pup to wait. He did not. It was the younger one that Don had smacked at the Abalone Bake. Hall had checked the wound on the dog's back, a neat two-inch cut. It had healed faster than he'd thought it would, aided, he supposed, by daily saltwater swims.

This morning Hall planned to knock on Roger's door again but it was still too early; the sun had barely come up. He looked for something to read or do while he had breakfast. There was a pack of cards beside the stacked board games and he took them down, dealing himself a game of patience. It was hard to concentrate, his thoughts returning to Sarah. He was a moron. Last night he should have just grabbed her and kissed her, properly, how he wanted to. How many chances did a man need?

A door closed somewhere in the depths of the guesthouse. Hall put the cards down. He was about to go down the internal staircase when instinct urged him to look out the kitchen window. In the garden below, a man wearing running shorts and a T-shirt was bent over, rooting around in the wood stack beneath the tank stand. The man stood up, glanced around as if to ensure no one was watching him, and walked up the hill toward the road.

Hall exhaled slowly. It was John Avery.

He finished his tea, watching Jane run the dogs through the white wash. He wouldn't tell her, not yet. There was no sense in scaring her unnecessarily. And for all he knew John Avery was merely returning some firewood or something. It was nothing that could not be sorted by a few deliberate questions addressed directly to Dr Avery.

As Hall washed his breakfast dishes, he spotted Roger Coker lumbering across the rocks. Abandoning the soapy water in the sink, Hall grabbed his notebook and jogged down the beach track.

People had said that Roger smelled like cat urine, that his hands were abnormally large and one of them was missing two fingers, that when he looked at you he didn't blink and it made you feel like he could read your thoughts. Hall had not believed any of it, had attributed it to the witch hunt he was witnessing. The first time he knocked on Roger's door he had not detected the smell on his body, combined as it must have been with the cat-reeking veranda. Now, crouched next to Roger on the rocks, he had to shuffle back as the sour odor sickened him.

Hall didn't describe the profile piece he wanted to write on Roger. Instead he talked about the history of the area and how Roger must know a lot about it, having lived here all his life. Roger stared unblinking at Hall, his hands tying a knot in his fishing line. When the knot was tied, he propped the rod on the rock.

'Yep, lived here all my life. Probably die here, too. My old man said his last prayers a few miles up that way.' Roger nodded back toward the gray beach and whitecapped surf. With two fingers shaped like a gun, he tapped his head. 'Tock. Gulls and sea eagles had eaten most of him by the time we found him.'

'Is that right?'

'Mum said that was what he always wanted.'

Hall made a perfunctory sound.

'To get eaten by birds – that wasn't what he wanted.' Roger's chuckle turned into a hoarse cough. 'No, he didn't want to live for a long time.'

Hall had heard the rumor about Roger Coker's father from more than one person. Apparently he had taken his own life on the bluff when Roger was a boy of ten or eleven. Hearing it from Roger was humbling.

'Sarah said your father was a carpenter?' Hall said.

'Yes. But he never got his papers. That was his problem. He was hopeless, my mum said. He couldn't finish things. He built a boat once. Just a small dinghy. It leaked. It's in the bottom of the lagoon somewhere.'

Hall laughed with Roger. This could make a really lovely, insightful story. A story that changed people's perceptions. Somehow, Roger had decided to trust him. Hall tapped his notebook.

'Maybe you could talk to me about fishing in the area?'

Roger stood up. He was taller than Hall. As if to fend off Hall, he held both hands up. The palms were flat and wide, his fingers flared.

'You shouldn't talk to strangers,' Roger said. 'Off I go.'

As Roger lumbered away across the rocks, Hall could not stop himself thinking about the size of his hands. Roger might not be a muscular man, but even with several fingers missing, those hands looked capable of snuffing the life out of a person.

Once they were clear of the wharf, Don wound the throttle up. Hall had no idea how fast they were going in boating terms but it felt like a hundred kilometers an hour: the speedboat was skimming the water. Wind rushing on his face, hand steadied on the bow, Hall momentarily reconsidered putting his hand up the next time the chief subeditor job was offered. It paid at least ninety thousand a year, which was a thirty percent increase on what he was currently earning. With that kind of money, he could afford to purchase a small but sexy speedboat.

They followed the coastline south, passing the guesthouse on the headland and the row of shacks nestled above the beach. Where the rocks ended and the sand began, a figure was running by the water's edge. As the boat approached, Hall recognized Sam Shelley, his long legs striding through the white wash. Even more interesting was the figure behind him. It was Simone, her sarong tucked into her bathing suit. Sam kept turning, glancing over his shoulder at her. Either they were racing, or she was chasing him. It reminded Hall of those vibrant, outdoorsy types of images used in cigarette advertisements in the eighties, before the tobacco companies were banned from having people in their ads.

In line with the lagoon, Don cut the engine. He pointed out the landmarks relating to the Anja Traugott and Chloe Crawford cases. It was interesting to see the land from the perspective of the ocean.

Don's observations were things Hall had heard before. Hall let his mind drift, nodding agreeably as the older man spoke. Don's way of speaking was unhurried; he was confident he would be listened to. Hall's father had been a man like that, a man quietly satisfied with his self-sufficient farm, his cattle dogs, his keen sons, his hardworking, uncomplaining wife. Such measured parlance was not a characteristic that you would expect of a man with such a verbose wife as Pamela. You would think Don would need to blurt out his thoughts in order to make them heard.

The boat drifted toward the beach, positioning them in line with the Coker block.

'He doesn't do himself any favors, that one.' Don nodded toward the green cottage.

'Roger Coker?'

'Queer.' Don's tone implied this was a bad thing.

'That's okay, isn't it?'

'Son, I'm not going to give you a biology lesson.' Don chuckled.

Right then Hall remembered where he had seen Don Gunn. It was in June 1994 at an Ulverstone rally titled 'Say No to Sodomy.' That was nearly ten years ago, but Hall's recollection of dates and political events was as precise as his capacity to remember names and faces. In any case, that date was an easy one to recall: it was the year the state's anti-gay laws were repealed by the United Nations Human Rights Committee. Oh dear. Hall wouldn't have picked Don.

'Now I know where I've seen you before.' Hall snapped his fingers. 'You spoke at a rally at Ulverstone alongside Pauline Hanson years ago, didn't you?'

Usually the mention of Australia's most prominent redneck politician provoked eye-rolling and sniggers, but Don nodded amicably, unembarrassed.

'I was toying with the idea of running in the state election at the time. It didn't pan out. In hindsight I probably would have won a seat.'

'There were three rallies across the state. I covered them all.'

'Ulverstone was our best event. We kept the idiots out.'

At the Hobart rally the police, for some reason that was never explained, had opened the doors and two hundred protesters had barged in, ending the meeting. Following this, the Launceston and Ulverstone rallies had charged a five-dollar entry fee, which had minimized the disruptions, although almost three hundred protesters held a candlelit vigil outside the Ulverstone rally. It was a topic that had divided the state.

'Well, it was a controversial issue.' Hall emphasized the past tense.

Don shrugged. 'You see, it's not what people do in privacy. That's not what everyone was concerned about. It was the age of consent that was the problem. And now it is legal for depraved men such as Roger Coker to sodomize very young boys.'

'You mean pedophiles in general, not Roger Coker specifically, I assume,' Hall said.

'Hall, I do mean Roger Coker. And I don't think his interest stops at young boys, either. He used to sit in those sand dunes for hours, and I can tell you he wasn't bird-watching.'

'Geez, Don, that's a big call.'

'Well, you're the journalist. These are the things you need to be aware of.'

Don switched the key too fast and the engine snarled. He muttered something about not flooding the engine and sat there, twisting the gold mesh of his watchband around his wrist.

Sarah executed a perfect pin drop in the center of the rock pool. Seal-swift, she sucked a mouthful of air then kicked her way to the bottom. Hall didn't want to follow. He felt jumpy today, as though he had drunk too much coffee when in fact he had drunk only one cup. There was no need to be nervous. From the moment he had jumped off the back of Don's boat, which she had held steady in the surf, she had acted as relaxed as if they had been friends for years. She wasn't one to complicate things; he should follow her lead.

Her dark shape circled the rock pool. The water looked inviting. Shades of green shot with crystal twirled above a subtropic rock reef, an ecosystem protected by granite walls. As Hall watched, the water changed color continuously: bright emerald switched to cool aqua; one moment the water reflected the blue sky before becoming as transparent as drinking water. A gap in the rock pool floor led to the ocean, and bubbles rose with each oceanic pulse.

Hall leaned forward trying to see. Sarah was no longer circling; her body remained head down at the bottom of the pool, her legs dangling upward. Impressive lung power. She could probably cut it as a synchronized swimmer, not that he would say that. She'd bite his head off. She emerged laughing, snorting water from her nose.

Above the rock pool was a cave. It was the kind of cave Hall would have liked to know about as a kid. Pirate games, castaway, the perfect hideout from where the rock pool could be secretly viewed. It was in this cave, Sarah said, that Roger Coker had slept for two nights when he ran away from home as a teenager.

Dripping water, Sarah sprawled beside him on the rock. Her body language was encouraging. When they first met she had covered her body with a towel after every swim; now she didn't bother. Instead of a bathing suit she was wearing what looked like an aerobics bra and sporty bikini pants. Her stomach muscles rippled every time she moved. They looked out to sea, attempting to distinguish distant whitecaps from the sails of the returning Sydney-to-Hobart yachts. At the bottom of the rocks, burnt-orange-colored kelp thrust up with each wave.

Arriving at the Bay of Fires last week, Hall had seen scrubby vegetation in shades of muted green, spiky dune grasses, a murky lagoon, and sea too cold to swim in. It looked different now. The Bay of Fires had a beauty that was not apparent on first glance. He remembered thinking the same thing when he visited here for the day with Laura. The open ocean, and the way the tree-covered mountains sat humble and untouched beneath the big sky, had gladdened him. That was a year before the breakup, and probably Laura had not even thought of sleeping with Dan. There were signs that she wasn't happy. It had taken Hall a long time to acknowledge this. For instance, that weekend she had not liked the motel he booked in a fishing town farther down the coast. She complained to reception that the bath was not clean. She hadn't liked the lunch he packed; he couldn't remember what it was now, but he recalled her feeding bits of it to the swans. And when they arrived back in Launceston, she had called him the 'traveling companion of the year.' He was flattered; then he realized she was being sarcastic. Apparently he had not initiated one piece of conversation during the three-hour drive. Hall had thought they were enjoying a companionable silence.

One thing he now knew for sure was that when a man was crazily in love with a woman, he wasn't an idiot for not seeing that she didn't love him in the same way. Laura should have told him how she felt. Not all women would be deceitful – Sarah's honesty, he imagined, might be brutal.

It caught him off guard when Sarah mentioned she was considering returning to Eumundi at the end of the summer. Maybe he had misread the situation, but he thought she was looking to start a new life in Tasmania. The conversation during their pub lunch had been clear; her ex-boyfriend had physically abused her. Something irrevocable had happened and she could never return. She hadn't gone into the details and Hall had not pressed her. It wasn't his business. But she couldn't go back. Hall had written feature articles on the subject for the weekend paper; a woman returned to her abuser on average eight times before she left for good. She should not go back.

'Men who don't respect women never will,' he said.

He took her silence for agreement and added, 'People don't change, Sarah.'

She nodded. She picked up a shell and threw it into the sea.

'Do you want to go back to the barramundi farm?' he said.

'Not an option.'

'So sell the house.'

'Renovator's dream. I wouldn't get jack for it.' Sarah climbed up to the jumping rock. 'You coming?'

He didn't want to jump into the rock pool. He had never liked jumping off rocks or bridges. Reluctantly, he followed her over to the edge, took a breath, and jumped. In the seconds he was in the air he noticed a flash of color moving across the tops of the rocks. Someone else was there.

Chapter 8

The day after the press conference, Sarah wanted to show Hall the rock pool. Hall had already planned to go boating with Don, so Sarah arranged with Don to drop Hall off at a precise point at the other end of the long beach. From there, it would be a short climb across the granite boulders to the rock pool. She could have gone in the boat with them, but she wanted to jog instead. It was pleasant running on the beach and she did not stop; she ran past all the shacks and the lagoon, she avoided a dead fairy penguin lying in the sand, and she only glanced briefly at the place where Anja's body had washed in.

She ran along the hard sand, through the white light that poured down everywhere on the beach, and her muscles and lungs began to hurt. Always, when she exercised, Sarah felt a sense of righteousness in the pleasurable pain. Forcing her body to do intense exercise was good for her. She concentrated on her breathing and let her rhythm slow into a steady pace. In front of her, as far as she could see, the beach was empty. There were no other footprints.

Yesterday, noticeably absent from the press conference was Roger Coker. Sarah had overheard several comments on this as she waited with the onlookers, who were all agitating for something to happen. Deliberately, she had stepped closer to Bunghole and his mates.

'Anyone would be here unless he had something to hide,' Bunghole had said.

Sarah had pointed out that, on the contrary, killers usually made a point of coming to gatherings like this.

'Look around,' Sarah had said.

Bunghole had not answered her but someone else had said, 'He's mad as a cut snake. Madder than his old woman.'

It was true – Mrs Coker was mad. Sarah had once heard her swearing at Mr Coker as he dragged driftwood up from the beach to burn as firewood. Crowlike, with her hunched back and a neck that swiveled with rough jerks, she hurried him along with language fouler than any Sarah had ever heard. Of course, she had heard worse since working on the fish farm.

At the press conference Sarah had positioned herself behind Don so the panning cameras couldn't film her. It had been interesting watching the crowd's interest in the television crews. Some people must have come straight off the beach as soon as they heard something was happening; beach towels hung from their necks and zinc smeared their noses. Others, such as Erica, who was wearing lipstick and a nice skirt, had had time to dress up in case they appeared on the news. Sarah had studied each face.

What she had told Bunghole was true. Someone at that press conference was a killer. One of the campers was her bet

– and she had not ruled out Bunghole. He was vile. As she had searched each face in the crowd for a sign of guilt or secret pleasure, Bunghole had bared his tongue lewdly at her. Sarah had stepped sideways so he could no longer see her.

Two other people had behaved inappropriately at the press conference in Sarah's opinion – Sam and Don. Cross-armed and cocky, Sam had grinned at Sarah the entire time. It was irritating. Holding his arm was Simone, her head dipped so her wide-brimmed hat hid her face. Don and Sarah's father had calmly discussed a turn in the stock market; the ordinariness of the topic was as discomfiting as the enjoyment on the faces of the campers. When someone muttered something about Roger, Don had turned to acknowledge the comment. Sarah had seen his face; he had been smiling. It was a nasty smile, that of someone who knows he did the wrong thing and is glad about it.

The silence was uncomfortable when Anja Traugott's parents had walked out of the shop. Crossing the park, the Swiss couple had looked out of place, from another time, like characters in a children's fairy tale. Their skin was pale and their clothes were dark. The father had answered the media's questions in halting English, but it was Anja's mother who Sarah could not get out of her mind. She had gazed beyond the gabbling reporters, her eyes shifting to each onlooker, one by one. The mother's face was contorted with rage and sorrow. It was a heartbreaking combination.

As Sarah ran, she imagined explaining to Anja's mother the conversation she had had with Anja. I'm sorry, Sarah silently rehearsed. I told her to go there.

What did Sarah want? Their forgiveness? It was a

conversation she would never have. Her words of regret were of no use to the Traugotts.

Throughout the press conference Hall had been in professional mode. He had remained on the edge of the media scrum and listened without looking, his head bent to his chest. Occasionally he had scribbled something in his notebook. She found his detachment attractive. When the press conference ended and the woman in charge had led the Traugotts away, an immaculately groomed woman approached Hall. They had spoken for a few minutes. Sarah noticed that the woman wore high-heeled pointy-toed shoes that sank into the earth as she walked away.

Sarah wondered what the woman had said to Hall. He had left before Sarah could speak with him. Thinking it over now, as she jogged along the beach, she knew she wouldn't ask him how well he knew that woman. That would be embarrassing.

The other annoying thing that had happened at the press conference involved Simone. Sarah had approached her, planning to engage in some friendly small talk to make up for the awkwardness in the shack the other night. Simone had greeted Sarah, and then, almost immediately, Simone's attention was diverted to a good-looking man who was coordinating one of the news teams. With his suit and gelled hair, he exuded importance. He had smiled at Simone and placed a hand on her arm.

'Excuse us.' He had barely glanced at Sarah.

Neither had Simone. They had marched across the park to where the Apple Isle TV news team gathered beside their vehicle.

Despite that it was now a day later Sarah still felt slightly rebuffed. Maybe Flip and Pamela were right about Simone – she was more interested in receiving attention from men than holding a conversation with another woman.

At the end of the beach Sarah stripped off her T-shirt and running shorts and strode into the water. She let the waves smash around her legs while she got her breath back. There was a boat one kilometer down the coastline, but it was too far away for her to tell if it was Don's vessel. She turned her back on the ocean and surveyed the beach.

Today, she had not stopped as she passed the place where Anja was found. She imagined the Traugotts standing there, looking across the whispering grasses to the empty beach, holding hands, tying their flowers to the driftwood so they wouldn't blow away. The man and the woman, forced to visit this island at the bottom of the world where their daughter perished. For them, Tasmania would be forever a place of death.

That morning the paper ran four pages on what it was calling the Bay of Fires Killer. There were photos of the Traugotts: standing alone looking at the headlines on the sign outside Pamela's shop, surrounded during the press conference, their tear-streaked faces bent together. There was also an incredibly beautiful photo of Anja which Sarah had not seen before. In Hall's article it was revealed that the police had a suspect. An east coast resident who was helping police with inquiries, whatever that was supposed to mean.

Hall had refused to name names when Sarah had asked him about it the other day. He would not even say whether she knew him. It was creepy, not knowing.

Sarah waded out of the water and stretched her body across

a warm flat rock. Fatigue caused her eyes to sting momentarily as they shut. Light pricked the darkness beyond her closed lids. Things she thought she had forgotten wafted through her sleepy consciousness: how Tasmanian summer sun never feels hot until a person is sheltered from the wind, the silence of a beating ocean, the deliciousness of unresolved desire.

Since the first night Hall had not touched her. Insecurity made her analyze their first night together, rehash each bit she remembered, until she wasn't sure what was real or imagined.

Jake said she fucked like a man. Although that was anatomically impossible, his meaning was clear. She wasn't soft or seductive; in bed she liked to ask for what she wanted. Apparently this was not a turn-on.

There had been opportunities for Hall to make a move. Maybe he wasn't interested in her in that way.

Erica said she was overthinking it. 'Unbutton your shirt and he'll take care of the rest of it,' she had advised. But that was the kind of demanding, intimidating behavior Sarah wished to avoid.

He liked her. Why else would he follow her down to the gulch in the dark, stand beside her for hours catching nothing?

The sun delivered a hot assault to her back. The sound of a boat engine drifted across the water. She opened her eyes. It was Don's boat. She ran into the shallows and waved so they would see her.

How many times had she sat above the rock pool as a teenager staring out to sea? Past Sloop Rock and the shadowy kelp fields the ocean's blueness merged with sky. Hours and days when perfect swimming weather meant there was no point fishing.

Diving to the bottom and swimming in tight circles to see the baby bull kelp, the starfish, and the cold-water coral growing in the underwater garden.

Beside her, Hall shaded his eyes and searched for yachts on the horizon. She was used to him now and his lengthy pauses. No longer did his silences induce her to chatter pointlessly. He didn't know everything about her, but he knew enough. He didn't call her by her surname or swear around her, and she appreciated that.

'So I came across something interesting,' Hall was saying. 'Don Gunn has connections to the One Nation party.'

Hall described a political rally where he had seen Don deliver a speech, years ago. Apparently Don had been unperturbed when confronted with his own homophobia.

'Don Gunn is sixty. Who isn't quietly homophobic from that generation in Tassie?' Sarah shrugged. 'In Queensland no one admits to being racist, either, but if there is an Aboriginal person sleeping at a bus stop, no one will even nudge him with their boot to see if he is dead or alive.'

Hall nodded. 'Don was quite nasty about Roger Coker.'

'One minute Pamela reckons Roger's got an overweight girl-friend staying at his place, next minute he's gay.' Sarah rolled her eyes. 'As far as I know, Roger's not gay. Don't mind Don. He's a harmless old bugger, really. By the way, Dad and Don didn't realize the council was thinking of designating a nudist beach near here. I'm worried they're planning to visit for a swim.'

'That should give my angry residents over there cause for complaint. Will they pose for a photo?'

'They might not be allowed to go. Pamela doesn't believe in nudist beaches.'

'I think I heard her say something about that.'

'Yeah. She got quite cross, actually. They were only joking about it. She told Don to shut up.'

'That man needs to learn to do what he's told.'

While they were laughing, a large wave showered them with what looked like liquid drops of sunlight.

'Nice one,' Sarah said, holding her palms upward to catch the droplets. 'This is a million miles from my old life. I don't want to go back up north.'

Immediately, Sarah wished she had not spoken. Hall wanted to talk about it. She rocked against her knees and didn't answer him properly. She wouldn't go back, but not for the reason he thought. His concern was so reassuring she could almost believe she was the wronged woman.

When she was with him she didn't feel that gnawing emptiness, that wide landscape of thought where nothing she had done or said was worthwhile. Loneliness was an unpredictable creature. Fishing on an empty beach, clearing out a gutter from the top of a wobbly ladder, checking over water quality reports at three in the morning; none of that made Sarah lonely. It was the last beer before closing, no plans for a Sunday, or some crap song from 1985 that reminded her with painful hopelessness of a time when she had been a hopeful teenager. Hall knew loneliness. They hadn't talked about it, but she could see it in his eyes. She suspected that, unlike her, he expected to feel that way forever.

Sarah let him talk for a while, then casually stood up and got ready to jump. Midair, she grabbed one knee, landing in the middle of the rock pool with a huge splash. Hall followed, arms flailing as though he was trying to slow himself down.

When he surfaced, he climbed out. Drying his face and neck, he looked up the hill with a concerned expression.

'There!' Hall dropped the towel and ran up the granite boulders. 'I've seen you!' he shouted.

Sarah hauled herself out so quickly she tore her knee on the mussels growing on the edge. She knew who Hall was chasing. She had seen Sam's long afternoon shadow undulating from out of the cave when they arrived. He disappeared into the casuarinas before Hall was halfway up the rock face.

'Give it up!' she yelled to Hall. 'You've lost him.'

'Why would he run?' Hall said as he came back.

'Sam is always spying on people.'

'Is that right? Don Gunn caught him peeping at Anja. Pamela told me.'

'He used to spy on me and Erica when he was a kid. Try to eavesdrop on our conversations. Erica used to flash her boobs at him, and he was so disgusted it made him run away; then he got older and that made him stay, so she stopped.'

'I feel sorry for him. He keeps thinking of excuses to come and talk to me. He's lonely.'

For the first time since Christmas Day, Sarah's indifference to Sam shifted slightly. She had barely spoken to him since the incident. Maybe she would agree to take him fishing next time he asked.

A yacht on the horizon, a white flag on the great slab of blue, distracted her. Hall saw it too and ran down to the edge of the rock.

'There's a returning yacht!' Hall waved even though the boat was ten kilometers out to sea. 'Ahoy!'

All week they had watched the racing yachts sliding down

the coast toward Hobart. By the time the yachts reached the Bay of Fires, the most treacherous part of the journey across Bass Strait was behind them. They were only a day's sailing away from the dockside festivities. A couple of days ago the yacht that would come last had passed. Sarah had felt sorry for it, but Hall had told her not to.

'Don't feel sorry for it! The last boat in gets the biggest cheer. Everyone loves a loser.'

Watching the swirling water, Sarah had a revelation. She needed to demonstrate it to Hall. Without warning, she ran down the rocks and dived across the kelp into open ocean. Cold wide water swallowed her. It was dark down there. When she emerged she floated on her back in the gutter by the rocks. Gradually, with each wave's returning wash, she floated seaward.

'Goodbye, Hall.'

'Come back. I don't like it!' Hall shouted. 'Your knee is bleeding, remember?'

'Do you see?'

She knew he didn't. Sarah closed her eyes and concentrated on the current. She was floating in a gutter in which the current ran from the rock pool straight out to sea. The current did not run straight around to the beach, as some people, such as Pamela, had assumed. With strong confident strokes, Sarah swam back toward the rock.

'Can you pull me up?'

She propelled herself over the kelp toward Hall's hand. He grunted with the exertion of dragging her up.

'What are you saying?' he asked.

'As I demonstrated, a dead person, tossed in, would float

straight out to sea. Never to be seen again. Shark food out there. But Anja landed on the beach, which means she must have been alive when she fell in.'

'Or alive when she was pushed in.'

'Sure. So, either she tried to climb out of the ocean and onto the rocks where you are standing. This would be hard to do alone. Or she would have swum around the rocks, toward the beach.'

Hall nodded. 'Continue.'

'The weather was rotten when Anja disappeared. Big surf. I would struggle to swim from here to the beach without being smashed on the rocks, or strangled in the kelp. If she's swimming to the beach, she's swimming against the current, because the current wants to drag her out to sea.'

'I don't think Anja Traugott was an Iron Woman.'

'No. The only way she could have ended up on the beach was if she was tossed dead, or alive, off a boat out at sea, or if she tried to swim around the rocks, drowned in the process, and drifted down to the beach. It's unlikely she would have ended up on that beach if she got caught in this current.'

'We don't know the precise spot where she entered the water.'

'No. But I've dived around here. All along here sucks straight out to sea. There is no natural drift to the beach until you get into that sheltered section past the bottlebrush up there.'

'What about the boat theory?'

'Don and Bunghole. That's your department. Ask them. Why would they do it, though?'

'We'll know more when the autopsy results come through.' Hall studied the dark churning water. 'I would not want to fall in there. So let me clarify what you have just said. Anja is alive when she lands in the water here. She tries to swim to the beach; she manages to swim clear of the gutter, which would drag her out to sea, but drowns and washes up on the beach days later?'

'You better give me an editorial credit.'

'A long shot.'

He obviously didn't think it was such a long shot. He was quiet as they walked back along the beach, and when they said goodbye at the bottom of the Averys' track, he asked her to explain the current movements once again.

It was pointless to compare people. Sarah had always hated being compared to anyone. But Hall introduced things to her that, in her experiences with other men, she had not had the chance to know she appreciated. A challenging conversation was one. Although they both voted for the Greens, the environmental party, their ideas often caused them to disagree. They had spoken at length about the practice of including hormones and antibiotics in the feed on ocean farms. Sarah believed in moderation – there was a science to it, after all – but Hall was adamant it would have long-term effects on wild fish and sea life populations. She never could discuss anything in depth with Jake. If she mentioned the prime minister or a foreign president he would just say, oh, that dickhead, and there would be nothing left to talk about.

Today, watching Hall watching the boat, his hands on his hips and his board shorts clinging to his thin thighs, Sarah had felt affection. His wholesomeness was another one of the things she liked. It was peculiar how the polar opposite of what attracted you to one man could be the precise thing that would attract you to another.

Deception, the thrill of an illicit relationship, had fueled her attraction for Jake. Hiding it from the others at work had been part of the fun. In hindsight, people weren't as stupid as the two of them had thought. When she had told Hall about it, the events turned into a self-deprecating story in which she was a lecherous boss and Jake an emotional moron.

'Don't screw the crew is the moral to the story,' Sarah had said.

Hall had laughed and she cut him off. 'Look, I don't want to slag him off. Women who slag off their exes often have more problems than the ex.'

Besides, it was boring to listen to. As her thoughts shifted back to Hall she grinned. For the first time since she left Eumundi, her thoughts about Jake had not been accompanied by a gut ache and cold sweats.

The next morning they jogged up the old tip road, past the first burned bridge, through the scrub and down toward the lagoon. It had been raining for most of the morning, and muddied water dredged the steep hillside. Sand and leaves washed between the paperbarks and clumped in a sticky mess around the base of bleached gum trees. As the ground flattened, they jogged side by side, occasionally bumping against each other. Sarah was still stiff from yesterday's beach run and it felt good to stretch her legs. Hall ran unevenly beside her; she could tell he didn't run often.

'He won't talk to me.' Hall spoke in rough puffs. 'He will if you're there.'

It was the third time he had asked her to take him to Roger's place. She didn't want to escort Hall there, not in his capacity as a journalist. It didn't feel right.

They paused at the bottom of the gulley. Dappled green light from the eucalyptus canopy cast patterns on the sand. Potable water flowed over the last river rocks before filling the lagoon. Hall scooped his cap through the water and poured it over his head. Beads were trapped in his stubble. He hadn't shaved since yesterday and it suited him, made him appear exotic rather than a middle-aged greenie.

'No stupid questions?'

Hall grinned. 'Deal.'

They resumed jogging. It wasn't that she didn't want to help him; it was more that she rightfully suspected that Hall was capable of a gung-ho approach to his stories, with people such as Roger being treated as collateral damage. She lengthened her stride and maintained a five-centimeter lead over Hall. It was a psychological racing tactic designed to dishearten and exhaust the second runner.

It didn't take long until Hall's breathing became alarmingly rough. Sarah, with satisfaction, suggested they walk it out. They followed the curve of the lagoon beach east. The gray sand was stained with yellow frothy arches that looked like washing-up scum. They talked as they walked, about nothing in particular – the bird sounds they could hear, the fishing trip Sarah wanted to take to a frozen lake in Minnesota one day, and how Hall had learned that Simone Shelley had once been a competitive figure skater in the United States.

Sarah didn't know that about Simone. In fact, she knew little about the American woman's past except that Simone had two dead husbands and ran a successful business importing home furnishings.

'Sounds like you're getting friendly with her,' Sarah said.

'Not too friendly, I hope. Although she did mention that she hadn't been to the Pub in the Paddock for many years . . . I told her how nice our lunch was and I think she was hoping for an invitation.'

'Right,' Sarah said.

Why would Hall tell her that? Either he was taking Simone out for lunch or he wasn't. It had nothing to do with Sarah. If he was hoping to get a reaction from her, he would be waiting for a long time. She continued walking, concentrating on the damp swampy smells around the lagoon.

They emerged from an inlet and the campsite became visible, snatches of color through the paperbark trees. It was an isolated spot to camp. The only access was by four-wheel drive along the swampy shore, and only then if the lagoon was not too full and there were no fallen trees blocking the beach. Not the most serene spot, either; midges and March flies bred in foul pockets of still water between the rocks, and there was no breeze to ease the intimate salty smell of low tide.

Roger had said the pink shells would be easy to find and he was right. There must have been close to one hundred of them. Sarah knelt beside the pile, swearing softly. She didn't need a measuring device to see they were undersized. At least half of the shells couldn't have been more than ten centimeters wide. Some were only seven; just babies. She glared in the direction of Bunghole's camp. Damn thieving greedy vandals.

'Don't go over there. There's no point,' Hall said.

'If I don't say something, who will?'

'We'll call the ranger. That's his job.'

Disgusted, she breathed in through her nose, out through her mouth, trying to control her temper.

Bunghole was stupid, too. It was illegal to shuck or shell abalone until you had brought it ashore and above the high-water line. This was so the shells could be measured. Any half-brained criminal would have shucked the undersized creatures in his boat and tossed the telltale shells over the side.

Roger crouched beside the cooking pit at the back of the house. There was no ocean view from here; bushy vines grew high above his fence. His smile slipped sideways when he saw Hall.

'What's cooking?' Hall said.

'Hall wants to do a story on you, Roger,' Sarah said. 'He thought you might agree if I asked you.'

Roger didn't answer. Using tongs, he slid a foil-wrapped package off the coals and across the wet grass.

'Snotty trevally,' Roger said.

'Funny name for a fish,' Hall said.

Sarah said, 'They're slimy. It's supposed to protect them from being stung by the jellyfish they eat. There's no scientific evidence to back that up.'

Roger peeled back a layer of foil, and steam hissed out into the rain. He fed himself a chunk of white flesh, nodding with satisfaction.

'Now that looks like a big one,' Hall said. 'Would have taken some muscle to bring that in.'

Roger folded the foil back around the fish.

'Where did you catch him, mate?' Hall didn't wait for Roger to answer. 'What kind of rod did you use?'

Sarah felt irritable – either from finding all those abalone or from Hall's comments about Simone – and Hall's blokey act now annoyed her. There was no need for Hall to pretend that Roger was a mate. Roger wasn't stupid. He knew what people thought of him. Several hot coals had fallen out of the fire and were simmering on the ring of sand around the pit. Roger nudged them in with his boot.

Hall was mumbling numbers, working out the size of the plot of land.

'How much land you got here, Roger? Is it an eighty-square-foot block? What would that be worth? Five hundred? Five fifty?'

'Dunno.'

Sarah tried to remember why Hall was there.

'Hall wants to write a story on you. You don't have to.'

'Three quarters of a million, easy.'

'Pipe down, Flynn.' Sarah was only partly joking.

No one spoke. The ocean fizzed onto the empty beach, and there was the muffled clatter of a car crossing the lagoon bridge.

'A storm's coming.' Hall nodded as though someone had asked him for a weather update.

'Take some fish,' Roger said before he disappeared around the side of the house.

'I guess that's a no,' Sarah said.

In the car, the fish sat between them on the bench seat. Its hot sweetness overpowered the Holden's dusty smell. Hall hummed as he bunched up an old handkerchief and wiped the condensation off the windscreen. Sarah's window was stuck open, and rain blew in as they drove past the empty turnip paddocks. Shapeless white water heaved in the bay below.

They ate the fillet in the guesthouse kitchen, straight out of the foil, without speaking.

Bursts of rain and sunshine fell in patches over the coastline, creating several small rainbows. As Sarah walked to the shop from the guesthouse, watching the colors appear and disappear, she heard someone call her name. It was Sam, hurrying through the sun shower to reach her.

'Wait!' he called.

'How are things?' Sarah said as he fell into step beside her.

'All right. It's a bit boring always going surfing by yourself.'

'I don't mind fishing by myself,' Sarah said.

She asked him if there were any interesting people his age at the camping ground and he shook his head. More than likely Simone would not want Sam to linger down there. It must be hard for Sam; there had never been a kid his age with a shack in the Bay of Fires.

'You were friendly with that girl Chloe who went missing, weren't you?'

'Sort of,' Sam said.

Sarah remembered what Pamela had said about Simone intervening in Sam's friendship with Chloe.

'There'll be a time when you'll make your own decisions about who you are friends with,' Sarah said.

'Mom liked Chloe.' Sam shrugged.

'Really? I heard your mother intervened outside the shop one day when you were talking to Chloe,' Sarah said.

Sam thought about it. 'I know when you mean. It wasn't like that. Mom needed me to help her get the jet ski into the water. Mom even asked Chloe to come, but she didn't want to.'

'Oh,' Sarah said.

'I haven't been banned from talking to you,' Sam said.

There was slyness in his tone. 'You told your mother?'

'She asked me where I'd been.'

'She asked? And you told?'

'Yeah.'

'What mother wants to hear about their teenage son's private life?' Sarah said. 'That's perverse.'

Sam's sunny demeanor changed. His expression turned sulky and he kicked the gravel as they walked.

'Mom loves me hooking up with hot chicks. That's why she was so pissed about what happened with you.'

'So I'm not hot, is that what you're saying, Sam? Thanks for letting me know,' Sarah said. 'Do you want me to itemize your physical deficiencies?'

He didn't. At the turnoff to his mother's place, Sam left Sarah. She said goodbye, but his response was sarcastic, as though she had been the one who had offended him. It bothered Sarah that Simone and Sam had been discussing her. Sarah was not secretive, but the less people knew about you, the better. In some ways her honesty had provided the catalyst for Jake's final outburst.

That night at the Pineapple Hotel, Jake had accused her of managing her team through sexual favors. Everyone drinking with them heard, even one of the Eumundi Barramundi owners who had popped in to the pub. A couple of people laughed. Sarah never tried to hide that she had slept with several of her staff. But what she did after hours did not affect her work, or her decision-making process as a manager. She had thought he was joking and told him that there were less time-consuming things she could do to keep a staff member happy besides sleeping with him. Jake was drunker than she was. His lips curled into an ugly sneer and he repeated himself, raising his voice to reach her across the pool table.

On the gravel road Sarah stopped, staring out to sea. The horizon was no longer visible; the ocean and sky were the same washed-out color. A prawn trawler had anchored in the bay for the night.

Sarah wished she had walked out when Jake started mouthing off. Instead, she had responded by giving the guy a hefty dressing-down, holding nothing back, just the way he served it. It was one of those volatile pub discussions that could swing to either anger or jokiness. Watching, their work mates laughed and some heckled. That made Jake furious. Sarah remembered thinking that when she did walk away, he would regret calling her those dirty names. He wouldn't speak to his dog like that. She did not recall crossing the car park or unlocking her car, but she did remember sitting in the driver's seat fumbling with the key when Jake caught up to her.

In the bay below, the trawler shifted on a current, swinging around. On board the fishermen would be heating up their dinner and getting ready for another uneventful night at sea. What a pleasant place to be.

On Pamela's kitchen table was her latest project, a pile of posters stating *A Killer Walks Free. Our Kids Can't.*

'Just drawing attention to the situation,' Pamela said. 'Darlene's helping.'

They had already pinned a dozen to signposts and trees along the main road.

'Who's Darlene?' Erica asked.

'Bunghole's wife. You know, the fat blond woman with the terrible regrowth? She's quite nice, actually.'

Flip sipped from her teacup. Her expression was one Sarah recognized from when her mother had fought with Erica about curfews or pocket money.

'This one,' Pamela said as she finished coloring in the wording on a larger poster, 'this one goes at the turnoff to the guesthouse. You won't be able to drive past without seeing it.'

'You need a photo of Gary to put on the poster,' Sarah suggested, 'so that everyone knows exactly who to look out for.'

Pamela missed her sarcasm. 'We can't do that, Sarah, because that would be defamatory. That's against the law. But I think to most people driving past the guesthouse it will be pretty clear who the poster is referring to. Having said that, it could be Roger Coker. I'm keeping an open mind.'

Two days had passed since Pamela telephoned the police and told them Gary Taylor had returned. They still refused to confirm whether he was the suspect reported in the paper.

'We're taking matters into our own hands,' Pamela said.

'You're a hypocrite,' Flip said.

Pamela's mouth dropped as if she had been slapped. Erica started to speak, but Flip held her hand up.

'No, I mean this.' Flip's voice wavered with emotion. 'We don't know Gary did it. It could have been Don or John for all we know. This poster . . . Your son is in prison for robbery. You shouldn't throw stones.'

Flip's hand stiffened into a clawlike hook where she gripped the teacup handle. Sarah had never seen her mother stand up to Pamela.

Pamela shuffled her posters into a pile. 'Maxwell has been charged and sentenced. He is repaying his debt to society. This is different. A killer walks free.'

Pamela pushed her chair back and busied herself in the kitchen. Erica and Sarah swapped looks. In their entire lives, Flip and Pamela had never had a disagreement.

In the shack's garden John was arranging tea tree mulch around the geraniums and daisies. He stopped what he was doing as Flip and Erica described the conversation at Pamela's.

'Pamela is ignorant and opinionated, and that is a dangerous combination,' he summarized.

Flip and Erica agreed. Sarah wasn't convinced that Pamela was any more opinionated than any person standing there, but she remained silent for once. Emotions were high and there was no point in stirring things up.

Her father plucked a caterpillar from the leaf of a pink geranium and squeezed the life out of it with his fingers.

'There will always be people like Pamela,' he said, rubbing his fingers on the fencepost to remove the dead insect. 'One has to ignore them.'

'Pamela was out of line,' Erica said.

'No. John's right.' Flip sat down on the garden seat. 'I shouldn't have spoken so harshly to her.'

'You don't want to get on Pamela's bad side,' Sarah said.

'There will be posters up about you next. "Felicity Avery Walks Free. Our Kids Can't!"'

'How about "Felicity and John Avery: Natural-Born Killers"!' Erica said.

The sisters laughed, but John frowned. He smacked his trowel on the bag of mulch.

'People in glass houses should not throw stones,' he said, his voice stiff. 'If Pamela starts jabbering rubbish about this family, she will be playing with fire.' His finger jabbed at the air, emphasizing each word.

'John, settle down,' Flip said.

'You tell her or I will.' He glared at Flip. 'People who spread rumors should be lined up and shot!'

'That's a bit harsh, Dad,' Sarah said.

'Come inside, everyone,' Flip said. 'It's time to start dinner.'

John continued laying mulch as the women went in. Sarah glanced over her shoulder. His head was shaking as he scooped mulch from the bag and flipped it onto the garden bed in his exact, methodical motion. She imagined he was silently rehearsing all the nasty things he wished he could say to his wife's best friend.

In the days that followed, Sarah caught more fish than she had in the past year. The ocean swelled and fell against the rocks with slow, satisfied sighs, simmering hungrily. Warm currents brought schools of silver trevally, full grown and hungry. She fished with shellfish, mussels and oysters, joking to Hall that the fish here were better fed than diners in any fancy restaurant. Hungry fish churned around the mince scraps she tossed as burley, reminding her of feeding times on the farm, when frenzied fish made the water appear to boil. She caught trevally with pilchards, flathead with squid tentacles, and a beautiful ten-kilogram yellowtail kingfish with leftover squid head. She threw back almost everything except the yellowtail kingfish. That was a rare catch. Down at the boat ramp Don and Bunghole were getting their backs slapped as their nets collected schools of parrot fish and mullet.

Roger had not made an appearance on the rocks or the beach for several days. There was a chance he had seen Hall on the rock next to her, sitting there while they waited for the bites, passing her the knife when it was time to clean the fish. If so, Roger would have shuffled away. This was a man who detoured into the sand dunes to avoid her when she was walking with someone else on the beach.

It occurred to Sarah that if he hadn't been fishing, he wouldn't have anything to feed his cats. Pamela had removed the cat food from her store shelves.

No smoke wound up into the wet sky from the chimney; no light was visible from any of the windows. Over the cottage's rusting shoulder, a cold vapor breathed across foam scum swirling on the ocean.

Sarah waded through knee-deep grass, thick enough to be infested with snakes. The Coker house always looked abandoned, with the broken-down, tire-less car in the backyard, windows covered with newspapers, and rubbish piled around the incinerator that was never used. The cats who usually dozed on the veranda sofa were absent.

Sarah rapped on the back door. No answer.

She strained to hear some kind of noise inside, but all she

heard were the bees dipping into yellow spiky flowers and a skink lizard scurrying across the floorboards.

When there was no answer to her second knock, Sarah turned to leave, the fish wrapped in newspaper under her arm. She was certain she had left the garden gate as she had found it, swinging slightly ajar. Now the gate was shut. Sarah flicked the latch but it was rusty and would not slide up. It didn't move at all. As she looked around the empty garden, her skin chilled. Whereas before the Coker property had seemed charmingly and curiously derelict, now it suggested utter neglect, an abandonment of humanity that had occurred long before the grass needed mowing or the walls needed painting. She tried the latch again but it did not move. The gate and fences were covered with thin mesh which kept the devils out and they were impossible to climb. Even if you could hoist yourself up a fence, wiry scrub and bushels of razor grass grew to all boundaries. Vegetation like that was tough to wade through. She laughed a nervous, humorless laugh. It was crazy, but she was locked in.

At the bottom of the garden was another gate which led to the beach. As she walked toward it, she scanned the yard for any suspicious movement, checking and rechecking the tank stand, the old car, the bloated sofa, and the house itself. Be smart, Avery, she repeated.

She sensed, rather than heard, the person. Under the tank stand, a shape shifted. Sarah paused. It was Roger, holding a black and white cat with unblinking green eyes. He was hiding.

'Leftover trevally. For the cats.' Sarah held up the parcel, deliberately not remarking on Roger's strange position.

Apart from one finger stroking the underside of the cat's

chin, Roger didn't move. Another cat, a beautiful gray creature with white boots, pushed against his leg.

'I thought there was no one home.'

'I'm sick of people coming here.' His voice was rough with anger.

'Who has been around?' She followed his gaze, up the rutted sandy driveway twisting into the dusty casuarinas. The police had visited Roger several times, and Hall had been down once, but otherwise she couldn't think of anyone else who would come.

'They hurt Grumpy. And Gretel has run off again. I can't find her anywhere.'

'Who hurt Grumpy?'

Roger crawled out from under the tank stand and sat on the grass hill. Gently he stretched the cat across his knees. One of its legs twisted the wrong way, the paw pointing outward.

'They kicked him. Could have belted him over the head with a stick. They kicked Grumpy. What did they do that for? Now he can't walk.'

The cat lay still while Roger ran his hand down its thigh. When his fingers reached the joint, the broken leg twitched and the cat let out a pained mew.

'Grumpy was shaking on the ground, the other two were licking his face, meowing. Ali was hiding underneath and wouldn't come out. I looked through the bush around here and I can't find Gretel. I can't look anymore because I don't want to leave the others. And now Gretel's been gone for two nights. Something's got her.'

Most people Hall had spoken to blamed Roger Coker for

the deaths. Women refused to swim off the lagoon beach near his cottage, and kids were still singing about Roger being a serial killer to the tune of the 'Teddy Bears' Picnic' song. Hall had visited the campground a couple of days ago, and the men were swearing about how hopeless the police had been. Pamela and Don were convinced it was Roger or Gary. Erica said she wasn't sure, but Sarah had heard her sniping about Roger. The police had not ruled anyone out.

Sarah opened her newspaper package. Inside were three thick, clear fillets that would sell in the supermarket for twenty dollars each. She broke the fish into small pieces and scattered it in the grass. The gray cat came forward and ate. Roger remained on the ground, nursing the maimed black and white cat. He waved a small piece of fish meat in front of the cat's nose, trying to tempt it. The cat sniffed at it but didn't open its mouth.

'He won't drink milk, either. Something is not right. He's crapping all over the place, on the carpet and on the couch. What's wrong with you, boy?'

When the fish was gone, she scrunched the paper up into a tight ball. Roger hunched over his cat. He looked fragile, a boy's frame inside an old man's body.

'I wish they hurt me instead,' he said.

Unfortunately, that was exactly what Sarah feared would happen next.

Erica's fiancé, Steve, arrived at dinnertime and the family ate outside, a simple meal of barbecued lamb chops and salad. Tired from a long day in the sun, everyone went to bed early. Barely any breeze had rolled off the ocean, and inside the shack it was muggy. Before Sarah crawled into her bunk, she opened the kitchen window. With five people in the small space, they would need air circulating.

Something woke her up from a deep sleep. The glow-in-the-dark numbers on her watch showed it was after midnight. Henry growled. There was a thumping noise, like someone stomping deliberately in the living room.

'Something is inside the shack,' Flip shrieked.

Sarah sat up and swung herself off the bunk bed. Steve stood in the bedroom doorway, shining a torch into the living area. He was wearing canary yellow underpants and nothing else. Sarah looked away. The dog, standing in his basket, growled at something under the table. Sarah moved closer.

'What is it?' Erica, still in her bed, called.

Henry barked again, and the creature under the table bounded across the room and hurtled onto the couch, sliding on the newspaper pages scattered there. Flip and Steve screamed. Sarah jumped back. She was unnerved, not scared. It was not human. She snatched Steve's torch.

Two frightened yellow eyes gazed at her.

'It's a quoll,' she said. 'Look.'

He was a young one with a reddish coat and the distinctive white dots. He was beautiful.

'Throw a blanket over it,' John said. He was standing on his bed.

'No, Dad.'

Flip dragged Henry into her room and Sarah opened all the doors. Eventually the animal found its way out and everyone laughed in relief.

'Oh my God,' Flip said. 'I woke up when he thumped

through the window. I knew something was in the shack, but I was too terrified to have a look.'

'Me too,' Erica said. 'Henry was going nuts, and I thought, as soon as he stops making a noise, we're all dead. Sorry, Henry, I didn't even try and save you.'

'I don't know what scared me more: having to disarm a murderer breaking into the shack or seeing you in those undies,' Sarah told Steve, grinning.

Erica giggled. Sarah laughed too. Their laughter gained momentum until, for a crazy minute, it was like they were teenagers again, laughing uncontrollably at a silly private joke.

'Stop it, you two,' Flip said as she closed the window.

Everyone went back to bed. Sarah lay down on her bunk, still smiling. Erica was fortunate, really – at least Steve got out of bed to investigate the noise. Look at Dad, yelling instructions from the safety of his bed. He was hopeless in an emergency.

Chapter 9

Hall knelt in the grass beside the guesthouse tank stand. Peering in, he tried to ascertain what John Avery had been looking for. At the end of the neat stacks of cut firewood he spied a glass jar. Checking for the redback spiders that liked to live near wood, he retrieved the jar. Inside was a key. It was old-fashioned, so not likely to be the key to the guesthouse, which had a dead-bolt on the front door. How strange.

'Can I help you, Scoop?'

Jane's flat tone startled him.

'I saw the bottle and was just wondering what it was. This looks like an old key.'

'Sure, you just stumbled across it. Fancying letting yourself into my bedroom one of these nights, were you?' She laughed. 'I'm joking. Don't look so scared. Yeah, that's my spare key. Make sure you put it back.'

'But you've got a deadbolt.'

'Upstairs. That's the key for downstairs.'

'Does anyone know it is there?'

Jane frowned. 'Why would anyone need to know that?'

'May I suggest you find a new hiding spot for it,' Hall said. 'Just until the police sort this case out. Peace of mind.'

'Why?' Jane took the bottle.

Hall sighed. He didn't want to frighten her. Remaining an impartial observer was becoming a challenge with this story. But it would be remiss of him to say nothing.

'What is it?' Jane said. 'Spit it out.'

'I saw John Avery doing something with the key.'

'Something lewd?'

'No! I saw him crouched down here, probably putting it back. You were on the beach with the dogs. I didn't realize the key was here when I saw him.'

Jane shoved the key back into its tank stand nook. She shook her head.

'I've known John a long time. I'll have a talk with him. Sometimes he checks on my gas bottles for me. Maybe that's what he was doing.'

Appeased, Hall went back inside the guesthouse to tidy up some work. His gut instinct had told him he was on a wild-goose chase as he poked around under the tank stand. He called Elizabeth and ran one of his latest theories by her. Based on Sarah's description of how the currents around the rock pool point worked, the idea of no foul play, accidental drowning, was worth considering. Elizabeth snorted.

'Until it's confirmed,' Elizabeth said, and he imagined her flicking her pen in the air at him, 'until we have an autopsy result, which could be another five to seven days according to your own reports, we have got an apparently defiled body and a murder. That's not being sensationalistic, that's the facts.'

He didn't admit it during their phone meeting, but she was right. Fifteen minutes later, glancing out the window, he saw Jane. She was still seated on the patio. She held no drink or cigarette, was not pulling weeds or poisoning bull ant nests. For once Jane sat, hands folded in her lap, staring at the ocean and beyond.

Hall filled the next few days with interviews. Elizabeth was harassing him for copy even though she had not printed several of his warm fuzzies, including Sam Shelley's message in a bottle story. Hall drove two hours north to Anson's Bay to investigate the serious erosion issues faced by a seaside cemetery. He also had a list of easy news stories he had been neglecting in favor of the murder story. Local planning issues, irate neighbors, human interest; stories that involved long phone calls listening to interminable backstories.

One morning he took a phone call from Allan Bennett, the retired racehorse trainer he had spoken to about Gary Taylor. Bennett had a story for Hall. His horse had escaped its paddock. What made it newsworthy, apart from the fact that Bennett was a well-known and popular racing personality, was the fact that the horse, Marbles, had won the Launceston Cup four times. No other horse had achieved this. The story probably would run on the merit of the headline alone, *Allan Bennett's Lost His Marbles*. Hall reminded himself to mention the story to Sarah when he met her later that evening – it would make her laugh.

It was late and the gulch was silent except for the ocean slapping the rocks. Hall held the net ready to scoop the squid before it fell off Sarah's jig. Bristly fibers from her fishing jacket brushed his bare arms. He could smell the back of her neck. She never smelled of shampoo or perfume, but of wool and sand, fresh bread and campfire. It was an organic scent that reminded him of the pleasant smell of his cat's fur after she had been sleeping on grass.

Hall had wondered why they weren't using a torch to catch the squid. He had heard that was what you used. Sarah explained that there were two kinds of squid, calamari and arrowhead. It was the arrowhead squid, which lived in deep water, that were mesmerized by torchlight. The calamari squid they were hoping to catch tonight were curious enough to come look at the light, but it wouldn't hold their interest.

'Squid jig works for me,' she said, checking it. It looked like a prawn with barbs on its tail.

'I see.' Hall tried to sound convinced.

'Concentrate,' she murmured, 'or we'll lose it.'

In the water the jig dipped. Hall scooped the net. The creature he lifted was translucent, tentacles wriggling from a cone-shaped head. Sarah slid it into the bucket and dropped the squid jig back into the water.

Hall's brothers enjoyed shooting possums; Hall found it abhorrent. He imagined his brothers marching through the bush on the farm, rifles resting on their shoulders. Outdoors under a huge night sky they would have heard nocturnal scrambling and wind churning through the treetops.

Reading and writing were Hall's hobbies, solitary pursuits pursued in privacy and indoors. Lately the only time he had been out at night, apart from walking home from work or the pub, was to attend the protest camp against the West Coast

Ring Road. But even then, camping in the Tarkine, the night was never silent. People sat around the fire singing or moved around the camp, making placards and plans.

High inside the Walls of Jerusalem National Park, or on Lake St Clair's pebbly beach, Hall had listened to the night. Hiking alone in the wilderness had been his tonic after Laura left. Often he had not built a fire, just sat in his sleeping bag in the doorway of his tent and listened to the nocturnal sounds of an ancient yet young wilderness. Up there in subfreezing temperatures and unpredictable weather patterns, the remoteness of the campsite reduced a man's loneliness. Waking up in the Upper Florentine Valley was infinitely better than waking up after a night at the Gunners Arms Hotel.

Listening to the hush of old-growth forests breathing or the ocean heave was similarly soothing. Sarah stared out to sea, her hands twitching the squid jig automatically. Calmness replaced the worried concentration so often present in her expression. Her hair had fallen loose from its ponytail and brushed each cheek. If he touched it, he knew, it would feel creamy in its softness.

'What are you thinking about?' Hall said.

'Murderers and horror movies. In horror movies, you only stay alive so long as you preserve your virginity.'

'If the last thing I do is make love to you before I die, I'll die a happy man.'

'You're full of shit, Flynn.'

He could see her smiling through the darkness.

They cooked the calamari on the electric barbecues in the park. It would leave too much mess, they agreed, to build a fire on the beach. Sarah cut the squid into rings and rolled each piece in flour, salt, and pepper. She didn't cook them for long, just enough to brown them. They ate them sitting on a blanket Sarah had arranged on the mossy grass growing between the ocean rocks and the scrub. Hall could easily get used to this. It had been hours since he thought of work and his empty house in Launceston.

When he remembered the evening later, he was surprised at how easily everything happened. Her body was softer than it looked in her bathing suit, the strong muscles on her arms yielding to the pressure of his fingertips. She closed her eyes every time he kissed her.

They did it in the missionary position, his shirt a pillow beneath her head. It was different from the first time in the guesthouse. Sober, his senses were heightened; he could hear the soft sound of her hair slithering across the blanket, he could smell salt water on her skin. Not since Laura had he made love sober, and it was like swimming naked; illicit yet pure. With each breath the ocean became an inaudible whisper and the stars dimmed behind the creeping sea mist.

Afterward, lying beside her, looking up into the starless sky, Hall sang. She knew the song – it was a Cold Chisel love song.

Sarah sang the next line. They laughed and started singing the chorus, forgetting the killer lurking somewhere on the land behind them.

Hall woke early and planned to walk along the beach to clear his head. Jane had other ideas for him. She was in the yard, moving a huge pile of chopped wood and stacking it under the Nissen hut's veranda. Hall did not mind helping. He whistled as he worked. His phone beeped three times, but he ignored it. It wasn't even eight o'clock.

'You don't want to answer that in front of me?' Jane said.

'It's not that,' Hall said. It was too early to allow Elizabeth to ruin his day.

Jane watched him, chewing her lip. 'Gary's your suspect, isn't he? The one helping police with inquiries.'

Hall shrugged. 'You know you never mentioned he lived near Goulds Country.'

'You never asked.' Jane shook a huntsman spider off a piece of wood and crushed it with her boot.

He watched her split another log with the axe. Why would she let everyone think Gary was in jail, or traveling overseas, or living with a girlfriend on the mainland, when in fact he was living no more than a couple of hours' drive away? Goulds Country was practically a ghost town, in dense bushland more than one hundred kilometers inland from the coast. Hall had accidentally-on-purpose driven up the unsealed logging road that led to Goulds Country with Sarah on the way home from their pub lunch. What had she said that day? The wilderness around Goulds Country was where someone would go who didn't want to be found.

'Did he do it?' Hall said as Jane stacked wood onto his arms.

'Don't ask me.'

It was her standard response. There were many things about Jane that Hall was curious to have explained. She didn't respond well to personal questions. He carried the wood to the stack, wondering what had made Gary Taylor move to Goulds Country. And what had made him come back?

'If you don't mind me saying so, people are going to think it strange, him turning up now,' Hall said.

'Gary is many things, but he's not a murderer.'

Hall could see Jane was firmly convinced of this. 'Fine. But you understand that's what people will say.'

Jane used her index finger to give the finger to an imaginary audience.

'You know that's the wrong finger.' Hall raised his middle finger and showed her the right way to give the finger. 'You're supposed to do it like this.'

'Says who?' Jane practiced giving the finger using Hall's technique. 'Doesn't feel right.'

'You're old school.' Hall laughed.

The six o'clock news ran Sam's letter in a bottle story straight after the weather. There was no television at the guesthouse, so Hall did not see it. Pamela did. They had recorded it on the Shelleys' front deck, and Simone had been done up to the nines, Pamela told Hall when he entered the shop to buy a coffee. The *Voice* was spread across the counter. With the tips of her French-manicured fingers Pamela tapped the newsprint photo of Sam on the rocks. It was a rotten coincidence. After holding Hall's story for over a week, Elizabeth finally decided to run it – the day after Apple Isle TV broadcast their own version of the story.

'*I* know how your deadlines work, but other people won't,' Pamela said. 'It looks like they had the idea first.'

Hall left the shop without buying anything. He was furious. Damn that Simone, and damn this stupid job. He damned himself for caring. Christ, it was a warm fuzzy, not worth getting angry about. But he was; anger twisted through his gut and he cursed Simone, and Apple Isle TV news, and Pamela for knowing that it would upset him. As the speedometer on his Holden reached fifty, he didn't ease the pressure on the accelerator. The wheels jarred over the corrugations and he took it up to sixty, then seventy. Only when the stick reached eighty-five and the expanse of ocean beyond the shoulder of the hill moved too fast for him to see it properly did he ease his foot back.

Four beers into the evening and Hall still hadn't filed the copy he needed to. He leaned back on his chair to view the fishing boats anchoring for the night. Three shacks stood between him and Sarah. Three Fibro, weatherboard, and tin dwellings and a couple of acres of saltbush. You could walk it in less than ten minutes. And then what? Stand outside in the dark peering in at the lantern-lit shack and the family sitting around the table playing Scrabble and sipping cups of tea? One of the Good Samaritans around here would report him for sure. Anyway, Sarah had probably gone to bed. She had told him she wanted an early night. They had plans to meet at the boat ramp just before dawn. That was hours away.

Pressed against the neck of his stubby, his lips curled into a wry smile. Take it easy, mate. You're getting soft in your old age. Images flickered through his mind: the shadows beneath each ribcage bone, the stretch marks like creamy spider webs on her breasts. In the darkness she was friendlier to him than she was in the daytime. Outside the shop the other day she had stiffened when he tried to hold her hand. She even pretended to search for something in her pocket. By the beach last night it was she who moved his hands across her body, madly, as though his touch was the only thing that she had ever wanted. She liked him, and the knowledge undid his doubts.

The computer screen turned to black and he rapped the keyboard. For the best part of the last hour he had labored over a boring story. It was a complex dispute between two shack owners concerning an illegal addition. His best quotes were possibly defamatory and he had spent too long trying to tweak it into something publishable. Earlier in the evening he had filed a story on the property glut which had taken just ten minutes to knock up. He was fast when he had the right material. Now that was a decent story. Real estate agents with windows full of coastal property and no buyers, land going cheaper than it had for a decade. No one wanted to buy in an area where a serial killer was at large. Surely that would feed the beast for today. He switched the computer off.

Jane was drinking on the patio as she did every night. She poured him a generous measure of gin, ignoring his halfhearted refusal. An hour later Hall felt calmer. He smoked Jane's cigarettes as she remembered better times. Jane talked about the days when politicians were motivated by a desire to represent the people who elected them. Hall was agreeable. It was unusually warm, even for January, and the midges weren't biting.

'Well I'll be,' Jane said when they realized they had attended the same tiny primary school in Buckland, at different times, of course.

It was unlikely their families were friends. Jane's father was a logger; Hall's parents organized logging protests from their self-sufficient farm.

'I didn't pick you for a greenie,' Jane said. 'Although you've got the right car for it.'

'Should I be insulted by that?'

'I always think it strange that greenies drive old cars which are more polluting than newer models.'

'What I find hard to understand are people who don't look past their next paycheck. You can't replace the old growth.'

'Where do you want to get your newspaper pages from? Brazil? You reckon they practice sustainable logging?'

'Logging here is not the answer.'

'It's easy to criticize people who can't wait for payday when your own lifestyle is secure. I bet you had lots of meat on the farm. Sausages and mince, that's all my mother could manage.'

'Let's agree to disagree.'

One of the dogs howled at something moving in the bushes.

'Diesel. Been jumpy since that fat penguin attacked him.'

Hall laughed. Don Gunn did resemble a well-fed penguin. 'You're not worried someone's skulking around here?'

'Wouldn't be the first time. I caught Simone Shelley's son over here more than once this summer. Last time he climbed up on the tank stand and was looking through the bathroom window at one of my guests.'

Hall sucked his cigarette the wrong way and wheezed. His mind churned through unclear thoughts. Why had she not mentioned this before? Sam Shelley. Hall hadn't considered him as a suspect. Had Hall been blindsided by the attention his story about the bikini top turning up had brought? No. That wasn't it. A seventeen-year-old boy with no friends who wanted to look at women in states of undress; it might not be socially acceptable, but it didn't make him a murderer.

Jane was watching him. 'Was before Anja got here.'

'What did you do?'

'Let the dog off. He won't do it again.'

Jane's laughter rattled from her body. This was not the first time Hall had seen her sense of humor accessed by tales of boyhood foolishness. Maybe she would have been less sour if she had raised a child.

'You would have been a good mum,' he said without thinking.

Jane tried to pour herself another drink but the bottle was empty. She lit a cigarette and sniffed. 'Story of my fucking life.'

In hindsight, Hall should have said good night then. Instead he found himself talking about the novel he wrote after Laura left. He had typed until his eyes were bloodshot every night for three weeks straight. Nearly two hundred pages about a sheep farmer whose wife slept with his best friend, a contract shearer. In the end, the farmer ran over the shearer with his tractor.

'It's fiction. I never tried to kill Dan.' Hall caught himself slurring; he was drunker than he had realized. He tried to remember what he'd had for dinner but nothing came to mind. Nauseated from the cigarettes, Hall went inside for a glass of water. When he returned, Jane was sliding her flip-flops on.

'Better call it quits,' she said. 'Got work to do tomorrow.'

He only meant to press his lips briefly to her ruddy cheek. As he leaned forward, Jane turned and their lips pressed together. Two seconds was all it took; her tongue felt furry in his mouth. His snorted laughter surprised them both.

'For God's sake!'

It was unclear who she was admonishing. The bottle and glasses clashed as she scooped them up and the screen door slammed behind her.

Half-drunk, half-stunned, Hall listened to his phone messages, his pen tapping on a fresh page in his notebook.

Elizabeth had called at ten p.m. Working late. Her message effectively put to bed a series of terse e-mails she had sent. It wasn't that she didn't like the property glut story, Elizabeth said; she was just hoping for more blood and guts, wanted him to come down hard on the police and their ineffectual effort to date. Get investigative, she suggested. He knew what she wanted, something gritty enough for the subs to slap a sensational headline across the front page. The message ended with Elizabeth's needling voice saying, 'This is your chance.'

For Christ's sake, did she want him to make something up?

At dawn Hall met Sarah and they walked around the top of the headland and down an overgrown beach track to Eddystone Cove. From where Hall stood beside Sarah on a flat rock he could see no shacks, no dirt roads, nothing but pristine sand and water. Hall watched Sarah slide bait onto her hook and then did his own, attempting to copy her deftness. The ocean surface swirled in response to a deep current. Cold air and his relief at having slipped away from the guesthouse without seeing Jane tempered Hall's hangover.

On the beach a dog dodged the white water. It must have escaped its owner. The distant snap of the dog's bark was the only sound in the quiet dawn.

Fishing in silence, Hall envied Sarah's ability to focus. Elizabeth and Jane had kept him awake well into the night.

Hall's line pulled. Was that a bite? Peering past the kelp into the deceptively tropical water, he looked for the end of his line. Imitating Sarah's smooth technique, he wound the line in. Something bounced out of the water and he furiously spun the reel.

'Got one!'

He swung the rod around and the fish flapped on the rock. It was ugly with brown blotches and big red eyes.

'I got one!' Hall shouted again.

He squatted beside his fish. It was swelling up, its mouth opening and closing with a strange sucking noise. Sarah clambered down the rocks to look.

'Chuck it back, mate.'

'You can't tell me that's too small.'

'It's a toadfish.'

'What's wrong with a toadfish?' Hall pulled the line toward him and the fish flipped a meter in the air.

'Poisonous.'

Hall was surprised by how disappointed he felt. 'I could take it back for the dogs.'

'If you want to kill the dogs. We can't even use that one for bait. Careful. He bites. Those little teeth can bite through fishhooks and bones.'

Hall held the toadfish while Sarah slipped the hook out of its mouth. She flipped it with the toe of her sneaker into the sea. It floated on the surface as though it were dead before disappearing into the shadowy water.

'Don't chew your fingernails or you'll get sick,' she added.

If Hall ever went to a fishing trivia night, he would want Sarah on his team. In the fortnight since he had met her, she had taught him more fishing secrets than he reckoned the *Voice*'s fishing editor knew. One of her tricks was to scatter diced steak into the water. When she did this, the surface erupted with tailor, pretty fish with blue-green backs and forked tails. She explained the secret was to scatter only tiny pieces of steak so you weren't feeding the fish, just tempting their taste buds. Sometimes she used cuttlefish or squid. Tailor were greedy; in a feeding frenzy they regurgitated so they could eat more.

Hall had not yet caught a fish he could keep, but if he did, he knew what to do. She had shown him how to hold a fish against the rock and cut under its throat in two decisive movements, letting it bleed before putting it in the bucket.

The sun was a dizzyingly bright ball above the horizon when they finished. Sarah had caught six tailor, which Hall carried back to the beach in the bucket. Up near the high-tide line a person wandered, stooping to pick up long fringes of seaweed which were shoved into a garbage bag. It was Jane. Hall recognized the skinny white legs and uncombed gray hair poking out of her black cap. He hesitated; there was no way to leave the beach without her seeing him. Unencumbered by the heavy bucket, Sarah was striding up the beach toward Jane. She was too far away to hear his weak call to stop. He repeated her name but she didn't hear. Any louder and Jane would hear his panic. By the time he caught up to them, Sarah and Jane were side by side, watching the dog.

'How are you, Hall?' Jane didn't look at him.

'Good. Tired. Got a lot of work to do today, you know how it is.'

'I wouldn't actually.'

Jane whistled with two fingers in her mouth. The dog didn't respond. She wiped the saliva on her shorts and shook her head. Hall squinted down the beach. The dog had something in its mouth. Driftwood or possibly one of the dead fairy penguins that had washed in with the storm. The dog tossed the thing up and pounced with his front paws, barking. He leaned down and rolled his toy on the sand. He looked like a black dingo, his hind legs straight and his tail beating the air.

Sarah handed her rod to Jane. 'I'll get him.'

'I'll go,' said Jane, but Sarah was already jogging down the beach.

Uncertain of what else to do, they followed her. Jane swallowed and exhaled; the sounds uncomfortably human on the empty beach. She wasn't going to pretend that nothing had happened. Damn it. She wasn't that type of woman.

'I enjoyed talking to you last night,' she rasped. She must have smoked almost a packet of Holidays as they sat on her patio. 'I don't get much chance for conversation with an intelligent man.'

'I was pretty fuzzy when I woke up this morning. Can't remember much. Sorry if I was out of line.'

'Cut it out.' Her lips were slack, her eyes hidden behind her black Ray-Bans. 'I misread the situation. All that gin didn't help. Sorry.'

'Jane . . .'

'Don't.' She stopped him with the palm of her hand. 'Something else I wanted to tell you. The other day you were asking why I didn't tell everyone where Gary was?'

'I shouldn't have asked. It's not my business, Jane.'

'Well, you did ask. So you can listen. There's no big mystery. It's simple. The man hated being married to me so much he had to go and live in a tin shed up the back of Goulds Country for fifteen years. No running water. Long drop – no septic tank. Gary doesn't even have a window to look out of. I didn't want everyone knowing.'

Hall felt for her. No wonder she was so bitter. All this time, knowing her estranged husband was a few hours' drive away. He didn't know who had it worse – Jane, so lonely in her empty guesthouse by the sea, or Gary, hiding in a humpy up in the sticks with only the other misfits and social rejects for company.

Down the beach, Sarah held the dog by the neck. She was waving. The wave went on and on. Jane dragged her garbage bag toward Sarah faster. Hall followed in the foul wake of decomposing seaweed.

Under Sarah's firm grip on its collar the dog jerked its head upward. A polished white bone was clenched between the dog's teeth.

'Help me get this out of his mouth.'

Around her the sand was ripped up from the dog's game. Half a dozen white bones lay where the tide had dumped them.

'It's just a bone,' Hall said.

'Are you an idiot? It's human.'

Stung by her unexpected vitriol, Hall gaped as Sarah whacked the dog on his snout. The animal ducked and ran backward in a circle, his jaw clamped on his prize. Jane kicked the bones into a pile and protected them with her garbage bag.

Feeling hopeless for just watching, Hall jumped on the dog

and wrestled it between his legs. Slippery with saliva, the bone was locked by the dog's jaw.

'Drop it.' Hall tugged at the bone.

'You'll break his teeth,' Jane shouted.

'Whack him on the nose, Hall,' Sarah said.

Hall let go, feeling foolish. The dog backed away, growling through clenched teeth at Hall, and sprinted up into the scrub at the back of the beach. Jane followed.

Sarah carried the bones up into the soft sand, away from the next high tide.

'What do we do now?' she said.

'I'll tell you what we'll do,' Hall said. 'Nothing. The person is dead. Another day won't hurt them. I will notify the police by close of business today. I promise.' This was front-page breaking news if he managed it properly.

'Jesus, Hall.'

Hall took a deep breath. 'If we ring the authorities now, it will be all over the evening news. I'm just proposing that we delay telling them by a few hours.' He held out the bucket of fish to Sarah. 'Please.'

She yanked it from his hand and he exhaled. 'I'm not hurting anyone,' he said as he picked up Jane's garbage bag of seaweed.

'Where are you going?'

'I have to make sure she doesn't tell anyone,' he yelled over his shoulder as he started running.

Hall wrote a draft of his story about the bones, ate lunch, wrote some questions for his next interview. He called the police at three p.m., too late for the prime-time evening television news to scoop his story. As he filed the story, after adding the standard police response, he decided that in fact he should call one of the radio stations. A radio interview would be a fantastic teaser for his story.

When he saw the police car speed past, he took his camera and walked down to the wharf. A crowd was gathering on the jetty. It was the best vantage point to watch the local police cordoning off the beach. Judging by the excited commentary, it was not fear or concern that motivated them to come out of their comfortable shacks and campsites but a macabre voyeurism.

'Human bones have washed up on the beach,' Pamela told him. 'That's the police there now. That could be our missing girl, Chloe Crawford.'

'I heard there were serrated cuts on the bones, like someone had had a go with a saw,' Bunghole said.

'Two words for you, Keith. Shark bite,' John said, and he shared a chuckle with Don.

'Jane Taylor's dog was playing with them. Isn't that disgusting?' Pamela said.

'Who said that?' Hall asked.

'Sarah told us,' Pamela said.

'I didn't say it like that.' Sarah acknowledged Hall with a nod and then returned her attention to the beach.

Hall walked to the end of the jetty and stood by himself. Roger Coker was crossing the dusty wharf. A hush replaced the chatter as he walked onto the jetty. Pamela and Don moved to avoid having to greet the man. Bunghole and his friends were talking about Roger in barely lowered voices.

'What the fuck is he doing here?' someone muttered.

Roger didn't hear. He grinned and asked what was happening.

There was a moment when it seemed no one was going to answer. Bunghole finally called out an answer.

'Bones, mate. What do you reckon about that?'

Roger kept smiling, his blue eyes scanning the crowd. He had his hands so deep in his pockets it gave his thin shoulders an awkward sloping posture. It looked like Roger was clenching and unclenching his fingers; the fabric of his trousers slid up and down his legs. Hall expected Sarah to assist Roger, to stand beside him at the least, but she was focused on the beach with her back to everyone. Hall stepped into the space between Roger and the crowd.

'Roger. How are you?' Hall asked.

'Very well, thank you. Very well indeed. I'm good, thanks. And how are you yourself?'

To halt Roger's nervous small talk, Hall explained about how he found the bones with Sarah. He outlined the story he had written for tomorrow's paper. With luck, Hall said, the police would be able to DNA and carbon test the bones and find some further information on the crimes.

Sam interjected, 'They'll be seal bones. Or whale.'

'Do you know how big whale bones are?' Pamela said. 'That's the stupidest thing I ever heard.'

'Stop it.' Simone's high pitch surprised everyone. 'His father was an oceanographer. Sam would know better than anyone what the bones are.'

Pamela rearranged her sunglasses on top of her head and made a face at Flip.

'Whatever.' Sam shook his long hair over his eyes. 'I'm going for a surf.'

'No!' Simone called as Sam pushed past the crowd on

the wharf. 'I don't want to be alone right now. No one should be.'

Simone followed Sam, and they finished their conversation near where Hall was standing.

'I feel so stressed and my heart is beating so fast it's like I'm about to have a heart attack,' Simone told her son.

'Okay, Mom.'

Hall felt sorry for the kid. Meanwhile, Bunghole moved closer to Roger. He was backed by a dozen men and women, some holding children. Bunghole had his hands on his hips, which were thrust forward, and his chin out, the typical stance of a short man who wished he was taller. Hall contemplated saying something to calm people down; but then again, if they didn't let their tension out now, it would re-emerge later, perhaps when he wasn't there.

'Coker. You could go over and sign your confession now,' Bunghole said. 'Save yourself a trip into town.'

'Maybe you should,' Sarah told Bunghole without turning around.

'Why should I?' Bunghole shot back.

'Just leave Roger alone. Let the police sort this out.' Flip's voice shook.

Bunghole's brother-in-law piped up, 'Nothing criminal about our lot. None of us have a son in jail for holding up Chicken Feed.'

The campers laughed. Pamela and Don squirmed. Sarah had mentioned their son was in jail for a gambling-related problem; she hadn't said he had tried to rob a two-dollar shop. Hall pretended to cough.

'Donald. Don't just stand there,' Pamela said.

'What do you want me to do?' Don said.

'Nothing! Why would I want you to do something? You never do bloody anything.' Pamela turned to Bunghole and his wife. She spoke without her usual careful enunciation; she sounded like Jane. 'Everyone here, at some point, thought it was you,' Pamela said, pointing at Bunghole, then her finger scanned across John, Flip, Erica, Sarah, Simone, and Don. 'They said you killed that girl.'

'Don't blame us. You thought it too.' Flip turned on Pamela.

'No. No, I never did. I've always said it was Roger Coker or Gary Taylor.'

'Only Gary since he turned up three days ago,' Flip said. 'Before that you said Bung – Keith.'

'Gary Taylor didn't do it. I knew the man. Speed wouldn't.' Bunghole had to look up to yell at Pamela. 'Probably was your husband; I'd do something like that if I was married to you. Blaming a man who's not even here to defend himself!'

Darlene ushered two of her children to the back of the crowd.

'Well, where's Gary Taylor been these last fifteen years? A man doesn't disappear for no reason,' Pamela shouted back. 'Don't you shout at me, Keith.'

John had stepped away, slightly distancing himself from the discussion but watching with an odd smile. Simone clapped her hands. She was standing between the two groups and kept clapping, slowly and dramatically, for longer than was necessary to get everyone's attention. This was more entertaining than a logging protest.

'All right, Simone,' Flip said.

Simone clasped her hands. 'What are you doing? What are

you thinking? Blaming each other. It's counterproductive. I remember the days when we were all friends, sharing the catch of the day on the beach, popping into each other's homes or the lagoon campsite. What has happened to you people? Shame. Shame.'

Flip groaned. 'That never happened. You live in a dream.'

'Maybe I do. But it's better than being part of this.' Simone gestured broadly at everyone.

The police crew on the beach were forgotten as the people on the jetty glared at one another. Overhead, a lone seagull flapped hard in the windless sky.

'Call it a night, I think,' Hall said to no one in particular.

Bunghole and his group left the jetty. They climbed into their various cars and flatbed utilities and drove away. Simone dragged her son by the hand toward her Mercedes. She opened the passenger door and sat inside before handing him the keys.

'I don't think he did do it,' Roger said. 'Gary wasn't here either.'

'We'll probably never know, Roger,' John said.

They watched the police, who were preparing to leave.

'I'm not standing here any longer.' Sarah pushed past everyone. 'I can't bear it. You all just stand here gawking and you don't even know what is going on. I'm going over there to find out.'

'Hey, hey,' Erica said. 'Make way for Miss Marple.'

Eager for relief, Pamela, Don, Flip, and John laughed. Sarah stopped, her face bright red. Erica's fluty flight attendant voice carried across the gathering.

'Yep, forget forensic teams and the *Voice*'s special investigation; we have our own sleuth. She found the body, she visits the crime scene every day looking for clues, she patrols the bush tracks and has itemized the tip! People, if you could stop throwing rubbish in there each day, that would help Sarah the Sleuth because she has to keep going back to update her refuse inventory!'

Everyone was laughing now. Even Roger, although Hall suspected he didn't know what he was laughing at. Sarah hovered, her cheeks flushed with embarrassment. She looked like she was about to swear at Erica. Her fists bunched up. Just as Hall was about to intervene, she walked away so fast she was almost running, crossing the empty wharf turning circle, away from the beach.

She would feel more embarrassed if Hall chased her. Feeling sorry for her, he wandered along the jetty. The water lapped the soaked remains of the Tasmanian oaks holding up the jetty floor. He crouched and rubbed his hand against one of the time-smoothed stumps. Over his shoulder, the remaining people faded in the twilight. Framed by the old fishing shacks and boatsheds with their peeling painted timber and stacks of broken cray pots, the scene looked ominous. If this were a movie, he imagined, the murderer would be watching through a slit in one of those sheds, biding his time as he chose his next victim. Pamela would make a nice twist, he thought, and then censored himself. There was no need to be nasty.

Hall left the wharf and drove back up the hill to the guesthouse. Between the scrub and the side of the guesthouse, well hidden from view of the road, a bronze utility was parked. It had a trailer attached to the back which was full of firewood. Hall stalled. Everyone said Gary Taylor drove a bronze ute.

Hall could not see anyone in the garden, but he assumed Gary was in the alcove under the Nissen hut where Jane stored her firewood. Quite clearly this man was stealing his estranged wife's chopped firewood.

Hall had noticed Jane chopping logs for several hours each day. It wasn't easy work – especially for a fifty-something-year-old woman. Hall considered his options. He could confront Gary. Or he could look in the guesthouse and see if he could find Jane. That would be more sensible.

Hall stepped into the main living room and waited for his eyes to adjust to the different light. A man jumped off the couch, knocking a newspaper to the floor. He did not pick it up. Hall had never met Gary, but he recognized him right away. Confident and guarded, Gary moved like a man who knew how to rely on himself.

Gary sized Hall up then walked to the sink. The soles of his boots flapped as he crossed the linoleum floor. He filled a glass with water and drank the lot in one long gulp. Jane was right; Gary had lived hard. The back of his neck was sun-worn and his matted hair looked like it would break a comb.

'If you're looking for Jane,' Hall said, 'she's probably downstairs in her apartment.'

Gary leaned over the sink, slapping handfuls of water over his face with both hands. As he rubbed his face dry with a tea towel, Hall noticed tattoos wrapped around both of his biceps. His hands were huge. One set of salami-thick fingers were marked with letters, tattooed into his skin by an amateur artist. The technique reminded Hall of that used by people who inked themselves in jail. Hall wished Jane would come upstairs.

'Can I help you with anything?' Hall said.

The large man shook his head. He filled the kettle with water and lit the gas stove. Why did he need to boil water? Hall looked out the window to see if Jane was pegging washing on the Hills Hoist. There was no sign of anyone; even the dogs were quiet.

'I'm Hall Flynn, from the *Tasmanian Voice*.'

Gary cleared his throat. 'So who is the murderer?'

Hall stared. 'I don't know.'

That wasn't true, not entirely. He did have a theory about what had happened to the Swiss woman. It wouldn't hurt to tell Gary. Hall started to explain, but he couldn't remember the Swiss woman's name.

'Accidental death,' Hall said.

Gary looked hostile, unsmiling. 'There are no accidents.'

Hall needed to let Jane know that Gary was here. If anything happened, at least Hall would know that he had given her warning. He moved toward the internal staircase as Gary opened a tin labeled leaf tea and peered inside.

'Teabags.' He sounded disgusted.

'There's no leaf tea,' Hall said.

Gary thought this was very funny. His laugh was loud and tobacco-rusty. He took two cups out of the cupboard. 'She never buys leaf tea. Want a cuppa?'

Hall nodded, but he did not relax until they were seated at the table, drinking cups of tea. Silence, Hall knew, was a good way to get your companion to speak. It seemed Gary knew the tactic. Eventually, it was Hall who spoke first. He asked Gary what he planned to do with all that firewood. Hall didn't accuse Gary of stealing, not outright, but hopefully his disapproval was implied in his tone. It was the least he could do for Jane.

'Leave it where it lands,' Gary said. 'The old girl can stack it where she wants.'

Hall leaned back in his chair, slightly embarrassed. Gary wasn't stealing the wood, he was delivering it. And Hall was as susceptible to gossip as any of those well-meaning shack owners.

As Gary drained his cup, Hall could see the letters on his fingers. One single blurry letter occupied each space between the knuckle and finger joint, together spelling JANE.

Chapter 10

From the beach, Sarah saw Roger pottering in his yard. He was tying bailing twine around the gate that led to his beach track. Judging from how much of the strong orange string he was using, he didn't plan to use the gate for a while.

Roger nodded gravely when Sarah told him she had placed the call to the ranger concerning the abalone shells.

'Maybe they'll leave you alone now they have this to worry about.'

'They won't leave me alone. I can't stop them and they know that.'

Roger stopped winding the twine.

'When I was at school I used to catch the country bus that runs down from Anson's Bay. Doesn't run anymore. The other kids called me names, horrible names. That was when Grandma was in jail. They threw my shoes out the window and made me sit on the floor. You don't want to know what Mum was like when I came home without my shoes. Other things those kids did I wouldn't tell a nice lady like you.'

'Oh, man.'

'People say children are cruel. It's not children. It's people,' Roger said. 'It's people who teach children to be cruel.'

It was the most words he had ever spoken to her at one time.

After Roger finished speaking, she placed a hand on him. Her thumb touched the underside of his forearm. She could feel the bone through his soft downy skin. Her fingers slid up and down, grinding over his coarse arm hair. It must have been at least a minute before he removed his arm from her grasp.

John Avery knocked on the open guesthouse door as he entered. He greeted Hall and handed him the day's paper. The front-page headline was huge. *Bones Wash onto Beach: Possible Human Remains*. In case readers of the *Voice* didn't draw the connection, there were photos of Chloe Crawford and Anja Traugott.

'I thought you'd be pleased to see your story on the front page,' John said.

'I am. Thank you.' Hall scanned his story to check that it hadn't been changed too much. 'You know, you gave me a fright the other day.'

'When was that?'

'A few days ago now. You were on the patio.' Hall gestured out the window. 'You were busy with something under the tank stand.'

'What are you talking about?'

'I didn't know who it was. I'm embarrassed to admit, I was startled until I realized it was you.'

John shook his head. 'Wasn't me. You must be mistaken.'

'No. It was you. Pretty sure.' Hall smiled in a friendly, non-confrontational way, looking at the paper to avoid John's scowl.

'I said, it absolutely was not me who you saw.'

He was lying, Hall was certain. 'Well, I must be mistaken. Pays to check your facts in my industry, doesn't it?' Hall held out the newspaper. 'Do you want this back?'

'No. I bought it for you. I have another here.' John licked his thin lips. 'Apparently there might be something on abalone poaching.'

'Really? Tell Sarah not to hold her breath. The ranger needs to catch them red-handed to lay charges.'

'She won't like hearing that.'

'That's why you're telling her,' Hall said, and John laughed.

The men shook hands and John left. Hall sat on the couch. Inadvertently, he was too involved in this murder story. Here he was, sleeping with the daughter of someone who could be a suspect. If he had had to give advice to another journalist in this position, he would simply tell him to throw down his cards and ask to be reassigned.

Warm wind blowing low across the farmland toward the coast collected flecks of dirt that stuck to the sunscreen on Sarah's skin. In the dry heat her beach towel had turned into salty stubble.

'Can you smell smoke?' Erica called from the other end of the veranda.

Sarah didn't answer. She had not spoken to her sister since the scene on the jetty yesterday. She sniffed; something was burning. Assuming it was someone barbecuing lunch, Sarah closed her eyes.

It was Pamela who warned them. She was driving to every shack, alerting residents.

'Fire's burning at the tip,' Pamela shouted as she came across the lawn. 'Don't panic. It's contained. No need to evacuate.'

Sarah and Erica jumped off their deck chairs. A single plume of smoke spouted out of the bush behind the lagoon. It curled into the blue sky until gusts of high wind tossed it. Erica sprinted inside to get her camera.

Pamela's rings glinted in the sun as she listed on her fingers the preparations she had made for a major bushfire. 'I've had the yard mowed, and the park. We have proper chemical extinguishers, three of them. I have fire blankets, two water tanks almost full, and two and a half lengths of hose. I've done everything.'

'You're making me nervous,' Sarah said.

Orange dustballs moved in both directions along the long straight road beside the beach – more traffic than Sarah had ever seen on that stretch. It was the only route out of there, unless you had a boat. She walked around to the front of the shack. The wind was offshore. As long as it didn't change, the shacks were safe.

'Back in the car, darling. I'm coming,' Pamela shouted to Don, who was crossing the backyard. The grass was long enough to cover his shoes. It could do with a mow. In fact, nothing about the shack was fireproof. Gutters stuffed with bird's nests and debris, wooden boards brittle from the harsh east coast sun. One loose spark on the roof and the structure would incinerate like kindling.

'You said you would be quick.' Don smiled. 'Are you having a cup of tea?'

'I'm coming.' Pamela rolled her eyes for Sarah's benefit. 'How many times do I need to tell him something?'

After Pamela left, Sarah sat watching the smoke. Within half an hour the sky was mottled gray. A wallaby burst from the bushes and hopped across the back lawn. The animal paused, ears twitching at uneven angles as he assessed his options. His brown eyes met Sarah's for a moment before he hopped up the hill, crossed the road, and disappeared into the scrub. Sarah went to find the mower.

The fire had started in the tip trench, probably by a flame igniting beneath broken glass, in Hall's opinion. Capable men from the camping ground tidied the tip surrounds, shoving discarded mattresses, broken cane cray pots, and anything that could catch a spark in the ditch. They used planks of wood and a crowbar to slide the items into the flames, jumping back as soon as they had done so. The fire was so intense, Hall could not stand close to it for more than a few seconds. A couple of wrecked cars had already been shoved in – a sensible move to contain the fire.

Hall and Jane bucketed water onto the grassy ground surrounding the tip. Jane had given Hall a scarf to wear over his mouth and nose to keep the smoke out, but his eyes stung. Even though he was sixty meters away, Hall could feel the heat coming through the eucalyptus scrubland. It was getting louder, crackling and belching bursts of black smoke. The St Helens volunteer bushfire fighters had arrived and ordered the spectators to remain in a clearing farther up the road. What was going to be a filler with a picture on fire management had turned into a half-page story on a disaster waiting to happen.

Hall wasn't trying to eavesdrop. But Pamela and Don, standing at the back of their Range Rover, were whispering, and it caught his attention.

'If you're sure it was him, Pamela, you need to tell the police.'

'I don't know. They've had enough people spreading rumors.'

'It's not a rumor.'

'I just don't want to say something and cause a heap of trouble if I'm wrong.'

Don muttered something. Hall pretended to check the batteries in his camera. Without turning his head he could see Don, his hands either side of an open Esky containing wrapped sandwiches and bottled water. Wearing his SES volunteer uniform, Don was prepared for any level of emergency.

'It probably wasn't even Roger Coker.' Don lifted the Esky. 'Your eyes are terrible.'

'I had to pull over to let him pass. It was the Valiant, no mistake.'

'So tell the police that.'

'Okay.'

'He deserves what he gets.'

'Watch your back when you lift that – I've got enough to do without you putting your back out again.' Pamela wasn't whispering anymore. 'Maybe you're right. Firebugs incense me.'

Hall tried to make sense of their conversation. He walked toward the tip area, standing as close to the heat as he could bear, and peered through the smoke at the roof of one of the wrecks. It did look like Roger Coker's black Valiant. If that was the case, what was it doing here and, more important, where was Roger?

By eight p.m. Sarah and Don had driven Jane's Land Cruiser between the fire and Pamela's shop more than ten times. Jane reckoned her eyes weren't good enough to drive in the glaring twilight, and Sarah wasn't arguing. A plastic water tank was strapped to the Land Cruiser's trailer. Sarah and Don's job was to fill it with water from the shop's concrete tank and bring it back to the fire. Bunghole and the other men were pumping water with Bunghole's generator. The plan was to wet down the bush on all sides of the tip and contain the fire. High winds were forecast – southerly, too, which would blow it right through the shacks. Roger's would be hit first, and if the flames were dragged with the wind, every other shack up to the boat ramp would be next. The timber frames would not stand a chance. Embers wafted through the air like shooting stars. It would be pretty if it wasn't so dangerous.

Trouble was, the fire was growing balls. Each time Sarah floored the accelerator over the crest of the hill, one hand on the horn to warn pedestrians, the flames had risen higher in the eucalyptus canopy. The air felt hotter, a hot dryer blowing through her open window.

Riding in the truck bed, Don smacked his hand against the roof.

'Back it up another inch, girl!' he shouted, and she released the heavy clutch. Don rarely raised his voice, but all afternoon he had yelled instructions at everyone.

'Almost. Stop.' Don jumped down and ran around to attach the pipe. She suspected he was enjoying it as much as she was.

Sarah was guzzling water from a Mount Franklin bottle when Jane stuck her head through the open window.

'Coker's not home and he's not here,' Jane said.

'Right.'

'Well, where the hell is he?'

'Does it matter?'

'If this turns, his is the first place to cop it.'

'Did you go down there?'

'Someone had to, didn't they?'

What Jane didn't say, but Sarah knew, was that Pamela had not bothered driving down Roger's potholed sand trap of a driveway.

'As long as he's not home, I guess that's all that matters.' She hoped his cats would smell the danger and flee. 'Jane?'

The older woman turned.

'Keep it to yourself, won't you . . . that we don't know where he is.' Absence could be mistaken for guilt. They didn't need people jumping to conclusions. Jane's eyes flicked to Don at the back of the vehicle. She understood.

'Gotcha,' Jane said.

At sunset the entire sky turned red and the ocean took on a strange glow. Driving hard, Sarah felt wired, as alert as when she was belting her mountain bike over rough terrain. Every second counted, every decision had to be the right one. Things that kept a woman lying in endless darkness worrying were irrelevant.

Hall heard the burning car's fuel tank explode as he ran, carrying buckets of water, down the sandy tip road with Jane. It sounded like gunfire. Startled, Jane dropped her water bucket. Hall picked it up and gave her a quick one-armed hug. Inside the black fog, men shouted. It was fortunate Bunghole and his crew had had the foresight to shove the car into the trench. If it had exploded outside the trench, flying debris might have injured someone.

Bushfires could move quickly, Hall knew, from severe to catastrophic in minutes. There were rules for survival. In the event of a fire, residents should either remain to defend their property, if they were capable, or evacuate early before escape routes become hampered by smoke or flames. So far this fire had remained in the tip trench, and the wind had not picked up as predicted. There was still time to evacuate. Hall mentioned as much to Jane.

'Maybe that explains where Roger Coker is,' she said.

'Evacuated?'

'Well, he's not here. He's not at home.'

The St Helens firefighters were busy dragging their hoses and yelling to one another. Hall raced over to them. He identified the man in charge by his badge. Quietly, Hall explained his fear that one of the wrecked cars might not have been empty.

'I could be wrong,' Hall said.

'I hope to God you are,' the fire chief replied. 'The blokes said it was empty when they shoved it into the pit.'

'We haven't been able to locate the owner of that car,' Hall told him.

'We'll check it out.'

It was not safe to examine the vehicle immediately. Hall continued to water the ground, watching the firemen and the fire from the distance. Heat spiraling from the burning wreckage made it impossible to stand close enough to see even the vague outline of what might have been Roger's car.

Hall stared through the darkness, watching the firemen move around the tip trench. If there was a human body in that sizzling hole, the person would have to be identified with dental records or DNA. Hall was not a forensics expert, but he was pretty sure the cause of death would be impossible to ascertain. If a man had been stabbed with a fishing knife, or suffocated with a plastic bag, or strangled with a piece of wire, no one here would ever know for sure. A fire of this size did its job thoroughly.

The creepiest thing was the possibility that the perpetrator was lingering in the well-meaning crowd fanned out in the bush clearing. It never did any good to speculate on murder suspects without solid evidence. But Hall could not help it. As he filled his bucket with water, he searched the grim face of every man there.

No one was secretive, no one was behaving strangely. John Avery had barely acknowledged Hall each time they passed on the track, but he was always serious. Sam Shelley, in contrast, had given Hall a cheerful thumbs-up as he worked alongside his mother. Don, riding in the back of the Land Cruiser, seemed more aggressive than usual. So did Bunghole and his brother-in-law. But hard work required aggression. Maybe, as Pamela had suggested to her husband earlier, it was suspicious that Roger was not here.

Sarah pressed her foot down on the accelerator when she heard the explosion. She was coming up the crest of the hill, and she leaned forward to watch the road even more closely, conscious of Don in the back. She could not work out what had caused the explosion. There was a wrecked car at the tip, but it had been there forever, and she doubted there was any fuel in its tank. They dumped their load of water and returned to the shop for more. She risked a glance at the Coker cottage as she drove past. No light in the windows, nothing to suggest he was home. As soon as they had this fire under control, she would have a closer look. Maybe he was hiding under the tank stand again.

Returning with the water, she braked hard as the Land Cruiser reached the Coker cottage. Don, seated beside her, braced against the dashboard with both hands.

'What are you doing?' Don said.

'I'm worried about Roger.' She squinted into the darkness.

'For goodness' sake, girl. If he's murdered those women, he deserves what he gets.'

Don's patriarchal assurance gave her pause. 'You know he didn't murder Chloe.'

'No I don't,' Don said. 'He very well could have done.'

'But . . .'

'Stop carrying on. Put your foot down.'

There wasn't time to dwell on it. Sarah continued driving to the fire, ready to do another water run. But when they got there, people were using words such as 'contained' and 'under control' to describe the fire.

'Simmering like a pork chop,' Don said as he climbed out of the Land Cruiser. 'I deserve a beer.'

Sarah remained in the vehicle, her hands on the wheel, the engine running. Everyone was standing around the trench, towels covering their faces, patting one another on the back for their handiwork. She did not share their exuberance. She reversed swiftly, tapping the horn until she was back on the gravel road.

Everyone became jovial once the fire was dead. Bunghole and the blokes worked the hoses, tossing their empty cans into the drenched, simmering pits. Pamela and Flip arranged food on a table with the merry efficiency of cake stand volunteers at a school fair. The St Helens firefighters inspected the tip, their heavy boots crunching over the hot ground. Hall hung back, watching as the last orange embers puffed foul-smelling black smoke into the night. Hall looked up the road, waiting for Sarah to come flying down in Jane's Land Cruiser again. At least twenty slow minutes passed before the fire chief approached him.

'Nothing,' he said. 'There's no one in the car. The police will do a full search tomorrow.'

Bunghole was listening, and he joined the conversation without invitation. 'That's right. Me and the boys were first to get here and the Valiant was empty. We shoved it into the trench so the fire wouldn't spread.'

Men moved in the shadows behind Bunghole, their eyes catching the flickering light as they listened.

'The right thing to do,' the fire chief said.

Hall posed the St Helens firefighters in front of their bush fire engine. They grinned, the comfortable smiles of men who knew they had done a good job. Everyone liked firemen. A round of applause was given as Hall took the last shot.

The fire was out, the danger was gone, yet Hall did not feel calm. In some men Hall saw smugness, a self-righteousness that gave their satisfaction with extinguishing the fire a malicious undercurrent.

Jane's Land Cruiser romped up the road as the firemen were leaving. There was room for only one vehicle, and the Land Cruiser veered onto the rough edge. People had to jump aside as it approached the group. It was being driven much faster than was necessary. Hall could see Sarah's serious face inside the cabin, her hand hard on the horn. On her last trip Hall had heard John tell her they didn't need any more water and she had ignored him, grimly shaking her head as she drove off. This time Hall went to her.

'You can stop now,' he said. 'It's all over.'

She jumped out of the cabin and stretched, scanning the fire site with jerky twists of her head. Almost imperceptibly, her body was shaking. Hall's eyes stung with every blink, partly from the smoke, partly from fatigue. He wanted a shower.

'Nothing more we can do here tonight,' he said. 'Shall we head off?'

Her lip curled into a frown. Someone handed her a can of beer, which she drank from before answering.

'I might have a couple. I'm too psyched to sleep,' she said, and walked across the clearing to sit down on the trunk of a fallen tree.

All that remained of the fire were simmering shreds of paper-barks floating on the lagoon and the acrid smell of burned refuse. It had been a hard couple of hours. No one wanted to go home; they sat on the backs of cars, on tree stumps and Eskies, drinking and swapping stories. Sarah sat alone, not wanting to chat, trying to control her body's shaking. Waiting for Hall to come over, she drank two beers in twenty minutes. It did nothing to calm the taut exhilaration in her body.

She wanted to tell Hall about her night, about driving the Land Cruiser through that ridiculous smoke, about Don's deceptiveness, and most of all about her concern for Roger, who wasn't at home. Sarah had driven to the end of the road, lights on high beam, searching for Roger. She had even checked the wharf, rolling past the boatsheds, which were now scrubbed clean of the graffiti. She wanted to hear where Hall had been, who he had spoken to. Mostly she just wanted him to sit beside her. She sipped beer and watched him wander around with his notebook. Soot marred his face, and when he pointed up the hill at something, there were sweat patches under his arms. He looked exactly how she liked a man to look.

Erica stepped into her line of vision. Her denim jeans, artfully frayed, were almost clean. Her navy woolen sweater looked brand-new; nothing about her gave the impression that she had helped to put out a bushfire.

'What do you want?' Sarah asked.

'We're going home,' Erica said. 'Walk with us?'

'Hmmm. Let me think about that for a minute,' Sarah said sarcastically. 'Actually, I think I have better things to do than be a human punch line for your lame jokes.'

Erica looked sorry. But that was precisely Erica's problem: she never conceded that she was wrong. Not once had Sarah ever heard Erica admit that she had screwed up. Anger and fatigue were a dangerous mix, and Sarah reminded herself to be silent.

'Come on. You have to admit, it is kind of funny how hard you've been trying to solve this murder investigation,' Erica said. 'If I were doing that, you'd make fun of me, too.'

Sarah glared at her sister. 'But you wouldn't try to find out who killed anyone. That's what annoys me about you. You never try to do anything unless you know you'll be good at it. You can't handle failure.'

'You don't look like you're handling failure very well.'

'What are you talking about?' Sarah hadn't told anyone about her final mistake on the fish farm, if that was what Erica was referring to. Sarah had not even mentioned it to Hall. It would be too hard to explain her absence from the farm that night without going into the details of her fight with Jake.

'Well, obviously your relationship failed or you wouldn't be here,' Erica said.

'My relationship?' Sarah shook her head. 'You want to give me some relationship advice now?'

'No.' Erica took a step back. 'I'm your sister. I don't like seeing you so sad. I want to help you.'

'You want to help?' Sarah said. 'Then fuck off. That would be the most helpful thing you could do right now.'

Erica was stung. Sarah had never spoken so aggressively to her. Erica turned and crossed the clearing to where her parents were waiting. Whatever Erica said satisfied them; they glanced at Sarah, who pretended not to notice, and they moved into the night.

Hall looked around for some drinking water. Pamela noticed and fetched him a bottle. It was cool on his throat. He splashed some on his eyes. Discontent festered beneath the cheeriness of everyone who had helped extinguish the fire. Names were mentioned. Some of the men were not holding back with their theories.

From the other side of the crowd he heard Sarah point out

that if the fire had been deliberately lit, the pyromaniac was most likely sitting around drinking beers right now.

'He will have dirty hands,' she said, showing her own soot-covered hands.

No one liked hearing that. Hall overheard one of the men sprawled on Bunghole's flatbed call Sarah a know-it-all dyke. He was glad she was busy talking to Jane and, as far as he could tell, missed hearing it. He didn't want to leave her here. She was shivering – and it was not a cold night.

He would make sure she got home safely tonight. He planned to return here in the morning, and he suspected Sarah would like to accompany him. Especially if he mentioned his suspicions that this burned-out rubbish dump might be a crime scene.

In the center of the crowd, Bunghole was stabbing the air with his cigarette, telling a story in a loud voice. As Sarah watched, he tossed the cigarette butt onto the ground and stomped on it.

'Some people are slow learners,' Hall murmured in her ear.

She grinned. 'Where's your beer, Hall?'

'Not tonight. I'm shattered. Need sleep.'

She hid her disappointment. 'You haven't seen Roger around, have you?'

'I'm heading up the hill now. Why don't you come and we can stop in at his place?' he said.

It was tempting, but then what? Roger wasn't home, she already knew that. Hall would drop her off at the shack and she could sit there in the quiet kitchen and drink a glass of Dad's port by herself. No thanks. Not tonight.

It was only when Hall stood up that she realized how much she didn't want him to leave.

'I liked your bones story,' she said. 'Possible human remains? When will that be confirmed?'

'The *Voice* police editor is looking into it for me. I think there will be a piece in the paper tomorrow.'

'You're holding something back.'

'Whatever the story is, it will be broken in tomorrow's paper. You'll have to wait.' He smiled and kissed the top of her head. He looked tired, older than forty. 'Get some rest tonight, Sarah.'

Hall left Sarah straddling the tree trunk with the motley group of men and women from the campground. He didn't like leaving her there. Walking home, he went over his leads out of habit more than interest. The police arson specialist would arrive in the morning to confirm how the fire had started. The fire chief said a burning cigarette butt was a likely culprit. When Hall voiced his concerns, the chief explained that several unmanned rubbish tips caught fire each summer and it was unlikely to be a homicide. Hall didn't mention suicide. He hoped his suspicion was wrong.

Hall shoved his hands in his pockets as he walked. Smoke stung his eyes; his throat was taut. He should have tried harder to persuade Sarah to leave tonight, even if that meant having to drag her away from the drama. It was silly mentioning his suspicions about a potential crime scene at the site of the tip fire. She didn't need another thing to worry about. Her fascination with the murder case saddened him. Perhaps in the morning she would be more relaxed. If not, he would take her for a drive, maybe to the Scamander Raspberry Farm or even as far as the Elephant Pass pancake parlor.

Halfway up the hill he stopped in the middle of the road.

Gas lanterns were lit inside the Averys' shack. He could see John, Flip, and Erica sitting at the table. It was a cozy scene. Certainly an image at odds with Hall's growing suspicions. But it was important to keep an open mind as a journalist. Otherwise he might as well pack his bags and go back to Launceston.

Sarah had promised to meet Hall outside the shop in the morning. Checking her watch, she realized that was in eight hours. The man beside her started singing and slapping his leg. Some of the other men, including Don, joined in. With Hall gone, things felt off-kilter. Mum, Dad, and Erica had left a while ago. Sarah couldn't remember why she had wanted to stay. She should have gone with Hall. Too late now. She opened another can of beer, flicking off the top too fast so that liquid fizzed down her arm.

'It's a boy,' one of the women called out.

A few of them laughed, but Sarah didn't smile. Nursing her beer, she slipped away into the darkness. She could have finished the drink and then said goodbye, but someone would only tell her to have another one, and she was worried she would.

Swinging her torch, she made her way down the sandy road. A man's shape emerged from the bushes. Startled, Sarah lurched sideways. Then she saw the fluorescent vest. It was only Don. Must have been taking a leak.

'You going? I should too. But I think I'll have just one more,' he said.

'Okay.' Sarah didn't feel like chatting. 'Have a good one.'

She didn't want to pick a fight with Don. He was almost like family to her. But she needed to hear him explain his abruptness when she braked outside Roger's place. Either he knew something she didn't or he was being an idiot, in which case she would tell him so. That's what family friends were for.

'Is everything all right?' Don asked.

'I'm confused, Don. You saw Roger up at Douglas River the day Chloe disappeared. He told me. Buying fuel.'

'You believe him?' Don said.

Sarah began walking down the road, waving without looking back. She was too tired to have this conversation right now.

Don called after her. 'Yes, I saw Roger and Les Coker at the Douglas River service station.'

Sarah shone her torch on his face and he blocked the light with his hand. 'Why not say?' she said.

'What was there to say?'

'Come on, Don.'

'What purpose would it serve? Roger was never charged. There was never a body, so of course no one was charged. In any case, they could easily have driven there and back in a day, and it's not my responsibility to provide someone with an alibi.'

'No, I don't mean that. Why didn't you ever mention it? When Pamela was ranting on about Roger, why not say?'

'You make your bed, you lie on it.'

Sarah frowned. 'Is that right?'

She walked away.

On her way home Sarah skirted the campsite. The abalone shells were gone. Either the ranger had taken them or Bunghole had disposed of them.

In the morning Sarah woke before her watch alarm sounded. She dressed and walked down to the shop to wait for Hall.

As she stood in the shadows, listening to nests of baby currawongs awaken, she heard Don. Braced over the rubbish bin, Don vomited with doglike yelps. He still wore his fire-fighting hard hat. Sarah moved away, treading lightly on the gravel. She had no intention of holding a conversation with a pissed bloke right now.

A clang sounded as something hit the ground. He must have knocked one of the signs over. If that wasn't enough to wake Pamela, Don's slurred voice carried loudly. Despite her disappointment with him, Sarah smiled when she realized he was singing a beer ad jingle. Good for him. She had known him all her life and never seen him drunk.

'Ya gotta work, work. Working hard, hard.'

The side door opened.

'You're useless.' Pamela's voice was harsh in the soft dawn.

Don kept singing. 'Sweating in the sun—'

'What do you think you're doing?'

Sarah peered around the corner to see Pamela march over and grab her husband by the arm. Her hair was tied with a scrunchie. Without makeup her face was colorless.

'Working up a thirst. A man . . . a man needs a beer . . .'

Pamela and Don lurched toward the stairs. Don was a big man; it would be interesting to see how she planned to get him up the steps.

'A man needs a beer, now he's done his work.' His voice cracked as he sang.

Above the banksias lining the road to the point, Hall's red cap bobbed. He was minutes away. Pamela would be embarrassed if Hall saw her outside in her nightie, berating her drunken husband. Sarah contemplated stepping forward, helping Pamela get him inside. She peeped around the corner. Don leaned on the stair railing, pointing at Pamela as he sang.

''Cause every man deserves . . . a Boag's Draught.'

'You're going to get more than that in a minute, boy.'

'I need a smoke.'

'You don't smoke.'

'We're celebrating . . . hey, hey, the fire's out.'

Pamela followed him up the steps.

'Celebration's over.' The door slammed.

Hall's and Sarah's feet crunched on the light layer of ash covering the road up to the old tip. Bullet hole-riddled tin sheeting was all that remained of the *No Shooting* sign; the wording was burned away. As they closed in, the air, warm from the charred ground, left a smoky aftertaste at the back of Hall's throat. Beside the track, yellow banksias and delicate blue wildflowers were dusty, blending with the muted browns and greens of the bush floor.

The tip was a moonscape, an old-fashioned apocalypse. Fire had devoured the plastic bags of household waste in the rubbish trench. All that remained was the metal frame of a cast iron hospital-style bed, a melted 1960s fridge, and two partly burnt-out vehicles. Without speaking, they moved toward the sedan-shaped car. Up close Hall could smell the sickly stench of burnt rubber and melted plastics.

'It is Roger's,' Sarah said. 'My God.'

Hall followed Sarah toward it and then stopped before he got too close. He could hear his editor's voice repeating the words 'crime exclusive' and 'front-page spread.' On the ground around the car lay five or six empty beer cans, brittle from the heat.

It was Sarah who climbed down into the pit, balancing on a fridge carcass, and peered inside the dirty wreckage.

'Nothing,' she called, adding, 'It's still warm.'

'The boot,' Hall said.

The boot lid was warped and poking up at an unusual angle. Sarah stuck a stick into the gap and paused.

'Shouldn't we wait for the police?' she said.

'They'll be here soon . . . but not soon enough if Roger's still alive in the boot.'

'Good God. I hope he's not alive if he is in here.'

A metallic crunch echoed into the silent bush as Sarah wrenched the boot open. Hall felt sick in his guts. Crazy, fearsome thoughts pulsed through his mind. He wanted to get the hell out of there, wondered if she knew how gutless he was, and imagined Roger cramped in the boot in terror, yelling futilely as the car incinerated around him.

Despite himself, Hall looked inside. The boot was empty.

'What now?' Sarah's voice echoed up into the bare treetops.

'We need to report Roger missing. At this point, as far as the police are concerned, they've got a small bushfire to investigate, not a missing person. You do it.'

He found the local police station number in his phone and handed the mobile to her. While she placed the call, Hall inspected the car. It was destroyed. The leather seats were burned down to the springs and the glass shattered. The tires were melted into lumpy rubber mounds. One of the wheels was missing. On the ground beside the trench was a spider lug wrench, the old-fashioned crossbar sort that loosened tire bolts.

Hall couldn't think what else to do, so he took out his camera and started taking photos.

Bravado and common sense eluded her. As Sarah circled the rubbish trench and Roger's burned car, sounds magnified: wind whistled in the canopy, Hall's camera clicked. Roger was dead. Once again, someone had asked her for help and she had done nothing. She fell to her knees, trying to breathe.

Across the dump yard Hall called, 'Are you OK?'

She waved him away, pretending to look at something in the pit. She felt his hand on her shoulder and cringed. It was embarrassing and she ignored him.

Hall did not take the hint. Instead, he tried to hug her, pressing her face against his shirt. She could feel his crumpled chest hair through the cotton.

'I'm here for you,' he said.

She laughed and he mistook it for a sob. It was like the script of a bad movie.

'Listen,' Hall said. 'I've thought about this a lot. You need a fresh start. You're welcome to stay with me in Launceston while you find a job. I've got a spare room.'

His tone was too passionate. The laughter dissipated from her throat. 'No chance.'

Hall looked hurt.

'I'm not looking for a boyfriend. I don't want to get involved.'

'We are involved.'

'The first night we met I told you I wasn't after a relationship.'

'Come on.'

'You could do better than me.' Sarah stepped back from the intensity of his gaze.

'Don't feed me lines like that.'

'I'm not convinced one person should have to fulfill another person's every need.'

They stared into the trees. Glimpses of the lagoon were now visible through the singed bush. It was a crap thing to do, but she walked away. He didn't follow immediately. It wasn't until she was well onto the sandy track leading to the main road that he caught up.

Sarah was walking so quickly up the road Hall could barely keep up without running. Someone was coming down the road toward them. It was Sam, his arms pumping and shorts hanging low over his hips. Sarah would have kept walking, but Hall grabbed the edge of her T-shirt and made her stop. He wanted to talk to Sam, and he didn't want Sarah to end the morning like this. Surely she could wait five minutes.

'Did you watch the fire with your telescope?' Hall asked Sam. 'How did it look?'

'Couldn't see much.'

Hall tried to ignore Sarah, who was shielding her eyes and looking toward the Coker place. Involuntarily, Hall followed her gaze. He could just make out the green roof and the stretch of grass in the front yard. There was nothing moving in the garden, nor on the porch; nothing to suggest Roger was home.

'I suppose the telescope doesn't see that far,' Hall said, turned back to Sam.

'Want to bet? You can see inside cars coming down the straight.' Sam pointed at the distant road. 'See who's driving. I saw you two making out in the canoe on the lagoon a few days ago. Near the bridge. Bet you thought no one saw you.'

'You're creepy,' Sarah said, and Hall laughed.

'I'm not creepy. Coker, he's creepy.'

'Roger is a good man.'

'Mom reckons he was trying to peep at her.'

'I have to go.'

'Yesterday. He was on our road.'

'He was going to drop a line in.'

'He had no gear on him.'

'What time, Sam? Which way was he walking?'

'After lunch. Heading away from here. North. That's Mom, though.'

'Your mother is an idiot.'

'Sarah.'

Sarah pivoted on the gravel and jogged off up the road. Hall and Sam regarded each other.

'Alley cat,' Sam said.

'Watch yourself.' Hall flinched at the harshness in his own voice.

'Easy. Just saying she's got a temper. We both know about that.'

'What?'

'You're not the only one who's been for a ride in her canoe.' Sam nodded. 'Don't worry. It was before you got here.'

'What a thing to say.' Hall felt sick.

'Ask her.'

'I don't believe you.'

Hall didn't wait to hear anything else. He walked up to the

guesthouse, panting roughly, as though he had been punched in the guts.

Gravity pulled Sarah down the steep driveway faster than her legs could move her. By the time she got to Roger's gate, her blood was pumping so hard around her body it drowned out the sound of the ocean.

The front door was swinging open. Inside, the house smelled like cat urine and wet towels. A teapot was on the table, and the remains of a meal – toast crusts and soup. A bucket in the sink catching drips from a leaking tap was overflowing. She shouted Roger's name, running from the kitchen to a bedroom to the built-in front veranda. In the front room her legs became wobbly. Sunshine illuminated the closed floral curtains, and the room glowed yellow and rosy. It was too warm, and her vision reeled sideways, forcing her to slide down to sit on the doorstep between the two rooms. Where was he? She blamed herself. Why couldn't she get it right for once?

The heat of Roger's sunroom, the strange subtropical glow from the curtains, the adrenaline flooding her veins, and the lack of sleep and dizziness overwhelmed every sense. Vomit clogged her throat. Inside her head, Jake's mocking drawl was loud. Everything he said, all those things, the things that other people thought about her, shouting out her problems from the Pineapple Hotel front stairs. Foul-mouthed lesbian. Fuck like a man. Fugly bitch. Ball breaker. That's what they call you. Goldfish. You eat your young. Maybe that nickname suited her. Anyone weaker than her, somehow, she betrayed.

Chapter 11

A flock of birds dipped shadows across the road and disappeared over the hill. There was a faint taste of something foul in the air. Hall's eyes stung. Once the birds were gone, there was no other sign of life, no boat in the bay, no sound of a car or of distant children playing. No sound at all except the dull churn of wave and ocean wind.

He kicked the gravel with each step toward the guesthouse. In the paddock the two brown mares were running, circling the electric fence perimeters of their enclosure. Dirt beat from the earth under their hooves. They went round and round, their manes tossing from the exertion. They shook their heads and whinnied. The sound was lost in the ocean's white noise, and the horses' performance was an unnatural mime.

Hall stopped at the guesthouse long enough to pick up his car keys and a bottle of water. The laptop on his bedside table looked ominously shut. He had not filed sufficient copy for days, but his thoughts were too scattered for him to care. As he passed through the kitchen, he noticed that the stack of board games, usually piled neatly on the bookshelf, had been rearranged. Scrabble was on top, precariously positioned so it looked as if it might slide off onto the floor. Hall marched over to straighten it. The cardboard lid had not been fitted properly. He took the lid off and was about to refit it when he noticed inside, on top of the board and the plastic racks for the letters, a piece of paper that had been used to record a score. Two columns of numbers, two sets of initials. It had been a close game. JA had beat JT by only four points. Hall crumpled the paper into a tight ball and tossed it in the bin.

Hall drove by the boat ramp and over a stagnant creek, barely seeing the road as he tried to sort his thoughts. Some were factual and easy to process: Pamela had seen Roger driving up to the tip yesterday afternoon; Sam had seen Roger walking past their shack, toward the unprotected northern beaches, around the same time and without fishing gear or a car. From what Sarah had said, this was a man who rarely left his cottage. And somewhere beyond these blustery empty beaches, where no one fished or camped or swam, Roger Coker's father had committed suicide. The man had put a gun to his head. Not just any gun; when John Avery confirmed the story, he had described a twelve-gauge duck-hunting shotgun. Those things didn't shoot one bullet. They fired a cluster of pellets. The idea of a man doing that to himself made Hall feel physically sick.

Hall's other thoughts didn't make as much sense. He went over everything Sarah had said to him, and he to her, trying to work out where it went wrong. But it hadn't gone wrong, had it? If she was fooling around with that kid before he even got here, there hadn't been a chance. Sam was full of shit. Trying to impress him and being gravely mistaken. But what if he was telling the truth? Stuff like that did happen. No wonder she was so aloof. Quite simply, she was not who he thought she was. He didn't judge her for that; who was he to say who someone could and could not have sex with? Hall had had his fair share of regrettable nights. It was his own naïveté that was making him slam the gears of his car and drive so fast that gravel sprayed up on his car's paintwork. Years of trusting his gut instinct had served him well; how could he have missed this?

And the Scrabble score sheet. What on earth had possessed him to pick up that piece of paper? If John Avery and Jane Taylor were having an affair, Hall did not want to know about it. It all made sense, though – John's sneaky appearances around the guesthouse, Jane's cagey references to her so-called private life. He felt sorry for Flip, too. With an empathy that surprised him, he felt sorrier for Jane. The couple of times Hall had seen Jane and John together, the professor had barely acknowledged her. That was cruel.

He forced himself to focus on Roger. The man had been missing, in effect, for seventeen hours. It was not a story. Suicides and suicide attempts were not reported. If a man threw himself into the gorge beneath the disused Duck Reach power station, you reported that a businessman was missing and his car had been found parked on Duck Reach Road. If a well-known person was found dead in his home, it took no more than three paragraphs to inform readers. No need to elaborate, and you never printed how he did it in case copycats took inspiration. The unwritten rule on suicide reporting was about the only time the media formed a united ethical front.

Past the last fisherman's cottage the gravel narrowed and then petered out. Rain had churned sand channels in the road. Farther along a closed gate blocked his path. Hanging on the gate was a sign that read *Trespassers Prosecuted*. Sarah had reckoned that the farmer hung it to keep the tourists out. The gate wasn't locked, and he let himself through. As the car bumped over the tussocks on the track to the exposed northern beaches, Hall checked his mirrors. There was no sign of any farmer. If it was true about the destroyed middens, the farmer might become trigger-happy if he spied a journalist on his land. He looked in the rearview mirror again. The sky above the bald paddocks was tinged with an indefinable redness, almost as translucent as smoke.

Hall's phone rang as he negotiated his way across the final barbed wire fence between him and the beach. His slacks caught, tearing on the wire, as he pulled his phone out. Elizabeth. Damn it.

She wasn't happy.

'I'll have some stuff for you later today,' he promised.

'I loved yesterday's story about human bones washing up on the beach. But today we're reporting that they were actually seal bones, Hall.'

'Yeah. We probably should have been more upfront about the likelihood of the bones being animal,' Hall said.

'That's not what I'm saying at all. You could have dragged that one out a bit longer.'

Hall took a breath. He exhaled. 'What, and give Apple Isle TV the chance to clear it up for us?'

Today's story on the bones, which combined Hall's reporting with the police editor's confirmation that the bones were seal bones, had made page five. When they were possible human remains, the story had been a front-page screamer.

To move the conversation along, Hall described the fire and the photos he had taken of Roger's burned-out car. Elizabeth, agitated, cut him off.

'The devil guy? What was his car doing there?'

'Not sure yet.'

'He lit it.'

'Don't know.'

'Well, what have you got? Did anyone die? Anyone injured? Otherwise it's just another bushfire.'

The fire alone didn't have legs; he didn't need Elizabeth to tell him that.

'I've got a few warm fuzzies you'll like,' he said.

He had shot the rural fire crew eating pies donated by Pamela, and the grinning blackened faces of a couple of local blokes who had strapped a ten-gallon drum of water to their truck to fight the flames. Feelgood stories about community spirit and everyone rallying together were the lifeblood of a regional tabloid like the *Voice*. Grisly headlines, rate increases, election results, and political scandals had their place, but it was names and faces that people wanted to see in their newspaper. The stories coming out of even such a minor rubbish fire were perfect warm fuzzies.

They weren't having the desired effect on Elizabeth.

'Warm fuzzies, that's cute. You should write down expressions like that. Hang on a sec . . .' Elizabeth's voice became muffled as she spoke to someone in the newsroom. 'It's what

I thought,' Elizabeth said. 'I've got nothing. I need a front page by lunchtime.'

It was a slow news day and she was panicking. Her anxiety and desperation were audible. Hall exhaled loudly enough for her to hear.

'Stop barking at me. Front page doesn't go to bed until six.' Elizabeth's problem was that she couldn't trust journalists and photographers to bring in the news.

Some days there wasn't any earth-shattering news. Those were the days when you gave your good space to the warm fuzzies. If Elizabeth would bother to spend a few hours on the street talking to her readers rather than breathing down the necks of journalists, she would learn that readers didn't want to read about doom and gloom every day.

'Don't tell me how to do my job, Hall.'

'What do you want me to do?'

Elizabeth was defensive. 'I can get any of the cadet reporters to fill my pages with human interest stories. You're a senior journalist and we need serious copy, Hall.'

Hall began to speak but she interrupted.

'Listen. You said the loner had his car firebombed. Sounds like he did it himself. Serial killer suspect starts fire. Police suspect destruction of evidence. There's your story.'

'Complete fabrication.'

'It's not. You said yourself he might have lit it.'

'I didn't say that, Elizabeth.'

'You didn't *not* say it, did you?'

She was a bitch. Hall told her he would get back to her and ended the call. It was people like Elizabeth who were responsible for the degradation of newspaper content. Yes, there was an art to finding an angle in an impossible story, but writing headlines before the journalist had the story was crap. Entertainment masquerading as journalism. He was half a kilometer down the beach before he remembered what he was supposed to be doing there.

Sarah was pretty good at predicting unusual weather patterns, but the dust storm took her by surprise. A foul westerly had been forecast; she did not know, however, that the farmer had plowed his turnip paddocks right before Christmas. Inside the shack, with a T-shirt covering her mouth and a snorkeling mask protecting her eyes and nose, she watched the murky sky as she built a card castle at the kitchen counter. Dust rushed up from the earth with each gust, billowing like dirty petticoats. Erica closed the windows and shoved towels along the base of the doors, but it was no good. Charcoal dust crept in. It coated the furniture and couches, blackened the pillows and duvet covers, settled on every surface, even in the cutlery drawer. Erica started cleaning and then stopped.

'This is driving me nuts,' Erica said.

'Wait until it's over.'

'No. Not the weather. You. You're sulking again. I'm sick of it.'

'Go away.'

'I won't. Mum told me to leave you alone, but I've had enough. What is wrong with you?'

'Nothing.'

Erica made an overly loud, exasperated sound. 'You're freaking weird about the murder. We all are upset by it, but no one else is riding their bike up in the spooky bush trying to get themselves killed, hanging around the crime scene, talking about it every night while they drink themselves stupid. And what is it with Roger Coker? You never cared about him before.'

Sarah nodded.

'But it's more than that.' Erica lowered her voice. 'Whenever you think no one is watching, you have the saddest expression on your face, like you're about to burst into tears any second.'

Sarah struggled to hold her composure. Leaning over the table, she cradled her head in her hands. She groaned quietly and the movement rocked the table. The card castle collapsed onto the floor.

'Oh dear. I wasn't trying to make you cry.'

'I'm not. Leave me alone, Erica.'

Outside the scrub rattled and the ocean seized in colicky fits. Under a hazy sky the world was in shadow. Erica dragged a chair over and sat next to Sarah, close enough that her bare knees pressed on Sarah's leg. Sarah didn't move away.

'I won't,' Erica said, draping an arm over Sarah's shoulders. 'No matter what you say or do, I won't leave you alone. I'm your sister and you're stuck with me.'

'Are you trying to make me feel better?' Sarah muttered.

Erica laughed. 'See, you're making a little joke already. Now talk to me.'

'All right.' Sarah's voice was barely audible as she listed everything that had happened in the past month. 'I punched my boyfriend in the face. I'm responsible for the loss of three thousand kilograms of prime barramundi. I told Anja Traugott to take a hike up to the rock pool even though I knew it was revolting and full of fish guts. I drink, it makes me feel like shit, and I drink more. And I've ruined whatever friendship I had with Hall. Do you want more?'

'Well,' Erica said. 'There are a few worrying items in that list. But a lot is not your fault.'

'Breaking Jake's nose?'

'Maybe he deserved it.'

'You're not supposed to say that,' Sarah said.

It was uncomfortable to verbalize what had happened but it was also a relief.

'I'm worried it will happen again,' Sarah mumbled.

'That you'll hurt someone?'

'Yeah.'

'Have you ever hit me? No. And I'm the most annoying person you'll ever have to put up with.'

'You're very wise, Erica.'

Erica smiled kindly. 'You won't do it again. You're a gentle, good person. I know you better than anyone.'

Sarah looked into Erica's eyes, feeling a familiar strangeness as she remembered that their eyes were the exact same color and shape. It was like looking into a mirror.

'I'm sorry I've been such a grump these holidays,' Sarah said.

'And I'm sorry for not being more sensitive.'

They laughed. Their glance conveyed an unspoken agreement on the oddness of their heartfelt talk. Despite feeling weird and emotional, the conversation was nice. Sarah bent down to pick the cards up off the floor.

'I still think you're annoying,' Sarah said.

'And I still think you're unhygienic and obsessive about fishing.'

'Good.'

Sarah finished collecting the cards and split the deck in two. She handed half to Erica and, without discussion, they each began laying out cards in formation for a fast-paced game which they had played since they were children.

Hall strode down the beach toward where he suspected Roger Coker had gone. The coast was wilder up here, low-lying rocks pounded by frothy, dirty swell. Bleached ryegrass and clumps of sharp cutting-grass grew next to the beach. The banksia and casuarina trees and ground-covering honeysuckle vines that grew around the other beaches were missing. Except for one giant gnarled gumtree, the farmer had cleared his land to the waterline. In front of Hall the northern sky was clear. Behind him, above the paddocks, the sky was dark.

There were no footprints in the gravelly sand, but that didn't mean anything. Hall hiked for nearly an hour before he saw someone in the distance. Sharp midday sun made it hard to tell if the figure was moving toward him, let alone if it was human. As he got closer, he saw Roger slumped on a rocky outcrop. For a horrible moment Hall thought he was already dead. Roger's hand moved. Sand stuck to his wet jeans, and one arm of his cotton shirt was torn. It was the first time Hall had seen Roger without a hat. His cropped hair was soft-looking, like a newborn bird's down.

'We're getting you home, mate.'

Roger was parched. He drank the water Hall handed him with thirsty gulps, his eyes dull like stagnant pools. After he drank, he smiled at Hall, the motion threatening to split the chapped skin of his lips.

'Last night was a dangerous night to be down here on the rocks . . . not much of a moon,' Hall began, but Roger wheezed deeply when he tried to answer.

Hall considered again the scenarios that had kept him awake last night. Did those louts from the camping ground rough Roger up and set his car on fire? Did Roger light the fire? And what was the lug wrench doing there? You didn't see that old style very often, and certainly not discarded on the ground at a rubbish tip.

Roger was dragging his feet in the sand. It wasn't clear what had happened, but asking a man why he had run away from home was like asking bereaved parents how they felt about their daughter being murdered.

It was a slow walk back. Hall held Roger's hand on his shoulder, taking the man's weight. They were the same age, but Roger's weather-stained hands and secondhand clothing made him seem decades older. It was getting harder and harder to breathe; the air was dry and dirty. It was gusty, too; in the distance black shadows bounced over the paddocks. Hall watched them for a while, blinking and rubbing his eyes, before realizing they were walking into a dust storm.

When they got back to the car, Roger sat down on the grass and took off his sneakers. He tipped the sand out of each shoe and turned them over, studying the soles. The air was thick with fine dirt. Hall covered his mouth and nostrils and told Roger to hurry up. He had seen colleagues gain a second wind on hiking expeditions, and the comedown from that deceptively exhilarating confidence could be more debilitating than the initial exhaustion. Roger tried to put his sneakers back on, but his feet wouldn't go in properly. Eventually he stood up, his heels hanging out the back of each shoe. The effort fatigued him. He gasped with each breath.

Steering the Holden across the paddock, Hall tried again.

'What were you doing up there, Roger?' Hall hoped he did not sound like he was fishing for a story. Fact was, a story was the last thing he cared about right now. 'I was worried.'

Roger didn't answer right away. 'Is that why you came looking for me? Thought I was shark bait?'

'I don't know.' The truth sounded melodramatic, like Hall was trying to be a hero.

'Anything left?'

'None of the shacks were burned. Your place is fine. The fire was out by midnight last night.'

Roger plucked at a frayed patch on the knee of his jeans with shaking fingers.

'Your car's gone,' Hall added. Roger didn't respond.

As they rolled back across the paddock, Roger slumped against the window. Hall turned the music off to let him sleep. They were back on the gravel road when Roger spoke again, startling Hall.

'They hate me. Those fishermen. Hate me.' Fatigue stripped his voice of any timbre. The man was wheezing. His body hunched around his neck, and he muttered about a range of disconnected things. Hall drove even more slowly, trying to isolate meaning in Roger's rambling monologue. 'One of their kids shot my tire out while I was getting rid of the rubbish. He thought I didn't see him. I saw him.'

'And then what happened?'

'I tried to change my tire. The nuts were too tight. And they were watching me. Yelling at me. My hands were shaking and I couldn't turn the nuts. When they threw the match into the rubbish trench, I bolted. I left my car there. I was scared.'

'Right.'

It made sense. Hall could imagine Roger's anxiety, taking his rubbish to the tip and running into a gang of campers. How frightening, to have your car tire blasted with a bullet. He could imagine Roger's terror as he crouched beside his car, bravely trying to turn stiff bolts with his wrench while Bunghole and his mates looked on, jeering, smoking, making threats. Up there at the tip, surrounded by silent unforgiving bush, the man would not have stood a chance against that mob mentality. At least they let him run away. But then what? They fought the fire alongside everyone else. They celebrated when it was extinguished. Was it too much of a leap to think that people capable of that could be inclined to cover up the murder of two young women?

'They say I killed those women. I didn't. I told the American lady I saw her boy. "Shut your mouth," she told me.'

'Do you mean Simone Shelley?'

Roger twisted his neck around and looked at Hall as though he were stupid. 'Yes. That's what I told you. She said, "Shut your mouth." And that is not a nice thing to say to someone.'

'Roger, where did you see her boy?'

'I saw him following that woman. The foreign one. She walked all the way up the beach and he did too, a long way behind her. Then he disappeared into the rocks above the rock pool. I was fishing off the rocks. I heard them yelling at each other, too. That is what I told her.'

The air was thick with dust and Hall switched on his headlights. The Holden was not airtight, and even with the windows and vents shut, black soot choked the cabin. The scene Roger had described was vivid in Hall's mind: the old fisherman watching the young man trailing the beautiful Swiss woman along an empty beach. Hall passed Roger's cottage and drove hard through the dust until they were on the other side of the national park. He took Roger to the St Helens hospital and left his own mobile number as the contact.

Returning to the Bay of Fires through the dirty smog, Hall wished he had stayed in town. A hotel on the high street had a vacancy sign out front. Instead, here he was, driving so slowly the dashboard chattered, sensitive to every gravel corrugation. Visibility was poor; he couldn't see the posts on the side of the road.

He was relieved when he finally turned into the Averys' backyard. He slammed the car door and ran toward the shack, kicking over one of the succulent pots in his blind hurry. Someone was holding the door open for him. They must have heard his car arrive, loud in the eerie silence. He ducked inside, his eyes watering, dirt clinging to the corners of his mouth.

'Are you insane going out in this weather?' Erica asked.

'I need to talk to Sarah,' he said.

For once Erica did not annoy him. She put on her earphones and disappeared into the bunkroom. Hall sat beside Sarah on the couch under the window. Outside, trees were dark smudges in the dust storm, the ocean shrouded in unnatural, unshifting fog. He could feel the tension in his neck, stiff and gnarled as tree roots. Rehearsing this conversation in the car, he had planned to start gently, to let her confess. If she didn't want to talk about it, fine. After all, it had happened before they met. Days before they had met. Four days. His words rushed out as if he were a jealous schoolboy.

'Sam Shelley said he had sex with you.'

'Is that what he said?' Her half-grin was furtive and hopeless, like that of the no-hopers lining the bench seat outside the Court of Petty Sessions. She already knew how this conversation was going to end.

'So it's true then?'

'I can explain.' Sarah crossed her arms. 'I have a problem . . .'

'I don't want to know.'

'A problem with alcohol.'

Hall clasped his hands while she described her lack of self-control after three or four beers, of waking up under a tree or on a park bench, of encounters with people whose names she did not know. These were stories he had heard before, from colleagues or mates. It was pathetic.

'That night with Sam. It was Christmas. I drank too much. I don't even know what happened.'

'Okay.' Hall tried to breathe slowly. His hands were clasped as if in prayer. He shoved them into his pockets. Conscious of Erica in the next room, he kept his voice low.

'Sam's saying . . . Well, he didn't say. He is implying that he had sex with you.'

'No.'

'So he's lying?'

'Just go . . .' She had her back to him so he could not be sure, but it sounded like she was crying. Anger rooted him to the spot.

'I feel sick,' he said.

She dismissed him with a wave of her hand. The mildness

of the gesture infuriated him and he forgot to lower his voice.

'He's boasting about it. He told me, "Don't think you're the only one to ride in her canoe."'

Girlish laughter came from the bunkroom. Sarah spun around, flushed with embarrassment or anger.

'Hall, it's none of your business.' For a fleeting moment, as they glared at each other, he experienced a surge of sexual desire for her. It did not last. 'Get out of here.'

The shack rattled as he strode toward the door. He opened it roughly, and the doorknob came off in his hand. Damn it, everything was going wrong.

'I'm really sorry. I shouldn't have said that. I'm in shock. And for what it is worth, I don't care. Okay? I don't care. I was just surprised, that's all.'

Hall placed the doorknob on the windowsill beside the door. Ashamed, he stepped out into the black afternoon. The sun gleamed like a fuzzy ball of light behind dark gauze. He didn't know if he could bear to see Sarah again.

'You did what with Sam Shelley?' Erica emerged from the bedroom while Hall thundered down the veranda.

'Shut up.'

'Slut!' Erica clapped her hands. Tears made stripes on the light dust that had settled on her face. It wasn't funny. 'I want details.'

'I don't know any.'

'Does his mother know?'

'Of course. I asked her permission first.'

'How drunk were you?'

'Paralytic.' Sarah didn't tell Erica about waking up in the dunes on a pillow of her own vomit. 'Really drunk.'

Sarah looked around the shack for something to do, a task to immerse herself in, but there was nothing. The storm was not abating, so there was no point in cleaning. Usually she enjoyed an argument. Not this one with Hall. It would be crazy to go outside while the air was thick as mosquito netting. Breathing would be like suffocating.

Hall knew. Who else would find out? She couldn't defend herself when she couldn't remember a thing that happened. She wrapped her arms around her stomach and rocked back and forth.

'What am I going to do?' Sarah murmured.

'You remember nothing?'

'Not a thing.'

'Hall will get over it. He cares about you.'

Erica leaned her face against the window, gazing toward the point and the Shelleys' holiday house.

'He's a slimy kid . . . he's always looking at my boobs.'

Hall was struggling to breathe normally when he knocked on the Shelleys' door. He took the wet cloth Simone handed him and wiped his eyes first, then his nose and mouth. The cloth blackened. She didn't comment on the strangeness of his being out in the dust storm.

'I'll get to the point, Simone,' Hall said. 'I think Sam knows something about Anja Traugott's demise.'

'First that revolting lunatic accosts me on the road. Now you accuse my son of murder.'

'I didn't, actually.' Hall controlled himself. 'You'd better let me come in.'

He followed Simone into her main room. She had covered her couches in sheets; everything else was coated in black dust. Sam was sitting on one of the couches.

'Sam saw her fall into the ocean.' Simone's words rushed at Hall. 'He didn't push her. He dived in after her but couldn't find her. It would have been impossible, with the depth and currents at the point.'

Stunned, Hall sank against the sheet-covered couch. Any uncertainty he had had about the verity of Roger's account of Sam's presence on the rocks when Anja disappeared vanished. He had almost hoped that Roger was deluded. Instead, all this time, Simone and Sam possessed information that could have alleviated everyone's fear.

'Why have you not told the police?'

'I only just found out. He just told me. He was scared. He's a kid, Hall. I've tried to do the best I could on my own—'

'Stop it. There's plenty of single mothers who have it tougher than you.' Hall needed to think. 'Sam. What were you doing up there?'

'I'm not a murderer.'

'Tell me what happened.'

'I got there. She was already there. She was climbing up the rock, one of the slippery ones, and she fell. Banged herself up over the rocks as she slipped down. Disappeared into the kelp.' Sam picked up a basketball and tossed it from one hand to the other.

'Continue,' Hall prompted.

'I dived in. Dived down deep, swam out, I couldn't find her. Waves were rolling, huge sets smashing the rocks. I was scared.'

'Why did she fall?'

'Maybe I frightened her. She got a shock and slipped.'

'You'll need to think of a better story than that, boss. That won't cut it with the cops.'

'I'm telling you the truth.' Sam's voice cracked.

'Why would he lie?' Simone put both her arms around Sam.

'Why did you keep this to yourself, Sam?'

'Who would believe me?'

Hall stared at the kid. The illogicality of Sam's and Simone's statements irritated him. 'That's not the point. No one is accusing you of murder. But you could have saved everyone the effort of looking for Anja's killer. Her parents . . . the grief they have endured . . .'

'I couldn't. They wouldn't believe me.'

'Why not?'

'Please, Hall,' Simone said.

'Why not?' Hall repeated.

Sam shrugged away his mother's embrace. He described how he had followed Anja to the beach and watched her sunbathe topless, more than once. On one of these occasions Don Gunn had caught him, and there had been a confrontation between the two men. Don had forced him to apologize to Anja. She had become angry and called him a pervert.

'She only made a big deal out of it because Don was there,' Sam said. 'The point is, she fell in. I didn't touch her. End of story. But if everyone knows I was there, and Don tells the police what he thinks he saw . . . Mom?'

'It was a horrible accident,' Simone said.

Hall eyed the youth. He wasn't a kid. He was taller than Hall, probably just as strong, no doubt fitter. Well-developed muscle rippled on his bare legs, arms, and neck. Brimming with testosterone. You couldn't blame him for being opportunistic. After all, nudity was not common on Tasmanian beaches. Hall was about to back off when an image of Sarah drunk, laughing, and letting Sam touch her smacked into his mind.

'Here's what I think, Sam,' Hall said. 'You followed Anja Traugott. To spy on her in the event she sunbathed topless. She realized you were there, got a fright, somehow fell into the sea. Manslaughter, if your lawyer is smart about it. But apparently you have a thing for looking through the guesthouse bathroom window, too. It's not going to be hard to prove you are morally reprehensible.'

Hall left then. He had reached his car when Sam jogged up the driveway. They faced each other in the afternoon's gritty shadow.

'You're stressing my mom.'

Hall didn't reply; he sat in the driver's seat and placed the key in the ignition. Sam held the door open.

'Get your hands off my car.'

'I shouldn't have said that thing about Sarah.'

'You probably shouldn't have.'

'What are you going to do? Are the cops going to turn up here?'

'Sam, I don't know. You're a good guy. Ring them yourself.'

'I can't.'

Hall tried to pull the door shut but Sam held on.

'Sarah wouldn't want anyone knowing about anything, would she? It's a close-knit community.' Dust stuck to Sam's face and hair; he looked like a fighter from the *Mad Max* movies. 'I remember the old days when everyone would share the catch of the day on the beach. Good times.'

'When women were safe to swim without being frightened into throwing themselves in the ocean, you mean?'

'She slipped. Nothing to do with me. You know it.'

For the fourth and, he hoped, the last time that day, Hall started his engine and drove into the dust storm. It was still thick, but perhaps it was settling. He turned toward the guest-house. Since he'd left the Averys', anger had ripped through him. For a brief interlude Sam's helpless stare and Simone's bewilderment had defused it.

He slammed the accelerator to the floor of the car. The tires clawed the gravel with a satisfying snarl as he sped up the middle of the road in conditions it was probably illegal to drive in.

Chapter 12

In the sanctuary of the guesthouse, Hall took two Heron headache tablets and watched the dust blow outside. It was morning, but through the window the coast was so dark, parts of it were unrecognizable. It was hard to imagine it would ever look normal again.

After a while Jane sat beside him, both of them comfortably quiet, sedated by the blackened world. For ages they did not speak, watching as the winds changed the patterns on the sky from corrugated lines to grand swirls to textured layers, as though it were a huge abstract canvas. Hall broke the silence.

'That's good you won't need any more firewood for a while,' he said.

Jane nodded. 'I suppose. Next thing I'll be in the slammer for accepting stolen goods.'

Hall smiled. 'You'll be okay.'

'Don't know why Gary's suddenly being friendly. Good luck to him.'

'Don't be like that. Maybe he wanted to see you. That's nice he brought the firewood.'

'And then he asked me for fifty bucks.'

'Did he?' Hall tried to contain his amusement, but it was hopeless.

He burst out laughing. After a moment, Jane joined in. Like two old mates, they laughed and laughed until Jane's laugh turned into a racking tobacco cough and Hall had to fetch her a glass of water.

Dust blew intermittently for most of the morning. It did not completely subside until mid-afternoon, coinciding with the turning of the high tide. By then every surface was covered by the turnip paddock's silky dust. It took Sarah and Erica three hours to clean the shack. Stools, cushions, armchairs, three different-sized tables, diving gear with rusting weight belts, and boxes of old magazines; everything went out on the back grass. Inside they wiped crevices with damp tea towels. Don helped them drag the heavy rugs outside. They slung them over the veranda railing and banged the dust out with a broomstick. Along the row of shacks, as birds cried out from their hiding places in the sooty scrub, everyone was doing the same.

As they shifted the mattress that served as the couch Sarah said, 'Don, I have to ask you.' At the same time Don said, 'I'm sorting out that matter we discussed the other night.'

They laughed uneasily.

'What worries me,' Sarah said, and she was pleased with the diplomacy in her tone, 'what worries me is that I had this crazy thought that you weren't honest about seeing Roger because there's something about him you don't like.'

'Not at all.' Don concentrated on arranging the dirty mattress against the railing, dragging it along a little bit, pushing it with his boot. 'It was as I said; it didn't seem important. But it's on the record now. I've spoken to the relevant people.'

'Good.'

Sarah was wiping down the outdoor furniture when Simone Shelley's green Mercedes stopped in front of the shack. It was Sam who climbed out. He ran over to her.

'You have to tell Hall I wasn't on the rocks with Anja. I was fishing with you. Tell him. Otherwise you're going to regret the day you lured me into your car,' Sam said.

Sarah didn't think twice. She grabbed Sam by the scruff of his neck and dragged him behind the fence so that Don and Erica could not see. Pinned against the wooden palings by his shoulders, Sam was stunned.

'Lured you into my car?' she said, her voice cold and low. 'Those are not your words. What kind of game are you and your mother playing, Sam?'

He didn't try to escape, so she loosened her grip. It took a lot of self-control. Her anger was like an unstoppable amphetamine rush.

'Listen, you little shit. Do not ever try to blackmail me. You don't know what you're dealing with.'

Energy from her rage fine-tuned her vision so that every detail of Sam's face was clear – the tiny burst capillaries on the whites of his eyes, crusts of white saliva in the corners of his mouth, and clear snot at the base of his nostrils. She clamped her fingers into a fist.

'Is this what you want?' She rocked her fist, back and forth, in front of Sam's face. 'You'd better tell me what's going on, Sam.'

Sam believed she was going to hit him. He was shaking. Sickened by herself, Sarah released his shoulders, and he collapsed onto his knees in the grass beside the fence.

'Mom told me to come here. I didn't mean for any of this to happen. She wasn't dead when I left her. Sarah, please help me.'

'Left who? Anja?'

'No. Anja drowned. I tried to find her. If anyone could have found her it was me. It wasn't my fault. Chloe was my friend. I would never willingly hurt her.'

Sarah could barely understand him, he was crying so hard. She reached out her hand to pat his head but pulled it back before she touched him. It was horrible watching a man cry. He had a cat scratch on his neck. It looked fresh, blood welling up beneath each prong, the skin around it swollen. She told Sam to go home, told him not to worry, that things would sort themselves out, but her words were uttered by rote, the kind of general thing you said to an upset person. After he left, she busied herself in the garden, pouring water over the dirt-caked succulents and geraniums, trying to compose herself. Her own temper frightened her. Had she scratched him? She examined her nails, but they were blunt and short.

When the shack was clean, all windows open to air it, the sisters rode with Don down to the guesthouse. Sarah's parents and Pamela were already there, helping Jane.

Hall's car was parked out front. Sarah recognized it before Erica did.

'There's Hall's car,' Erica said.

'I'll head somewhere else,' Sarah said. 'Enough people here.'

'No need to leave, Sarah. Everyone's here,' Don told her. 'Teamwork today. One in, all in.'

In the main room Jane and Pamela stood on a table, reaching up to unhook the decorative fishing net from the ceiling. Flip and Simone were on the ground, hands stretched out to take it. Each woman was smiling at Hall and his camera. They did not notice Sarah. Neither did Hall. He had his back to her. He looked at once familiar and devastatingly distant.

She left. As she walked down the ramp, she could hear Jane urging Hall to hurry. She couldn't hear Hall's response, only the women's laughter at whatever he said. Good chance that was the first photo ever taken of those four women together.

Even with excellent pictures, it was unlikely that Hall's dust storm cleanup story would run. Elizabeth wouldn't read past the first paragraph, unless she was reading it aloud to the newsroom for a joke. She had done that before with shoddy cadet reporters' copy. For this warm fuzzy to run, it would need to be a very quiet news week – unless of course by chance there were dust storms blowing all over the state. As far as Hall knew there weren't, but he continued photographing the women cleaning the guesthouse. Concentrating on work was the only thing keeping him from calling the police station and venting his concerns about Sam Shelley. He had felt rattled when Simone strolled in, offering to help Jane. Robotically, he had nodded at her and continued arranging and taking shots.

For a crazy moment he had considered calling that bird-brained spin doctor Ann Eggerton. That was when he knew he was not thinking with any intelligence. She would have a press release typed up and issued to every news outlet before he even got off the phone.

He heard Sarah's voice as she walked up the guesthouse ramp. He took several more shots while he composed himself. When he turned around, she was gone. Erica and Don stared back at him, complicity mirrored in their expressions.

Hall crossed the room so quickly he accidentally kicked a dustpan and broom. He didn't stop to pick them up. Sarah was already halfway across the lawn.

'Wait,' he said.

She paused. She looked upset, and he wanted to hug her. That would be the wrong thing to do.

'You need to ask Sam Shelley about Chloe.' She spoke without looking at him, her jaw clenched, her lips severe. 'I don't know what the story is, but he knows something.'

'What's happened?'

'I don't even know if he's telling the truth. He said, and don't quote me, he said, "She wasn't dead when I left her."'

'Do you want to go somewhere and talk about this?'

'No.' Sarah continued to look away, her gaze fixed on the other side of the yard where the dogs paced as far as their chains would allow. 'And his mother. She's involved. He all but said it. One more thing: the tip used to be an old tin mine. There are a few disused mineshafts in the bush behind it. I might be way off here, but I saw Sam in the bush, directly behind the tip. The week before Christmas, before you got here, before everything happened.'

Hall processed the details. He would get to the bottom of

341

this immediately. He began to thank Sarah for sharing the information, but she was already walking away.

Hall was considering how to catch Simone alone when she stepped onto the guesthouse veranda, rolling a bucket of dirty mop water. Hall took one side of the handle, Simone took the other, and they carried the heavy bucket toward the grass.

'I'm so glad we're still friends,' Simone said, standing back as Hall poured the dirty water onto some bushes. 'I was worried you were cross with me.'

She adjusted her red bandana, tugging at a loose lock of hair that had fallen free.

'I'm not cross.' Hall gave an exasperated sigh. 'I'm reporting on a possible double murder. You need to be honest with me. My patience is wearing thin.'

His aggressive tone startled her. She glanced at the guest-house. 'Please, Hall. Not here.'

'You want to sit in my car? Or yours?'

'Sit in mine. It's behind the concrete tank. Out of the way.'

Inside the green Mercedes it was cool and dark. Hall had never sat in a luxury car, but the experience was lost on him. He found his notebook and spun his pencil in his hand, choosing his words carefully. He had only one chance to make this conversation work.

'So you have me where you want me,' Simone said.

She turned the keys and the air-conditioning came on. Music did too – a jazz tune with a fast trumpet-driven tempo – and she lowered the volume.

Every conversation Hall had held – with Sam, with Sarah,

with Simone, with Roger, with anyone in the Bay of Fires – ran through his mind. Odd comments, observations that had not made perfect sense, his own interpretation of the various relationships among them all; Hall mentally shuffled the fragments of information like pieces of a puzzle.

'You're a good mother, Simone, but you need to get your son a lawyer,' Hall began. 'Chloe Crawford. Buried alive in a mineshaft behind the tip.'

Simone took off the red bandana and folded it on her lap. She appeared utterly relaxed, waiting for Hall to continue. The only sign Hall could perceive of her nervousness was her mouth. She kept licking her lips. It was not a mannerism he had observed her doing before. He was pretty certain she was not aware she was doing it.

'It's a heartbreaking tale,' Hall said. 'Teenage lovers, a summer holiday romance, she breaks up with him, and his reaction is explosive and violent. And that poor little girl, cowering in the mineshaft, praying that her parents would find her.'

'She wasn't buried alive.' Simone sounded teary. 'They had an altercation and he put his hand over her mouth. She was yelling at him. He only wanted her to be quiet. She was unconscious when he came to get me. Sam tried to do the right thing. But it was too late. Chloe was dead when we returned. I took her pulse. She was in a strange position and must have suffered asphyxiation while he was gone. It was awful, Hall. Sliding her into the mineshaft, that was my idea.' Sobbing, Simone covered her face with her hands. 'A mother does things for her son, Hall. I've already lost two husbands. Should I be expected to lose my only son, too?'

'She asphyxiated?'

'It's not the worst way to die, Hall.'

'Chloe Crawford left her parents' cottage with a surfboard under her arm. She was going surfing. Can you explain how she ended up in the bush?' Hall stared straight ahead, concentrating on Simone's voice rather than the way she kept stroking her own arms.

'Sam and Chloe paddled their surfboards across the lagoon. They walked up into the bush a little way, planning to kiss. It was, as you say, an innocent romance. And it went wrong. Maybe she got scared. I understand her family is quite religious.'

'And her surfboard?'

'Everything was tossed into the mineshaft. What were we supposed to do? We're not trophy hunters.'

Simone turned to face Hall. Teardrops sat on both her cheeks. She didn't try to wipe them away. He could not look away from her dark blue eyes. For a surreal moment, a feeling of déjà vu washed over him. He was a teenager again, sitting in a car with a beautiful girl, waiting for her to give him permission to touch her. In reality, Hall realized, Simone was waiting for him to make a decision.

'You're not trophy hunters.' Hall sounded harsher than he intended to and Simone's little smile faded. 'So how did Sam come to have Anja Traugott's bikini top?'

Simone smoothed her hair. She folded her bandana into a triangle and wrapped it over her head, tying it in a jaunty knot at the base of her neck.

'Hall. No one wants to be a bad person. It's not in a human being's nature. I don't think it is. But we all have to do whatever is necessary to survive. I'm not evil. I know you know that.'

In the spacious vehicle Hall felt cooped up. Through the tinted window the sky was darker. The air-conditioning was working too well, and Hall had goose bumps on his arms.

'I'm a loving mother. I want Sam to experience love and enjoy his sexuality. I've always been very open with him about life. But women can be cruel, Hall. I know you know that – I can tell.'

Hall raised his palm to stop her from talking. 'I'm sorry, Simone. You need to inform the police. I won't do anything until you have done so. You have my word.'

As he placed a hand on the door handle, Simone placed her hand on his leg. It was a slender hand and seemingly weightless – he could barely feel it through his jeans.

'Hall, I have another worry you might be able to help me with.'

'Yeah?'

'Sam turns eighteen next month. The law is quite clear in Tasmania.' Simone's voice was melodious. It had quavered before. 'It is a crime for anyone to have sex with a seventeen-year-old if they are more than five years older than the seventeen-year-old. It's an awful situation.'

'I don't see your point, Simone.'

'I'm uncertain what to do . . . I've always been on good terms with the Averys.'

Hall smacked her hand off his knee. He knew where this was going.

'I would never tell you how to do your job, Hall. But maybe it's enough if you could tell the police that you found Chloe's body. I doubt it will be intact. It's been a year. But at least they can close the case. It will probably look like she fell into the mineshaft. I've always worried that those mineshafts pose a danger.'

'Are you serious?' Hall asked. 'Are you blackmailing me?'

Simone had stopped crying a few minutes ago, but tears remained on her cheek. She wiped them with the edge of her bandana.

'Blackmail is a dirty word, Hall. We're not in a mobster movie.' She turned the key again, this time igniting the engine. 'Now, can I drop you somewhere?'

'No thanks.'

Clutching his pad and pencil, Hall walked away from the Mercedes. He heard the purr of its engine blend into the seaside sounds as Simone drove off.

Hall trudged up the sandy track. His leather shoes rubbed painfully against his heels, and his hatless head burned. The refuse tip was very different from the day after the fire, when he had come with Sarah. Today, stripped trees revealed an airy view of turquoise water and a white curl of sandy beach. The tip smelled clean, like charcoal rather than decomposing household waste or burnt synthetic garbage.

Hall skirted the trench, only stopping when he reached the edge of the forest beyond the tip. Thirty meters in, where the fire had not burned, the bush was thick. Sharp grasses and wiry, delicate ferns grew from the hot sandy soil, shaded by parched-looking gum trees. In theory, he was looking for Chloe Crawford's bones or the remnants of her personal possessions. Human remains were extremely unlikely. Anything would do. It didn't matter to Hall. Anything belonging to Chloe would be front-page news and would allow the police to solve the case.

Hall stepped into the bush, thumping his feet to warn the black snakes he was coming. Sarah had said she had seen Sam in the scrub as she rode her bike up the tip road. That was before the fire, when the vegetation was thicker, so Sam could not have been too far in. Common sense told Hall he would find nothing. Journalists didn't simply walk into the bush and discover a dead body that the police and local search parties had failed to find. Still, Hall had nothing more productive to do, so he continued to look, zigzagging through the scrub behind the tip, banging his feet on the ground, looking for anything odd.

It was easy to see how people became lost in the wilderness. Tasmanian bush grew horizontally, not vertically. Above his head, in the area where the fire had not been, the canopy was thick enough to prevent a helicopter pilot from seeing a person on the ground. Surrounding Hall on all sides, the bush looked the same, pale sap-oozing tree trunks and insects buzzing around the yellow wattle shrubs. There were no landmarks. But Hall would not become lost; if he walked downhill he would end up on the beach or by the lagoon eventually.

Hall spotted the mineshaft at the same time that he heard the noise. He panicked and spun around to see who was following him. For a crazy moment he worried that Simone had trailed him. Beneath the shadowy gums there was no one, just empty, indifferent bush. He heard the noise again and exhaled. It was a kookaburra, the bird's sharp laugh-like call sinister in the quietness. Hall turned his attention back to where he suspected the shaft to be. It was the topography that drew

Hall's eye to it, the way the earth on all sides gently sloped downward to a central dip. The ferns and bracken grew more thickly here, too, perhaps an indication of once-disturbed soil.

He didn't want to stand too close, for he was afraid the ground would give way beneath his weight. He found a long stick and separated the ferns covering the hole. Indeed there was something in there. Stepping closer, Hall peered in, momentarily forgetting his own safety. Down several meters, wedged against a rotting wooden paling, the yellowed curving edge of fiberglass was enough confirmation that Simone had been telling the truth.

Sweat ran down his back, soaking his shirt and the top of his underpants. He stumbled back to the tip clearing. Checking for jack jumper ants, he sat on the ground under a shady tree and nursed his head in his hands. Jane was talking about moving to Launceston and getting a job at the supermarket where her cousin worked. Pamela had refused to walk alone on the beach since the day Anja was found. Roger Coker was being harassed to the point where it had become life threatening.

Hall could solve this case. He didn't have every fact, but he could give the police enough information. Anja Traugott's final minutes were a mystery. He doubted Sam had pushed her into the ocean. Frightened her, more likely. Still, Sam had been following her, and not for the first time, and consequently she was dead. Two beautiful young women led to their deaths in the Bay of Fires.

It would be the biggest murder story to come out of Tasmania in years. So why was Hall Flynn sitting under a gum tree with his head in his hands? What was he doing even deliberating over this? It wasn't his job to be judge and juror. By saying nothing to the police, he was guilty of withholding information. The thought made his stomach tighten.

But the image of Sarah facing a charge of unlawful sexual intercourse with a minor made Hall feel ill. Initially Hall had tried to not think about the few flimsy facts he knew about Sarah and Sam. When that failed, he had considered each fact, linking them together as though he were weighing up the workability of a formulaic news story. Removing his emotion from the matter had been sensible; objectively, he decided, it did not matter who she had slept with. Most likely, Sarah did not know Sam was only seventeen. Even Hall had assumed the kid was older. The problem was, most people would react in the explosive way Hall had when they heard about it.

Frustrated, he jumped to his feet. There was no one he could discuss it with.

Three garbage bags taped tightly had saved Hall's laptop from the dust. He checked his e-mail; nothing from Elizabeth. Nothing from any of the subeditors, either, not that he had filed any story in the last few days that was complex enough to require them to contact him for further explanation.

Hall typed up his quotes relating to the dust storm and tried to arrange them. In his mind he knew what to do, how to write a workable lead, how to massage the story to intrigue the readers. It was a no-brainer; the stupidest cadet reporter could do it. The longer he sat there, trying not to feel his blistered heels and sunburned neck, the angrier he became. His mind refused to focus. In the garden below, one of Jane's dogs was barking. The sharp howl hurt his head. Eventually he slammed the computer lid shut. He thrust his shoulders out the window.

'Shut up, you stupid mutt,' he yelled.

Sarah heard him knock eleven times. Frozen on the top bunk, she counted each gentle rap. Where the curtain did not meet the window frame, she held the fabric in place, in case he tried to peer in. In between the knocking his footsteps thudded down the veranda toward the beach. He stood there for ten minutes, probably scanning the headland and rocks for her. Lying on the shaggy green bedspread, staring at the Alvey reel hanging over her head, she willed him to leave. She didn't want to hear his apology. She didn't want to hear about her inadequacies. She knew them.

His footsteps returned along the veranda and stopped at the door. He tried the handle. She had locked it. She imagined him trying to see past the yellowed hula girl curtain, hoping to see someone sleeping on the couch who could tell him where she was. His bristly face and the smell of his skin were more real to her than the bedspread's aged mothy scent. She could feel his hands that were larger than hers, she could hear his rich voice as though he were murmuring in her ear.

As the Holden's engine started up, she rolled off the bunk. Bright daylight hurt her eyes. Five minutes felt like hours as she waited until the car emerged through the bush to cross the lagoon. He turned up the long straight road toward the hills and highway. She watched until the vehicle disappeared into a wall of gum trees. A faint orange cloud was all that remained.

The dry smell of fire dust lingered in the air. A filmy layer of soot draped the ocean like black chiffon, leaving dark arches on the shore. She placed both hands on the railing and for the first time since she left Eumundi, Sarah cried without restraint.

A seagull was under attack by the flock. The lone bird swooped and ducked but had no hope. The other birds pecked him in midair. He landed on the rock not far from Hall. Some of his feathers were broken. Fluffed up, he hunched his shoulders and charged at the bigger bird facing him. His opponent charged back. Screeching, flat necked, they beaked each other. More birds descended in a high-pitched war cry. The lone seagull rose up and flew out across the ocean. The others became airborne but did not follow.

She had not answered his knocks. He knew she was there. Her fishing gear was on the veranda, her Blundstone boots beside the door.

Time to think and the chance to talk to her were the two things he needed. Neither was forthcoming. In his pocket his phone beeped and he ignored it. He didn't trust himself to speak to anyone from the office right now.

The next morning, summer cricket commentary rang out from the radio as Sarah scanned both aisles of the shop. It was as she thought; Pamela and Don had not returned the canned cat food to the shelves.

'Are you still out of Whiskas?' Sarah said.

'You hungry?' Pamela laughed.

Don pushed his chair back and disappeared into the kitchen. He returned with a cardboard box containing the cat food cans and several packets of dried cat biscuits balancing on top.

'I was planning to have this done already. I assure you. We got sidetracked.'

'Good catch,' Pamela shouted.

With no major new developments in the investigation, Anja Traugott was no longer front-page news and the newspaper stack had been moved off the counter. In its place was Erica's card display. The card at the front showed two dead crayfish with their pincers and mouths touching. Underneath the photograph Erica had written *Happy Valentine's Day*.

'Is Roger still in hospital?' Don asked.

'He's on a drip. He's probably got pneumonia.'

'Oh dear,' Pamela said, and then swiveled to listen to the radio commentary.

'They hit a six!' Don pumped his arm, and Pamela clapped.

Sarah was halfway out the door when Pamela stopped cheering.

'Where did Roger run to anyway . . . up near Anson's Bay, was it?' Pamela asked. 'Mental as anything. Just like his father.'

'I'll let him know you send your regards.' Sarah slipped through the plastic strips.

As she walked down the stairs she heard Pamela say, 'She can be a real cow sometimes.'

Two weeks ago Sarah would have stuck her head back inside the shop and let Pamela know she had been overheard. It would be worth it just to see the embarrassment on Pamela's face. Instead, she marched along an animal track running south above the beach in the direction of the lagoon.

'You just missed her, darl. Sarah was here fifteen minutes ago,' Pamela called as Hall entered the shop. Her voice was raised to be heard over the cricket commentators blasting on the radio. She looked fresh in a yellow sundress.

'Actually, I need to confirm a few things if you've got a moment,' Hall said, brushing his hair with his hands so he would not look so disheveled. 'I wasn't looking for . . .'

'Never mind.' Pamela smiled kindly. 'What did you want to ask me?'

Hall considered how to phrase his question. He didn't want to alarm them, or give fodder for gossip. He certainly did not want to reveal, at this stage, the distressing find of Chloe Crawford's remains in the mineshaft behind the tip.

'Don told me he encountered Sam Shelley, on the beach, watching Anja Traugott sunbathe,' Hall said.

'Talk to Don.'

Hall hadn't noticed Don sitting behind the magazine rack. Don lowered the volume and nodded.

'I just wanted to know, did you speak to Simone about that?' Hall said.

'Pamela did. We thought it best if we kept it to ourselves.'

'What was there to say?' Pamela interrupted. 'A young guy looking at a pretty girl on the beach. That's life. We told his mother.'

'Right.' Hall maintained a mild tone.

'Yes, we've had a few funny things with Sam, haven't we, love?' Pamela said.

Don grunted.

Pamela continued. 'I've had to sort it out. Sam's mother is so useless. I'll tell you, Hall, because I like you, but it's not for publication. Darlene from the campground saw Sam hiding in the bushes near where the women relieve themselves. She would have made trouble if I hadn't calmed her down. I asked Don to have a little talk with Sam . . . didn't you, love?'

'You didn't tell the police,' Hall said.

'I thought about it, Hall. But what good would it do? I don't have much time for Simone, but I wouldn't do that to her.'

'It could be related to the investigation.'

'Well, that thing with Anja happened days before she disappeared.'

'You didn't think it might help the police, knowing everything?'

'No. Frankly I didn't. If someone looks at a topless woman and that makes him a murder suspect, then you might as well go over to that nudist beach and start arresting everyone now.'

The campers were packing up to go home. Trailers were connected to cars, square patches of flattened grass lay where the tents had been. Litter fringed the site; bottles, food scraps, and wisps of toilet paper. It was interesting that they were leaving now. Usually the campsite remained established, in some form, until the Australia Day long weekend. Sarah had planned what she wanted to say, had rehearsed it silently as she walked down here. Just a friendly warning, were her chosen words. Roger's not the easy target you think he is. Some of us are looking out for him and we don't like what we've been seeing.

Sarah's sneakers sucked against the wet sand on the edge of the lagoon. Half a dozen men and women loitered around the smoldering campfire. She reconsidered instigating the confrontation. They were leaving, after all. Roger was in the hospital and would be safe tonight.

But the campers would return at Easter, and again next Christmas. She had come down to the campsite to speak her mind and she would do so. They'd tell her where to go. They were probably pissed already. It was widely known the wives drove everyone home at the end of their holiday. Sarah crossed her arms and waited for someone to turn around.

Bunghole saw her before the others did.

'To what do we owe this lovely surprise?' He grinned sarcastically as he threw some camping equipment into the back of his Hilux.

His smile slid off his face as Sarah let him have it. She didn't hold back, even when his wife came over and positioned herself between them. Darlene was a big woman, and Sarah took a cautious sideways step. She had seen women fight inside and outside the two Eumundi pubs. It was ugly; they ripped hair and clawed fingers into each other's eyes and noses.

'Anytime I see you, or hear you've been anywhere near the Coker property, you're going to get it.'

Bunghole nodded. 'And you're going to give it to me?'

'Don't underestimate me.'

'Coker is a bad egg,' Darlene said. 'Face it.'

'He's not.' Sarah couldn't believe how calm she was being. This was going well. 'Physically, Roger Coker would be incapable of killing. He's got one good arm that shakes all the time. He can barely get bait on his hook.'

No one spoke. Sarah looked around. Most of the campers did not make eye contact with her. Darlene, at least, looked sympathetic, just as she had that day outside the shop when Bunghole's milk carton almost hit Sarah in the head. Were they finally getting it? When they plotted to hurl road kill at the Coker cottage, when they attacked Roger's cats, when they accused him of murder, had they harbored the suspicion that they were mistaken? She had not expected them to be receptive to her. She wondered if they regretted their action. Perhaps they finally saw their suspicion of Roger as a misplaced diversion from another night swatting mosquitoes around their campfire.

'If you're done, you can get the fuck out of here,' Bunghole said.

So that was how he wanted to play it. Fine.

'By the way, did I see the ranger out here the other day?' she said.

'I dunno. Did you?'

'Wonder how he knew about you? Must have had a good tip-off.'

Hands on her hips, Sarah waited for one of them to speak. She wasn't sure, but it could have been Darlene's sister who threw the first can. It hit Sarah on her arm. Someone else threw a rubber thong which slapped the side of her head. Her body stiffened with rage, but their laughter pushed her back. She jogged out of the campsite, taking a shortcut through yellow buffalo grass that whipped her bare legs.

Hall's gear was in the Holden; he'd paid Jane in full. She knew he was standing there, waiting to speak to her, but she betrayed no sign of it except for pulling weeds faster than before.

'Jane,' he began. He wanted to say goodbye and wish her well. Her hospitality had been decent, in its own unique way.

Jane swung around. Sweat shone on her reddened neck. It had dampened the armpits of her T-shirt. She wiped her hands on her jeans and took a breath.

'Life's too short to beat around the bush,' she said.

'Let sleeping dogs lie,' he offered.

He had a gut feeling about what she was going to say, and he didn't want to hear it.

Jane was speaking to the sea. 'The other night, when we both drank too much, that was a mistake. I've apologized to you already.'

'Water under the bridge,' Hall said, reverting to feeble clichés in his foreboding.

'Hang on. I've always spoken my mind. I think you know I am interested in having a relationship with you.'

Hall was speechless. He felt ill. It was childish, his reaction. It wasn't as if Jane had given an explicit description of what they could do sexually together. She wanted his company. Nothing wrong with that, he repeated silently. Inside his pockets, he rubbed his sweaty fingertips together. More than anything else, he felt deeply sad for her.

'I'm so sorry, Jane,' Hall said.

'Fair enough.' Jane nodded.

A heavy silence hung between them.

'This is not the life I would choose if I had a choice,' Jane said.

Hall looked around, trying to understand her. Her mature garden was full of delicate beauty – the fragrant herbs, the flowering succulents, the lavender and yellow roses. But there was also the hard stubby grass and faded house with its broken windows and, downstairs, the bedroom she had slept in alone for far too long.

'But it's my life. I don't want it screwed up,' she said. 'Appreciate it if you could keep this to yourself.'

'Of course.'

'You get what I'm saying, Hall? I have a private life.'

She almost smiled, watching Hall to see if he comprehended her implication. An image of her and John Avery making love appeared in Hall's mind. Did she discard her crankiness with the faded red flannelette nightshirt he had seen flapping on the Hills Hoist? He could not imagine her being warm and cuddly. He almost shuddered.

'I understand,' Hall said. 'And I assume you are not speaking about Gary.'

'I am not talking about Gary.' Jane started digging again. 'No. He's a bag of shit.'

'We all have our regrets, I guess,' Hall said.

She dug and tossed the soil a few more times before shoving the fork in hard. 'I've never had a man who didn't let me down.'

'You're an angry woman, Jane.'

She shrugged.

'You have to get over it,' Hall said.

She didn't answer.

He added, 'It's not healthy to be so angry.'

'People have said to me, "Are you planning on being this bitter for the rest of your life?"' Jane said. 'Maybe I am.'

'Jane . . .'

She flicked her hand in his direction, dismissing him. 'You've made yourself heard.'

Poised on a rock beyond the old jetty, Sarah looked like a fisherwoman in a painting of a nineteenth-century fishing village. The bare wooden jetty, the empty sea, and the muted green vegetation that matched her clothing conveyed a peaceful sadness. From his position up on the road, Hall recognized her powerful swing as she cast out. There was no way she could avoid him. He cut through the yard of a vacant shack and followed the winding track down to the sea. He moved slowly, carefully picking delicate pink flowers with tiny thorns that cut his fingers, navy blue blooms, and cottontails. The task gave him time to collect his thoughts.

In Launceston his rundown house had rooms with bay windows overlooking the gorge cliff grounds. From the wooden verandas you could hear gum trees rustling and peacocks calling out at dusk. His house had broken balustrades and five blocked chimneys. It needed fixing, a diamond in the rough. That was what he wanted to tell her. But first he needed to tell her everything that Simone had told him.

When Sarah greeted him, she seemed agitated. She kept looking across to the wharf and up at the track Hall had come down, as though she expected someone to be following her. No one was.

She continued to fish as he updated her on Roger's condition in the hospital. He was sick, still not breathing properly, but it was not pneumonia. She seemed pleased that Roger's illness was not as severe as they first thought, although she did not say so.

Two days had passed since their confrontation about Sam Shelley. He could see she was no longer angry, but her indifference hurt him more. He had thought about penning his thoughts. He said things better on paper than he did face-to-face.

'Simone confessed everything,' Hall blurted out. 'I know what happened to Anja and Chloe.'

He explained almost everything Simone had said in the

Mercedes. Sarah listened, her forehead creased with worry, and he decided he would not tell her he was certain that Chloe Crawford's body was in the mineshaft behind the tip. Knowing Sarah, she would hike up there and take a look. It would not be good for her. Sarah had seen one dead body and that was enough for anyone.

She cut him off. 'Why are you talking to me about all this?'

There was no way to put it except bluntly. 'Simone is threatening to have you charged over Sam.'

'Is this an ultimatum?' Sarah's lip curled and he could see her blood-red gums.

'God, no.'

'Well what, then? I don't care what you do. Why are you even telling me?'

'I'm telling you that I know what happened to Anja and I think I've located Chloe's body and I'm not writing the story. I'm not following it up.'

'Slow down. Are you insane?'

Hall knew he was rambling as he explained his plan. He would do as Simone suggested, and let the police work out the details. Perhaps Chloe's death would look accidental; that would depend on the forensics. He felt sorry for Sam. Simone deserved to stand trial as much as Sam did, but Hall doubted she ever would.

'She was awful, Sarah,' Hall said. 'I've never heard a woman be so callous, so cruel.'

'Sounds like you're blowing a good story,' Sarah said.

Hall stared, frustrated with her lack of emotion. 'Sarah, breaking this news would be any journalist's once-in-a-lifetime story.'

'Don't do this for me, mate. I'm not worth it.'

He grabbed her hand and she snatched it away. He felt stupid, a schoolboy making a fool of himself.

'Why are you acting like this?' he said.

'Like what? You got what you paid for. I never false-advertised.'

'Don't be crass.'

'Please go.'

Her voice sounded emotionless, the way it did whenever she spoke to Bunghole. Hall stalled, tasting the salt spray on his lips, watching how the afternoon sun dimpled the water. The beauty of the afternoon ocean heightened his disappointment.

There was something else he had planned to tell her. It was none of his business. But a tiny part of him hoped she didn't really want him to leave. If ever they were to have something more together, he had to be brutally honest.

Using gentle language he explained about John and the key. He kept his eyes on the sea as he outlined his embarrassing initial suspicions and his regrettable secondary suspicions when he found the score sheet in the Scrabble box. Sarah listened, nodding, winding and releasing her fishing rod.

'I know about it, Hall.'

'You do?'

'Can't believe they're still at it. Yuck. It's been going, on and off, for twenty years.'

'Oh.'

'Mum and Erica don't know. I always thought they didn't need to.'

He put a hand on her shoulder. Her torso shook as she

wound the reel in. It was still shaking as she released it. Gently, she removed his hand.

'Hall. Go back to town and your teenybopper girlfriends. I'm not interested in you anymore.'

Hall left her alone on the rocks. As he walked up to the guesthouse, he hoped not to pass anyone. If he had to speak, even to say hello, Hall feared he might cry.

Sarah glanced at the wildflowers Hall had left on the rock for her. The bunch was tied with a piece of plaited dune grass. No one had ever given her flowers.

Her head hurt, worse than the meanest hangover she had ever endured.

What a shocking turn of events. Simone and Sam Shelley. If someone had suggested it to her at the beginning of the summer, Sarah would have laughed in their face. But now it didn't seem so farfetched. A drunken flashback of Sam in her hire car on Christmas Day began to form in her mind. Sitting beside her, Sam had mentioned his mother in some peculiar context. Sarah could not remember exactly what he'd said, except that she had felt uncomfortable, which made her suspect he had spoken of Simone after their physical encounter. What Hall said was true: if Sam did push Anja into the ocean, if Sam did suffocate Chloe and dispose of her body, it was impossible to prove. Regardless, Hall was mistaken and deluded to keep this theory from the police.

Whether the murder case went to court or not, Simone Shelley might hold Sarah's encounter with Sam over her head forever. The realization startled her enough that she slacked the line and lost a decent chunk of bait.

The only non-depressing thing about the conversation with Hall was his news about Dad and Jane Taylor. Hall's demeanor was severe and churchlike as he described the affair, as though he were informing her that someone had died. Sarah had never been entirely certain about the relationship between Jane Taylor and her father. It was something she tried not to think about.

There had been funny things over the years that could have exposed an unpleasant set of circumstances. These oddities, such as nice bottles of port or gin going missing from the liquor cabinet which neither Sarah, Erica, nor their mother had a plausible explanation for, or their father's unexplained absences from the shack, his habit of taking long walks late in the evening, could easily be dismissed as inconsequential. It was easy enough to tell herself she was imagining any familiarity in the interactions she had witnessed between her father and the guesthouse owner.

Sarah sighed. Long ago, when Sarah was fifteen or so, she had been staying alone at the shack with her father. John had kissed her good night and gone for a walk, as was his custom. When she woke early to go fishing, he was not in the shack. It had not bothered her until, casting her line from the headland, Sarah watched her father emerge from the track that led up to the guesthouse. Father and daughter eyed each other. Their ensuing conversation revolved around the safe topics of fishing and ocean conditions.

Hall was right about one thing: it wasn't anyone else's business. There was no sense in living your life worrying about how other people lived theirs. And maybe Sarah's mother knew but chose to ignore it.

She wondered if Hall had been expecting to cast a line with

her. She had not offered him any of the raw chicken she was using for bait when he picked up her spare rod. Her decision was made. She was satisfied that he had helped Roger, but there was an implication in the way he told her about it that suggested she should be grateful to him. He had paused after he told the story, as though waiting for her to provide the conclusion. Sarah had merely nodded. Hall had done what was required, that was all.

Sarah slid fresh bait on her hook and sighed. Who cared if she did sleep with Sam? It wasn't like she would have forced him. She poised the rod over her shoulder, whipped the line out to sea. She didn't care what Hall Flynn, in particular, thought about it. He was not morally superior.

But while he was beside her on the rocks, she had searched Hall's face. All she had seen was the same crinkled kindness she had recognized in him from the start.

Hall drove by the wharf, along the high road above the shacks and the sea, past the lagoon, and along the straight gravel road leading out of the national park. He was not worrying about the danger of sliding off the slippery gravel. The sign to Sloop Point caught his eye as he entered the eucalyptus shade and he signaled left. He doubted he would ever return, and he wanted to sit by the rock pool, for just five or ten minutes. Time to take a breath.

The rock pool was peaceful. Nothing disturbed its smooth, cool surface. As he peered in he could see the beautiful seaweed fronds floating languidly and the starfish and shells clinging to the rock wall. It was as tranquil as it had been the day he visited with Sarah. In the open sea, glistening twists of kelp reared with each oceanic pump. Hall leaned his back against the cold stone and watched gulls circling the white peaks of Sloop Rock. At the other end of the beach the Averys' shack was indistinguishable from the hillside.

He thought back to the first murder story he had covered, as an earnest cadet reporter. The victim had been his age, a seventeen-year-old boy who had died in police custody. As well as horrific injuries to his face and head, the boy had severe bruising on the inside of both thighs, as though something had been held there with considerable pressure. Two years after the boy died, Hall had sat with the mother in her pretty house in Riverside. He could hear her broken voice as though it were yesterday: 'I wanted to know every detail of what happened to my son. But now when I think about him, that's the first thing that comes to mind – his final terrified minutes.'

Anja's parents were better off thinking she drowned in the ocean than that she was chased, half naked, down the rocks by a psychopath. And Chloe's parents were better off thinking she died accidentally stumbling into a disused mineshaft than that she was suffocated by a deranged boyfriend. Even if Hall forgot about protecting Sarah and the case went to court, the Shelleys would never tell the truth. Hall was certain of it. Roger was not a reliable witness. There was a chance that police forensics would find something on Chloe's body to connect Sam to her, but in reality, date rape was hard to prove, let alone when the victim's corpse had been exposed to the elements for a year.

A text message came through on his phone. It was from the HR guy. It said:

Your editor is concerned that you are not answering your phone nor have you filed any copy recently. Please make an appointment with me.

Hall reread it. He hadn't filed anything decent for days, hadn't returned any of Elizabeth's calls, either. And now, obviously, she had held another meeting with that kid from HR. Hall typed: I quit. He pressed 'send' before he could change his mind.

Without thinking, he swung his arm back and hurled the mobile phone as hard as he could. It bounced off the rock and disappeared into the ocean. That phone was company property; they could take the cost out of his last paycheck.

He sat down hard on the rock. Twenty-three years. No gold watch, no farewell lunch. Not even a bottle of cheap champagne while they stood around the desks. It wasn't the way he wanted to go.

Waves rolled in, splashing over the rocks, not making it far enough to disturb the rock pool's perfect blue surface. It was the same warm summer sky, the same dappled sea and circling gulls, but for the moment it held no charm.

Simone's green Mercedes was parked in front of her holiday house. Sarah stood at the edge of the Shelleys' garden, deliberating whether or not to go in. She had the option of not visiting Sam. She could let it go, let things run their course. There had been the same option with Jake that night at the Pineapple Hotel. In hindsight, she should have gone home well before the confrontation began. She should have refused to respond when he pretty much called her a whore, in the pub, in earshot of her entire staff. When he stood in front of her car, she should have waited until he moved rather than jumping out and confronting him. But this situation with Sam was not going to escalate. Not today. She had not had a drink for three days. Her mind was calm.

Her tentative knock echoed in the quiet afternoon. Sam came to the door. His eyes were bloodshot; either the ocean was extremely salty or he had been crying. It sounded like he deserved to. But that was not why Sarah was here. She wanted to apologize for what she had done wrong.

Sarah did not lower her voice.

'I'm not here to have a go at you. I just want to talk to you about . . . what you said to Hall.'

'I can't remember.'

Sam shoved his hands in his pockets and looked at his sneakers. They were laced tightly, the laces tied in neat bows, the first time she had seen his sneakers done up.

'I said something about riding in your canoe,' Sam said.

'Something about me and my canoe?'

'I'm sorry. I was trying to impress the reporter.'

'Look, what happened at Christmas was my fault. I'm dealing with the reasons behind it, just so you know.' Shame rushed over her, flushing her cheeks. 'I'm sorry. For giving you beer and for everything else that happened.'

Cooking sounds came from inside the Shelleys' house, reminding Sarah and Sam that they were not alone. Sarah could smell garlic and onions frying. Whatever anyone said about Simone, her son was well looked after. Sam stepped outside and closed the door behind him. The sun was in his eyes now and he squinted.

'You didn't do anything.'

'Sorry?'

'Christmas Day in your car. You were smashed and singing songs, but you didn't – there was no canoe. You let me feel your tits and—'

Sarah's face heated with embarrassment. 'Shut up.'

'You told me to piss off.'

'Enough information.'

Relief coursed through her, a salve on her soul. To Sarah, his revelation was as thorough as a rushing king tide that flooded the beach and removed all debris as it sucked back to the ocean. She almost thanked him. She had no memory of doing anything sexual with Sam, but in her experience that did not necessarily mean nothing had happened. She felt like double air-punching. Instead she turned to leave, waving her hand without looking back.

'Wait.' Sam followed her up the dirt steps to the road. 'What about Anja and Chloe?'

'Nothing to do with me, Sam.' Sarah felt even more relief as she uttered the words.

'It wouldn't have happened like it did if the women hadn't wanted to come with me. Tell Hall that. I jumped in after Anja, I tried to save her. I didn't mean to hurt Chloe. Mom says it's partly their fault—'

'They asked for it?'

Sam slumped his face toward the ground. Right then he didn't look like a soon-to-be eighteen-year-old man – he was a frightened boy.

'Sam. Just tell the truth.'

Walking down the gravel road, Sarah vowed never to drink

rum again. She had made the promise before, usually during the nauseous wakeful sleep, the prelude to a violent convulsive vomit. This time she was sober and she meant it.

People said when you asked for forgiveness, you felt lighter. Sarah didn't feel lighter. She felt focused. Her mind was not convoluted with anxious kaleidoscopic emotions and nervous thoughts colliding. She was thinking straight. Sober, in control of her thoughts, and all she could think of was Hall.

Chapter 13

Under a gloomy sky, far out where the continental shelf dropped away and the ocean turned from turquoise into a dark watery void, Roger caught a blue-eye trevalla. According to Don, who watched with unconcealed envy as Roger showed it off down at the boat ramp that morning, no one had come home with a trevalla that big since 1993. It had to weigh twenty-five kilograms at least.

'Where's the press when you need them?' Don said. 'This is front-page stuff.'

Hall had been gone for a week, and for a moment Sarah thought Don was talking to her. Then Roger swiveled around, his whole face squinting in the sharp morning sun. He laughed a snorting laugh. It was the first time she had seen Don speak directly to Roger.

'You nuts? You want to queue up to drop your boat in?' Sarah said.

The fish was impressive, but what escaped the pressing crowd was the fact that Roger had motored all the way out there in his tinny. He was either brave or stupid; a patch of black rain clouds boiled on the horizon. His tinny was so light that a four-foot wave could flip it. He had caught the fish on an Alvey surf rod which Sarah had lent him. She probably would not have lent it to him if she had known he was going out so far in unpredictable conditions. But then again, Roger knew the ocean. If something bad had happened to him, even if he was using her rod, it wouldn't have been her fault.

Roger, ruddy-faced and grinning, held his catch up to the sky. It was a magnificent fish, more than a meter long, its scales shimmering in shades of bronze and turquoise. For once Roger didn't try to conceal his deformed hand.

Hall had been home in Launceston for a week when Ann Eggerton left a message on his landline. He almost didn't call her back. He no longer worked for the paper and had no desire to listen to her condescending condolences over his abrupt resignation. Halfway through tidying up his garage, curiosity got the better of him.

'I've got some news about Anja Traugott,' Ann said. 'I thought you might want to know. Your replacement told me you were on gardening leave.'

'I'm listening.'

'We're releasing the final results from the postmortem later today. I'm just waiting confirmation from the Swiss consulate that the Traugott family has been informed.'

'Yes?'

'Accidental death from drowning. Lacerations on her face and legs are consistent with having fallen from the rocks. Other injuries are consistent with decomposition from ocean predators.'

Ann explained it was difficult for a forensic pathologist to prove with complete accuracy that death by drowning had occurred. Circumstance and elimination of other causes of death were considered.

'There's more. They excavated the mineshaft behind the tip that you told us about. They took a great deal of forensic evidence to Hobart yesterday. You're a bit of a hero, Hall, stumbling across that.'

'No I'm not. Tell me, has anyone come forward with further information about Chloe? Any witnesses?'

'Early days, Hall.'

Hall sat down on the sunken sofa in his sunroom. He picked at the yellow daisy pattern imprinted in the worn fabric while she prattled away about the difficulties the forensics team faced in determining a cause of death for Chloe. Once the police had taken her body away, there had been a couple of interesting calls to the Crime Stoppers hotline. Ann refused to elaborate, except to predict that the police would solve this case in due time. Hall listened without interrupting. This was good news. Maybe tonight he would be able to sleep properly.

'You're the best in the business, Ann.'

'One other thing,' Ann said. 'You didn't hear it from me, but we might be looking for a media liaison for our Burnie office soon.'

'Not a chance in hell.' He had almost said not a fucking chance in hell.

'Oh.'

'I'm joking. Thanks, Ann, but I need a break from the front line.'

'I understand.' She liked that; in her voice he could hear

satisfaction with the implication that her job was as difficult and meaningful as a journalist's.

Charred trees surrounded the tip like thin, naked survivors. Broken glass spun sunlight. Even Roger's wrecked car had an aspect of beauty, its vintage lines evoking a bygone era. A red bauble, a Christmas decoration, lay surprisingly intact in the ash. Sarah picked it up. It looked like one from Pamela's tree. Christmas seemed like months ago, a blur of sadness. How morose she must have seemed to her family, sitting in the armchair drinking beer after beer. She had barely spoken to anyone that day, had barely raised her stubby for any of the toasts. Things had changed a lot since.

Early this morning a television crew had been driving around the area. Don had seen unmarked police cars coming out of the tip yesterday. Pamela speculated that new evidence had turned up, suggesting that a skeleton had been discovered in the tip, or a weapon. Sarah's father pointed out that there had been many items thrown in there over the years that could be used as a weapon. Blunt fishing knives, rusted shards of corrugated iron, cooking pots, bricks, tools; John's list had gone on and on. Erica said she no longer believed they would find anything. Not here in the burned-out tip, not in the lagoon if Don's idea of dredging it ever happened, not washed in by the next big storm.

Sarah listened to their predictions, keeping what knowledge she had of the facts to herself.

Last night was the first time she had slept properly since before she punched Jake. Every night since she'd left Eumundi, Sarah had woken several times from lurid dreams in which she lost control and physically hurt people she cared about – her mother, Erica, Henry the dog. Lying awake in bed she would rationalize the dreams, but reality was worse. Nothing, no justifying, could change what she had done to Jake. Her biggest fear, exacerbated by a tiny, mean voice in her head, was that she would do it to someone else. That being a man-basher was her fate.

Last night was the first time she had felt confident that this would not happen. It wasn't a promise to herself, or a guilty reaction, it was a fact. She knew, without doubt, that the situation with Jake was a mistake she would learn from. For the first time in weeks, Sarah slept past the stifling silent early hours and woke to the now comforting sounds of her family beginning the day.

Sarah crouched down to pick up the Christmas decoration. How it survived the fire, she had no idea. Without thinking, she tossed it onto the front seat of Roger's Valiant. It occurred to her that it might confuse the investigation, that the television crews might turn it into a story. She grinned.

Riding her mountain bike back to the shack, she noticed a glint of green metal through the trees. Parked at the top of Roger's driveway was the Holden. Her stomach flipped. Hall Flynn, too gutless to drive down the sand trap driveway. She smiled. She peered in the window and noticed he had cleaned the car. There was a new yellow sticker on the back window. *An Alvey Reel Fills the Creel*. He must have stolen it from her tackle box. She paused for a moment then pedaled hard for home, smiling a smile so wide it made her cheeks hurt.

* * *

Hall walked toward the little blue shack with the red geraniums. Someone had been shucking abalone on the wooden picnic table; the shells were scattered on the grass. The bloated technicolored surfboard Sarah and Erica called The Pig leaned against the bunkroom wall. Wet bathing suits were spread on a banana lounge; he recognized the budgie smugglers as John's tight-fitting racing briefs, and Flip's red one-piece. The familial intimacy of the tangled swimsuits halted him. Perhaps he was intruding, had intruded enough already on this family's summer holiday.

Sarah strode around the corner before he had time to rethink his plan. She carried a shovel in each hand.

'You were at Roger's for so long I thought you must be planning to spend the night there.'

'I'm sure he'd let me camp on his veranda couch if I need to.'

'You're dreaming. That's the cats' bed.'

It was important to explain to Sarah why he was here. He weighed his words. The main thing he had planned to say was that he didn't want to leave things like they had been left. Instead, Sarah handed him a shovel.

'Come on. I need your help.'

On the beach Hall leaned on the shovel while Sarah dragged her toe through the damp sand, drawing the lines for the trench they were about to dig. She explained that the lagoon was full and washing into the edges of the dune grass. It wouldn't take much work to dig the trench to release the pent-up tea-tree-stained water into the ocean. Some people were concerned that it was environmentally bad to meddle with the lagoon. It would upset the natural ecosystem, drain the lagoon of micro fish food. They were idiots. The lagoon was pushing against the sand that lay between it and the ocean; it would break through of its own accord any day now.

He had expected questions about Anja Traugott or Chloe Crawford. But Sarah did not mention any of it. She didn't even ask why Ned Keneally's byline was now running under the *Bay of Fires Killer* banner.

'Let's start work,' she said.

She jammed her shovel into the sand.

Deep down the sand was heavy. It slumped off the spade before it could be removed from the trench. Sweat stuck Sarah's clothes to her skin. Beside her Hall panted with exertion under the harsh afternoon sun. He was too exhausted to talk, and that was a good thing. Half an hour before he'd looked like he was about to have an emotional meltdown. He'd had that thoughtful half-smile and made too much eye contact. He was back, and she was glad to see him. Hopefully, he would just accept that things would be okay without having to talk about it.

It wasn't long before the beach became crowded. Sarah directed everyone where to work; Erica and Steve were to dig halfway between the lagoon and the sea, John and Flip halfway between there and the lagoon. Jane Taylor grunted with a shovel on her own. Several curious families who had rented some of the fishing shacks wandered along the beach to watch as progress was made. Some of them dug with their hands. A new group of people had set up tents in the campground beside the lagoon. Some of their children joined in. Simone and Sam Shelley were the only ones missing.

Hall asked Flip where they were.

'Gone, Hall,' Flip said. 'She had urgent business back in the States. They left yesterday. She told Pamela they could only get business-class tickets at such late notice. I went past their place and it was all closed up like it was winter.'

'Shame,' Hall said.

'It is a shame when people have too much money to enjoy the simple things.'

Hall didn't comment. Perhaps, as he suspected, Sam had rung the Crime Stoppers hotline. Perhaps the police had even approached Simone. Hall could imagine her feeling that there was no choice except to whisk her son away.

He studied the beach dig. Sarah had gauged the lagoon's shape, its fullness, and plotted the most strategic spot to dig the trench. In two hours they had dug a forty-meter trench in the middle of the beach. Either side of it, fifty meters of digging remained when Don and Pamela arrived with bottles of champagne and the Weber.

Later in the afternoon only three meters remained between the trench and the lagoon. Sarah whistled and everyone stopped work. Pamela opened another bottle of champagne, and a couple of kids from the campground poised themselves with their surfboards. Knee-deep in water in what was the dry trench, Hall tugged on Sarah's arm. The wall of sand between them and the lagoon quivered. Hall watched it nervously. Any moment now a measureless torrent of water would storm through the weak sand wall, gobbling everything in its path.

'Maybe we should stand up there with everyone else?' Hall said.

'Timing it is the challenge.'

A trickle of water oozed through the damp sand. It was tea-tree brown, definitely not seawater. Hall moved down the trench and hoisted himself out. Sarah followed. They barely made it out as the pressure from the lagoon exploded. It was louder than Hall expected; the sound of sliding sand, the *slish* of mud. A cheer rose up, and parents pulled their children back as the huge water rushed forward to the ocean. It gutted the beach and surged into the sea, the azure water swamped with a tea tree stain, yellow and frothy.

Sarah whooped. Others clapped and hooted. One kid jumped in with his surfboard. He was the first person to plunge into the water, and he skillfully rode the current out into the ocean. Steve clutched a boogie board, holding on as the tormented water ripped out to sea. He was a strong guy, and he made it look difficult. Sarah rode The Pig surfboard along the rushing waves at the edge of the gutter, using her upper-body strength to steer. She had told Hall she expected him to follow.

Above the noisy rush Hall was aware of a conversation being conducted in self-conscious tones. He did not mean to eavesdrop.

'I've got some rubbish Felicity wants to get rid of,' John Avery was telling Jane.

'Trailer is there if you want it. Three o'clock I'll be around.'

'Done.' John nodded curtly.

Jane watched him walk away. Not a measured glance, Hall noted, just long enough to confirm he was leaving. Dr Avery strolled around the lagoon to where his canoe nestled in the dune. Jane met Hall's gaze, holding it until he looked away.

'You can see that too?' Roger spoke from behind Hall. 'No one else can.'

For a moment Hall contemplated feigning ignorance. Instead he said, 'How do you know?'

'I'm smart.' Roger's eyes narrowed as though he were looking into the sun. 'Real smart.'

On The Pig, Sarah coasted out into the ocean. Hall did not want to follow. It wasn't getting in that was the hard bit, it was getting out. If he rode that boogie board, he knew he would careen out to sea, marooned in the grungy water.

John's canoe shot down the lagoon toward the entrance. Water gushed under him; he tapped the water with the paddle in a futile attempt to steer. As the canoe entered the opening, it was seized by frothing water and spun in circles toward the ocean. John frantically tried to control the canoe. Jane cackled. Flip shouted for him to be careful.

'She's right,' Roger said. 'He should be careful. If he wants to make it back to shore in one piece. That lagoon will flick him out into the southwesterly circular current and whoosh . . .'

Roger tapped the air as though he were a magician wielding a wand.

'You reckon a body wouldn't come back?'

'I know a body wouldn't come back.'

Hall paused. His mind sorted previous conversations, rearranged small details, recalled notes he had taken. Stop it, man. It's over. He moved away from Roger, toward the rushing water.

It would be days before the sea would return to its natural color. Rain fell in the Blue Tiers, trickled through old-growth sassafras and myrtle forests, filled ancient rainforest creeks, flushed the St Columba and Detention Falls, nursed freshwater salmon and platypus, gushed into the Two Rivers and watered Pyengana dairy farms, trickled through unnamed tin-mining creeks, soaked through the Sloop and Piccaninny marshes before draining into the Chain of Lagoons. Now it was being returned to the ocean.

Pamela, Flip, and Jane sipped champagne. Hall stepped into line beside them.

'Come on, Hall, we're all waiting for you to show us your stuff,' Pamela called.

The others, tipsy, hooted in agreement. Reluctantly, Hall toyed with a button on his shirt. He wasn't a strong swimmer; how humiliating if someone, Sarah probably, had to rescue him. He knew he should wait until the torrent calmed. The canoe looked like it was spinning out to sea.

Erica was on the edge of the river, undecided whether to jump. She knelt down, her boogie board held out. She looked over her shoulder to see who was watching her and rolled her eyes and laughed. In the churning, directionless shallows, Sarah yelled directions to her father.

'You'd be an idiot to swim in there,' Jane said.

He had not noticed her move around to stand beside him. Her eyes were smiling.

'Here's your excuse.' She held out a champagne-filled plastic cup for him to take.

Sarah wrapped her towel around her waist. It was cold now that she was out of the water. Over the roar of the draining lagoon Sarah couldn't hear Roger and Hall's conversation. Roger gestured with his fishing rod at the sea, and Hall was talking and counting on his fingers. She came closer and listened. Large schools of mullet were sweeping up and down the coast. Hall thought he might have a chance of catching something.

'Roger, don't make it so easy for him,' she interrupted. 'In the morning, Hall, I'm going to get some trevalla, if you're around.'

Mullet were too easy. Not a sport fish. If Hall wanted to catch something other than a toadfish, it should be a trevalla. It would test him. It would test her, too; the frustration of standing back watching while he potentially lost the fish off the line might be more than she could stand.

Acknowledgments

This novel began as a story written at the kitchen table in the precious, fleeting hours that my babies slept. I never really believed it would be published. The person who waved the magic wand is Julia Kenny from the Markson Thoma Literary Agency. She is an amazing, creative, sensitive, and clever editor who transformed my manuscript into a novel. Julia spent countless hours editing *Bay of Fires* and apparently effortlessly found a wonderful publisher in Reagan Arthur Books (an imprint of Little, Brown) and Headline Publishing Group. I was fortunate to have two gifted editors work on my manuscript. Together, Headline's Imogen Taylor and former Little, Brown editor Andrea Walker improved *Bay of Fires* with their insightful and intelligent editorial suggestions. Julia, Andrea, and Imogen made this novel happen. We have never met, but have worked together from opposite sides of the world, and this book is a kind of collaboration. Many thanks to Reagan Arthur and her hardworking team, including Ben Allen, Marlena Bittner, Amanda Lang, and Sarah Murphy. Everything they do exceeds my expectations. Thanks to Julianna Lee for the gorgeous cover artwork. Freelance copy-editor Amanda Heller and proofreader Audrey Sussman put the finishing touches on the novel, and I am comforted by their high standards. I am grateful to the wonderful, passionate people at Headline: Imogen Taylor, Frankie Gray, Holly McCulloch, and Laura Esslemont, all of whom are generous in sharing their talent and their time. I thank Siobhan Hooper for creating the beautiful jacket.

Thank you to the fantastic people from Hachette Australia who worked on this novel: Matt Richell, Carolyn Chwalko, Anna Hayward and Asha Mears.

I am extremely grateful to the staff in the School of English, Media Studies and Art History at the University of Queensland, where I wrote this book as part of a master's degree in creative writing. *Bay of Fires* owes a big debt to Venero Armanno; in particular, he was influential in transforming the novel from an odd love story into a murder mystery. Veny was generous, honest, and encouraging, and I feel lucky that he was my thesis advisor. The theoretical research I did under Hilary Emmett's exceptional guidance broadened my mind and the scope of this novel, such as the focus on single women. I received a five-thousand-dollar University of Queensland Completion Scholarship, which was helpful as I finalized the draft of my book. I was fortunate to have two accomplished writers kindly read my manuscript: Laurent Boulanger and Marion May Campbell. They both advised me well on how to improve the novel. I also thank Stuart Glover, Bronwyn Lea, and Julienne Van Loon for their creative ideas in the early stages of writing.

My brilliant University of Queensland writers' group

– James Halford, Jessica Miller, Sree Ramachandran, and Matt Sini – gave ruthless, thoughtful criticism that improved my writing. Over the years, my friend Eleanor Limprecht has read many terrible drafts of my writing, and she has given heartfelt feedback for which I am appreciative. I am lucky to have worked with talented writers such as these.

The scraps for a story come from many cupboards, and so do the motivation and inspiration for a first novel. Firstly, thank you to my parents, Kaye and Nick Gee, and Lucy and George, Sophie and Paul, and Steven. I'm grateful to have such a close, encouraging family. In particular, I thank my mum for fostering a love of reading in all her children.

In the real Bay of Fires Conservation Area there is no village, no shop, no guesthouse, and no large campground. There is a group of family and friends who love the Bay of Fires area and together with my family we have shared many beautiful summers. I thank you all.

I am grateful to my wonderful teachers Mrs Forster, Ms Davies, and Mrs Bryan from West Launceston Primary School for teaching me to read and write. English teachers are special people, and I thank those at Launceston Church Grammar School, especially Mr Fairfax, Mrs Frost, Mr Leo, and Miss Pitt. Other teachers encouraged my passion for storytelling and language, in particular Mrs Bailey-Smith, Mrs Bower, Mrs Evans, and Mr Harris.

My first job as a journalist was on a Sydney newspaper, the *Village Voice*, and I wish to thank owner-publisher Kylie Davis and her staff for training me. During my time there as a cadet reporter, and eventually as the editor, I learned how to interview and how to write professionally.

I am grateful to fish experts Stuart Atherton and Paul DeIonno for allowing me to interview them about fishing. I hope I have not exposed too many of your fishing secrets!

The biggest challenge I faced in writing this novel was finding the time to write. This was made possible for me by the people who cared for my children at various times in the past few years: Sarah Newman, Amy Duncan, and the wonderful people at Kindypatch Paddington, Jahjumbeen Occasional Child Care Centre, and C&K Paddington Community Kindergarten.

My lovely mothers' group gave me invaluable friendship as I wrote this novel – words cannot express what you all mean to me. Many others showed their support and interest in various ways, and I thank the Gee, Embery, Alvey, and Bell families, Helen Bennett, Ron Bennett, Madeleine Gallagher, Louise Grayson, Simon Groth, Dana Lomer, and Tim Velema.

I also wish to acknowledge the many strong, inspiring women in my family, especially my two grandmothers, Margaret Embery and Diana Gee, who are very much missed.

Finally, most importantly, thank you to my husband, William, my children, Scarlett and Miles, and my cat, Jet, for being such a nice family.

This novel was indirectly inspired by two separate tragedies: the disappearance of Nancy Grunwaldt and the death of Victoria Cafasso, both overseas visitors to Tasmania whose cases remain unsolved. This is not their story. I simply wish to acknowledge these two women.

BAY
OF
FIRES

Bonus Material:

About the Author
The Location of the Novel
An Interview with Poppy Gee

About the Author

Poppy Alice Marguerite Gee was born in Tasmania, Australia, in 1977. She comes from a large Tasmanian family. Her mother's business is the manufacture of Alvey fishing reels and Poppy has been surrounded by the craft of fishing all her life. Tasmania's old growth forests are also at the heart of her family; they are a livelihood for some, whilst others have dedicated their lives to saving the forests from destruction. These, often polarising, characteristics of life in a rural Tasmanian community have coalesced in the many strands of this novel.

Although this is Poppy's first novel, over the past decade she has worked for numerous newspapers and magazines as a journalist, book reviewer and editor. She also teaches journalism and creative writing.

Poppy holds a Bachelor of Arts in English, and in 2011 completed a master's degree in Creative Writing at the University of Queensland, for which she received the Dean's Award for Excellence. This novel contributed to her master's.

Poppy now lives in Southeast Queensland with her husband, two beautiful children and two cats, in a timber cottage, built around 1860, which leaks when it rains.

The Location of the Novel

Tasmania is a small, sparsely-populated island at the southern end of Australia. Poppy has spent many summers on its east coast, in the Bay Of Fires Conservation Area. At its heart is an area called The Gardens, where this novel is set.

The Bay of Fires village is a creation of Poppy's imagination; in reality there is no camping ground, guest house or village shop in The Gardens. It consists only of a small smattering of shacks and the beach, named one of the *Lonely Planet* travel guide's top ten in the world. Although completely wild, the area is known as The Gardens because of the delicate wild flowers which grow there.

The Bay of Fires gained its name in 1773 from Captain Tobias Furneaux after he noticed fires burning all along this stretch of coast, signs of the Aboriginal people then living in the area. Evidence of their presence remains today, in the lost middens for instance – the old aboriginal feasting sites that intrigue Hall in the novel.

An Interview with Poppy Gee

What is it about the Tasmanian land and sea scape that inspired you to write this book?

The Tasmanian school holidays are quite long, and as a child I spent three months every summer on the east coast. Where we stayed there were no phones or electricity and visitors were limited by a ruinous gravel road that provided the only access. For children, there was nothing to do but explore the beaches, coves, lagoons and forest. In my mind I know intimately every rock formation on the beach, the way the water ripples around the headland, the many shades and textures of the sand, and the shape of the kelp under the water as you snorkel through the reefs. I love this area. The beauty is understated, but it grows on you. From a writer's perspective, Tasmania makes a great character: the beautiful island is wild and remote, fragile and complex, and the forest and oceans have the potential to be absolutely merciless.

Do you think there is something in small communities that binds them together in an unusual way?

When people know that their neighbour has no one else to turn to, they step up to help. Australia regularly suffers natural disasters – bushfires and floods, mainly – and without fail ravaged communities rally to repair the damage. It's not easy to ignore each other in a small community, which is a good and a bad thing! It's easier to keep a secret in a city; in less populated places people tend to know much more about each other. What appeals to me as a writer is that a small community acts as a microcosm of society – a range of diverse personalities who are forced to interact.

The book has a subtle environmental slant – is this something that you feel strongly about?

I do feel very strongly about the preservation of the environment. Tasmania has incredible areas of old growth forests and unique flora and fauna. This has to be preserved. Tasmania also has the lowest socio-economic level of any Australian state and there is a compelling argument to maintain employment opportunities through industries such as forestry and mining. My heart sides with protesters who chain themselves to trees to stop them being logged, but I believe as a society we need to think on a global scale. In the novel Jane Taylor, the guesthouse owner, says, 'Where do you want your newspaper pages to come from? Brazil? Do you think they practise sustainable logging there?'. There needs to be a global solution for logging, mining and fishing. Obviously I don't know the answer: these issues worry me. It's so important that we don't destroy precious, irreplaceable eco-systems.

Both Hall and Sarah are strong but flawed characters. What was it about human nature that you set out to show?

My first instinct as a writer is to find a character's compassion. Even the most hardened criminal has a human side. In real life, I think people want to be treated with dignity and respect. Dignity is such a fragile thing, and it can be a casualty of personal relationships. Sarah and Hall have emotional wounds that affect their behaviour. In a nutshell, I try to show the importance of kindness, and how a simple thing such as being shown kindness can make a huge difference in a person's life.

You use nature to emphasise the 'creepy' elements of the book. Why is it that you felt this was effective?

Australia has an obvious range of creepy natural elements which are fun to write about. Most visitors to Australia have a giant fear of our poisonous snakes and spiders, and of crocodiles, sharks and sea creatures. I even met one person who was worried a Tasmanian Devil might chew his way into his tent. On a more subtle level I use the moods of the land and the sea to reflect that of the characters. When Sarah is living in the tropical town of Eumundi, the natural imagery is very fertile and verdant, with lots of rain and lush overgrown plants. At this point she feels like her life is out of her control. In contrast, in the Bay of Fires village where most of the action is set, the landscape is more muted, and possibly restrained. This reflects her changing headspace. I was inspired by how nineteenth-century writer Thomas Hardy, in particular in his novel *Tess*, uses landscape to explore the experiences of his characters. My use of nature to create creepy scenes was a small part of this idea.

Alcohol abuse underlies some of the actions in this novel. Is this something you feel is prevalent amongst small communities?

My thoughts on alcohol abuse are not so much that it is prevalent in small communities, but that it causes problems in society in general, especially in Australia where heavy drinking is considered normal and even encouraged. Everyone I know has a tale to tell of an alcohol fuelled event that went horribly wrong. Alcohol is socially acceptable but it causes heartache and regret. Moderation would be a great solution – unfortunately that is not part of Australian culture.

Both Sarah and Jane Taylor are single-minded, strong women. Did you want to create a feminist slant in this novel?

Absolutely. I'm fascinated by how women have been represented in literature historically, in particular single women. Traditionally the spinster figure has been ridiculed and reviled, and I wanted to explore that and attempt to contribute a different representation other than someone who is marginalised. For example, Jane Taylor appears to have the qualities associated with the spinster-figure – she lives alone, she's a social misfit, she grows herbs like a witch would – but the fact that she is single permits her an integral role in the plot. Jane interacts secretly with male and female characters. These interactions are not always truthful or positive, but they give her an agency denied to coupled female characters. Widow Simone Shelley is also empowered by the fact that she operates alone. She decides what information she shares with other characters, a factor which influences the resolution of the murder mystery. In real life I like self-reliant women, so that influenced my writing of my characters.

What are you writing next?

A murder-mystery set in a ski village in Tasmania. It is told through the alternate perspective of a poppy-farming mother and her teenage daughter. This was a really fun novel to write. It is set in Quoll's Nest Ski Club, one of the oldest ski lodges on the mountain. As everyone settles in for a fun, boozy ski week they discover that a woman who was lost in a blizzard the previous winter actually met with foul play. The cloud of suspicion hovers over certain members of the Ski Club, as well as several young men who operate the ski tows and live in staff quarters next door. Once again, I am drawing on some of my experiences as my family used to ski on a tiny mountain in Tasmania.